THE RIB O...

Southwest France, early in the 13th Century; a young woman is taking her dying father on a long journey to undergo a strange initiation ceremony. Grazide, the daughter of a blacksmith is deeply disturbed by what her father has insisted she should do. This is the era when many inhabitants of the region are involved in heresy, principally the unorthodoxy known as Catharism.

The story starts at a time when she is growing up in a small village. It is a time of conflict. Northern French forces have been recruited by the Church into a war against the heretics, the Albigensian Crusade and the land is being systematically despoiled, its people ravaged. Her village and her family are not unaffected. As she matures into womanhood she finds her independent nature and her self-determination opposed by the misogyny of the age. Despite this she struggles to assert her belief in her own autonomy.

As the story unfolds we follow events that encompass the aftermath of war, the building of model new towns known as bastides, and the devastating Papal inquisition that seeks to eliminate heresy from the region once and for all.

This is a novel whose strong narrative carves out a vivid picture of these turbulent times - at the same time exposing the forces that seek to oppress a woman who strives to take possession of her own life.

Andrew Chapman is the author of three previous novels, *Beyond the Silence*, *Ikon* and *The Leaving*, all published by Pilrig Publishing. He lives in Worcestershire, England.

For my grand daughters

Emma, Issy, Bella, Liz, Eleftheria, Sylvie and Angelica

CONTENTS

A note about language

In the thirteenth century the language spoken in the south western regions of France, which included the lands of the Count of Toulouse, was Occitan - a romance language. I have used Occitan place names for some of the locations, principally the village/bastide town of Vilanòva (modern French *Villeneuve d'Aveyron*) and the town of Montalban (modern *Montauban*). I have used the modern French name for Toulouse (Occitan *Tolosa*) to avoid confusion. Words such as joglar, ostal, bailie, plaça, sauvatèrra are in the Occitan form. Their meaning can be found in the glossary.

PRINCIPAL CHARACTERS
PART ONE - HERESY

Arnaud Lamothe	a blacksmith in Vilanòva
Grazide Lamothe	daughter of Arnaud *(qv)*
Guillaume Lamothe	elder son of Arnaud *(qv)*
Pierre Lamothe	younger son of Arnaud *(qv)*
Bethane Noguès *née* Guiraud	of Vilanòva
Brother Bernard	a Waldensian itinerant preacher
Fabrisse Guillon	a widow of Vilanòva
Father Jean Vital	a priest in Vilanòva
Galtier Foulcaut	a weaver and a Cathar goodman
Gervais Targuier	a crippled boy, childhood friend of Grazide
Guillaume Guiraud	of Vilanòva
Phillipe Noguès	a shepherd
Prior Roger	the head of the monastic community in Vilanòva
Raimond	a monk in Vilanòva, later Prior
Sybille	a widow and a Cathar believer

PART TWO - BASTIDE

Aurimonde de Sella	a trobairitz
Bertrand de Castillon	a consul of Montalban
Géraud de Rabastens	a surveyor
Giufré da Costa	a Catalan mercenary
Magali de Gramazie	a widowed head of an ostal in Montalban
Pierre de Vals	a Waldensian doctor in Montalban
Pierre-Guillaume	son of Grazide
Pons Grimoard	Seneschal to Count Raimond VII

PART THREE - INQUISITION

Brother Ferrer	a Dominican friar and inquisitor
Hugues Dubois	a priest in Vilanòva, after Jean Vital
Sicard d'Alaman	Seneschal to Raimond VII, after Pons Grimoard

PREAMBLE

Heresy in 13ᵗʰ Century Southwest France

It is easy to forget how much the medieval mind was obsessed with heavenly salvation. In all levels of society there was a preoccupation with the fate of one's soul after death. It is fair to say that that concern is not, in most instances, anything that governs day to day life in modern Western society.

In the late 12ᵗʰ and early 13ᵗʰ century world of orthodox Latin Christianity that salvation was to be gained through observing the sacraments of the Church, baptism, attendance at Mass, confession and the like, all mediated by a clergy who were quite often seen as venal and corrupt. In addition a doctrine of purgatory was developed, a time after death that the soul was purged of its sins before entry into the heavenly realms. Remission of time in purgatory could be gained by making pilgrimages, going on crusades, making generous donations to churches and abbeys or even purchasing indulgences granted by the Pope. The Latin Church grew rich and powerful on these proceeds.

Heresy, a deviation from what is regarded as the true faith at any one time, has always been present, even from the earliest days of the church. There have been many heretical movements over the centuries, some more bizarre than others. The ones that feature in this novel are those that that later came to be labelled as Catharism and Waldensianism. These both appeared around the latter part of the 12ᵗʰ Century and were quite distinct from each other.

The heresy that was later labelled as Cathar appeared in Northern Italy and Southwest France in the second half of the 12ᵗʰ Century. It probably derived from an earlier heresy in Bulgaria named after a priest called Bogomil. It was a dualist belief that maintained that there were two Gods, one good God who reigned in heaven and the spiritual realm and one bad God who was the creator of all people, animals and the material world. The proponents of this heresy regarded themselves as true Christians, descended from the Apostles in a line of succession conferred by a type of baptism known as the consolamentum. Those who were 'consoled' in this way undertook to lead an ascetic life, shunning carnal relations, the eating of meat and maintaining a devout and sinless existence. These 'perfects' or goodmen/goodwomen as they were known could then be assured that after death their souls would return to the spiritual realm from which they had been banished. To die in an unconsoled state would mean that one's soul would transfer to another individual, even to an animal.

It was not possible for the majority of people to undertake such a rigorous, ascetic life but a type of *consolamentum* was developed that could be administered to a dying individual which would ensure the salvation of their soul, even if their previous life had been one of sin and self-gratification. This religious movement was very popular and was a thorn in the flesh of the orthodox Latin Church whose Popes declared it heretical.

The Waldensian heresy was completely different. It had appeared in Lyon, France in the late 12th Century with a man called Pierre Valdes. He sought to emulate the life of his Saviour, the Jesus of the Gospels, by leading a poor, itinerant life of preaching and healing. Some amongst his followers practised medicine. Waldensians preached in the vernacular and in public places. They saw no need of churches or sacred buildings and were certainly not licensed by the ecclesiastical authorities. They were similar in their embrace of poverty to the later followers of St Francis of Assisi. Despite this Franciscans were approved of by the Roman Pope. Waldensians were declared heretics.

After various unsuccessful attempts to bring these perceived heretics back into the orthodox fold Pope Innocent III had had enough. In 1208 he declared a crusade against the heresy in these southern lands. It became known as the 'Albigensian Crusade' - the city of Albi being seen as a hotbed of heretics whom the invading forces labelled 'Albigensians'. A large number of Northern French lords were persuaded to take up the Cross and join the crusade. It is likely that many of them were as much motivated by the prospect of land-grabbing in the domains of the Count of Toulouse, whose fiefdom extended from Provence to the Atlantic coast, as by any kind of holy war.

TIMELINE OF THE CATHAR WARS

1209   Start of the Albigensian (or Cathar) Crusade, initiated by Pope Innocent III

1213   Battle of Muret. King Peter of Aragon and Count Raimond VI of Toulouse defeated

1214   Sack of the castle of Morlhon by Simon de Montfort

1215   Magna Carta signed by King John of England

1215   4th Lateran Council presided over by Pope Innocent III

1216   Pope Innocent III dies. Succeeded by Honorius III

1218   Death of Simon de Montfort at the siege of Toulouse

1222   Death of Raimond VI. Succeeded by Raimond VII

1223   Truce between Raimond VII and the crusaders

1226   Crusade of King Louis VIII of France

1229   Treaty of Paris which ends the Cathar wars

1231   Inquisition initiated by Pope Gregory IX

MAP OF QUERCY AND THE ROUERGUE IN THE 13ᵀᴴ CENTURY

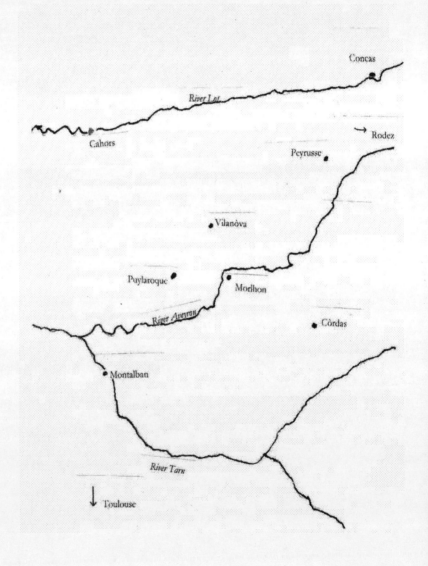

PREFACE

CONSOLAMENTUM

1223

The smell is overpowering. A few candles gutter in the draught from the low door, enough to allow a dim light in the room. She can just make out two figures in the penumbra, hooded and dark-robed. Standing, still, waiting. She moves forward and kneels in front of them. She is unsure if this is required. The genuflection makes her feel uncomfortable, compromised.

One of the two, the taller man, reaches forward with an outstretched hand and touches the top of her head. She can hardly feel it through the thick weave of her hood. She moves backwards. There is silence.

A groan. Two men are carrying in a litter, a rough construction of wood and rope. Lying on it is her father. His eyes, caked with dried pus, are closed. She has cleaned them as best she can but it seems he has no use for them now. In his extremity he is seeing little.

They lay the litter on the ground. A crackling sound as its weight settles into the reeds, newly laid as a covering for the floor. She stares down at him, scarcely able to believe that this is her father. His strength is gone. The bulky muscles of his arms and shoulders, product of years of wielding heavy hammers, have withered away to nothing. She can see the skeleton beneath, as if it were anxious to escape from the flesh now that its time has come. She notices the white scars that have replaced much of the skin of his forearms, legacy of years of work with hot metal.

But it is the smell that is new. He has been vomiting for weeks, vomiting away the great substance of his body. His limbs are now thin and wasted whilst his lower belly has become more and more distended. He had neglected the symptoms at first, despite her entreaties. No need to fuss, daughter. Just some rough bread; those bakers are fools, worse still maybe crooks. Using bad flour and poisoning folk who need to make an honest living.

But it was not foul bread. He had stopped eating. The vomiting, the distension continued. His flesh began to fall away, his face gaunt, his eyes became wide and staring. It is as if they could already see what lay ahead. Then the pain had started. He never spoke of it but she could see how he was suffering. She had sought some help from one of the monks. He was a man known for his skills with herbs and recipes. His libations made no difference. In the end her father refused to take them.

She had known he was dying but could not find the means to talk of it, the way into that conversation. Later she realised that he knew well enough. He had started to talk about the goodmen. This was a surprise. Rarely did he speak of such matters. He had raised her as best he could, taking her to Mass on days of obligation but never talking of matters of the soul. She cannot remember how it was before her mother died; she had been too young. All she knows is how it has been with him. What memories she might retain could be just dreams, constructions in her mind, phantasms that could tell her of the warmth of being loved. In the austerity of her father's care she knew the need for it.

Surprising then when he spoke of the goodmen. She had heard the talk of heresy. She knew that it infected the village. The sauvatèrra, the sanctuary village of Vilanòva, dominated by its Priory and a church whose structure, or so she was told, was an image of the Church of the Holy Sepulchre in Jerusalem. She had kept herself apart. She knew little of what these heretics believed.

"Grazide. You must take me to the goodmen." That was what he had said.

"Why, father? Where are these goodmen?"

"Talk to Guillaume, he knows."

She had sought out Guillaume, the man who hired out his pair of oxen for the ploughing. "You need to take him to Corbarieu. It is a long journey but there you will find the men he seeks. You can be sure that people will help you if you say that you are taking him to the goodmen."

And it had been so. Their neighbours had lent them a small donkey cart, just large enough for her father to lie down in. She had travelled south until they met the river Aveyron. There she had found

4

a boatman who agreed to take them the rest of the way. Travelling downstream on the river was a gentler means of transport for a sick man. The boatman was skilled, negotiating the rapids with care so as not to disturb his suffering passenger.

For his condition had worsened. Now his vomit was turning dark brown and had the smell of shit. She had helped him as best she could but soon the stench pervaded the whole boat. She could hardly bear to face him. The faeculent odour of his breath would as likely make her heave in turn.

Eventually the boatman had left them at a small quay. "You'll have to walk the last bit," was his advice but he stopped long enough to find two men who would carry the litter, not a hard task for its wasted burden was light enough. She had offered them money but they refused when she told them that he was to be taken to the goodmen. They did not complain of the smell.

Now he is lying on the floor. The taller man steps forward. He is looking at her and his gaze is both gentle and severe at one and the same time.

"What is his name, daughter?"

"Arnaud, sir. Arnaud Lamothe."

"And you?"

"Grazide. I am his only remaining child."

"Why have you brought him here, Grazide? What prompted you?"

"It was his wish, sir. As you can see he is dying." She stares down at her father, supine on the litter. He is still now except for the laboured movement of his chest. His Adam's apple is prominent and gaunt. With each breath it is pulled down, as if he were struggling to extract a vestige of life from the air around.

"I can see that, daughter. Does he wish to be consoled?"

She is at a loss to answer him. The consolamentum she had heard it called. She knew little more than that.

"I believe so, sir. He insisted that we bring him here."

The man steps back into the gloom and says nothing. For a while there is only the sound of the dying man's agonal breathing.

The second man comes forward. "I believe we must be quick if his soul is to be saved. Madam, would you leave us?"

Her cheeks redden as a sudden anger rises up in her throat. "I cannot leave him. He is my father." Are these men intending to exclude her?

The man's expression is severe. "Are you a believer, madam?"

"I'm not sure what you mean." Her tone has now hardened with determination. Surely these men do not intend to deprive her of her last moments with her father.

The other man mutters something to his companion who speaks again. "This is no place for a woman."

Grazide slows her speech. "I am not going to leave him now."

"Very well, but you must be certain not to say anything of what you see here. It could be a danger for you." She is silent at this warning. She understands what it implies.

The taller man is speaking now. His voice is low-pitched. She has to strain to hear the words. "Bless us, have mercy upon us. Amen. Let it be done unto us according to Thy Word. May the Father, the Son and the Holy Spirit forgive all your sins."

She is surprised to hear this incantation, spoken in her own tongue. The priests and the monks only speak the liturgy in Latin. Father Jean had taught her Latin so the words are familiar. The goodman repeats the words three times and then she hears the words of the Pater Noster, again in her own language.

The tall man addresses her. "Grazide Lamothe, it is clear that your father cannot speak for himself. I need to know that he has been a believer of our faith and has not done any injury to us nor owes us any debts." She nods in assent even though she has no idea of whether it is true.

He looks down. "Arnaud Lamothe, will you agree to maintain the usages and prohibitions of the faith? Do you wish to be consoled?"

6

He is staring at her father. He appears to take the dying man's silence as assent. "Let us proceed."

The second man lays a white cloth across the body in front of them. It exaggerates the contour of his swollen belly, rising and falling with each strained breath. He places a book on the cloth as gently as he can. The dying man groans at the unexpected weight.

The taller man is speaking again. "This baptism in which you are being consoled has been instituted by Christ, preserved by the apostles, passed by goodmen to goodmen until now and will continue thus until the end of the world." He takes the book in his right hand and places it on the dying blacksmith's head, holding it still. The second goodman places his hand on the book as well. They pray together for a few moments. Finally they step back.

"Daughter, your father has been consoled. You can trust that his soul will re-join his heavenly Father after his death."

Is that it? She cannot speak. Her mind is a jumble of thoughts but there is an anger deep within her, an anger that reaches down to her very guts. She cannot speak.

PART ONE

HERESY

CHAPTER 1

June 1209

The track leaves the village of Vilanòva from the north gate. It winds around the plots of cultivation, corn, vegetables, a few vines, that surround the small habitation. A village that is hardly a hundred people strong, that is if you discount the monks. Arnaud is following the path down a gentle slope towards the start of the trees. The ground is rocky under his feet.

The forest is sparse here. Stubby scrub oaks, never large enough nor close enough together to make a canopy. The sun shines through the leaves, illuminating patches of clearing with here and there small, marshy bogs. The track is clear enough for him to push his handcart with ease. He has made this journey so many times. He weaves his way through the trees, recognising familiar ruts and potholes, the exposed rocks that could break a wheel if he hits them too hard.

Arnaud has never understood why the charcoal burners have to live so deep in the forest. It is a good two hours walk to their camp, longer coming back with a cart laden with charcoal. Still, he never minds the journey. It makes a break from the days of sweltering in the heat of the forge. He has left the girl with Na Lisier. The old woman likes the company though the nine-year-old can be difficult at times, seeming to be closed in on herself.

It has been hard to deal with her since Allemande's death, taken by a fever that would not submit to any ministrations. The girl had never cried, never asked for her mother after that. Her brothers, both older, had shown more upset at their mother's death than had little Grazide. He tried to do his best with her but she was beyond his reach, as if isolated in her loneliness.

The forest is thicker here. Taller oaks, ash and chestnut combine to create a dense canopy. The shade is darker and the path less distinct. Even so the journey is familiar enough to Arnaud, he has made it enough times. There is no difficulty in finding the charcoal burners, the familiar smell of wood smoke drifting on the breeze tells him he is nearly there.

The forest opens up into a wide clearing. In the centre is a rough wooden hut. Next to it he can see an active kiln, its conical shape as high as a man. The smoke emerging from its top is thin and blue. Arnaud knows that means the process of carbonising the wood inside is almost complete. There are distinct holes scattered around the surface of the kiln. A figure can be seen to be filling some of them in with soft earth.

Arnaud calls a greeting, "Fellow. Good day to you." The man turns away from his work and stares at the blacksmith. His expression shows he resents the interruption. He makes no reply. His face is blackened by years of exposure to wood smoke, lines of concentration are deeply etched in the grime. Arnaud recognises him, he makes this trip often enough, but he does not know the man's name. Another charcoal burner emerges from the hut. Stockier than the first with shoulders as broad as those of the blacksmith.

"You're back, Arnaud. Need more coal?"

"That's right," he indicates the empty cart, "Can you fill that with a load?"

The stocky man grunts, which Arnaud takes to mean yes. Arnaud follows him around to the back of the hut to where a large pile of charcoal awaits him.

"Help yourself. There's a shovel there," he nods towards the heap. Arnaud realises that he is going to get no help with loading his cart. It is always the same. These charcoal burners are a rough lot, living on the edge of civilised society and often mistrusted. Yet Arnaud has never had a problem with them.

He sets to and soon the cart is loaded with its dusty, black load. His hands are now blackened but he is used to that. After a day in the forge it is hard to get them completely clean. He reaches for the purse that is tied to his belt.

"Here's your money," he hands over a collection of coins. The man takes one and bites it, then he counts the remainder.

"Is that right? Twenty-five deniers?"

The man nods then turns away without a word. His companion is still working on the kiln, blocking the air holes. Arnaud guesses that the firing is about complete. It will have been going for seven days, needing constant attention. These sylvan artisans rarely leave their glade.

It is a slow journey back to the village, hard work even for a man with the strength of Arnaud. After an hour he stops for a rest beside a dew pond. He takes a drink and fills up his water container. The sun is high in the sky and the day is hot. From where he is sitting he can look down over the forest towards the village. Further on he can make out the line of the pilgrim road that runs from the northeast, the road that leads on to the gorges of the river Aveyron to the south and then beyond.

His unfocused gaze does not notice a small cloud of dust rising from the road below him. He is lost in thought, resting to gather strength for the last part of his journey. It is only when he hears the whinny of a horse, carried across on the breeze, that he sits up. He peers in the direction of the sound, his hand up to shade his eyes from the sun. He notices the dust cloud. It is getting nearer.

Now he can see more. Horses with men astride, metal glinting in the sun. He hears the jingle of armour, the tramp of footsteps. In a moment of panic a thought hits him. They must have passed through the village, just a few miles back. At once he remembers the news he had heard the previous week. A travelling wool merchant who turned up in the village with a story about the sacking of the small castle at Puylaroque, some ten leagues or so to the south west. His account was second-hand and vague. Arnaud assumed it was no more than a touch of bother between local lords. There was enough of that. Not unwelcome, it kept him in work sharpening swords and making chain mail. Even so, sacking a castle sounded a bit extreme. He had thought no more about it at the time.

But now here is something much more threatening. What is this force that is kicking up the dust along the pilgrim way? He screws his eyes to make out detail. He sees a banner at the head of the procession, a white bird with outstretched wings set on a blue background; it signifies that the force is being led by an important man. He counts around thirty mounted knights followed by a large contingent of foot-soldiers. He can make out their pikes, pointing to the sky. Behind them are carts pulled by mules and donkeys. There are women amongst them, rough-looking mountain women. Occasional shouts float up to his hearing, then a snatch of song.

Arnaud slips down the grassy bank to remain unobserved. Whoever or whatever this force is he does not want to get mixed up with them. But what have they done back at the village? As soon as they have passed on he grabs his cart and bumps his way back home as fast as he can.

There is a small crowd gathered around the west door of the church when he arrives. He is relieved to see that there are no signs of depredation from the passing force. Even more relieved when he sees Na Lisier in the crowd, holding the hand of his daughter Grazide, her two brothers standing nearby. People are chattering, their voices taut with anxiety. Arnaud abandons his cart and pushes his way through the crowd towards his daughter.

"Grazide. Boys. Come here." Grazide lets go of the hand of the old woman and runs to her father, grasping him around his waist. For a moment he is shocked by this show of emotion. It is unexpected, unfamiliar.

"Papa. We've seen soldiers. Lots of them."

Now his boys are by his side. The elder of the two, Guillaume, gesticulates with excitement as he speaks. "Hundreds of them, father. And horses. I saw a man with a sword two arms' length long. It was huge."

Beside him his younger brother, Pierre, is more subdued but still anxious enough to gain his father's attention that he pushes Guillaume aside. "They wore crosses, Papa. Red crosses. What does that mean?"

14

Arnaud does not reply but he knows the answer. These are the crosses of crusaders. He remembers the stories that his grandfather had told him. The old man had been on a crusade against the infidels many years previously. He had told the young Arnaud of his pride in taking up the cross, of wearing it stitched on to his clothing. He hardly spoke of the horrors of the campaign. Few of his friends who had joined the forces of King Louis had survived to make it back home. The thought of crusaders on his own soil chills Arnaud's bones to the core. What are they doing here?

In the crowd he spots a monk that he knows, Brother Raimond. The blacksmith pushes his way through the throng and grasps his shoulder from behind. The monk turns.

"Arnaud. Hello. Did you see the procession?"

"Only in the distance. I was returning from the forest," he points across the square to his loaded cart, black in the sunlight. "Who are they? Where are they off to?"

"They're the forces of the Bishop of Le Puy, Bertrand de Chalencon. Didn't you see his standard?"

"But they're wearing crusader crosses. What are they doing in our lands?"

"Perhaps you haven't heard, Arnaud. The Holy Father has preached a crusade against the heretics that infest our land. It is a holy war. None too soon, in my opinion."

These are harsh words to Arnaud's ears. He had heard of heretics though had never met a single one of them. There had been a strange man in the village at the last annual fair who called himself a follower of Valdes. He seemed gentle enough. He expounded the scripture in their own tongue. How, in the name of God, was the Pope going to wage war on such benign individuals? Can't all be bad, though. Knights need armour and soldiers need weapons. Work for blacksmiths; that will be an opportunity.

Already rumours and fabulations are spreading through the crowd. Talk of horrors and disasters abound, constructed from the collective of frightened minds. Arnaud rounds up his children and takes them away; he does not want them infected with the common panic. Even so the two boys run ahead, wielding imaginary swords and shouting "Die, heretic! Take that!" Grazide clutches his hand tightly. He can see the fear in her eyes.

He unloads the contents of his cart into the fuel store at the forge. Enough charcoal to last till Lammastide he reckons. That is unless he gets an influx of extra work, thinking of the impending hostilities. Back at his home, his ostal, Na Lisier is cooking vegetable broth over the fire, food enough for the five of them but his mind is uneasy. If war comes then famine follows on. It is inexorable; how then to protect his family?

CHAPTER 2
February 1210

It has been a hard winter, harder than most. The food stores are being rapidly depleted. Arnaud worries about how little salted pork they have left. Na Lisier does her best but for most of the time all she can put on the table is a thin gruel with some coarse bread. Hunger plagues the village.

Hunger drags at him as he works. Some days it is hard to wield the heavy hammer. These days the boys help him in the forge; Guillaume, now fifteen, is strong enough to hold the fiery metal whilst his father hammers it into shape. Pierre keeps the fire going, shovelling on the charcoal. He is tall enough now to pull down the bellows handle, just within his reach. The pair of wood and leather bellows keep up a steady blast of air that turns the fire bright yellow. The smoke funnels up through a hole in the roof, the wooden roof tiles blackened by the years of use.

Yet Arnaud is more at peace here, working in the forge. His mind can focus on his work and that shuts out all the disturbing news that infests the village. Stories of the sack of castles and cities in the south. Lurid accounts of massacres, of armies from the north all wearing the red cross of crusaders. Tales of atrocities that are at one and the same time horrific and chilling, captives burnt at the stake, innocent women and children brutally murdered. Talk of heretics and of heresy, it all seems far away to Arnaud. He has enough to worry about nearer to home. There is always less work in the forge in winter so he supplements his income with casual work for the monastery, repairing walls, clearing ditches, anything that can put a little bread on the table.

And there is much to be done at his ostal. Na Lisier helps out but Arnaud often finds himself doing women's work, cooking, fetching water, collecting wood for the fire. It has been hard since his wife Allemande was so cruelly taken from him. He still misses her. He knows the boys are missing her too but Grazide has shown nothing.

No tears, no questions. So withdrawn, he knows nothing of what she is nursing in the shell of that detachment.

"She's a girl, Arnaud," says Na Lisier as she stirs the pot. "Girls keep themselves to themselves."

"What can I do with her? She hardly speaks to me. Or her brothers. Silent as the night."

"Give her time. She'll come round."

"I don't know. Maybe she'll never come out of it. I don't know what to do."

But little changes. Grazide seems like a silent wraith to him. Not only has he lost a wife, he has lost a daughter too. He talks to Brother Raimond about it. Arnaud has little time for most of the monks in the Priory but Raimond seems an exception, more approachable.

"Perhaps she needs some schooling." says the monk. "Something to bring her out of herself. I could talk to Father Jean."

Arnaud knows that the parish priest, Father Jean Vital, tutors some of the village children. "But he only takes boys."

"Maybe he'd make an exception. I'll talk to him if you like."

It is soon decided. Father Jean is approached and terms are agreed. Arnaud wonders to himself whether this is money well spent, money he can ill afford at the moment.

Grazide shows little reaction to the news that she is to visit the priest once a week.

"Who else is going, Papa?"

"There'll be others. Father Jean will teach you numbers, writing, things like that."

"Will there be other girls?" Grazide has few friends, perhaps only the strange boy, Gervais. He is ten years old, the same age as Grazide. He walks with a limp and has a palsied arm, his speech slurred. Perhaps because of this he is shunned by the other boys in the village. Somehow Grazide can get through to him, they are often together, playing in the fields outside the village or just sitting on the step outside Gervais's house.

"I don't know. Maybe," but Arnaud knows it is unlikely.

"Perhaps Gervais can come too. Can he, Papa?" Arnaud does not answer, never happy about her friendship with the cripple.

Father Jean's lessons are given in the church of the Holy Sepulchre. In the north apse are large wall paintings. Grazide knows them well enough. She has often crept into the building to look at the figures, their bright colours lit by the afternoon sun. Often she will stand for hours in front of them, staring up, not moving.

From time to time pilgrims come into the church. Strangers carrying bags across their shoulders. She shrinks behind a pillar when they appear, fearing to be discovered. She can hear them muttering prayers, kneeling on the cold stone floor, lighting candles to place in the wooden rack at the side of the apse.

She wonders what motivates them. Her unformed mind has not yet appreciated the universal desire amongst ordinary folk to seek salvation after death. Such preoccupations find no foothold in her young consciousness. To her death is just an absence. One day a person is here, the next gone. She imagines that that must have been how it was with her mother. She has no memory of her except for an enduring sensation, a feeling of being loved.

On one wall of the apse are painted three images, seemingly ordinary working people. Not saints, not monks or priests, no haloes. One, a man in a purple cloak carries a staff in his left hand. Around his shoulder is slung the strap of a bag that hangs over his right hip. There is an emblem on his bag. His long, curled hair is surmounted by a broad-brimmed, dark hat. Who is he, she wonders? Perhaps a pilgrim. He wears a pair of shoes that look well-made and sturdy, just what you would need for a journey of such a length.

The second figure is hooded, no hat, and carries a long, slender staff. In his left hand he holds a curved horn which he blows with obvious vigour. His cheeks blown out, his mouth pursed around the mouthpiece. He is surrounded by substantial bushy trees. Flowers are scattered across the sandy-coloured ground. Perhaps he is a huntsman, thinks Grazide. She can hear the call of his horn, sounding through her head. She imagines the baying of dogs, the squealing of the terrified boar. Sometimes she spots boars when she accompanies Papa to collect the charcoal, often hears them rustling in the undergrowth.

But it is the third figure which, in the end, draws most of her attention. It is a woman in a red cloak, also carrying a staff. Her head is enclosed in the folds of a wimple and surmounted by another wide-brimmed hat. On the hat is a symbol; now she realises that the same symbol is on the bag that the first two figures carry. It is the scallop shell, the image of the shell that she has seen along the pilgrims' path and on the door lintels of the hostel in the village. The shell of Saint-Jacques. Na Lisier has told her that these symbols mark the path as it wends its way for hundreds of leagues, over the mountains in the south to the city of Saint-Jacques, Santiago de Compostela. The old lady talked of a vast new cathedral that has been built where the bones of the saint now lie. Often Grazide has imagined joining these pilgrims. What must it be like? To walk for weeks, even months on end to some distant city. To be driven by an inner need, even in her young mind perhaps she can begin to understand.

For this woman is more than just another pilgrim. Grazide stares at her face, gentle and calm and then Grazide knows. This is her mother. She is certain that it is her face even though she has no memory of it. Now she imagines she can hear her voice, speaking love to her little daughter. Grazide knows it is her. Whoever painted this fresco must have known her, perhaps used her as a model for this holy painting. This is a safe place for Grazide, this is her sanctuary. She can immerse herself in its peace, her own special place of pilgrimage.

The creak of the door from the Priory breaks into her absorption. She slips out of sight. She can hear footsteps. Peering around the pillar she spots the figure of Father Jean. Only then does she remember that this is the day and the hour for her lessons. She can hear the cries of the boys playing in the dust outside the north door of the church. The priest has not seen her but she can see that he is carrying a heavy book. He sets it down on a table in the central nave.

The light from a circular window high up above the pillars casts a pool of light around the book and the table.

From behind the pillar she watches the figure as he walks into the eastern apse where the high altar is raised up on a wooden dais. He moves behind the altar. Now he is out of sight. Just then she hears the sound of the main door. Someone is opening it slowly, carefully. Perhaps it is a pilgrim, weary from the long walk from Concas, seeking the solace of this holy church. It cannot be the boys. They never come in until the priest goes out to summon them.

The figure is cloaked and hooded. Grazide cannot make out her face but she is in no doubt that it is a woman. The figure looks about her, perhaps adapting her eyes to the gloom for a moment. Then she moves swiftly across the nave into the eastern apse. She disappears behind the altar.

Now there are quiet voices. A forced quietness such that Grazide cannot hear what is being said. Nonetheless she can hear agitation in the woman's tone, interspersed with the low firmness of the priest's speech. In their restrained whispering they are arguing.

Suddenly she hears a clap, the sound of a hand on exposed flesh. There is an immediate cry and Grazide shrinks behind the pillar as the hooded figure runs across the nave, clutching her face and making for the door. She hears it being opened, forcefully this time. Light spills into the narthex. The woman has gone.

A few moments later Father Jean emerges and strides towards the door. She hears him calling the boys and within minutes they are in the church, sitting on the hard floor around the table in the nave. As unobtrusively as she can she comes around from behind the pillar and joins them. The priest settles down on a wooden stool and the lessons begin. She joins in the recitation of numbers, one, two, three, four, onwards and onwards. On her slate she forms the ones that she has learnt, the angular four, the rotund eight, but her mind remains with the scene that she has just witnessed. Not understanding yet knowing it was unusual. She had not recognised the hooded woman but there was something familiar about her appearance. She folds the memory into her silent mind as she traces out the numbers.

CHAPTER 3
1212

On most weeks of the year a market is held in the square in front of the church. It is a concession from the Prior that has been established for a century at least. Concession it may be but the rents, tolls and taxes charged make for a healthy income for the Priory. Along with the tithes levied on the villagers the religious house is well provided for. Even in the hard winter of two years ago the monks did not go hungry.

Wednesday is market day. Stalls are set up in the shadow of the church. Some weeks the produce is sparse, those times when crop and fruit yields are meagre, but there are other seasons when the tables groan with the weight of a glut. Often there are fish for sale. Rough-handed fishermen from the Lot and the Aveyron bring in their crates of trout, salted carp and eels, paying their toll to the treasurer of the Priory, an austere monk who patrols the stalls, making sure that no one fails to come up with their dues.

In the corner of the market stands a stone block, its centre hollowed out to create a measure for corn. The treasurer keeps a careful eye on the stallholders using it, seeing that their bags of grain are of a uniform content. Most weeks Arnaud has a stall in the market. The two boys act as vendors though sometimes Guillaume is needed in the forge so Pierre does the selling on his own. Grazide is by his side, silent and observant. Ironware is laid out on the table, cooking pots, nails, mattocks and other tools for use in the house or the fields. Grazide likes to set out the display in an orderly pattern, large pots at the back, nails arranged in size order. When an item is sold she rearranges the wares to conceal the gap. After two years of lessons from Father Jean she is quite adept at both counting and writing. She keeps a tally of the sales and the takings ready to hand these over to her father at the end of the day. Arnaud then knows what he is due to pay in taxes to the treasurer.

It is the first Wednesday in July, a day when the heat of the sun drives many of the stallholders into the shade. Pierre remains with the ironwork table. Grazide seeks out the trees in the corner of the square. A small crowd has gathered there. As she approaches she sees that they seem to be watching a single figure standing in the darkness of the deep shade. Not just watching but listening too, for he is speaking to them.

He is dressed poorly. A rough brown tunic and belt, no hat and no shoes. His face is burnt brown by the sun but it is his eyes that attract Grazide's attention. Deep set in dark hollows they glint like bright blue jewels. Poor and undernourished he may be but rarely has she seen someone so filled with life. He is holding a book with both his hands.

"Brothers and sisters. You hear the gospel of Christ at Mass but can you understand it? No, it is spoken in Latin, gibberish to most of you, I guess. Only the priest understands it so what do you do? You rely on him to tell you what it means." There is a murmuring from the crowd at this, an insistent rumble. The man continues, "Let me read this to you. It is the Gospel of Saint-Jean. Listen closely." He lifts the book and starts to read. "In the beginning was the Word, and the Word was with God."

Grazide listens enthralled. He is reading in their language. She can understand what is being read. The words tumble from his book and whirl around in her mind. She does not know what to make of them but she can understand what is being read. The preacher has stopped his reading and now addresses the crowd again.

"My life is dedicated to bringing you the word of God. I am one of the Poor Men of Lyon. Like Our Lord we are, all of us, poor in possessions but rich in spirit. We all know that we are saved by the atoning death of Christ. You too. He is the sinless one who bears all our sins. Don't believe what they tell you in there." His arm points across to the edifice of the church that looms over the market square. "There is no purgatory. It is an invention. There is no need to buy indulgences, they are scraps of paper of no worth." Grazide hears gasps from some of the women in the crowd. "And all those relics, they have no power to save you. They are just old bones. Who knows

24

where they come from? They could be animal bones for all you know. They are powerless to save you." The rumble from the crowd grows stronger. The preacher's voice is rising a tone. "Don't waste your time and money going on pilgrimages, lavishing your hard-earned resources on large and beautiful buildings. You will find no salvation there. The gospel of the Lord does not need cathedrals or churches. It can be heard anywhere; in barns, in your homes, even in the open air."

Across the square Grazide spots two monks. They are making their way through the stalls towards the crowd. She sees that the preacher has spotted them too. "May God bless you, brothers and sisters," he says, and in a moment he has disappeared.

At the sight of the monks the people disperse. Grazide hears snatches of conversation, People wonder who this man is, where is he from? Does he speak the truth? The preacher has made an impact, that is obvious to her. She wonders what Father Jean or the Prior Roger would say were they to know what was being preached outside their church. She re-joins her brother at the stall.

"Any more sold, Pierre?"

"No, nothing much. Just a few nails."

She rearranges the display. "When did Papa say we should pack up?"

"Not sure. When the rest go, I suppose."

"I think we should go now. There are not many people left. It's too hot for them today."

Pierre agrees and together they collect up the wares, loading them in wooden crates on the hand cart.

There is no one at home when they get back to the ostal. Gathering up the takings she slips down the winding street to the forge. Smoke is rising from the hole in the roof. Papa and Guillaume must still be working. She hears the rhythmic ringing of steel on iron.

On such a hot day the heat from the fire is oppressive. She stands in the far corner watching her father wielding the heavy hammer. Guillaume is holding a bright yellow-heated metal block in the long-armed pincers. Papa is beating it into shape. After every few blows he transfers the cooling block back to the fire and pumps on the bellows arm. The blast restores the bright yellow heat to the metal and the process is repeated.

Hanging on the wall next to her are arrays of completed work; rings to go in the noses of oxen, horseshoes, harness fittings, hand axes and much more. She likes to finger the worked metal, now cool and solid.

Arnaud spots her in the corner and stops his work.

"Well, daughter? Home from the market? How did we do today?"

"Not so well, Papa. Here's the takings." She hands him the bag of coins. There is little weight in it. Arnaud frowns.

"You're quite right, daughter. What's going on? We usually do better than this."

"I'm sorry, Papa. I don't know. Maybe it's the heat." She has already decided not to mention the preacher. She resumes her silence.

Arnaud sighs. "Ah well. Maybe it'll be better next week. What do I have to pay that bloody treasurer?"

"Ten deniers, Papa." Her father grunts, takes the bag and returns to his work.

Packing up the stall early means that she has time to herself for a couple of hours. She does not need to be back to help Na Lisier prepare the food until later. Leaving the forge she turns down the street towards the north gate. Out in the fields she passes some of the women from the village working on the land. Without stopping their work they nod a greeting as she passes.

She loves the woods. Here she can be alone. She seeks out her favourite spot, a small ledge on a steep bank, shaded by a tall chestnut tree. From here she can watch yet not be seen. A few rabbits feed on the turf of the wood's floor. High overhead she hears a 'scree', the mew of a buzzard circling high in the sky, on the lookout for prey in the wood below. It is quiet yet she can still hear the distant clang from the forge

She stretches out her long limbs on the slope. She is tall for her age, already almost as tall as her brother, Pierre. She is watching everything, no detail escapes attention. Here are the small birds; blue tits, careering through the foliage like aerial tumblers, fat bullfinches tearing at berries on the conifer leaves, hedge sparrows rooting in the litter of the wood's floor. She sees them all, familiar and reassuring, her mind rested. Communal life in the village is hard to accommodate for Grazide. So often she does not know how to be, how she should behave. Easier to be silent, easier to be alone.

The strange preacher has disturbed her. Not his appearance, nor his poverty of dress. It is always meeting people's eyes that she finds difficult and his blue eyes, deep set in their dark pits, unnerved her. She could never have met his gaze. Looking away is always her defence; looking down. People might call her demure, shy even, but that is not how she feels to herself. She has her world inside her; at times it is a precarious construct but, however fragile, it is a place where she can feel safe.

A breeze has got up. Just enough to shimmer the light through the trees. Her mind adjusts to the change as she looks around. It is only then that she spots a figure down below her. A man is approaching along the woodland path from the direction of the village. As he gets closer she recognises him. It is the preacher, the thin man in the shabby brown tunic. He carries a staff which he uses to clear some of the brambles that encroach on the path. If he carries on along the path she knows that he will pass close by. As if by instinct she slips down the slope, seeking to make herself invisible.

It is a futile move. He must have spotted her for he calls out, "Hey there, daughter." Grazide feels an updraught of fear fill her body. She dares not move. She is silent.

"Peace to you, girl. Don't be afraid. I mean you no harm." Now he has stopped on the path, just below her. "Does this path take me to Peyrusse?" His tone is gentle enough to undermine her fear. She sits up and points to the east, nodding at the same time.

"I'm right, am I?"

Now she can find her voice. "Yes, sir. That is the way"

"Thank you, daughter"

For a moment Grazide is affronted. He is too familiar. Why does he call her daughter? Yet she can detect a calm in his voice. Her heart beats less fast in her chest. "Take this path. In half a league you will join the pilgrims' way. That goes to Peyrusse." Many times she has walked these paths, she knows the patterns, the junctions, the short cuts. Now her curiosity is aroused.

"It's a long day's journey to Peyrusse, sir." She notices that he is still barefoot. "You may not reach it by nightfall."

"That is not a concern. I'm used to it. I can sleep anywhere."

"Why do you go to Peyrusse?" She is remembering the man's preaching in the square, just a few hours past. "Are you going there to preach?"

"That is my calling, daughter. I am bound to preach the Word, that is my calling."

She moves down the slope. The preacher has sat down on a fallen tree trunk that crosses the path. She sits down next to him.

"I heard you preaching in the square up there." She points back to the village.

"I know, daughter. I saw you."

Once again she is discomfited. She does not like to be noticed. But by now her interest is aroused. "Those things you said. About purgatory and relics. It is not what the priest tells us. He says we are all sinners and have to atone for our bad deeds. But you say we don't. How do you know?"

The man smiles at her. "These are deep thoughts for a child of your age. Tell me, what should I call you?"

Her face reddens, she is uncomfortable with familiarity but she answers him, "Grazide, sir. Grazide Lamothe."

"Grazide. A good name. I am Brother Bernard. People call us Waldensians. Followers of Pierre Valdes. He died seven years ago. Came from a large city, Lyon, a long way from here. There are many of us now and we spread far and wide. The Poor Men of Lyon we call ourselves."

"Are you monks?" Grazide could not imagine the monks of the Priory embracing this degree of austerity.

"No. Just ordinary people like you. But we study the scriptures just as the monks do. It's just that we don't live in special buildings with beds, basins, refectories and the like. Our church is all this." He waves his arm around the woods about them, "the world in all its magnificence. Our Lord praised the lilies of the field. We embrace all of God's creation."

Grazide is silent. Such words are unusual to her. She can never imagine Father Jean speaking like this. She wonders how her father would react were he to hear them. Dismissive probably. "So much nonsense" he is likely to say. "A working man like me has no time for such blather." But it is no blather to her. Somewhere deep within her it triggers an emotional response. Nothing that she can recognise but in its gentleness it stirs a memory that is unreachable. Yet stirs it enough to bring with it a warmth, a warmth she knows she longs for. She casts her eyes down as she mutters "I have to go, sir." She turns and clambers back up the slope, running to get away. She does not look back. She has to get away.

It is towards sunset. Grazide is stirring the pot that steams over the kitchen fire. From the rafters hangs a dried ham, well out of reach of the cat. The hearth is surrounded by cooking utensils, pots and pans, jugs and basins. Na Lisier is sitting on a bench at the table, chopping up herbs to be thrown in the pot.

"Na, did you see the preacher in the square this afternoon?"

The old lady starts and crosses herself with a rapid movement, knife still held in her hand. "No, I certainly didn't but Guillaume told me of it. You didn't listen to him did you, girl?" The old lady's face darkens. "No good will come of it. Listening to those heretics. You should stay away from all that."

"But why? He seemed a good man. Where's the danger in that?"

The old lady stands up, waving the knife in the air in her agitation. "Danger? There is danger with those wandering heretics. Have you not heard of what's happening down in the south?"

Indeed Grazide has heard the reports. They come with travellers that pass through the village. Pilgrims returning from Spain speak of castles being besieged, mass burnings of prisoners and laying waste of the countryside.

"But that won't come here, will it Na?"

The old lady crosses herself again. "Pray that it doesn't, young lady," she pauses, "and stay away from those vermin. We shall all be infested if we give them any encouragement."

Grazide cannot associate vermin with the gentle Brother Bernard. Why is the old lady talking like this?

Na Lisier is grumbling on under her breath. She has seated herself again and resumes her chopping with increased vigour. Grazide cannot catch what she is saying, so indistinct is her mumbling. That is not until she hears the words "What would her poor mother think, listening to such vermin."

Grazide turns away. She hates it when Na Lisier mentions her mother. She wants to close her ears. She remains silent and the old woman quietens down.

Her brothers appear through the doorway, sitting themselves down on the bench by the table. Guillaume turns to Na Lisier. "What's cooking, Na? I'm starving."

"Me too," echoes his brother, Pierre "What's in the pot, Grazide?"

Grazide does not reply. It is only the usual potage. A few slices of the ham, vegetables and Na Lisier's herbs. She reaches down five bowls as her father enters.

"Are you boys cleaned up?" His voice is gruff.

"Yes, Papa" says Pierre. Grazide notices that their hand washing has been perfunctory.

30

"Come on then. Let's eat." Her father pulls up a heavy wooden stool to the head of the table.

Grazide ladles out the stew into the bowls and passes them across to Na Lisier who places them in front of Arnaud and the two boys. She puts a loaf of bread on the table and places her bowl next to Guillaume, edging him aside. "Move down. Make some space." Now she is next to her father. He hardly seems to notice her.

Na Lisier pauses from her noisy slurping. "The girl's been listening to heretics. I told her, no good will come of it."

Grazide flushes. Just at that moment she hates Na Lisier, hates her interference, hates her poisonous mind.

"Is this true, Grazide?" Dark lines appear across her father's forehead. His tone is threatening.

"Only for a moment, Papa. He left soon after I saw him." She was determined that she was not going to reveal the second meeting.

"You be careful, daughter. Those people are dangerous. Don't you let that priest of yours know you've been consorting with heretics."

Why all this prejudice, she thinks? What harm is there in this gentle man? Her face reddens but her eyes are downcast. She says nothing.

"It'll be the road to hell, following those wandering idiots." Arnaud has raised his tone. She recognises the signs for they are familiar. They are in for a rant. "They're spreading like rats. Just let those crusaders know about it and they'll be tearing down our houses, burning them to the ground. Then where'll we be?"

Surely not, thinks Grazide. This is a sauvatèrra, protected by the Peace of God is what Father Jean says. Nothing like that will happen here. She notices that the boys are quiet during this exchange, their heads down over their bowls of potage.

Later, after Na Lisier has gone and Grazide has cleared up the bowls and pots, she goes to her bed in the adjoining room. She and the boys share the bed, set amongst the few casks that the ostal owns. She tries to keep to the far side of the bed and get to sleep before the familiar rhythmic grunting comes from Pierre, keeping her awake. Her mind cannot stop turning over the events of the day. Pierre lets out a moan and is still. Now she can drift off to sleep.

CHAPTER 4
1213

Though Arnaud is troubled by his failure to get through to his adolescent daughter he is heartened by his two sons. Guillaume at seventeen now has the body of a grown man. Arnaud works hard to train him in the skills of a smithy but the boy is a slow learner. His younger brother Pierre, now fifteen, is the brighter of the two even if he has not yet attained the physical maturity of Guillaume. Arnaud looks on his small family with pride. It has not been easy, raising a family with no wife by his side, he thinks. Guillaume will be an adequate successor to him once he no longer has the strength to wield the hammer. He knows that one day age and decrepitude will end his career as an artisan.

He has no doubt that Pierre will find employment elsewhere, his quick wit will guarantee that. Best to pass the business on to Guillaume, the boy would struggle otherwise. Grazide will marry in due course, he has no doubt of that. That will be a relief to him when the time comes. In the meantime he will carry the responsibility of caring for her, even though he finds it hard to understand her, to break through the carapace of reserve that she always presents to him. Allemande, his late wife, would have been able to manage her better. If only he still had her with him, how much easier his life would be.

But events in the wider world are set to disrupt his hoped-for plans. Any expectation that the crusading war that rages in the south will leave Vilanòva unaffected are soon dispelled. In the early spring Segard de Puylaroque, seneschal to the Lord Ozil II of Morlhon, (the local lord whose domains include the village of Vilanòva), appears in the village. Word has got around that he is coming so a small crowd has gathered outside the main door of the church when he rides into the square. He dismounts. An accompanying page takes the bridle of his horse.

Standing on a wooden box, for he is a man of short stature, he addresses the men and women gathered around him.

"Good people. I come here to address you with the authority of your Lord, Ozil de Morlhon. He has been charged with raising a force to join the great army of his liege lord Raimond VI, the Count of Toulouse. We will rid our country of the false crusaders who, under cover of the cross, have ravaged our land, destroyed our homes and terrorised our people over the last four years. In accordance with his loyalty to the great Count Raimond, your lord now seeks brave and strong men who will join us in this great cause."

Pierre, Guillaume and Grazide are in the crowd, listening. Their father stands beside them, his face expressionless. Pierre glances at his brother. The older boy's demeanour is quite different. His eyes are lit up, he is standing tall. "Pierre, we must join them. Come on, it's a great chance," but Pierre looks doubtful, almost frightened. Along with other young men Guillaume has raised his arm and is cheering; an increasing roar echoes around the square. Pierre looks to his left and sees that his sister, Grazide, has joined their father. Both are now staring at him but saying nothing. He wants them to speak, wants to know what to do. Grazide is motionless.

"Come on, Pierre," calls his brother, "it will be great."

Pierre can see that Guillaume's blood is up. The younger boy is torn, part wanting to join this exultation, part terrified. He looks again at his father, as if searching for guidance. Arnaud must have seen the look on the younger boy's face for he says "You two boys are too young for this. There are plenty of others who will go" which is correct for young men are pushing their way to the front of the crowd to respond to the seneschal's call. A scent of male aggrandisement is in the air, galvanising the young men of the village.

"Oh, come on father" says Guillaume. His cheeks are flushed, his eyes brightened, there is little doubt that he is taken up by the fervent atmosphere. "I'm old enough. If I can swing a hammer in the forge I can wield a sword. Why can't I go?"

"You're too young boy. In any case I need you here."

"I'm not too young. I can fight like any man. You've got to let me go. Pierre can stay and help you out. It's a great opportunity for me."

"Don't you dare disobey me, Guillaume. You are staying here. Now come away." Arnaud seizes both boys by the arm and frogmarches them away from the throng. Neither of them can free themselves from his blacksmith's grip. Guillaume's head is hung low, as if in shame. The other villagers stare at the departure of the father and his two young sons.

Despite the absence of the two Lamothe boys a considerable contingent of young men join up with the Lord of Morlhon's forces. In one way the people of the village are proud of their sons, bravely marching off to war. On the other hand there is an undercurrent of anxiety, an apprehension which is compounded as time goes on.

News come to the village from time to time. Count Raimond VI is mustering a huge army to resist the crusaders. It is gathering at Toulouse and an army of King Peter of Aragon, resplendent with over a thousand knights from across the Pyrenean mountains is marching to join them. There is a general expectation that the hated crusading force under its new leader, the northern lord Simon de Montfort, will finally be driven from their southern lands. Peace will be restored.

For a while no more news finds its way back to Vilanòva. If this lulls the people of the village into a sense of security that complacency is soon to be shattered. Word comes from a travelling merchant, one of the few that still dare to carry on trade in these turbulent times, that the two opposing armies have met at Muret, just south of Toulouse. Despite being heavily outnumbered Simon de Montfort has routed the southern army and King Peter of Aragon has died on the field of battle. The defeated army is scattered. Soon comes news that twelve young men from the village have perished. Their families are devastated. Worse still are the reports that the crusaders under the Lord Simon de Montfort are criss-crossing the land just to the south of them. Castles are being besieged and destroyed, people slaughtered and crops pillaged by the invading army.

Guillaume is much subdued at the news of the death of many of his friends. Survivors of the carnage eventually make their way back to Vilanòva, some with horrific wounds, hands amputated, faces slashed and scarred. The two boys try to talk to the returnees but find the latter reluctant to speak of what they have been through.

Grazide cannot fail to hear of the turmoil but she folds the news within her, outwardly appearing unmoved where the other children of the village are as perturbed as the adults, like chickens in a coop with the fox prowling outside. Only this is a fox wearing the cross of Christ.

On Christmas Day she attends Mass with her father in the Priory church. Most of the village are there, filling the nave and the apses, their numbers swelled by pilgrims. A small band of them on the road to Saint-Jacques have rested over the feast day in the hostel. Their fervency in responses outdoes the lack of enthusiasm of the locals. The latter act as if unconvinced of the redemptive power of a Mass administered by a priest whose lack of personal probity is the subject of much village gossip. Na Lisier had spoken of it in Grazide's hearing more than once. "No better than the rest of the fornicating men of this village" was the old woman's complaint. Grazide did not understand what 'fornicating' meant. She dared not ask her father or her brothers. In any case she quite liked Father Jean. Whilst sometimes strict in his admonishments during her lessons he had never done anything to hurt her. She gave him the respect due to a man in his position. She could do little else.

As the priest drones on her eyes wander across to the painted walls of the north apse. To contemplate the figure of the woman pilgrim is a comfort for her. Was this how her mother was? Can she really remember such gentleness of her gaze or is it just from looking at this image? She is sure that there was a warmth, a warmth that she has never experienced since. Staring at the picture she can rest in that imagined embrace. Sometimes it is all that she can live by, that emotional memory. All that she can rely on.

Mass is over and the congregation spills out over the square outside the north door. It is one of those winter days when the light is bright and clear under a blue sky. The sun, though low in the sky brings a promise of warmth to come. She loops her arm in her father's as they walk back to their ostal. Na Lisier has killed one of the chickens so there is to be a feast today for the celebration of the birth of Our Lord.

On the edge of the crowd she spots a recognisable figure, gaunt, dressed like a pauper. It is Bernard, the Poor Man of Lyon that she encountered a year ago. He seems to be talking to a small bunch of pilgrims, recognisable by their thin staves and the small scallop shells of Saint-Jacques sewn on to their tunics. He appears animated in his speaking, waving one arm to emphasise his words. It is clear to her that he is preaching.

She is anxious. This is dangerous for him. Preaching in the open like this. Since her meeting with him the previous year she has learnt from Father Jean that these men, these Waldensians, are deemed heretics by the church. She cannot understand why. After all they preach the Gospel of Christ in a language that everyone can understand. Their poverty is no false affect, its reality contrasts with the affluence enjoyed by the monks and the clergy. Before she met this Poor Man she had thought such munificence of the Church was normal, customary. Now the contrast is arresting. How can these people be labelled 'heretics' when they follow the way of Jesus? Yet so they are and she had heard the stories of how the crusaders are seeking to root them out; tales of betrayals and burnings that frighten her when she hears of them.

She releases her hold of her father's arm. "I'll see you at home, Papa. There's someone I just want to see. Won't be long." It was obvious that Arnaud has not spotted Brother Bernard for he does not hinder her, turning away with a grunt of acknowledgement and striding off down the narrow lane to their ostal.

Grazide crosses the square. The man has gone, vanished down one of the winding streets of the village. She follows the narrow road, just wide enough to take a cart. It takes her to the south gate, an insubstantial barrier that fills a gap in the low wall surrounding their village. She imagines an invading force attacking them. This wall affords little protection. She does not want to think more about that.

Bernard is standing by the gate. He is chewing a piece of bread that someone, imbued with the spirit of Christmas, must have given him. His face lights up when he sees her.

"Grazide. Peace be with you, daughter."

"And with you, brother." She stands and stares at him, not knowing why she is there, what she can say.

"It is a blessed day, is it not?" he waves an arm around him. "The birth of Our Lord, what a beautiful day."

How can he speak like this? Does he not know what is going on in the world? They call him a heretic and would hunt him down if they knew where he was.

"Where are you going?" her voice is insecure, tempered by her anxiety for his safety.

"I'm on the road to Morlhon. I should make it by nightfall."

"Morlhon. Why Morlhon?"

"My fellow brothers should be there. We arranged to gather at the castle. The Lord of Morlhon is good enough to give us refuge there. There is much of the Lord Jesus' work to be done in these parts. Morlhon is a good base for us. We can travel by the roads, by the river Aveyron too."

Does he not know the danger? Surely he has heard what Simon de Montfort's army is doing. "Is it safe, Bernard? There are stories."

His tone is dismissive but gentle. "We are protected, Grazide. We do Our Blessed Saviour's work. No harm can come to us." He smiles yet she is unconvinced. Her anxiety builds within her. She hardly knows this man but yet she cannot remain indifferent to his fate. Then she has an impulsive thought.

"Let me come with you, brother. I can be your companion."

He seems taken aback by this outburst; his expression changes. Now he speaks with a firm voice. "That cannot be, Grazide. I must travel alone." His tone becomes gentler. "I am touched that you care but your place is here." He reaches out and touches her arm. "God go with you, daughter."

As he turns to leave through the gate she calls after him "Bernard." He pauses in his step and looks back. Grazide cannot find the words to say. They are locked up in her tightening throat. She stammers a weak goodbye, turns and runs back into the village. She does not notice her friend Gervais, the cripple, standing in the shadows. He has been watching and listening.

Winter turns into spring but the village does not seem to be the place of safety that it always was. The rumours of war build up like grey waves rolling on to a beach. People are mourning the loss of their sons, those bright boys that have not returned from the battle at Muret. Families struggle to get the seasonal work done, preparing the soil, clearing the ditches, the sowing, the lambing and the shearing of the sheep whose flocks wander the causse, the elevated plains to the north.

At Easter comes the news that Simon de Montfort has failed in a siege of a castle in the Agenais, over to the west and is now making his way east along the Lot valley. The Lord of Morlhon, Ozil is fortifying the garrison in his small castle just four leagues to the south. It is a well-placed fort, perched on the steep slopes above the valley of the Aveyron. The lord's family, retainers and the inhabitants of the small village that surrounds the castle can find good shelter there if trouble comes. Once again the Lord's men are back in Vilanòva, mustering recruits to help defend the castle if an attack should come. This time Arnaud sees that he cannot hold his boys back. There is a grim determination in the village that a stand has to be made, all able young men must come forward. Even so it is with a heavy heart that he lets his sons go. Nevertheless he tries to affect a stoical stance, "It won't be like Muret, lads. You'll be holed up in that little fortress and the bloody crusaders will probably pass you by. They'll have bigger fish to fry elsewhere."

His words might have been a comfort to Grazide had she believed her father. She is less optimistic. She remembers that Bernard and his fellow Poor Men of Lyon had gathered at Morlhon at Christmas. If they are still there and the crusaders get to hear of it she doubts that the little castle would be ignored by Simon de Montfort. In any case the lands of the Lord of Morlhon, including their own village, would be an alluring prize for any invading force despite most of its revenues having been sold off to the Bishop of Rodez over the past few years. Grazide has a head on her shoulders that is cannier than most fourteen-year olds. Her years of lessons with Father Jean have not been wasted.

There is more than enough work in the forge to keep Arnaud busy. Now the boys have gone again he struggles on his own. He looks to his daughter, now nearly fourteen years old. She is a tall girl, he thinks, has inherited her mother's strong limbs as well. "Grazide. I need you to help me in the forge. Can you do that?"

Grazide frowns, she seems reluctant. "I'm not sure, Papa. I'm not as strong as Guillaume and Pierre."

"No. I know that, but you're growing. I think you could be useful to me." Arnaud is not so insensitive that he cannot see that his daughter is frightened. "There's nothing to fear, girl. I will teach you; we can take it slowly."

Grazide pauses, then nods agreement, her eyes averted from his gaze.

"Good. We'll start tomorrow," her father is not going to allow her to change her mind. He needs the help.

To begin with he teaches her to lay and start the fire. She learns how to pump the paired bellows that keep up a steady flow of air. He sees that she enjoys that, is pleased that she has a good fire going when he starts work in the forge each morning. It is more difficult to get her to help with the hammering and forging. She wears the long leather apron that Pierre had used but she winces when the sparks fly as he hammers blocks of hot metal. He shows her how to use the tongs to hold the block on the square anvil, how to stand to avoid losing her balance. In time she grows in confidence and her reluctance begins to wane.

Today he is making a new sledgehammer head. Together they hammer it into shape, he using the heavy implement, she a lighter one. The anvil rings true like a bell, the sound floats out over the roof tops of the village, out into the fields outside the perimeter wall. A reassuring sound for the people of the village. A craftsman at work, sign of a settled community whatever may be happening in the world around. They take from it whatever comfort they can.

Now he needs to make a central hole for the handle. The block is returned to the fire. Grazide pumps the bellows and the metal reddens into yellow then white heat. Arnaud transfers it to the anvil with heavy long-handled tongs. Grazide uses the lighter, one-handed tongs to steady the block. With her other hand she uses a wooden handle to hold a stout metal punch. Her father wields the heavy hammer as he beats the punch down into the centre of the block to create the hole which will take the wooden handle of the implement. He has prepared lengths of ash, now hanging on the wall of the smithy, ready to be inserted once the work is complete. Finally the punch is driven right through the sledgehammer head. Arnaud transfers it to a wooden barrel of water beside the anvil. There is a loud hiss and steam fills the gloom of the forge.

There are other days when she joins her father in the regular trip to collect the charcoal. She likes these expeditions to the charcoal burners. She is never put off by their sullen demeanour.

The scrub oaks are putting on new leaves, beginning to hide the barren, black branches of winter. Often she and Arnaud come across pigs, snuffling in the deep beech litter for any sustenance they can find.

As the weeks go on she relaxes into the work. In the darkness of the forge, lit only by the glow of the fire, she feels closer to her father; not just the physical closeness of working together but a change in the way father relates to daughter, daughter to father. Now that she is sharing his work he talks to her in a different way, more on a level, perhaps more understanding.

For she is growing up fast. The physical work in the forge is bulking up the muscles of her arms, she is broadening her shoulders. Her breasts are beginning to enlarge. Now she has seen the blood spotting on her undergarments. Na Lisier has noticed too as she does the family washing. The old lady is consoling, which is a surprise. "It is nothing to fear, Grazide. These are just the flowers that bloom when you become a woman." She shows Grazide how to use menstrual cloths when her time of the month comes around. Grazide is glad to know that she is normal, that she is maturing. By now she is ready to leave her life as a child behind. Womanhood seems to beckon though she has little conception of what it entails. In the end she has no mother on whom to model herself. She knows she is going to have to discover on her own what it means to be an adult woman. She will not learn that from her father, will not learn it from Father Jean. She is on her own.

Summer Term 2020

Monday 20 April	**First day of Summer Term**
Thursday 23 April	**Year 8 Parent-Teacher Consultation Evening**
Wednesday 6 May	**CTC Committee – 8.00am**
Wednesday 13 May	**FPP Committee – 5.30pm**
Wednesday 20 May	**Full Governing Body – 6.00pm**
Thursday 21 May	**Summer Chill Concert**
Friday 22 May	**Year 13 Leavers' Day**
Monday 25 to Friday 29 May	**Half Term**
Monday 8 June	**Parent Forum**
Wednesday 10 June	**FPP Committee – 5.30pm**
Tuesday 16 June	**Sports Day**
Thursday 18 June	**Reserve Sports Day**
Wednesday 24 June	**CTC Committee – 8.00am**
Friday 26 and Saturday 27 June	**Summer Concert**
Tuesday 30 June	**Year 12 Induction Day**
Thursday 2 July	**Year 6 Transition Day** **Year 11 Prom**
Tuesday 7 July	**Year 6 Parents' Information Evening**
Wednesday 8 July	**Full Governing Body – 8.00am**
Wednesday 8 July	**Senior Citizens' Tea**
Thursday 9 July	**Key Stage 3 Presentation Evening**
Wednesday 15 July	**Activity Day**
Thursday 16 July	**Activity Day**
Friday 17 July	**Last day of Summer Term**
Thursday 13 August	**AS / A Level Results**
Thursday 20 August	**GCSE Results**

Spring Term 2020

Monday 6 January	**First day of Spring Term**
Thursday 16 January	**Year 11 Raising Achievement Evening for parents**
Wednesday 5 February	**CTC Committee – 8.00am**
Wednesday 5 February	**Governors in School Day – 10am**
Wednesday 12 February	**FPP Committee – 5.30pm**
Thursday 13 February	**Year 9 Options Evening**
Monday 17 to Friday 21 February	**Half Term**
Thursday 27 February	**Year 10 Parent-Teacher Consultation Evening**
Monday 2 March	**Parent Forum**
Tuesday 3 March	**Year 12 UCAS Evening**
Thursday 5 March	**Year 9 Parent-Teacher Consultation Evening**
Wednesday 11 March	**Extended Learning Day – all students**
Wednesday 18 March	**Full Governing Body – 6.00pm**
Thursday 19 March	**Year 7 Parent-Teacher Consultation Evening**
Thursday 26 March to Saturday 28 March	**Whole School Production**
Friday 3 April	**Last day of Spring Term**

Autumn Term 2019

Wednesday 11 September	**CTC Committee – 8.00am**
Wednesday 18 September	**Full Governing Body – 6.00pm**
Wednesday 25 September	**FPP Committee – 5.30pm**
Thursday 3 October	**Open Evening**
Thursday 10 October	**Year 13 Parents' Consultation and Target Setting**
Thursday 17 October	**Year 11 Parent-Teacher Consultation Evening**
Wednesday 23 October	**Sixth Form Open Evening for prospective students (Year 11 Into Sixth Form Evening)**
Thursday 24 October	**Autumn Chill Concert**
Monday 28 October to Friday 1 November	**Half Term**
Thursday 7 November	**Year 12 Parents' Consultation and Target Setting**
Monday 11 November	**Parent Forum**
Wednesday 13 November	**FPP Committee – 5.30pm**
Thursday 14 November	**Extended Learning Day**
Thursday 21 November	**Year 7 Parents' Transition Workshops**
Wednesday 27 November	**CTC Committee – 8.00am**
Wednesday 11 December	**Full Governing Body – 8.00am**
Sunday 15 December	**Carol Concert**
Wednesday 18 December	**Senior Citizens' Carol Concert and Tea**
Friday 20 December	**Last day of Autumn Term**

Ashlyns School

Governor Calendar

2019 – 2020

CHAPTER 5

It has been less than a day's journey for Guillaume and Pierre to reach the castle of Morlhon. Although small, the castle is well defended by its position overlooking the river Aveyron. Built in the time of the Lord Ozil's grandfather some seventy years previously it is a reassuring refuge for the people of the area.

The two brothers are changed from the callow youths of the previous year. Now it is the younger Pierre who has grown in confidence, his older brother seeming to have lost the youthful sense of adventure; it has been replaced by a reserve, withdrawn and cautious. The few accounts that he has heard from the returning young men in the previous year appear to have had their effect on Guillaume. They have turned him into a sullen, introspective young man. More and more he relies on Pierre to take the initiative.

The two young men reach Morlhon by early evening. Crossing the Aveyron at La Peyrade they follow a steep path through the woods that takes them to the castle. The path traverses a cliff face and they enter the castle through a low door. Following a dark passage through the rock they emerge into the open space of the castle courtyard. Above them looms the solid mass of the keep. The curtain wall on the opposite side to the cliff edge is strong and high. It incorporates the main gate, a heavy structure constructed of thick oak. Outside the walls the land slopes steeply uphill to the hamlet above. The crenellated tower of a small church can be seen on the skyline. The slope between hamlet and castle is lightly wooded, mostly with scrub oaks.

The open space within the castle walls is full of people; many of them young men like themselves. They recognise faces of their neighbours from Vilanòva. Pierre hails one of them, Aimèry Targuier, older brother of Grazide's strange friend, Gervais. Like them he had not been at Muret. "Hey, Aimèry, what goes on? Is this where we sign up?"

"Pierre. Good to see you. Over there," He indicates the keep. "The steward is in there. That's where you go."

The two brothers join a crowd of men surrounding the door to the keep. Some of them are older than the boys, rough looking men, many of them sporting impressive scars. One man has lost his nose, his face dominated by the two open nostril holes has the appearance of a hideous gargoyle. Seated at a wooden trestle table is the steward. The brothers soon reach the front of the queue.

"Names?"

"Guillaume and Pierre Lamothe, sir," says Pierre. The steward writes then raises his head to look at Pierre.

"How old are you, boy?" His tone is sharp. Pierre lies, "Eighteen, sir. My brother here is twenty."

The man grunts. "So, what's your work?"

"We work for our father. He's a blacksmith."

"Is he indeed? Where are you from?"

"Vilanòva, sir."

The steward's stern expression weakens a little. "Ah, yes. I know, Arnaud the blacksmith. He's done a good deal of work for us."

"I know that, sir. We helped him. He's been very busy."

"OK. Through there," he indicates the keep. "They'll kit you out. Food's later. Next." He dismisses them with a nod.

Kitting them out is perfunctory. Both brothers have their own swords and helmets. They are given heavy leather over-garments but no chainmail, which worries Pierre. Food is bread and a thin soup, enough to satisfy their hunger after the day's travel.

With so many assembled in the castle there is little space for accommodation. Men bed down in pallets on the floor of the hall and refectory; some sleep outside in the courtyard. Pierre and Guillaume are not discomfited by this. They can get a good night's rest.

The Lord Ozil is seen from time to time. A slight, dark-haired man in his early forties. Pierre wonders whether he has the strength or the will to resist the dreaded de Montfort and his crusaders. The reputation of these latter goes before them, accounts perhaps exaggerated by the fear that grips the whole region. Word is that now they are in the valley of the Lot, just three days march away. The tension in the castle of Morlhon is tightening.

In anticipation of trouble the people of the small hamlet, a short distance up the hill from the castle, have moved into the castle itself. Women, children, even dogs and cats make the overcrowding unbearable. It is then that Pierre notices a small band of men, barefoot and wearing brown tunics. They move amongst the crowd and seem to be calming some of the turmoil by their presence.

One of the mercenaries nods toward them and mutters to Pierre, "Bloody Waldensians. I've seen those buggers before. If word gets back to de Montfort that this stupid lord has them holed up here we're in for trouble. He won't pass us by if he thinks he can torch a few heretics." The man spits in the dust in disgust.

Later in the day Pierre comes across one of the Poor Men, sitting on the ground in the shelter of the curtain wall. "Pardon, sir. Are you a Waldensian?"

The man smiles. "That's what people call us, brother. We prefer 'Poor Men of Lyon'. That's what we call ourselves." He pauses for a moment. "Where are you from, young man?"

"Vilanòva. Vilanòva d'Aveyron. North of here."

"Ah yes. I've heard of it. Our brother Bernard was there last Christmas."

Pierre wonders what to make of this. The prospect of a link with his home was seductive. "Is he here, this Bernard?"

"Certainly. Do you want to see him? I can take you to him." Pierre nods agreement and the man stands and leads the way.

Brother Bernard is working in the kitchen. He turns when the two enter. "Greetings, brother. Are you looking for me?"

"Bernard. This young man's from Vilanòva. You were there, weren't you? Last Christmas."

Bernard is peering into Pierre's face. "Yes, I was, but I don't think I remember you, young sir. Tell me, what is your name?"

"Pierre. Pierre Lamothe. My father is Arnaud Lamothe, the blacksmith."

"Lamothe? Then do you have a sister?"

"Yes, sir. Grazide. She's younger than me."

"Of course." The man claps his hands making the connection. "Grazide. Yes I know her. A very serious young woman, as I remember. But a wise head on her. Are you like her?"

Pierre blushes. "I couldn't say, sir. To be honest she's a bit of a strange one at times. But she is my sister and I love her."

"As indeed you should. Well, remember me to her when you return home." Bernard smiles and resumes his work.

These words startle Pierre. Does this man not realise what danger is in store for him, for us all? Does he really think that I shall be going home? He says nothing of this encounter to Guillaume. His brother, perhaps under the influence of the mercenaries, seems to be regaining some of his fighting spirit. Like them he looks as if he is spoiling for action. Pierre's sense of foreboding grows as each day passes.

In Vilanòva news that the army of Simon de Montfort is moving east along the valley of the Lot spreads trepidation amongst the people. They know that their village is undefended. Most of the young men have responded to the Lord Ozil's call to Morlhon. The walls of the village were hardly intended as defensive when the village was established, over a hundred years ago. Like the four stone crosses in each corner of the sauvatèrra they were more symbolic than practical, marking out the space where the Peace of God obtained. These walls, substantial enough only to deter vagrants and petty criminals from entering, would be overrun by a crusading force as if they were made of straw.

More cool-headed voices, amongst them Arnaud, try to calm the general perturbation. "They'll not be interested in us," says the blacksmith, "we have no heretics here. They'll be sure to pass us by." These days the people of the village have been more inclined to listen to Arnaud. The directness of his speech and his prestige as a skilled artisan have served to mark him out as a man of authority. At the same time there has been a decline in the clout of the Priory and the Prior. People are showing greater reluctance to pay their tithes; stories of monastic largesse abound as do the gathering rumours concerning the behaviour of Father Jean, the priest. By now it is an open secret that he entertains a mistress in the form of a young widow, Fabrisse Guillon. Some are outraged at this concupiscence on the part of a man of God but by many his behaviour is tolerated; a forced celibacy required of lay clerics has always seemed unreasonable to most people, particularly the men of the village.

Prior Roger and his monks, meanwhile, are reinforcing the locks and bars on the doors of the church. If trouble is to come the solidity of the building will make a good refuge, being the only stone construction in the village apart from the encircling wall.

Arnaud is right. The crusading force passes within a league of the village on its route from the river Lot at Cajarc to the Aveyron crossing at La Peyrade. They do not divert to menace the village. De Montfort's intelligence is accurate. The heretic protector is Lord Ozil de Morlhon so that is where the invaders must go. Their leader's zeal at rooting out heretics is compounded by an equal enthusiasm for toppling minor lords from their castles and acquiring their lands.

Simon de Montfort did not figure much in the early stages of the Crusade. A minor lord from near Chartres, away to the north, he took the cross to enhance his reputation as well as to increase his political influence. In these more northern Occitan lands there are few of the Albigensian heretics that he had been persecuting in the south. But for Simon any heretic will do, he has learnt that there are Waldensians holed up in Morlhon so that is where he is heading; finer details of the nature of their heresy are of no concern to him. They will all be fuel for the fire.

Simon's technique for attacking castles is direct and swift. Not for him the prolonged siege of attrition, seeking to starve out the occupants of the defending stronghold. He has no time for that. And it is just so this day when his force of crusaders approaches the village of Morlhon. They are a large company, most have been home over the winter, their crusading obligation of forty days having expired after the previous summer's campaign. They have been well provisioned in their march from the Agenais in the west, the fertile Lot valley had yet to have been ravaged by war so there was no shortage of supplies. They are spoiling for a fight.

Their first action is to torch the hamlet above the castle, now deserted by the inhabitants. The small wooden houses burn well and soon the lookouts on the battlements of the castle see a pall of grey smoke rise from the landscape. Now the crusaders turn their attention to the castle.

Their mobile war machines are trundled down the slope towards the castle. Men with axes clear away the scrub oaks to allow their passage. Once lined up they hurl stone missiles over the curtain walls of the castle. So crowded are the people inside that many hit their target, crushing people and animals alike. A band of foot soldiers advances on the main gate and soon a fire is lit at its foot. Water is poured down from above but it hardly impedes the inferno which is quickly reinforced with more fuel.

Now a huge battering ram is wheeled forward. Its canopy protects the soldiers from arrows fired from above. The heavy log with its solid iron nose is hung from suspensory chains and men are systematically hurling it against the gate. Within minutes the gate splinters and is breached. The inside of the castle is revealed.

Lord Ozil has lined up his fighting men behind the gate. Guillaume and Pierre are amongst them. When the gate falls they pour out to engage with the enemy. There are shouts of 'Mors Lion' from the defenders as sword clashes on sword, cries of anguish and terror. Pierre and Guillaume fight side by side, swinging their heavy swords, cutting and stabbing. But it is to no avail, the skirmish is soon over. The forces of the Lord of Morlhon are quite outnumbered. The dead and wounded lie scattered on the ground amongst severed limbs, spilled entrails, brains and blood. They are trampled into the earth as the next battalion of invaders charge into the castle courtyard. They meet with very little resistance for most of the fighting men are dead.

48

Women and children huddle in a corner of the open space, held back by a disciplined group of crusaders. Another body of men soon break into the keep and moments later emerge with the Lord Ozil and his terrified wife. They are led off in chains.

Within the space of an hour the ancient house of Morlhon has fallen. The Lord's sons have died in the fight, they lie amongst the dead. Many of the women and children are slaughtered outside the castle walls. The remaining inhabitants are scattered. Their homes destroyed, there is nowhere for them to go. Some have escaped through the castle exit above the escarpment, seeking shelter in the woods below. Amongst them is the figure of Aimèry Targuier. He has escaped the slaughter by hiding in an empty wine barrel in the kitchen. Once the fighting has died down he slips away to hide in the woodland below.

The small band of Waldensians are led out from the castle keep, tied together in a line with rope around their necks. Soldiers erect seven stout poles in a space in front of the castle driven into the ground in a tight circle. Each one of the brothers is tied to a post. Brushwood is piled around them. They are all silent.

A sergeant comes forward with a blazing torch and thrusts it into the pyre. Within moments flames have engulfed the seven men. Smoke hides them from the watching soldiers. A huge cheer goes up. "Death to the bloody heretics!" A cruel joy lights up the faces of the watching crowd. Their cheers of joy drown out the agonised screams that emerge from the victims engulfed in the conflagration.

More fuel is fed on to the fire until all that is left is a pile of ash, interspersed with charred bodies. All the time the Lord de Montfort has been watching the spectacle from higher up the slope. Seated on his charger he has a look of grim satisfaction on his face.

Over the course of the next two days de Montfort's men systematically dismantle the castle with hammers and pickaxes. They destroy the crops and farm buildings around the hamlet. Cattle are slaughtered and butchered, grain stores are plundered. By sunrise on the third day the crusaders have gone. Lord Simon will allow no delay, he must move on. It is a devastated vista that he leaves behind, smouldering buildings, a destroyed castle, bodies everywhere. Morlhon is no more.

Later that morning a figure is spotted crossing the river at La Peyrade. It is a tall girl; the hood of her cloak is up. She takes the footpath that her brothers had taken some days previously, up through the oak forest, up towards the castle of Morlhon.

It is Grazide. She had slipped out of the village earlier that morning, before the sun was up. She has no thought as to why she takes this path. A sense of foreboding drives her on. As she ascends she sees smoke rising from over the ridge of the hill. Soon she reaches the castle but, to her horror, it is a castle no more. Its battlements are torn down, there is rubble everywhere.

Outside the main gate she comes across bodies strewn all over the sparse woodland. With horror she spies the pile of ash and charred remains that must have been Brother Bernard and his companions. Over in one corner is an elderly lady kneeling beside another body, its skull split open. She sobs quietly but incessantly. Bodies everywhere, panic grips Grazide. She goes from one to the next, at the same time seeking yet never wanting to find. Her brothers, are they here?

The question is soon answered. A body lies face down, blood has soaked his leather tunic. She recognises the fair hair. With considerable effort she rolls the body over to be greeted by the face of Pierre, all life drained out of him, his eyes glazed and fixed open, unseeing. It takes all her resolve to stop the horror from overtaking her. It seeks to rise up in her gorge. In a quick movement she turns away, fearing what she will see next.

She is as well to fear. Just a few paces away she spots her brother, Guillaume. He lies supine, his throat cut open with a wide gash. His life drained away on to the green earth, now soaked in dark red, congealed blood. She can suppress the horror no longer. Her head laid back she lets out a prolonged, terrifying scream. Not a scream that one could ever think a young girl could produce, a scream of loss, a scream of desolation.

Nothing happens. Nothing moves. Death is fixed and solid. Death cannot be reversed, it is now part of her life, has been part of her life for as long as she has memory.

Later she cannot recall how she made the journey back home; her whole self was numbed. As she staggered into the village late that night she was met by her father. There were no words. He could read on her face what had happened.

The following day they retrace her steps to the ruined castle of Morlhon. Together they bury the two boys, marking the site with a metal cross that Arnaud has brought with him. There is nothing that either of them can say, just an agonised silence punctuated by the ring of metal on metal as Arnaud hammers the cross in place. Grazide knows she has grown up on that day. No longer a daughter, no longer a sister. She is a woman.

CHAPTER 6

The death of his two sons has diminished Arnaud. He is a man hollowed out by grief. To see them so mutilated, to bury their bodies in the hard ground, all this is written on his face. He walks with a heavier step; his body is bowed as if the weight of their loss compresses him down.

He is by no means the only bereaved parent in Vilanòva. Many other families have lost a son or a brother in the slaughter at Morlhon. Yet Grazide can see a further dimension. It is as if his grief is compounded by a further, greater loss. He has hardly ever spoken of his wife, Allemande, in Grazide's hearing. Never told her of her mother, what she was like. Nothing, until now.

In the forge one day she is making nails. The work of blacksmithing must go on. Arnaud would have neglected it but Grazide cajoles and encourages him to keep some work going, after all they still have to eat. He stands at the entrance.

"Your mother would be proud of you, daughter." Grazide stops what she is doing and lays down her hammer. She does not meet his gaze, this is so unexpected.

"Would she, Papa?"

"She was a good woman. She loved you dearly, Grazide," he swallows hard, "and she loved her two boys." He cannot continue. He turns away, wiping his arm across his face in a vain effort to hide the tears.

"Did she love you too, father?"

He is struggling to speak. "I don't know. She was my wife. I don't know."

"Oh, Papa. I'm sure she did." She moves across the floor of the forge towards him, seeking to take him in her embrace. He steps backwards, as if to avoid her.

"I don't know. I can't remember. I can't think about it." It seems as if this brief exchange is more than he can encompass. He turns away and is gone.

Grazide remains standing, motionless. Her heart is racing. He has hardly ever spoken of the death of her mother, almost never acknowledging that she had ever existed, that she had borne his three children. Now here he is a broken man, his two boys gone. Yet Grazide sees that there is a further neglected sadness, a grief postponed which is tearing him apart.

She returns to her work. The banality of hammering out nails can shield her from all that churns within her. How can she herself grieve the loss of someone of whom she has no memory? She does not know what she looked like, cannot remember the sound of her voice. Yet there is a memory, somewhere a fragment of knowing that she was loved once.

She misses her brothers. Guillaume with his dark seriousness, Pierre's smile and his cheerfulness, teasing his little sister yet at the same time appreciating her. She had never questioned why they had to go off to fight, why any of the young men of the village had to. It was part of life. Boys grow up into men, men are strong, men have to fight to protect their families, their lands.

But now she does question. The futility of all their deaths has changed her. She begins to see that there is another kind of strength that differs from that convention. It is a strength that she begins to feel within herself. Perhaps the companion of her developing physical strength, perhaps it has always been there, waiting for time and events to let it show itself. Not a masculine, *faux* heroic strength but nonetheless a real potency, a determination.

Not that any of this can reduce the horror of what she has seen. The bodies of her brothers, hacked to death in a bloody confrontation; the burning of that innocent Bernard and his fellow Poor Men. All these horrors and to what end? Surely there is nothing in what she heard from Bernard that warranted this destruction. Father Jean speaks of the crusaders as servants of God, doing his will in the world. He points to the prowess of their conquering success as evidence that they do the Heavenly Father's work. If that is so, thinks Grazide, I want little to do with such a God.

54

She continues to attend her lessons with Father Jean, even though her work in the forge occupies more of her time. By now she can read Latin and understands what she is reading. She can write, both in Latin and in her native Occitan. Father Jean allows her to read the bible texts to herself but he is always insistent that he explains what they mean.

A change has come over the priest recently. Often he seems distracted when tutoring his young charge. These days she is his only pupil. Sometimes he forgets to turn up at the appointed time for their lesson. By now Grazide is aware the rumours that he has a mistress, the young widow Fabrisse. Grazide has overheard Na Lisier talking in subdued tones with other old women of the village in the marketplace. She misses much of what is being muttered but she does catch something of what Na Lisier is saying.

"She's quite open about it, that Fabrisse. Coming and going to the Father's house at all hours."

"Yes," another woman replies. "I've seen her too. My neighbour surprised them in the church one day, hiding behind the altar, if you please!"

"That's awful," another has chimed in. "Disgusting. In the house of God, carrying on like that."

"And she isn't the first. Not by any means. That horny old devil has deflowered a good few others in the past."

Grazide does not want to hear this. She turns away and drops a metal door hinge on to the display of nails on her stall. It makes a loud clatter. The women's faces turn towards the sound. They stop their chatter and move away.

Grazide likes Fabrisse. The widow has shown kindness to her on occasions. It contrasts with the way Na Lisier still bosses her about. She can see that the old woman is becoming frailer. There is less that she does for the ostal now that Grazide is growing up. Nevertheless she does not seem to be able to stop herself from treating Grazide like a child, like a servant even. Her father does not appear to notice what is going on.

These days Grazide feels uncomfortable when she is with Father Jean, knowing what the people of the village say about him. She is aware that the priest is becoming more abrupt with her. One day she is reading the first two chapters of Genesis, translating it to him out loud as she reads. She has studied these passages before, on her own, so it is not a difficult exercise.

"So there you are, Grazide. That is how our Heavenly Father created the world and all that it contains. Plants, animals and then his greatest creation, Man. Made in his own image and Lord of all the earth.. The Lord God ordained how it was to be. Adam was ordered to name all the beasts of the field. Finally he named she who was fashioned from his own rib, Woman. Woman came out of man, there to serve her master and to be a companion to him. You see how our Heavenly Father has prescribed the order of things."

Grazide makes no reply to this. Father Jean does not expect to be questioned so she keeps quiet.

"That will be all, daughter. I will see you next week." She hears the side door of the church shut as he leaves.

Left on her own she takes up the scripture that they have been studying. Taking her time she reads it through again, for something has puzzled her. There appear to be contradictions in the account of how Man and Woman were created. It mystifies her. There is a confusion which bewilders her.

Then, on a third re-reading, the solution jumps out at her. There are two accounts of the creation of human beings, not just one. There is the familiar story of Adam's rib being used to create a subservient, dependent woman; destined to be a companion and helpmeet to the Man. That is the account in the second chapter of Genesis but in the first chapter there is a different account: 'And God created man in his image; in the image of God he created him, *masculine and feminine he created them*.' Women and men created as equals. That apprehension surprises her the more she thinks about it. Father Jean has taught her that the Bible is the Word of God, that the writers of the Holy Book are directly inspired by God. Yet here, at the very beginning, there is an inconsistency. Not one clear account of creation but two. How can the divinely inspired account contain two such disparate versions?

And her next thought is as disturbing as it is subversive. Why has the Church chosen the second reading, that in the second chapter, as its account of creation? In particular why has orthodox religion (for she has heard this phrase more often recently) used it to ordain the relationship between men and women? This thinking is making her breathless. Can she talk to Father Jean about it? Her instinct tells her that there could be danger there. Is this what is meant by heresy, of which there is so much talk?

There is no one she can tell about this. With a pang of despair she realises that she could have talked of it with the Poor Man, Brother Bernard, were he not a pile of ash dispersed to the winds. The cruelty of the world, of her life, presses in on her. She feels more and more alone.

This surprising insight brings about a change in her relationship with Father Jean. Whilst she knows she cannot speak of what she has discovered in her reading of the first two chapters of the Bible, she becomes more critical of what he is telling her. Even so she rarely voices her obduracy. She senses that he has recognised the change in her; his reaction is to be more dogmatic, more overweening than before. Now he is more likely to reprove her, less given to encouragement.

And her sixth sense is picking up something else which is making her feel uncomfortable. Perhaps it is knowing about his mistress and the other stories of his past, unpriestly behaviour. She cannot identify just what it is that she senses but she cannot put the feeling out of her mind. She wishes on the one hand that she could end her lessons with the priest, yet she is still hungry to study more, to learn more. There is nowhere else that she can satisfy that need.

Sometimes she talks with her father about it. "Papa, now that I'm doing more and more in the forge, can I stop my lessons with Father Jean?"

"Why would you want to do that, daughter?"

"Oh, I don't want to," she is hesitant, "but there is less and less time for it. You need my help."

Arnaud grunts. "That's as may be but you need education, even though you're a girl."

She bristles at that. "Even though I'm a girl. What do you mean?"

"Well, if I still had sons they might need the learning."

"What are you saying, Father?"

Her father frowns; she can see that she is making him cross, yet something within her drives her to persist. "Why do you make me take all these lessons anyway? None of the other girls in the village have to."

"I have my reasons, girl," yet he shows no willingness to share them with her. "Come on, we've work to do. Enough of all this." He starts to pump the bellows; the fire begins to roar.

Grazide feels frustration. Why will he not explain? What does he expect of her? She talks to some of the other girls in the village. She has never felt very close to any of them but she wants to know what they think about their future. What do they expect from life?

"A husband," says one, Ricarde. "My Papa says he'll find me a good husband. Mother says such beings don't exist in Vilanòva but that makes him angry."

"Sometimes I think about becoming a nun," this is her dreamy friend, Margarethe. "It must be lovely to be that peaceful." Grazide doubts this. In any case she knows that Margarethe is needed to work in the fields along with her sisters; her family is one of the poorest in the community.

"Babies. I love little babies. I want as many as possible once I have a husband," says Guillemette. She is a tall girl like Grazide. She is unaware, thinks Grazide, of what child-bearing entails. The risks, the

58

pain. They all know of mothers who have died within hours of giving birth, blood pouring from them in an open torrent.

"What do you want, Grazide?" says Margarethe. "You can read and write. Are you going into a convent or something?"

Grazide does not know how to answer. She is sure that taking the habit is not what she wants to do, becoming a nun.

"With all those muscles you'd be a match for any husband," says Ricarde, "he'd not dare to put one over you." The girls laugh at this. Grazide knows they are laughing at her as well. She hates people talking about her size or her strength. For a moment she hates her father for making her work in the forge. In her anger she resolves that the last thing she wants is a husband, a controlling man like so many in the village, beating their wives at a whim.. Why do these girls accept such behaviour as the norm? Would Papa have beaten her mother had she lived? He has never lifted a finger against her, nor her brothers. Perhaps that is unusual.

The girls disperse. Only after they have gone does Grazide notice her childhood friend, Gervais, sheltering from view in the shadows. Since working in the forge she recognises that their relationship has waned.

"Gervais. Is that you?" The young man limps forward into the sunlight.

"Oh, yes. I see it is. What are you doing, Gervais? I haven't seen you for ages."

"I've been around but you probably don't notice me these days."

"What do you mean? Why wouldn't I notice you? You're my friend."

"Am I? Still?" There is a note of pleading in his voice which she does not like. "All your learning and now you're becoming a blacksmith. You've no time for a cripple like me."

Grazide is taken aback at his way of speaking. Self-deprecating yet resentful of her at the same time. "I don't know what you mean, Gervais. I haven't changed." The moment she says these words she realises that they are not true. She has changed, changed in so many ways not just in her physical development or her learning.

He moves closer to her. Now he is smiling. It is a lop-sided smile and one eye glistens.

"So, you're still my friend, are you Grazide?" He reaches out one hand and takes hold of her upper arm. Close enough now for her to feel his breathing, overactive and pressing. She shrinks back but he tightens his hold.

"Stop it, Gervais. You're hurting me!"

He does not let go. "Be my friend, Grazide. I want you to be my friend."

"Gervais. Stop. You mustn't do this!"

"But I have to. I want you, Grazide. Let me hold you."

She is gripped by a sudden feeling of revulsion. With a great effort she pushes him away. He stumbles backwards. "Don't do this, Gervais. I don't want it."

He is sneering now. "Oh, you don't want it, do you? I'm not good enough to be your friend now. You with all your learning don't want a cripple like me. I know what's happening. I saw you with that heretic man. You're not interested in me no more."

"Gervais, stop it. You are being cruel. Stop it." She feels tears well up, frustrated by this exchange. "I can't stay." She turns and runs from the square. Gervais is left standing alone. She does not look back.

CHAPTER 7
1218

Since the destruction of Morlhon some four years previously life has been hard for the inhabitants of Vilanòva. So many of its young men were killed in that brief but bloody devastation. Families struggle to keep up the incessant work in the fields, many plots of land that would have supported wheat or vines lie untended. Brambles and nettles abound. Women and girls are driven to neglect domestic duties to labour long days in the fields. There is never enough to eat.

Tithes still have to be paid. Since the collapse of the House of Morlhon all the rights over the lands have been passed to the Bishop of Rodez, a man determined to extract as much as he can from his domains, but less production means less tithes. The Bishop is forced to tax the market trade more heavily to compensate. To the people of Vilanòva it feels merciless.

The Priory suffers too. Prior Roger is ageing rapidly and his discipline over the brothers in his community declines. Monks, unwilling to work in the fields, attach themselves to families, demanding food and support. The consequent resentment in the village towards the church grows as fast as morale declines. No longer does Vilanòva feel like a sauvatèrra where the Peace of God prevails.

Some relief occurs when the news comes of the death of Simon de Montfort, leader of the crusading army. Travellers bring accounts of his demise, killed by a stone shot from a catapult during the siege of Toulouse.

"Surely this will mean the end of all the troubles now," is Arnaud's response to the news. Grazide is less optimistic. There are bound to be others ready to fill the warlike boots of de Montfort, men waiting for their moment of glory. The war on heresy, for that is what it is being called, seems likely to continue.

Four years have wrought a change with Grazide, now fully grown, dark haired and blossomed into maturity. Work in the forge has given her a powerful frame. Arnaud is clearly proud of his daughter. "Look at her," he says to his friend, Guillaume Guiraud as they share a jug of wine. "She's the strength of any man but a sight more graceful. And she has a bright head on those shoulders, what with her reading and writing."

"Aye, man," says the other, "she's a fine young woman. You must be proud of her. Makes up for losing those two boys of yours. She still doing the learning with that old priest?"

Arnaud nods. "When she has the time. I need her in the forge most days though there isn't much work at present."

"No. I guess not. Hard times for all of us, it is. Though maybe it'll get better now that bastard de Montfort's gone."

"Oh, aye. Maybe." The two men lapse into silence.

There is a creak of the door as Grazide enters. Her arms and hands are wet from washing at the pump.

"Good day, lass," says Guillaume. "Been working hard?"

"Just a bit." She turns to her father. "Papa, Gaubert Teisseire's been in. He needs a new hoe."

"He's not paid me yet for that last lot of nails I did for him."

"I didn't know that. I said we'd do one for him. He needs it by the end of the week."

"Well, he can go and whistle for that. When I get my money I'll make him his hoe."

Grazide frowns. "Papa, you know his family's having a hard time. His boys were killed as well."

Arnaud interrupts. "All of us are having a hard time, daughter."

In the past Grazide would not have persisted, recognising her father's intransigence. But times have changed. "We all of us have to help each other, Papa. That's always been the way. Come on, be reasonable."

Arnaud's head is lowered. He is muttering something under his breath. Neither Grazide nor Guillaume can hear him.

"Cheer up, Arnaud," says Guillaume, as if to interject some relief into the tension. "Your girl is looking after your interests, getting you work."

"Not much use if I'm not bloody paid!"

Grazide gasps with frustration. "For heaven's sake, Father. Be reasonable." She turns and goes into the adjacent room; they can hear her moving about in there.

After a pause Guillaume speaks. "Arnaud. You're a lucky man to have her. She'll make someone a useful wife one of these days."

The blacksmith does not reply. He is staring into his mug of wine. The late afternoon heat is subsiding. A cockerel crows.

Arnaud does not want to think about Grazide and marriage. By now he depends on her help, not just in the forge but around the ostal. Since old Na Lisier died two years ago it has fallen to Grazide to keep the domestic life going, cooking, cleaning, fetching water, her days are full. Arnaud could never manage without her. He is not sure he wants to lose her to a husband.

In any case he cannot think of a good match in the village. Most families are suffering from the prevalent austerity as much as he is. It would mean looking further afield. Maybe a good marriage for her, then he would take on an apprentice. That would work. Perhaps he could afford to pay for a young girl to come as a servant, keep the house in order.

Or perhaps there is another way. He has had his eye on Bethane, his friend Guillaume's niece, for a while now. She is a buxom young woman. Word has it that she had a fling with that old goat, father Jean, when the priest had tired of the widow Fabrisse. They say that it did not last long. These days she is married to the shepherd, Philippe Noguès but her husband is away with his sheep for most of the year.

Over the last few months Bethane and he have had a few occasions to talk, usually after Mass on a Sunday or at the market on Wednesdays. Arnaud is aware that she shows some interest in him even though the conversations never extends beyond the trivial or the short-lived. He will bide his time.

It is worth the waiting. On a warm autumnal afternoon he is returning with a cartload of charcoal from the forest. He stops to rest and such is the effect of the heat, lies down in a shady glade. Just as he begins to nod off his attention is alerted by the sound of footsteps approaching along the path, coming from the direction of the village. He sits up and sees that it is Bethane. She carries a basket which is part-filled with chestnuts. Her head is bared, her light brown hair glints in the sunshine. Seeing him seated on the ground she speaks, "Greetings to you, Arnaud. That's a heavy load you have there."

"No heavier than usual. I'm used to it."

She sits down next to him. "Do you mind? Can I sit here?"

Arnaud is horrified to find that he is blushing. "Of course." He moves along to give her space.

"It's a lovely day, isn't it, Arnaud?"

"Yes. No doubt. A lovely day."

"I've been collecting chestnuts. Look how many I've found."

He stares into the basket. "That's impressive."

She lies back and yawns. "You know what, Arnaud. I think I want you to make love to me." She is smiling but not looking at him.

Arnaud's heart races in his chest. He does not know whether he is amazed or shocked. Can he take her seriously?

She continues, "Come on, Arnaud. I've always fancied you." She is stroking his arm, gentle strokes but enough to awaken a dormant longing in him. Too long a longing he thinks as she pulls her tunic over her head.

That he acceded to her request surprised him when he recalled the incident later. He had thought that such pleasures were a thing of the past for him. Even greater is the surprise when the interaction is repeated. Not just once, it becomes a regular occurrence. Their affair is now common knowledge. Arnaud fears how his daughter would react were she to hear of it.

And she does hear of it. There are few secrets that last long in a small community like Vilanòva. What is a surprise is that the revelation comes from Father Jean.

"I hear your father is falling into the sin of concupiscence, Grazide. Did you know that?" He sits back, smiling.

64

This is a shock. Her face betrays it. She is unused to such gossip coming from the priest. He is usually austere in his dealings with her, a dogmatic pedagogue most of the time. On top of that she is aware that the priest is hardly one to point out other people's moral lapses. She knows his reputation. For a moment she is tongue-tied.

"What do you mean, Father? What are you saying?"

"Do you not know, daughter? Your father and Bethane Noguès. It is scandalous."

This is too much for Grazide. She is seized with anger. She jumps to her feet and advances on the priest. "How dare you say these things," she shouts. "The whole village knows about you and your filthy behaviour. Don't you dare say things about my father. He is a better man than you, even if you are a priest."

Father Jean appears unmoved by this outburst. He remains seated, a half smile on his lips. Grazide's fury grows. "You smug bastard. Have you nothing to say? Everyone knows you are a fornicator, a randy old goat!"

The priest's expression changes. He stands up. Now they are face to face. His eyes are narrowed, his lips compressed. "That's enough, woman. Be silent."

Grazide struggles to find words. In her frustration she pushes him in the chest. He staggers back. Now his face betrays surprise but only for a moment. It changes to a menacing leer. "You need to be taught a lesson, you whore." In a quick movement he grabs her by both arms. His face is in hers. "No one speaks to me like that."

Grazide is paralysed with fear. She cannot react. Now he is scrabbling at her clothing, pulling up her tunic, tearing at her linen undergarments. She finds her voice at last. "Get off me, you bastard."

His breathing is stertorous now, his eyes widened. She feels his arousal, pressed into her. With a sharp movement she brings up her knee into his groin. He lets out a cry of pain but does not release his grip. With grim determination she pokes her fingers into his eyes. Now he staggers back, moaning, leaning forward, grasping his genitals. Grazide summons up all her strength, the strength that has been honed over the last four years, the strength that can wield a heavy hammer to beat the molten iron into submission. She brings down both fists together on to the back of his neck. He falls to the floor, still groaning. Grazide stands back from the prone figure. She is panting, both with the exertion and in her anger. The priest tries to get up. With one last effort she spits in his face, turns and runs from the church.

Her father is not in when she gets back to the ostal. No one has seen her leave the church and run through the village. Her heart is racing with a sense of outrage that threatens to overcome her. How dare he? How dare he treat her like this? Just at that moment she hates him, hates the Church, hates God. Is this how women should be treated? Is this what was ordained? She sits at the table. Now the sobs are coming, heavy throbbing sobs that take away her breath. The anger and fury are turning into a sense of desolation. She is on her own, there is no one that she can turn to, no one at all. Now she knows how much she misses her mother, the mother she hardly remembers. She is inconsolable.

Sometime later Arnaud returns from the forge. Entering the room he senses that all is not well. Grazide is sitting at the table, her head in her hands. Her eyes are red, she has been crying. There is no sign that she has prepared the evening's meal. "What's this, lass? What's up?" She does not reply, does not look up at him. He sits down on the bench, facing her across the table. It is unusual seeing her like this. "Something must be up, girl. Have you been crying?" She shakes her head with a furious movement, as if wanting to deny this. "Come on, Grazide. It's not like you to cry. What's upsetting you?" His tone is as compassionate as he can make it, not easy for a man normally gruffer and more withdrawn. "You can tell me."

Grazide lifts her head and stares him in the face. "What is this about Bethane Noguès, Father?"

Arnaud has been dreading this moment. He knows well enough that village gossip would sooner or later come to his daughter's ears. "I wanted to tell you, Grazide. It's just that I haven't been able to find the moment."

66

Her face flushes red. "Can't find the moment? So you left me to find out on my own. Find out from that" she stutters but the words will not come, "that loathsome priest."

"Have a care, daughter. You can't speak of a man of God like that."

"Man of God!" she spits the words out as if they were poison in her mouth. "He's no man of God."

"What has he been telling you? About me and Bethane?"

"He said you were sinning. Some long word, I don't remember it. But I knew what he meant."

"I'm sorry. I didn't want this to hurt you." He searches in his head how to explain himself to his daughter. "It's been hard, all these years since your mother died. Hard to be on my own."

"But you're not. You've got me. You had Guillaume and Pierre until they were taken from us. Isn't that enough?"

How to explain to her that it is not enough? Arnaud cannot find the words. He regresses, instinctively reverting to a familiar patriarchy. "I'm not discussing this further, girl. There's nothing to be said." He stands up from the table.

Grazide shouts, "That's not fair, Papa. You can't just say that. What's going on? You have to tell me".

"No, I don't. And you need to curb your tongue." As he speaks these words he is aware that he rarely speaks to his daughter like this, hardly ever in the past. "I don't want to upset you but this is no concern of yours."

"What! No concern? You and Bethane? I remember the word now, the word that Father Jean used. Concupiscence. What is going on?"

Her father moves to the door. "I'm going out so you can calm down and control yourself. Get on with the food. I've had a hard day, I'm hungry." He needs to get away, aware of how incompetent he has been in handling his daughter's interrogation. Just at this moment he would like nothing better than for her to be married off. He hates himself for thinking so. He needs to find Bethane, it is a pressing, physical need. Some way to calm the entanglement of his feelings, to escape from what he is doing to his daughter.

The following day Grazide is working in the forge. She is on her own. Arnaud has gone to collect another load of charcoal. He will be away for hours. She is sharpening tools, one of the mainstays of a blacksmith's work in a community such as Vilanòva. In the gloom of the forge she does not notice a figure standing in the shadows. The person speaks. "Grazide."

She looks up. Standing in the corner is Bethane Noguès. She is cloaked, her hair covered by the hood. Grazide recognises the plain features of a local woman, not ugly by any means but not what one could call beautiful. Grazide has known her for most of her young life but has never been in any way close to her. She knows that she is married, her husband is a shepherd, away for much of the year following his flock on to the summer grazing on the causse. It is a shock to see her. Grazide is confused. She says nothing but returns to filing down the blade of a hoe.

"Grazide. I must talk to you." Grazide nods but continues to rasp the file over the metal blade. The sound echoes around the forge. "Grazide, I'm sorry. Your father told me what happened. I wanted to explain."

The young girl stops her filing. "Explain? How can you explain? There's nothing to be said."

"But there is. Arnaud and I, we have these feelings for each other."

Grazide cuts in, her voice sharp. "Don't tell me. I don't want to hear. Please go." The other woman does not move. "Please go, Bethane. I've got work to do."

Bethane is pleading now. "I must talk to you, Grazide."

"There's nothing that I want to hear from you," she restarts her filing with renewed force.

"Stop it," her tone is abrupt enough to cause Grazide to stop what she is doing. "Listen to me. You may not like it, you may not approve but your father and I have found something important for each of us. He needs that, though you may not see it."

Suddenly Grazide does see things, she sees them clearly. In her mind she takes a step back and perceives her father, a lonely man who has needs. Here is a woman willing to meet those needs. Her father is no better nor worse than any other man in the village. This plain woman is doing what she believes to be right by him. Grazide can see this but only by withdrawing, by detaching herself. She is no longer a daughter, she cannot determine how he should behave any more.

This new insight makes it easier for her, there is safety in detachment. She cannot be hurt. "If that is so I am glad for you," she says. "My father has his own life to lead. You must do what you think is right."

The relief in Bethane's voice is obvious. "Oh, thank you. I knew you would understand. There is no need for you to be upset by this. It will all be well, I'm sure it will."

Grazide's response is to smile but say nothing. What this woman does not know is that whatever her father and his new woman have between them is no longer her concern. In the end it is easier that way.

It is an adaption that is useful when, later, Bethane moves into the ostal with them, sharing her father's bed as his mistress. It appears that her husband, Philippe the shepherd, tolerates this arrangement. The affair between Bethane and her father becomes a fixture which seems to take it off the menu of village gossip. Such liberality is not unusual.

Grazide never speaks of what happened with Father Jean but she never goes to him for lessons again. She is now absent from Mass. It is unnoticed by most people, her father is aware of it but it never becomes a matter of conversation between them.

CHAPTER 8

1220

Any expectations that the death of the hated Simon de Montfort would bring peace to the lands of the Count of Toulouse prove to be optimistic. Sporadic violence continues though none comes close to the village of Vilanòva. Apart from the continuing ravages of the crusading army there is now further danger from bands of mercenaries. Deprived of gainful employment with either the Northern French invaders or the forces of local lords they make travel through the woods and forests a risky undertaking.

Refugees begin to turn up in the village. These are not the usual pilgrims on the trail to Santiago. There are fewer of the latter since journeying has become so dangerous. People who have been displaced from their own towns and villages begin to arrive, perhaps knowing that it was once a sauvatèrra. Many come from further south where the violence continues to rage.

They are welcomed. The people of Vilanòva have need of fit, young immigrants to replenish the depredation of the population occasioned by the loss of so many young men in the wars. Accommodation is found for them in the vacancies of ostals.

By now Bethane, Arnaud and Grazide are settled into a co-existence which is never comfortable, least of all for Grazide, but allows for an adaption that is truce-like. Bethane agitates for the three of them to give refuge to a visitor. Perhaps she hopes that another member in the ostal will relieve the tension. Arnaud makes no objection, Grazide is silent on the matter.

And so space is made for a woman. Another man in the ostal would create complications, all three of them can see that. Sybille is a young widow, as are many of the women seeking asylum. She has travelled in a group, women and men, from further south, somewhere around the town of Montalban. She is a quiet person, never keen to relate what has driven her to take the path of a refugee. She walks with a limp; observing her at a quiet moment Grazide can see that her left leg is shorter than its fellow. She walks with her left foot turned in, a stumbling gait that always seems to threaten to trip her up. Yet she rarely falls. Her pointed features give the impression of a sharp woman but in her conversation, when she does talk, she is quite the opposite; relaxed, almost untroubled. Grazide, though they share a bed in the ostal, finds her an enigma.

Sybille and her companions settle into the village. They appear to be pious, regularly attending Mass. It becomes apparent that one of their number, a man named Galtier Foulcaut, is their leader. He is billeted in the ostal of Guillaume Guiraud, Bethane's uncle. They soon learn that he is a weaver by trade. This looks as if it might cause difficulties with Na Mazaler, one of the matriarchs of the community who is their resident weaver. It soon becomes apparent that there need be no concern. He makes it clear that he has no desire to displace Na Mazaler. Instead he settles down to becoming a carder, straightening out the wool from the fleeces to turn into yarn for Na Mazaler to weave. He likes to make frequent trips out of the village, often into the woods, sometimes joining the shepherds as they take their flocks out on to the causse for grazing.

Grazide can see that he has a presence about him. It is as if he carries an authority. Not the kind of authority that she has seen from Father Jean Vital, the priest, nor even of Prior Roger, the latter being far less dogmatic than the former. No, it is a quiet, relaxed authority though she has no idea from where it comes.

Over the next few months, Vilanòva settles down once more into what is almost a steady state. More labour to help work the field plots outside the village brings better harvests. In a way there is a kind of peace which has not been experienced for many a year.

The decline of the Priory goes hand in hand with this growing autonomy of the community. Less and less are the people dependent on the will of the Prior or the absent Bishop. Old age and decrepitude have reduced the numbers of monks that the villagers support. With the deaths of any of the brothers there are rarely young replacements to fill the gaps. But the Bishop of Rodez is a determined and a shrewd man. Shrewd enough to see how the community of Vilanòva is changing. Collections of tithes have been becoming more fragmentary. Prior Roger is becoming enfeebled by an early onset of old age, his grip over the Priory and the village is weakening. The Bishop is alert to the bellwether of religious decline and its subsequent effect on the village.

In an uncommon visit to Vilanòva on Easter Day, he calls the people together in the market square and makes an announcement. "Dear people of Vilanòva. As your Bishop and Lord I decree that I shall appoint two prudhommes to represent you in the future. I ask you that you put forward two names for my approval as representatives of you all. Choose carefully for they must be upright, God-fearing men who will have your interests at heart. I give you until Pentecost to come up with the names. Then I will make my decision."

Prior Roger and the priest Jean Vital are standing beside him. It is apparent that the prior is unaware that his position is about to be usurped for he is smiling benignly. Grazide, who is on the edge of the crowd can see that his mind is far enough gone to fail to appreciate what is being proposed. Not so the priest. His face is set as hard as stone, his lips pursed. For a moment it looks as if he is about to speak but one look from the Bishop silences him.

Into Grazide's mind comes a thought. The Bishop speaks of 'prudhommes', specifically two men. Never a mention that the village might choose a woman, a 'prudfemme'. The overpowering male authority of the Church is blatant and obvious, the power of the masculine imposed on an older, southern culture where the voices of women have traditionally held equal weight with those of men. That, to Grazide's perception, has been the old way. The Bishop's decree has come down on that with the weight of a block of masonry.

Nevertheless to most people of the village this small degree of autonomy is welcome. Over the next six weeks the discussions range back and forth. Grazide is reluctant to join in; for one thing she is aware that what these two prudhommes are actually going to do has not been made clear. Do they have power or authority? What if they are incompetent or even corrupt? How can they be got rid of?

In the end a consensus emerges. The two names put forward to the Bishop on the Feast of Pentecost are Bethane's uncle, Guillaume Guiraud, the hirer out of oxen, and Grazide's father, Arnaud Lamothe.

"Congratulations, Father. I am sure you will be an excellent prudhomme, whatever it entails."

Arnaud is astute enough to recognise his daughter's gentle cynicism. He grunts, "we shall see, Grazide. We shall see."

The Bishop accepts the nominations. There is a small ceremony held a month later at which Arnaud and Guillaume are instituted. The Bishop does not attend so it falls to Prior Roger, still smiling benignly, to present each man with his document of authority.

In the months that follow their appointment the two prudhommes discover what their commission entails. If either had entertained any hope that they would have the authority to bring about change that would be of value to the community they are soon to be disappointed. In effect they find themselves either having to resolve petty disputes amongst the inhabitants or aiding the Bishop's men in the collection of tithes. Neither task gains them any popularity, quite the opposite in fact.

All this activity takes Arnaud away from his work in the forge. More and more the commissions for metalwork are being left to Grazide to fulfil. It is fortunate that she is proving to be more than capable. With her developing skills it is as if she treats the raw iron as her friend, coaxing it into shape rather than beating it into submission. Arnaud has noticed this and it is a source of pride for him.

"Daughter, you're becoming a first-rate blacksmith." He sees her development as a skilled artisan, her strong stature, her perceptive eye as a product of his tutelage. Perhaps he is fortunate that he does not hear the counter-current that rumbles through the village gossip; that it is unnatural for a woman to be doing this work, that she is some kind of freak, a man-hater, that no good will come of it. Arnaud is not cognisant of this tittle-tattle. Neither is he aware that some folk believe she should be married off. A good strong husband would put an end to all this nonsense.

For herself Grazide knows she needs help. "Papa, we need to get an apprentice if I'm to carry on with the work of the forge. You seem to have little time for it nowadays."

"I know, I'm sorry. Being a blasted prudhomme is becoming a burden but I suppose someone has to do it."

Grazide senses that despite its irritations carrying the title is a matter of pride for her father. She is under no illusion that he is going to give it up.

"Can we afford an apprentice, though?" he says.

"Of course we can." Not only has Grazide taken on the blacksmith work, she also keeps a close eye on the income. "We're getting enough work these days. We can afford it."

Finding the right candidate is not easy, though. There are precious few young men who might take it on. Even Grazide knows she would be creating a stir if she were to appoint a woman. In the end she finds a suitable candidate from amongst the group of refugees that have swelled the village population of late, Pierre Foulcaut. He is nephew of the enigmatic Galtier Foulcaut, both of his parents had been killed during the fighting around Toulouse. Grazide speaks to his uncle. "Are you willing to let him be apprenticed to me? I can teach him the trade." It appears to her that there is a reluctance in the older man.

"I am not sure this is appropriate, madam."

"I can assure you, sir, that I have enough experience to instruct him. If you doubt me, why not speak to my father?"

The older man stiffens. "That won't be necessary. I give my consent for now."

And later you might withdraw it, thinks Grazide. What is his objection? Surely he is not swayed by the misogynist gossip that bounces around the village. He seems, to her at least, to be above that sort of thing.

It is agreed, as are Pierre's terms of employment. He proves to be a fast learner. In a way he reminds her of that other Pierre, her long-dead brother. Trade in the blacksmith's forge flourishes over the next few months.

It is the best time of the year for Philippe Noguès. Spring lambing is over, it is time to lead his rejuvenated flock from its winter pasture around the village. Away to the north west, up on to the high plain of the causse. These are the summer feeding grounds. The wiry grass of the limestone uplands combines with the wild herbs to make good fodder for his sheep to convert into meat and wool. Philippe loves to feel the warmth of the spring sun on his back as he goes about his work, caring for his charges who, conversely, seem to have a facility to find many different ways to die. Sheep are not stupid, thinks Philippe, but they appear to have no desire for a long life. He is a skilled shepherd, good at keeping them alive. With his dogs he can keep away the wolves that would otherwise prey on the defenceless sheep given half a chance.

Today he is sitting on a bench outside a caselle, one of the dry-stone shelters that are dotted around the high plain, enjoying the sunshine. His flock is scattered across the landscape, either gently cropping the pasture or drinking at the dewpond. Even in spring water is scarce, the dewponds that generations of shepherds before him have created all over the causse are a godsend.

The caselle is stone built. From the outside it has the appearance of a large beehive. One door at the front, no windows but a hole in the ceiling to allow smoke from the fire to escape. Inside a wooden platform allows a straw mattress that is his sleeping arrangement. There are times when he gets to share his rough bed, those times when he is visited by women from the nearby hamlets, looking to buy his sheep cheese and willing to bestow their favours on him for a few coins. Philippe is happy with this existence. It was quite a relief when the blacksmith, Arnaud Lamothe, took over his wife, Bethane. A difficult woman to live with, remembers Philippe. Forever complaining when he left her to take his sheep away yet nagging him incessantly when he was at home. He was usually glad to get away. No, the outdoor life on his own with the occasional fuck, no questions asked, is good enough for him. He makes a wiry figure. His skin, darkened by the sun, fits tight to his bones. His hands, forever greasy with lanolin from handling the sheep, are big and strong. He gives off an odour that betrays his profession.

Sometimes he shares a caselle with a fellow shepherd. All of them are on the move throughout the summer; there are caselles scattered about the causse to give them shelter. At these times the shepherds pass the night hours telling stories, passing on news and gossip. There is plenty of that these days. The wars, whilst mostly in the south, have had an impact. Philippe lost most of the flock one year to a ravaging force that was passing through and sought to provision itself with sheep meat. That was a bad time. It took a few lambing seasons to repair the damage.

Tonight there are two of them sitting beside a good fire outside their caselle. His companion, one Barthelémey Maurs, had been making the sheep cheese that day. Philippe had had a day's shearing, both men are tired from the day's labour. Talk meanders along as they sit under the stars. Their dogs are lying still beside them, chins on front paws, making the most of the warmth from the fire.

"Some good fleeces you've got there, Philippe. They'll fetch you a good price at the fair next September."

"Maybe. Maybe not." No one could call Philippe an optimist. "Times are not so good these days."

"It's these bloody wars. Folk don't have the money they used to have."

"No. I'll be lucky to sell this lot."

Barthelémey changes the subject. "Saw that strange man again last week. You know, the one who often turns up around here."

Philippe knows who he means. An austere man, tall, wearing a dark cloak. Philippe had met him once. "He comes from my village,

Vilanòva. Turned up there with a bunch of others last year. Comes from down south, they say."

Barthelémey grunts in acknowledgement. A silence descends on the two. In the distance they hear the howl of a wolf. At once the dogs are on their feet.

Philippe calls to them. "Steady down there. It's a long way off."

Barthelémey is more cautious. "Maybe, but I think I'll just take the dogs over there. Just to be sure."

Left on his own Philippe's mind wanders back to the man that they had been talking about, Foulcaut, that was his name, Galtier Foulcaut. They had met back in the early spring. Foulcaut had helped with the lambing for a couple of days. Now Philippe remembered some of their conversations. It had been strange talk, difficult for the shepherd to understand. What he did remember was something about two Gods, one good, the other bad. It was strange. The shepherd had not thought about it until now. What he did recall was how gentle the tall man was, he had peace about him that showed in his eyes, in his speech. Philippe would like to talk to him again if he could.

Barthelémey returns with the dogs. "All's well. The sheep were a bit spooked so I've brought them in closer to here. The dogs will keep them safe. Time for me to turn in, I think." He disappears into the caselle. Within minutes Philippe can hear his gentle snoring.

He looks up at the stars, spread across the open sky. Were they put there by a bad God? That's what that man said. Everything created, stars, earth, animals, trees and men, all created by a bad God. Surely that cannot be. To a man that lives as close to the natural world as Philippe it makes no sense. Yet when he goes to Mass, hears the preaching of the priest, that rascal Jean Vital, all he is told is how his soul is damned unless he earns repentance for his sins. Philippe thinks about the women that he entertains in his caselles. Is his a sinful life? Is he going to pay for it in the end? He kicks down the remnants of the fire and joins his fellow shepherd in the caselle. Sleep comes quickly enough to blot out his ruminations. Tomorrow will be another day.

Philippe and Barthelémey had previously agreed that they should move the sheep on the following day. During the night clouds have gathered from the west, the wind has changed direction. By dawn it is raining, the slow steady rain that, once started, never relents. Shepherds welcome the rain. The soil of the causse is thin and dry, not good at holding the water so it percolates through the limestone bedrock. It finds cracks, channels that go deep underground. Philippe knows of caves in the landscape, nothing more than holes in the rocky ground. Some of them are big enough to allow a man to ease himself into the darkness, then they open out into large caverns. By the light of his candle he can see passages going deep into the darkness. Always the constant dripping of water, however dry it is outside.

He has heard tales of underground rivers. Idle shepherd-talk he guesses, probably made up to liven up the chitchat around an evening's fire. Still, sometimes he comes across springs, small streams that emerge from the ground. That water has to come from somewhere. Philippe is glad enough of it for his sheep, even the dewponds can sometimes run dry under the heat of the sun. Yet the springs continue to run. He has never known them to dwindle.

The two men, cloaks of rough wool pulled up over their heads, lead the flocks across the causse. They head for the north-west. At this time of year the pasture should be good, the sheep have exhausted the present grazing over the past week. It is time to move on. Part of life for shepherds is this transhumance. An age-old pastoralism, it suits Philippe.

They move slowly keeping half an eye out for stragglers. There are always some sheep who think they know best and are inclined to set off on different paths. Sometimes they whistle the dogs to bring them back. Once restored to the flock the wanderers will not drift off again.

It is a life that suits me, thinks Philippe. He welcomes the open air, the space. A winter confined to the village is more than enough for him. Folk are difficult at such times. Food is scarce, hunger does not lead to good relations; grumbles, bitchiness are prevalent. He tries to avoid it himself. And Bethane, he tries to avoid her too. She seems content enough with the blacksmith. Philippe and Arnaud have always rubbed along well enough. Even knowing that the blacksmith has commandeered his wife does not disturb that. Live and let live, that is the way that Philippe sees it. It is a contented man, then, who trudges the well-worn path to the new grazing grounds. He and Barthelémey rarely talk when on the move; it seems to be the accepted custom.

By mid-afternoon the rain has stopped. Warmth returns with the appearance of the sun. An eagle circles high in the air, quartering the flat plain of the causse on the lookout for a rabbit or even a straggling lamb. There are rarely any of the latter. This season's crop is growing well, by now sturdy and energetic, match for any marauding raptor. The shepherds spot an isolated caselle over on the horizon. "That'll be a good spot for tonight," says Barthelémey, "looks like there's no one there."

"Aye, good enough. We'll bed down there tonight. It'll only be a few more leagues tomorrow." Over to the left, quite far off, he spots a small hamlet. Maybe there'll be customers for his cheese there though any other transactions are unlikely with Barthelémey sharing the caselle with him.

As they approach the stone hut a figure emerges from the interior, stooping down to pass through the low doorway. A tall man wearing a black robe. Philippe recognises him at once. Galtier Foulcaut, the leader of the refugees that arrived in Vilanòva last year. He stands motionless in front of the caselle, smiling at the two shepherds as they approach. "Greetings, brothers. We are all well met."

Philippe's tone is abrupt. "How come you are here, Galtier? You're a long way from home."

Barthelémey looks intrigued. "Is this the man you were telling me about, Philippe?"

"It is. I don't know what he's doing here."

"I can answer that," says Galtier Foulcaut. "My journeys take me far at times. I have been in that hamlet over there, meeting the folk."

Philippe is still suspicious. "Meeting folk? What's that for, brother? Are you a preacher?"

"No, not really. But I need to talk with people, spread the word."

Barthelémey intervenes. "Well, you can talk with us. You are welcome to share the night here if you want. We have bread, and some good cheese."

"Thank you, shepherd. Bread is good but I cannot touch cheese." Philippe waits for an explanation but none is forthcoming.

Night falls, a fire lit they settle down to eat. They have a rough loaf of bread to share. Galtier picks it up, appears to bless it then breaks off pieces and passes them around.

"So, why no cheese?" says Barthelémey. "Us shepherds, we live on it."

"Cheese is made from milk, is it not?"

"True."

"And milk comes from a beast that has borne offspring, from the coupling of animals."

"Yes, but so what?"

"It is the work of the devil. All created matter is and I have sworn to abstain from all that comes from such fornication."

This sounds ridiculous to Philippe's ears. Surely the procreation of animals is a natural thing, as natural as the seasons, as day following night. All God-given.

"So what about you then?" Barthelémey is pressing him. "Don't you have a wife and children?"

"I did have, but once I became a goodman I put them aside."

This revelation silences the two shepherds. Philippe wants to hear no more. He knows Galtier for a kind man, gentle in his ways, but how could such a man throw his family aside?

Conversation dwindles as the fire dies down. All three men settle down to sleep. Philippe lies awake under the stars, driven from the caselle by Barthelémey's snoring. His mind wanders back to the conversation that seemed so strange to the shepherd. There is no doubt that this man is one of those heretics that he has heard tell of, the hounding of whom is justification for the crusading wars that have torn the country apart for years now. Is it these bizarre understandings of God and the devil, of creation and life that have brought down the wrath of the Pope and the Church on the land? In Philippe's eyes such heresy hardly seems worth it. Yet he finds Galtier to be a good man, perhaps there is more truth in what he propounds than can be found in the dogma of priests and monks. Philippe is as concerned about the fate of his soul as anyone. The path to salvation that Father Jean preaches, sacraments, confession, penances and purgatory seems harsh. Does this man have an alternative, an easier, kinder way, even if it means forswearing cheese?

CHAPTER 9

Bethane runs her fingers through the thick, black hair. Arnaud's preference is to keep it well-trimmed so this is a regular task for her, cutting and delousing. As the scissors peel away the curls of his hair she notices the tiny little ovoid shapes clinging to the strands. She lets them drop to the floor. She will sweep them up later and tip them into the fire, giving them no chance to infest anyone else. She has a well-developed sense of cleanliness, inherited from her mother no doubt.

When she first moved into the ostal she had taken it upon herself to clean up her new lover, Arnaud. He took some persuading to allow her to scrub away at the soot-engrained lines of his body but she was persistent. It is easier now. These days he spends little time in the forge, his duties as a prudhomme have supervened. To all intents and purposes Grazide is the blacksmith now. She has not inherited her father's tolerance of dirt and keeps herself clean enough, even by Bethane's exacting standards.

Bethane reaches for the fine-toothed comb and begins to rake through the hair that remains uncut. Her keen eyesight picks up the shapes of the lice buried in the dark. She removes them and crushes them between her finger and thumb, enjoying the satisfying slight crunch before dropping them to the floor. These moments with Arnaud are special for her. He will talk more at such times; she likes that. There are not many opportunities for such intimacy.

Satisfied that his scalp hair is cleared she puts down the comb. "Let's have your things off now." Arnaud knows the drill. He pulls off his tunic and his linen undershirt so that he is bare to the waist. He has a fine growth of chest hair, as curly as that on his scalp and nearly as thick. She sits in front of him and carefully searches out the body lice. She finds a few that have made a home in the forest, happy to suck his blood for the nourishment they need.

Whilst she works away he lifts his right hand to stroke her hair. She knows this is a sign that he will reciprocate the ritual for her. She smiles to herself. She knows that he will search her long hair in the same way and then remove her clothes, ostensibly to search her more hidden hirsute growth. He never finds any little crabs there but still she returns the gesture. She delights in seeing his member stiffen and rise as she runs her fingers through the bushiness of his pubic growth. She is aroused herself by now. It has become a well-worn pattern for them both but nonetheless welcome.

Once passion is exhausted they lie for a while under a rough blanket, their longing satisfied. The straw mattress rustles under their movement.

He begins to talk about Grazide. "I am proud of the girl," he says. "She stuck to her learning even when boys of her age gave up. Her mother made me promise to have her educated, made me promise when she realised she was dying. At the time I could see no sense in it. What does a growing girl want with all that reading and writing? Didn't seem natural to me yet Allemande made me promise. I couldn't break my word to a dying wife. Then, as she has grown up I have begun to see what a difference it has made. She is more independent, more self-reliant. She has to be, I suppose, seeing she has no mother and both her brothers are gone. I can see that. But these days I cannot get close to her, understand her. There always seems to be a holding back; it's like she has a shell around her. Now she's doing my work most of the time. Folks say that is not natural, her being a woman and doing the work of a blacksmith. She should be married off by now, they say. I thought that once too, but she shows no signs of wanting it. Maybe they are right, it is unnatural. Maybe she wants to be a man. She could be. She's strong enough, she knows her own mind."

Bethane listens without interrupting. It is not often that he talks in this way. She has no wish to halt the flow but part of her wants to break in. She has her own view of Grazide. Theirs is an uncomfortable relationship, particularly living in the same ostal. The younger woman made no objection when Bethane moved in but these days, even though she is occupied enough with the work in the forge, she seems to resist giving up her place as the woman in the ostal. Bethane has taken over the cooking, cleaning and the washing for

Grazide has no time for such work. Bethane does not look for gratitude but she finds it hard to accept the resentment.

Since the refugee woman, Sybille, has moved in as well matters have become even more complicated. Bethane finds the newcomer to be strange, almost other-worldly. She accepts that it was her prompting which led Arnaud to offer asylum to the newcomer but it is making life in the ostal difficult. Often she wishes it was just Arnaud and her. Life would be easier then, Bethane thinks to herself.

Sometimes she misses her husband, Philippe. She is surprised how tolerant he has been, what with her taking off with Arnaud. Living with a man who stinks of the sheep that he spends his days with, that is away for more than half the year, was never easy. But he was a kind husband, never beat her. Not much of a performer under the covers though. Not like nowadays.

She glances at the still body lying beside her. He has fallen asleep and is snoring, a quiet, contented snore. Arnaud has never beaten her either but he has his moments, ordering her about, sometimes shouting. His daughter ignores him when he is in that sort of mood. To Bethane it seems as if the young woman is out of reach, unassailed by any degree of masculine domination. Perhaps that is why she has never married.

Bethane keeps these thoughts to herself. She knows well enough how the confidences of one day become the village gossip of the next. She may have friends amongst the women of the village, people to chat to when washing clothes in the stone basins that are fed by the spring below the village, but she is wary enough to keep these thoughts to herself.

She does have a confidant, nonetheless. It is late afternoon and she is taking a break from the work of the day, sitting on the stone bench just outside the Lamothe ostal. The heat of the day is fading as the shadows lengthen. She is drowsy so fails to notice the man approaching. It is her uncle, Guillaume Guiraud, back from the fields. He sits down beside her.

"Uncle. I didn't see you coming."

"No, lass. I can see that," he laughs, a short and circumscribed laugh. "You looked well away there."

"Just getting a break. Arnaud and Grazide will be home soon."

"Yes. I guess they will. It's been a long day today."

She notices the sickle in his hand. "Harvest's started, has it?"

"Only just. My wheat has ripened so it's a good day to crop it. There's rain in the air."

Bethane remembers this about her uncle. He has a good nose for the weather. The other men rely on him for his predictions, he is rarely off the mark.

"A good crop, is it?"

"Not bad considering. Bit of rust down the bottom corner, mind you. Can never get rid of that bugger."

Bethane is used to the mild profanity, it does not offend her. She has other things on her mind. "Uncle, can I ask you a question?"

If he is taken aback at this request he does not show it. "Right, niece. What do you want to know?"

"It's about my Arnaud. Well, not exactly about him, it's about Grazide."

Guillaume frowns. "What about her?"

Bethane kicks at the dust under her feet, she is searching how to phrase this. Before she can answer her uncle cuts in. "What's a woman doing, playing at being a blacksmith? Is that what you're asking?"

"Yes, or not quite. It's just that she shows no sign of wanting a husband. Living, all of us, in the same house, it can be difficult. I never know where I stand."

"Stand? With her you mean?"

Bethane pauses, thinking. "No, not actually. Where I stand with Arnaud." She blushes to mention her liaison with her uncle's friend.

"Ah, I get it. How long's he going to put up with it, you mean. Daughter and you and that refugee woman under one roof."

86

"I suppose so. We're not husband and wife. Cannot be whilst Philippe's alive." She starts to cry quietly. "One day he may just ask me to go. Throw me out."

Guillaume puts an arm around her. "Come on, niece. Don't cry. I'm sure he'll not put you out. I know Arnaud. He wouldn't do that."

"I'm not so sure," she speaks through her tears. "If Grazide turns against me he might take heed of her. That would be the end of it for me."

"Why would Grazide take against you? What have you done?"

"Nothing. At least nothing that I know about. It's just that she is so difficult to fathom. I don't know what's going on in her mind. She never talks to me about these sort of things."

"Come on, lass. Dry your tears. I tell you what I'll do. I'll talk to Arnaud, just careful-like. See what he's got in his mind. I'm sure there's nothing for you to fret about. I'll have a word."

"Thank you, uncle," she smiles weakly, "you won't let on what I told you about."

"No, of course not. I'll find a way to sound him out. Don't you worry, lass."

Bethane looks relieved. She stands up, gives her uncle a kiss and disappears indoors without a further word. Guillaume remains standing, his sickle swinging from his right hand.

CHAPTER 10

Every year, on the fourteenth day of September, there is a Fair in Vilanòva. It is the Feast of the Holy Cross, the day when the inhabitants of the village welcome in folk from far and wide. Much eating and drinking and many opportunities to buy and sell a great assortment of surplus produce from the working of the land. Artisans, amongst whom are Arnaud and his daughter, do a good trade in the products of their labours. In the previous few years impoverishment had afflicted the community, the Fair had been a paltry affair. Now that the fortunes of the village are picking up a renewed enthusiasm for a jamboree is growing amongst the people.

Arnaud and Guillaume, prudhommes, encourage the participation of as many people as possible. The square in front of the west door of the church is packed with stalls. Tables full of baked bread jostle alongside those of butchered lambs and fish from the rivers Lot and Aveyron. Flies are everywhere. Na Mazaler, the weaver, stands behind bales of colourful and patterned cloth that she has been labouring to produce over the long year since the last Fair.

In the shade, under the trees on the edge of the square, are joglaresses, female minstrels who entertain the crowds with lively chansons. Small groups have gathered around the performers, their plaintive sing-song floats across the hum of the Fair. Other joglars, men, entertain with poems and bawdy stories, ribald laughter and back-chat punctuating their acts.

Grazide wanders through the crowds. Her father is looking after their stall for a while so she is free to circulate. Ever since she can remember she has enjoyed the day of the annual Fair. As a little girl she loved to search out the animals; goats, sheep, rabbits. She longed to have one of these as a companion but knew well enough that they were destined for the pot. Their ostal had never had a dog. She would like to have had one but her father had no time for such ideas. There are dogs that roam the village but they studiously avoid eye contact with any humans, intent only on some important project of their own. Philippe Noguès, Bethane's estranged husband, has a pair of dogs but they are working animals, fierce enough to take on a wolf if needs be. They used to frighten the young Grazide.

In the far corner of the marketplace she spots Sybille. She is standing with Galtier Foulcaut and a few others of the refugees. They seem distanced from the general festivities, looking on with expressionless faces. She is surprised to see that Philippe, the shepherd, is with them.

She stops to watch some small boys who have been attracted to one of the sideshows. A gnarled old peasant that she does not recognise is calling out in a quavering voice, "Come and catch the rat. Win a prize. Come and catch the rat."

He stands beside a large wooden board that is propped up at a steep angle. Down the centre of the board is a long tube that ends a couple of hands' breadths from the bottom. For the payment of a small coin the competitor is handed a stout, short staff. The old man produces a piece of hose stuffed out with dried peas; this is the rat. He holds it above the top of the tube, calls "Ready!" and lets it go. The competitor, usually a small boy, has to whack the rat as it emerges from the bottom of the tube and hold it in place. If the whacker is successful a slightly larger coin is presented as a prize. It turns out to be much more difficult than it looks and few of the young competitors succeed. The old man's purse, hanging from his belt, becomes fuller and fuller. Grazide moves on.

Looking up from a stall where she is examining some earthenware plates she comes face to face with the priest, Father Jean Vital. She wants to turn away but he is speaking to her. There is a smile on his face that does not extend to his eyes. They remain cold, holding her in an unflinching gaze.

"Well, Grazide Lamothe. It's a long time since I've seen you. You never seem to be at Mass these days."

Grazide cannot speak. She would try to escape him but the crowds are pressed tight against her. Bit by bit she feels an anger rise within her. How dare he speak to her in this way after what he tried to do to her? What right has he to dominate her still? She stares at him but makes no reply.

It appears that the priest is at an impasse. He shrugs his shoulders. "Oh well. I suppose you have your reasons," and turns to walk away. It is all that she can do to restrain herself from screaming at his retreating back. Her fists are tightened but she holds herself still.

The crowd around the stall has dispersed a little. Grazide feels a gentle tug of her sleeve. She turns to see the figure of Fabrisse Guillon, the widow whom Grazide knows to have been a one-time mistress of the priest. Fabrisse has been kind to her in the past.

"Grazide, my dear. Come away." The older woman takes her arm and steers her away. They walk together from the market, around the north side of the church where there are few people about. "You must not let him upset you, Grazide." By now tears are glistening in Grazide's eyes. Her mind is racing. What does Fabrisse know? Does she know what the priest tried to do to her?

"He is a despicable man, Grazide. Don't let him upset you. I know him of old."

A feeling of panic grips Grazide. "But what? What do you know?"

Fabrisse sighs. "I was a foolish woman. I allowed him to take over my life. It was a terrible mistake and I know that I shall pay for it one day. I thought he loved me, at one time I thought that," she pauses for a moment, appearing to collect herself, "but it was clear he didn't. He dropped me like a stone. No reason, no explanation. Now I can see him for what he is. You must not let him damage you, my dear. Don't give him the power over you."

Grazide is listening in silence, shocked at what she is hearing. The revelation of the older woman encourages her to speak. "I have never told anyone of this, Fabrisse. Can you keep this a secret?"

Fabrisse nods. Grazide is overwhelmed with a feeling of relief. She needs nothing further for her to trust this woman. "He tried to rape me."

"Oh God, my poor love. What happened?"

"I managed to fight him off. I think I hurt him."

"I'm glad of that. He deserves it, and much more. Did he hurt you?"

"No, I wouldn't let him." At this she cannot contain the flood of tears that are brimming in her eyes. She is sobbing, the anger that she felt before now turned to relief. Fabrisse holds her tight, her arms encircle the younger woman. For a moment Grazide feels safe, safe in a way that she can hardly remember.

"Thank you, Fabrisse," her voice is small now, emptied. Fabrisse kisses her on the cheek. "Come on now, I'll walk you home."

As they return to the square the stallholders are beginning to pack away their wares. It is late afternoon. Along one side of the square, opposite the west door of the church, they see Guillaume Guiraud supervising a group of men. They are constructing an edifice of wooden benches to make a grandstand for an audience. Grazide has heard that a group of players had arrived in the village the previous day. They are to put on a performance that evening once the Fair has been cleared away.

"Are you coming to the play?" says Fabrisse.

"I think so. I'm not sure."

"I'll sit with you, my love. It's a play about Adam and Eve, or so I'm told. It's not often we have travelling players come to Vilanòva."

An hour later they are in place on the stands. All the seats are taken, there is an expectant hum from the audience. There is a clear space in front of the west door of the church. The door itself, and its surrounds, are covered with an array of flowers and plants, small trees have been uprooted and lean against the portal. On the opposite side of the acting area is erected a large wooden frame over which hang two highly coloured curtains, reds, blacks and yellows painted on the fabric. A man appears.

"Good people of Vilanòva. Pray silence for our performance, the *Play of Adam*!" There is a small cheer from a rowdy group in the audience. The man continues. "Here in your village is depicted

Paradise," he indicates, with a dramatic gesture, the display over the west door. "God's creation for his masterwork, Adam and his wife, Eve."

"And over here," he walks across to the pair of curtains, "are the Gates of Hell." Catcalls from the ribald spectators greet this announcement. The man signals for silence. A hush falls over the audience. From a far corner comes the sound of three singers, chanting an introduction. Around the corner of the church come two figures, one dressed in a full robe over a white tunic, the other a man wearing nothing but a long, tight-fitting garment like a tube, as if he were naked.

The fully dressed figure speaks.

"Adam,

I have now formed you of earthly mud.

I formed you in my own likeness.

Since you're an image made of clay,

Do not rebel against my sway.

A good companion, you'll perceive.

This is your wife, her name is Eve."

From around the church emerges the figure of Eve, dressed in a similar fashion to Adam, her female shape is undisguised. Grazide is immediately struck by the grace of her body, slim and feminine. Her auburn hair glows in the evening light.

"This is your wife, she is your spouse.

To her you ought to be faithful.

You'll love her and she'll love you too.

She should take heed to your command.

From your own side I made her too

So she's not strange, she's part of you."

The audience listens intently. The story is familiar to most of them, they have heard it expounded in the homilies of Father Jean. Grazide recognises the second creation story. She is probably alone in knowing that there is a previous story from the first chapter of Genesis, man and woman created together, created equal.

The play continues. A lively Satan makes his appearance from the Gates of Hell and debates with Adam who spurns him. In seductive tones the devil inveigles Eve's attention. Now he is telling her of the joys of eating of the tree of Knowledge of Good and Evil.

"That fruit, on the forbidden tree

Has powerful efficacy.

That has power and grace."

"How does it taste?" says Eve.

Grazide's attention is at once seized. The woman is asking about knowledge but she says 'How does it taste?' Not 'What is knowledge?' She asks not about learning, a matter of the mind, but 'how does it taste?' a matter of the body, the sensual.

The play goes on. Grazide recognises the familiar message. Woman is not to be trusted, woman is weak and feeble, not capable of the higher thoughts of the mind but rooted in sensuality. Adam must rule her. Cast out of Paradise he rails against her, beats her, blames her for their downfall. Around her Grazide hears murmurs of approbation from some men in the audience. This is what they want to hear.

At the end of the play the applause is loud and long. Grazide does not join in. As she walks home that phrase resonates through her whole self. 'How does it taste?' Not a world of mind and body; the one, *Mind*, masculine and dominant, the other, *Body*, feminine and subordinated. Secondary as Eve is secondary to Adam, formed out of his rib.

No. Grazide has seen an alternative, a world where mind and body can both exist as equal, neither dominating the other. A world of both thinking and feeling. It is an alternate world that she has seen; more genuine, more authentic. Her eyes have been opened.

These thoughts occupy her mind as she waits for sleep to come that night. As her mind drifts towards oblivion they are replaced by an image, the figure of a slim, auburn-haired woman encased in white. The Eve of the play she has just seen.

Arnaud Lamothe and Guillaume Guiraud had had much to talk about in organising the Fair. The blacksmith fell naturally into the role of instigator. Guillaume seemed easy with that, always happy to adopt a subsidiary position. Even so he was diligent and hard-working, implementing rather than proposing plans and ideas. It was Arnaud who had heard of the travelling players and conceived the idea of staging a play for the populace. It was Guillaume who made the long journey to Rodez to seek them out and negotiate their appearance at the Fair.

The two prudhommes thus work well together. Prior Roger has relinquished any role that he might have had in running the community. The Bishop's representatives only appear twice a year when there are tithes to be collected. In this way the life of the village is becoming more stabilised. There are fewer disputes between neighbours; Arnaud's authority, though never oppressive, is firm enough to regulate the social life of the community.

But through all this time Guillaume has not forgotten his promise to his niece. How is he going to raise it with his fellow prudhomme? Arnaud has never talked about his cohabitation with Bethane. Guillaume has no difficulty in understanding why she left Philippe, her husband, for the more masterly figure of the blacksmith. She was always wilful as a child and that streak in her has persisted into adulthood. It was quite a relief when her father and mother married her off to the shepherd. They both died soon afterwards, perhaps feeling that their job was done.

Guillaume likes Philippe but he had doubted at the time whether the shepherd would be able to contain Bethane, let alone satisfy her. It was no surprise when she took up with Arnaud. To Guillaume it seemed a natural course of events. It seemed the same to most of the village. Father Jean had alluded to it in some of his homilies without actually naming names. This cut no ice with most people, knowing what they knew about the hypocritical priest's own predilections.

Yet Bethane has told him that she feels uncertain, unsure of her place in the Lamothe ostal. Guillaume wonders whether the difficulty is really with the daughter, Grazide. She is an unknown factor as far as Guillaume can tell. Surprising how she has taken over the smithy trade, even more surprising is how good she is at it. Yet that is never going to help her find a husband. That is what Bethane wants, for Grazide to marry and move out. That other woman, the refugee Sybille, she will not stay. Guillaume is sure she and the other refugees will move on sooner or later.

Funnily enough he has noticed that Philippe, Bethane's estranged husband, is to be seen in the company of the refugees more often. That seems strange. Philippe is known as a solitary man, happy enough to be away with his sheep for months on end. Guillaume gives it no more thought, more pressing is how he is going to approach Arnaud about his niece and her worries.

The opportunity finally presents itself at the end of the day of the Fair. Arnaud, having paid off the players, puts his arm around his fellow prudhomme's shoulders. "Well, that's all done. Seems like a great success, that play."

"It certainly was. The players told me that they've never had such a lively audience. They'll come back next year, no doubt."

"Aye. That would be good. Nice to have a play about all that Adam and Eve stuff. Much better than the priest's boring homilies. Tells us how men and women should be."

"That Eve, she was a shameless one. And getting turfed out of Paradise. Women, always bringing us trouble."

Arnaud looks at him closely. "Is that what you think?"

Guillaume detects an edge to his fellow's voice. He blushes and stammers, "No, no. Not really. No, I'm glad for women. Where would we be without them?" Perhaps a strange thing for him to say, his own wife having died some years back. That loss was something that he shared with Arnaud, both of them widowers.

"You never married again, did you, Guillaume?"

"No. Never seems to be the right time or the right person. I'm content enough though." He realises that this conversation is verging on dangerous ground. Perhaps Arnaud feels the same for neither man speaks for a few moments.

In the end Arnaud breaks the silence. "Do you have a problem with me and Bethane? Is that what you're driving at?"

This is getting almost too uncomfortable for Guillaume. He cannot look the other man in the face. "No, no. That's not it. No, that's all fine by me, you and Bethane."

"She's a good woman. I need a good woman like her. A man has needs when he's been on his own for so long, don't you agree?"

Guillaume nods assent though doubts whether he feels the same. Through his confusion he sees a path to take. "Arnaud, I'm glad for you. So you and Bethane, that will last, will it?"

Arnaud looks at him with a querulous stare. "I don't see why not. Philippe doesn't seem to object."

"You're not going to ditch her then?"

"Why on earth would I do that? She's a good worker. The house is clean, she cooks well and between you and me," he leans forward in a gesture of conspiracy, "and I know you're her uncle but I have to say she's a really good fuck. I'm not going to ditch her." He sits back with a grin on his face. Guillaume's own face reddens. Even so he is determined to continue.

"But what if Grazide wants her out? It must be difficult, two women in the same ostal."

"Grazide? She's too busy in the forge. She's not likely to want to go back to cleaning and cooking. No, don't you worry about Grazide."

"But it must be difficult, the two of them. And you've got that refugee woman as well."

Arnaud laughs. "Oh her. She'll never say boo to a goose. I hardly notice that she's around the place. She'll move on sooner or later, anyway."

At last a wave of relief floods over Guillaume. He has done what he promised his niece he would do. As far as he can fathom, the outcome will reassure Bethane. He will speak to her and put her mind at rest. Just so long as she continues to be a good fuck, he thinks to himself.

Philippe Noguès is back from the summer grazing grounds on the causse. He has left his flock in the care of his fellow shepherd, Barthelémey. He reckons he can rely on Barthelémey, not the brightest of men but trustworthy. Philippe has business to do and, in any case, he always tries to get back to Vilanòva for the annual Fair. His two mules are laden with fleeces that he hopes to sell during the festivities.

But there are other matters on his mind. In the past he has hired himself out as a shepherd. It is never an arrangement that brings him full satisfaction. The pay is meagre although it is supplemented by the provision of his food. Late last year he had taken the bold step of borrowing money, a substantial amount, to buy sixty sheep to call his own. Working for himself is more than satisfying but it has left him with a considerable debt. No doubt over the next few years he will be able to pay it off using the profits from the sale of the lambs and the fleeces that he shears every April. But Philippe feels oppressed by the debt; he wants to unburden himself of it. Over the last few months, out on the causse, sitting by the fire under the stars he has hatched a plan. Now he is returning to the village to implement it.

The difficulty is that it involves the blacksmith, Arnaud Lamothe. Philippe has always rubbed along well enough with Arnaud but when Bethane left him and shacked up with the blacksmith the situation became more delicate. Not that Philippe minds too much; life with Bethane was fractious most of the time. Philippe is glad to get away to the summer grazing each year. He is a man who values his independence.

Bethane's ditching of him was a cause for scandalous gossip in the village, but only for a short while. Sometimes it hurt when the old ladies of the village would waggle their little fingers at him, thinking that they were not observed. He knew they were hinting that Bethane's desertion was linked with a degree of inadequacy on the part of the shepherd. That hurt but it bolstered his resolve to stay away from Vilanòva and its scurrilous inhabitants as often as he could.

Philippe's plan is simple. He wants to find a partner, a sharecropper, who would take part-ownership of his flock. The money that such a benefactor might invest would enable Philippe to rid himself of his debt much sooner. Such arrangements were not unusual, sometimes they profited both parties well, sometimes they failed. What he needs is a partner with enough spare cash to sink it in such a venture. Such people would be hard to find in a small village like Vilanòva but Philippe knows that the blacksmith business is flourishing. He has heard that that success is down to the daughter, Grazide, who does most of the work in the forge. Some people are shocked by this but others appreciate that she has become highly skilled. Producing good, reliable tools is important to them, they do not care about the gender of the artisan who creates them.

Philippe reckons then that Arnaud could be a potential financial backer. His crafty shepherd's brain also surmises that he might have another advantage over the blacksmith; the latter owes him one having filched his wife from him. Philippe begins to feel cheered by his plan. He is sure that it will work.

The shepherd turns up at the Lamothe ostal one evening. Bethane and Grazide are out, Philippe had made sure of that. As he enters he sees Arnaud sitting at the table, a pitcher of wine in front of him.

"Greetings, Arnaud." The seated man looks up sharply. When he sees who it is his face falls. "I hope I don't disturb you, Arnaud."

Arnaud grunts. "No." There is no doubt that he is flustered, embarrassed even, which is unusual for him. "Philippe Noguès. Take a seat."

The invitation is cold but Philippe ignores that. He smiles and sits down opposite the blacksmith. "Thank you."

Arnaud proffers the pitcher and a mug. "Wine?" Philippe nods and Arnaud pours the dark red wine and passes the mug over.

"You're probably wondering why I'm here," says Philippe. He can see that the other man is discomfited; Philippe can guess why. No harm to let him stew in that uneasiness for a while, there could be an advantage in that. The blacksmith merely grunts.

"How is Bethane?" continues the shepherd, stirring the pot a little. This elicits another grunt but no further reply. Silence falls; Philippe takes a sip of his wine. He can see that this strategy is going nowhere. Time to get to the point.

"I have a business proposition for you, Arnaud."

The other man's face lightens. Perhaps he is relieved that the marital domestic difficulty is not the reason for the shepherd's visit. Philippe presses on, outlining his proposition and suggesting terms. Arnaud turns out to be responsive to what the shepherd is advocating, life as a prudhomme has given him a taste for negotiation. It is not long before terms are agreed. Arnaud stands and offers his hand. They shake on the deal and it is done. Both men settle down to finish off the wine, happy with their new liaison as business partners.

The door opens and Grazide appears, followed shortly by Bethane. Grazide looks surprised to see the shepherd drinking with her father. Bethane looks shocked, her face flushes and she turns to escape.

"Hold on there, wife," calls Philippe. He cannot resist using the title even though all present consider it redundant. "No need to bugger off. Arnaud and I have made a deal. We're partners now."

"A deal?" This is Grazide, her eyebrows raised.

"Yes, daughter. Just a bit of sharecropping of his sheep," Arnaud indicates Philippe. "Good for us all, I guess."

Philippe does not fail to notice the relief on Bethane's face. Perhaps she imagined that she was part of the share-cropping deal. Perhaps she is.

"Father," says Grazide, "How much have you put in? Did you not think that I should have been involved in this?"

This obviously annoys Arnaud, his former embarrassment channelled into fury. "I am the head of this ostal, let me remind you, daughter. I do not need to consult you or anyone else, least of all a bloody woman!" He moves to raise his arm. Philippe is shocked, shocked that his new partner could explode like this. And to his own daughter. He looks across at Grazide, her face is set firm. He sees in that instant that there has been a shift of power in this ostal. He wonders to himself whether he should have done the deal with the daughter rather than the father.

Bethane moves forward and puts a hand on Arnaud's right arm. "Calm down, my love. There's no need to shout at your daughter." Philippe is amazed at how this appears to diffuse the blacksmith's rage. The man's arm drops to his side, he slumps down on the bench. Time to go, thinks Philippe. He slips out through the door, glad to leave this domestic perturbation.

CHAPTER 11

A short distance outside the village, on the road to the south, lies a small chapel. It is dedicated to Our Lady of Grace; part of the domains of the Priory. Next to this chapel is a small orchard, tended by the monks but by now somewhat overgrown and neglected. A lack of pruning has allowed the apple and pear trees to produce a burgeoning of green growth but the small fruits are hard and sour.

Nevertheless it provides a space of shade for travellers on the road. In the cool of the evening Philippe Noguès is wandering down that road, his mind full of the scene that he has just left. He is cheered by the fact that a deal has been struck but that cheer is tempered by a fear that it may not work out as well as he might like. Passing the small chapel he spies a small gathering of people over in the corner of the adjacent orchard, under the trees. Most of them, men and women, are seated on the ground. One figure, tall, imposing and gaunt, is standing. Not near enough to hear what is being said it is nevertheless obvious to Philippe that this man is addressing the seated group. He moves closer and recognises the figure. The strange man that he met out on the causse, Galtier Foulcaut. Galtier has seen him for he calls across and beckons the shepherd to join them. "Hey there, Philippe Noguès. Come and sit with us."

Philippe approaches cautiously. He remembers his previous encounter with this Galtier. By now he is pretty sure that the man is a heretic but some of what he spoke made sense to the shepherd. Phillipe has little time for the priests, bishops and monks of the Church. Hypocrites most of them. Knowing this man to be a heretic does not put Philippe off, just enough of a renegade to make this an attraction.

He joins the group, sitting beside them on the grass. One or two mumble a word of welcome. All the refugee band are there with the exception of Galtier's son, Pierre. I guess he must be clearing up at the forge, thinks Philippe. He had heard that the boy had been taken on as an apprentice by his new business partner, Arnaud.

There are others there, under the fruit trees. He spots Na Mazaler the weaver, and Fabrisse Guillon. Philippe is surprised to see the widow and one-time mistress of the notorious Father Jean Vidal in this company. Galtier Foulcaut has resumed his address.

"I expect many of you saw that play on the day of the fair. Adam and Eve, Paradise and the Devil. I expect you know the old story, how Adam's sin is laid on the whole of humanity, you included. But it isn't like that. That's the story put about by the Church. You are laden with sin so you look about desperately for salvation. I tell you, the sacraments of the Church, baptism, the Mass are powerless to help you. The bishops may sell or grant you indulgences but they are worthless." The preacher is getting into his stride now. Philippe listens intently. These words are music to his ears, however seditious they may be.

Galtier goes on to expound a different story, an alternative cosmology. "Know," he says, "that there are two worlds, one visible, vain and corruptible, the other invisible, incorruptible and eternal. It was the devil who created the children of this world, the world we can see and touch, the world in which we live out our paltry lives. We are born of blood, of the will of the flesh and the pleasure of man. Everything created in our material world is the work of the devil. Set against that is the heavenly world, the domain of God and his angels, outside and apart from the real world. Saint-Jean's Gospel says that Christ's kingdom is not of this world. It is the world where souls live in the eternal life of God. Our troubles began," his voice is becoming harder and louder, "when the Devil and his angels invaded the heavenly world, did battle with the Archangel Michael and came away with a third of the creatures of God. It is these", now he is thundering out the words, "that he implants in human bodies and in the bodies of lower animals. These lost souls are then doomed to transfer from one body to another until such time as all shall be brought back to heaven. And how can they be brought back to heaven? Only when the soul reaches the body of a goodman or goodwoman, one who has been consoled."

Philippe is mystified. What is this 'consoled'? He looks up and sees that Galtier Foulcaut is looking straight at him.

"What is this consolation? Why, it is a blessing passed down from the Apostles themselves by the laying on of hands. A direct line. I have been consoled which is why I am known as a goodman. I have repented of all my sins. I have promised to forgive all men their sins, to keep the commandments of Christ, to hate this world and its works and all things which are of this world. I cannot eat the flesh of animals for they have been born in sin, I must not swear an oath, I must live a blameless life." A life without cheese, remembers Philippe. Now he is beginning to understand.

"But you, even if you cannot accept the consoling baptism, must still honour the goodmen in your midst. Support us and help us and you will be blessed. When your life is coming to an end you can be consoled by any one of us goodmen. That way you can die in peace knowing that your soul will rejoin your Heavenly Father in the higher realm. The way of a goodman in this world is hard and not for many to endure, but for you there is joy in the knowledge that you can die with all your sins forgiven, can die in the hands of the goodmen, die and your soul will go straight to God."

He ends his homily there. From the bag slung over his shoulder he pulls out a wineskin and drinks. The people on the ground begin to talk to each other. From what Philippe can ascertain it is apparent that many have heard such ideas before. He finds himself talking to Fabrisse. Her eyes are reddened, it seems she has been in tears. Philippe places a hand on her arm. "Are you all right, Fabrisse?"

She sniffs. "Oh, Philippe. What wonderful words. I feel as if a weight has been lifted from my shoulders, a burden that I have been carrying for years." Philippe cannot think of how to answer this so he says nothing. "Did you not find him wonderful? I have never heard anything like this, it's as if a whole new world has opened up for us."

Philippe feels the need for caution. "You have to be careful, Fabrisse. You know they call this heresy."

"Oh, I know that. But it cannot be bad. He's a good Christian. Now I know my soul is waiting to be released to join God in heaven it's," she pauses, searching for a word, "it's magnificent."

Philippe feels himself being swept along by this enthusiasm. Part of him wants to allow the tide to carry him with it, another part is suspicious, even fearful. He knows, they all must know, that the fate of heretics, if discovered, can be the stake. True the wars have left their small corner of the southern lands alone over the few years since the sack of Morlhon but things could change. The natural caution of a shepherd tells him it is a dangerous belief in dangerous times.

The following day Philippe returns to his flock on the causse. Before he leaves he seeks out the goodman, Galtier Foulcaut, to donate a fleece to him. The tall man receives it with thanks. Philippe kneels in front of him and receives his blessing, accompanied by a touch of his hand upon Philippe's head.

"Peace be with you, brother Philippe. Your gift will not go unrecognised."

The following night he is reunited with his flock, relieved to find that under Barthelémey's care there has been no depredation from wolves, nor sickness amongst the ewes. It is the season that the rams must service the females, mustering up their inexhaustible taste for the tup. Barthelémey is pleased to hear of his friend's successful deal with the blacksmith. He is also intrigued to hear more about the goodman, Galtier Foulcaut.

"Tell me more about him," says Barthelémey.

"He is a man like any other. His flesh, his bones, his shape, his face are all exactly like those of other men. But he says he is one who walks in the way of justice and truth, the way that the Apostles followed. Goodmen do not lie. They do not take what belongs to others. Even if they found gold or silver lying in their path they would not pick it up unless someone made them a present of it. Salvation is better achieved in the faith of these men called heretics than in any other faith." As he speaks these words he recognises that he is beginning to accept this as the truth. There is no turning back now.

Barthelémey is impressed. "I always thought there was something about that man. He carries an authority about him but it's a gentle authority. Not like the bloody priests," he spits into the fire, the spittle causing a small burst of steam when it hits the red heart of the blaze, "lording it over us common folk. Hypocrites!"

"We have to be careful who we talk to, Barthelémey. It is dangerous stuff, all this. We don't want to end up roasted on a stake."

Barthelémey shudders. "True, brother. I'll keep my trap shut." Somehow Philippe finds this hard to believe, his fellow shepherd has a liking for gossip as fervent as the fishwives on the river Lot. He will have to keep an eye on him.

Back in Vilanòva the heretical ideas of Galtier Foulcaut have gained a fresh momentum. They spread from ostal to ostal, from conversations between travellers on the road, from hearing the doctrine preached in private gatherings. It is approaching wintertime and there is more opportunity for talk around the kitchen fire in the long, dark evenings. Like the plague it spreads from person to person. Fabrisse, one of the earliest converts, is undiminished in her enthusiasm. In due course she incorporates her friend, Bethane Noguès, into the growing circle of 'believers', the designation that they have attached to themselves.

The appeal of the new faith to someone like Bethane is not difficult for Fabrisse to understand. Bethane is living in a permanent state of concupiscence with the blacksmith, Arnaud, much as Fabrisse herself was with Father Jean. The younger woman must be shrewd enough to see that her perpetual sin, at least that is how the Church would judge it, can be redeemed by a single ceremony at the end of her life. She has become a convert.

One afternoon Bethane talks to her uncle, Guillaume. She is helping him with mucking out the shed where he keeps his two oxen. As the pile of manure grows in the yard she expounds what she understands of the new belief.

"It's not God that causes bad things. It's the devil. And it's the devil that makes everything in this world. But we can get on with life

107

just so long as we honour the goodmen and get consoled before we die."

Guillaume has heard something of this though his niece's account seems a bit garbled and selective. "But this is heresy, niece. These are dangerous ideas."

"Poof! Where's the danger in it? That priest is going to do nothing about it, he's too busy finding his way up women's skirts."

"That's as may be, but just be careful who you talk to. I'd hate to see you getting hurt by this." Guillaume is cautious. After all he is a prudhomme, he has a certain standing in the village. He cannot be seen, on the outside anyway, to be condoning heretical beliefs.

Contagion cannot be subdued once it has embedded itself into a small society like that of Vilanòva. Guillaume's initial reserve is replaced by, if not an enthusiasm, a level of interest. To be a believer but not to have to undergo this new baptism, the consolamentum as it is called, has as much appeal to him as it does to many others in the community. He is not certain that he understands the new cosmology; two powers, one spiritual, one material. That is of little interest to him. His sympathies are more likely to be gained by the condemnation of the Church that the new understanding incorporates. Being one of two prudhommes in the village has exposed him to enough of the venality that infects the clerical powers. His dealings with the Bishop of Rodez have not been comfortable; the Priory and its monks are a constant drain on the community and as for the behaviour of the parish priest, it is outrageous.

Arnaud and he have common ground on this but they are powerless to do anything about it beyond grumbling. As prudhommes their major duty is to enforce the collection of tithes, a task which is getting more and more difficult. The ordinary working people are less and less inclined to offer up a tenth of their produce, particularly when times are hard. All in all there is a resistance in the community which only helps to foment the spread of the heresy.

In this atmosphere it is inevitable that before too long Guillaume feels emboldened to raise these issues with his fellow prudhomme. Many times he has been on the verge of mentioning them but caution has held him back. In the end it is Arnaud who opens the door for him.

"What am I hearing about this man Foulcaut? Have you heard what is being said?"

"A little." Guillaume remains cautious, not certain that he should speak of it to Arnaud.

"What little? Is it heresy? Do we have a problem here?"

"Oh no. I don't think so. Not a problem. It's just a few new ideas, as far as I can make out."

"What new ideas? What do you know, what have you heard?"

Guillaume swallows hard and summons up the little courage he can muster. Bit by bit he expounds the doctrine that is being preached. He tries not to give any hint that he approves of what he is recounting.

"Where have you heard all this, brother?"

"From one or two folk."

"What folk? Who?"

Time to be frank. "Well, one is Bethane. She heard it from Fabrisse who attended one of their meetings."

"What meetings? I've heard nothing of this." By the raised tone of Arnaud's voice Guillaume can see that his fellow prudhomme is becoming alarmed.

"It was in an orchard. The one by the chapel of Notre Dame. Bethane says Fabrisse was very taken with the new ideas."

"Does she? She's said nothing to me. Is she a convert too?"

Guillaume is feeling braver. "I think you should ask her that yourself." Guillaume never likes to be the passer-on of gossip or hearsay at the best of times; particularly not now.

"Perhaps I will. We have to be careful about all this. It could cause problems for the village."

Guillaume does not need him to explain. Word has come from elsewhere in the south of the burning of heretics and destruction of the houses of supporters of the heresy. Even though the crusading wars have left Vilanòva alone for some years now, that armistice could change. The two men agree that they should keep their ears to the ground over the next couple of weeks. That seems prudent but Guillaume has the inkling of a suspicion that his fellow prudhomme's interest has been kindled. Perhaps there is an appeal in the new faith to a man who lives with a woman who is another man's wife.

Bethane is surprised when Arnaud does raise the topic. She has wanted to talk to him but has never been able to find a way through the gruff exterior of her lover. They are in bed together, talking in low tones so as to not disturb Grazide and Sybille, asleep in the adjoining room. They are adept enough in their lovemaking to be restrained yet passionate. Bethane has a natural talent for finding ways to please him. She is glad of that, she knows it is a good part of the cement that holds the two of them together. Arnaud is lying back, panting gently from his exertions. Bethane lies on her side observing him, close enough for her breast to be resting on his arm.

"Your uncle tells me that you've been talking with the widow Fabrisse."

"Fabrisse? Oh yes. From time to time."

"About a meeting. Was that it?"

Bethane sees a way in. Her inclination is to rush through it but good sense warns her to tread carefully. "Yes. She did talk about a meeting she went to."

"Was it that Foulcaut man and his band of followers?"

"Yes. I believe so."

"Come on, Bethane. Why are you being so cagey? Tell me what it was all about. Your uncle Guillaume has told me what he knows."

In her relief Bethane launches forth. "They say that if we believe we can be baptised in some sort of way before we die and all our sins will be forgiven. Our souls will go straight to heaven. Oh, Arnaud. It sounds wonderful, it is such a relief to know that."

"Hold on, woman. Surely there's more to it than that."

"Oh yes, well I think so. I don't really understand the other stuff. Something about the Devil and God."

Arnaud is silent for a while. Bethane cannot contain herself for long. "Just think, my love. We can go on living like this without any guilt or fear of eternal punishment."

"There must be more to it than that, though."

"Probably there is, I don't know." An idea comes to her and in her enthusiasm she cannot keep it to herself.

"Why don't we ask Galtier Foulcaut to come and eat with us? Uncle Guillaume could come too, and Grazide. Then he can tell us all about it."

"I'm not sure, woman. It could be risky. I am still a prudhomme, don't forget that."

"At least think about it. It could be wonderful." In her eagerness she is oblivious to any dangers.

In the end Arnaud agrees. A week later he, Bethane, Sybille and Guillaume are gathered in the kitchen of the ostal, seated at the table. A pot simmers over the fire, the smell of herbs in the bean stew fills the atmosphere, mingling with the smoke from the glowing charcoal. There is a knock on the door and the latch is lifted. They all stand and Galtier Foulcaut enters. He nods to the assembled company.

"Greetings to you all. Thank you for your invitation."

Arnaud steps forward. "Welcome to our ostal. Please take a place here," he indicates the head of the table. The tall man inclines his head in acknowledgement.

Where is Grazide? thinks Arnaud. She should have finished in the forge by now. Galtier sits and the rest of them follow his lead. He picks up the loaf that is placed in front of him. He breaks off a piece and holds it up, his eyes closed. "Blessings be on this food and on those believers gathered here."

It is at this moment that they hear the door latch being lifted again. Grazide enters, her tall stature enhanced by the full-length smock that she wears for her work in the forge. It is dark in the ostal, a single candle on the table contributes a weak light. She peers through the gloom at the small assembly, looking around the people seated at the long table. At last her eye alights on the figure of Galtier Foulcaut, still holding the blessed bread in his hand. The shock on her face is plain for all to see.

She turns to face her father, glaring at him, her eyes narrowed. As if to forestall her Arnaud says, "Come and sit, daughter." His tone is stern, commanding.

The tall woman says nothing. She turns on her heel and walks quickly out of the ostal. The door bangs behind her, the sound echoing around the shocked silence her anger has left behind.

CHAPTER 12

There is a tension in the Lamothe ostal that lasts throughout the long winter months. Hunger exacerbates that disquiet; the supplies of salted pork and dried legumes are dwindling rapidly. Some days all that Bethane can produce is a thin soup, not much more than water boiled with paltry herbs, a small lump of pork fat added to make some consistence.

Grazide stays away as much as she can. There is little work in the forge, some sharpening and repairing of folk's agricultural tools mostly, yet she never returns until nightfall and is gone before the other ostal members have risen in the morning. She does not know what to do with her anger; she finds it hard to identify its true origin. Yes, she knows that much comes from the way her father behaves towards her. When she was a child he was a reliable Papa, seeming to take a pride in her. When she started working in the forge he showed how much he welcomed her involvement. Then he became a prudhomme and ever since he has left the work to her alone. It was her idea to take on an apprentice, the young Pierre Foulcaut. Arnaud seemed disinterested.

Grazide enjoys the work. When there is little in the way of commercial employment, as there is this winter, she has taken to initiating projects for herself. More creative, more artistic. She has learnt how to work in sympathy with the metal, moulding it to her imagination. She plans to try and sell her artisanal products at the next Fair in September. Yet there is more to her anger than the reaction to an over-bearing father. She cannot rid herself of the memory of what Father Jean, the parish priest, tried to do to her. That assault could be reason enough for her anger but it is magnified many times because the outrage came from a man she had trusted, her teacher and, she had supposed, her spiritual father. And there is more that fuels her feeling of affront. Beyond the physical, lustful attack she now perceives a shocking assumption. An assumption that women are objects, there to be used, exploited even. In the eyes of the Church, and thus of common society, she is downgraded, second class.

Grazide knows that this perception has come in part from the reading of the alternative Genesis creation stories. Women subservient in the ancient story of Adam's rib.

And then this new insight had come to her, vividly exposed in that single question from Eve in *The Play of Adam*. When offered the fruit of the Tree of Knowledge she responds, '*how does it taste?*'. For too long women have been falsely cast as inferior, created from the rib of Adam, deemed fit only to serve and support men. Men are characterised as thinking, knowledgeable and wise; women as sensual, flippant and unreliable. That false dichotomy has served to keep her, and all women, subordinated. Grazide's whole being now rejects this. Eve's apparently naive question joins together the two worlds of knowledge and feeling, both become equally available to women as well as to men. Both raised from the dust, as in the account in the first chapter of Genesis, they have equal access to those two supposedly opposed worlds.

In the following spring it comes as a shock to her when her father announces that he is returning to work in the forge.

"Why Father? You have always said that you have no time for it."

"Maybe I did but I reckon I have time enough now. Guillaume can carry on with the prudhomme work. They can find someone else to take my place. I've had enough."

A suspicion is growing in Grazide's mind. "So what am I to do then? Am I to give up the blacksmith work? Has someone been talking to you?"

"That's my business, daughter. My mind is made up."

"They have, haven't they?" Her eyes narrow. "They've been talking about me."

"Perhaps they have but, as I said, that's my business."

"It's my business as well, Father. I have a right to know what's being said about me. Come on, you have to tell me."

Arnaud lets out his breath in an audible gasp. "All right then. I'll tell you. The Bishop's bailie was here last week. They think it's wrong that you are doing a man's work, it's unnatural. It's against God's law."

"Do you think that too? You encouraged me."

Arnaud declines to answer that question. "They want you out of the forge. It comes from the Bishop." His tone becomes more sympathetic. "I'm sorry, Grazide. He is quite insistent."

Grazide explodes. "Well, fuck him!" Her father winces at the obscenity but it fails to restrain her. "Fuck them all and their interfering, hypocritical ways."

"Stop, daughter. That's enough. I will not hear any more of this. You are to stop work. I am taking over."

"So what am I to do? Do they have suggestions, these high and mighty men?"

"Yes, they do. And so do I. We need to find you a husband before you get too old to be married off."

Grazide screams, a scream of rage and impotence. "You cannot treat me as an object to be sold off. I am a woman and I am a person. None of you can treat me like this." By now tears are pouring down her cheeks.

"There's no need to be hysterical, woman. That is how it is going to be. We shall find you a husband, that is the right and proper way. I want to hear no more of this."

Grazide's only instinct is to escape. She turns and starts to run down the village street towards the western gate. Suddenly she stops, turns, her face contorted with rage.

"And who is he to be? Who is the lucky man that will marry this blacksmith?" She flexes her right arm to demonstrate the strength of her biceps. "Who will dare?" She turns away and is gone.

Arnaud could have answered her question straightaway if he had had the courage. He has already identified a possible candidate, Aimèry Targuier, elder brother of Grazide's childhood friend, the cripple, Gervais. Arnaud remembers how Grazide used to be a close companion of the younger brother when they were both children. Aimèry had escaped from the carnage at the sack of the castle of Morlhon, no one quite knows how. He had survived the fighting which had deprived Arnaud of both his sons.

The Targuier ostal was just a street away from Arnaud's. The boys' father, Etienne, was a pig herder who had a parcel of land and a small vineyard outside the village wall. He had grazing rights for his animals in the oak forest that surrounded Vilanòva. Their winter quarters, for those that had not been slaughtered for butchering, were in a shed attached to the ostal. That contributed to the particular smell that attached itself to the occupants of the ostal, Aimèry amongst them.

Arnaud has had the appropriate conversation with Etienne. The dowry that he could offer was a handsome amount. Blacksmithing is a lucrative trade in comparison to the subsistence farming that most in the village rely on. Arnaud has no sons to leave his money to so he can afford to be generous. Even so, Etienne has his doubts about the proposed match.

"I'm not sure if my boy will be up to it, neighbour. He's not exactly a forceful character."

"Forceful enough to tame my daughter you mean?"

"Well, she is sort of", for a moment the pig herder hesitates, "a strong lass."

Arnaud can see that, despite the lavish dowry offer, he is going to have a job to persuade his fellow parent to approve the liaison. "I know, she's a big girl, and she's strong but isn't that an asset in a wife? Your lad will have no trouble in ruling her, so long as he goes about it the right way. She'll be a good wife to him."

If he is honest with himself Arnaud has similar doubts but there are few candidates in the village, so many of the young men had been killed in the fighting. He cannot afford to be choosy. He needs to settle the deal; he is aware of the Bishop's displeasure if he fails to do so.

Both fathers shake hands on the arrangements and agree to break the news to the prospective married couple. Arnaud is not relishing the prospect but is determined to be firm. In his mind he can see what is best for his daughter, she needs to be ruled in this. Not for a moment does he ponder what her mother might have said, were she still alive.

His anxiety is justified. "Marry Aimèry Targuier? That milksop who smells of pig shit? You must be joking, Father." Arnaud wishes he were, but he cannot back down, the deal is already done.

"He's a good, honest young man. He'll make a fine husband for you."

"I don't want a husband," she spits the words out like pieces of gravel. "I told you. I don't want one."

Arnaud tries to placate her. "I know daughter. I know you feel like that now but what happens when I'm gone. You'll need someone to look after you. Aimèry will be a good husband to you. I'm sure of that." In his heart Arnaud has never felt less sure but he cannot backtrack now.

"And what does Aimèry have to say about this?"

Arnaud's patience is leaving him. "I've no idea. It's not up to him. It's an agreement between me and his father. He'll go along with it."

"I'm sure he will," her tone is sarcastic, "he'll jump at the snap of his father's fingers. I know him."

That's probably right, thinks Arnaud, beginning now to regret having started this whole business. "There's no point in arguing this, Grazide. My mind is made up. You are to marry Aimèry Targuier." She opens her mouth to speak but he cuts across her.

"No more! No more of this nonsense. You will do as I say." He is dismayed to find that he has raised his arm to her. In a flash she has grabbed his wrist. He can feel the strength in her grip. Her jaw is set firm.

"Do not dare, Father. Do not think I will let you strike me." She releases her grip and he lets his arm drop. "I've had enough.

117

Enough of all this." He wants to speak, to console her, his only child, but something within him prevents that. Not so much pride, more an expectation laid upon him; this is how a father must be, controlling a wayward daughter, master in his ostal. He cannot be gainsaid.

If ever Grazide needed reminding that she is on her own it is in this encounter. Leaving her father she takes herself out of the village, tracing the path to the woodland beyond. Her heart is bursting with both anger and fear. Surely he cannot make me marry. How can he think I could accept that poltroon, Aimèry, as a husband? The thought of it stokes the fires of her affronted indignation. It is not just the choice of Aimèry, it is the idea that she has no control. The decision is made for her. She knows that her anger, her resistance will be seen by others to be just a female petulance. Women are not equipped to make rational decisions, their shallow emotions need to be ruled by a cool, masculine detachment is what folk would say.

She returns to the ostal after dark and goes straight to her bed. A little later Sybille climbs in beside her as is usual. Both lie in the gloom but sleep cannot come to Grazide. Quietly she begins to weep, small sobs that she tries her best to stifle. She feels the other woman's hand on her arm, gently stroking her.

Grazide turns on her side to face Sybille. Her dark-adapted gaze can just make out the angular features of her bedfellow. "Sybille. What am I to do?" She speaks in a hushed voice.

"To do? About what, my dearest?"

"I am told I am to marry Aimèry Targuier. I cannot. I absolutely cannot." Her tears are flowing faster now. The other woman takes her in her arms.

"There, there. That is horrible."

"It is. It is. How can he make me? There's no escaping it."

Sybille speaks in measured tones. "No one can make you do what you don't want to do. No one has the right to do that."

Grazide is surprised to hear these words from Sybille. They are quite unexpected. "Do you mean that? Is that true?"

118

"Yes, I mean that. Perhaps I wouldn't say it to anybody. I like to keep such things to myself. But I can say it to you."

At last some relief, thinks Grazide. Perhaps this quiet, withdrawn woman can be an ally, though she has no idea how. She feels the tautness of her distress relax a little. It feels good to be held by this woman. She senses Sybille's embrace tighten in response; there is a relief in the physical contact.

After a while Sybille's hand moves down. Now she is stroking Grazide's thigh. She feels her lifting her shift upwards. The gentle but expert exploration is exhilarating. Grazide lets herself be swept along by the passion it engenders. All her anger, her distress is overtaken by the older woman's skilful embrace. Grazide has never experienced such delight, again and again as their two bodies come together throughout the long night. It is a turning point for her, a revelation that abolishes any shame.

The cock has crowed before she sleeps. When she wakes, Sybille has gone.

Grazide's defiance, for that is how he sees it, has cast Arnaud into a dilemma. He knows that, for all his bluster, he is not going to be able to force her into an unwanted marriage. Yet he fears for his reputation in the village, a man who cannot rule his own ostal is likely to be derided as impotent, weak. Above that is also the displeasure of the Bishop if Arnaud fails to see his daughter safely contained in wedlock.

There is still enough compassion in him to appreciate Grazide's view. However much she might defy him she is still his daughter, his only remaining child. He has invested so much in her since her mother died, she still retains a special draw on his heart, deeply embedded by all that has passed between them.

He was distressed that she had reacted so strongly to Galtier Foulcaut's presence at their table the previous year Had she stayed she could have heard what the goodman had to say. To Arnaud's ears it made so much sense; if Grazide could have heard it perhaps her

119

antipathy would have lessened. It could have been a bond between them.

He himself had heard enough to be convinced. As he has now discovered in conversations with others he is not alone. His fellow prudhomme, Guillaume and Bethane's estranged husband, Philippe, number themselves amongst the 'believers', support for the true faith which has grown in the village of Vilanòva.

But the greatest surprise to Arnaud is to find that the parish priest, Father Jean Vidal, has become a secret supporter. The blacksmith learns this one day from the priest's former mistress, the widow Fabrisse. They have met at the village well. Fabrisse is filling a large water pot, Arnaud offers to carry it back to her ostal for her. Walking slowly they make their way back; conversation between them is desultory until Arnaud mentions the name of Galtier Foulcaut. At this point the widow's eyes light up, her whole face is enlivened. Arnaud can see that she is a supporter, a believer probably.

"And the amazing and wonderful thing, Arnaud," she says, "is that Father Jean is one of us too."

"Father Jean? You're joking. How do you know this?" Arnaud is well aware that the errant priest is not Fabrisse's favourite person since his rejection of her some time previously. She has changed her tune, he thinks.

"It must be kept secret but I heard it from Na Mazaler." If the weaver knows it there's little chance that it is going to remain a secret, thinks Arnaud.

"That is a surprise but it's surely dangerous ground for a priest. What if the Bishop suspects?"

"Oh no, he won't. Father Jean carries on with his public duties just as before. It's only in private that he thinks the way we do."

Arnaud cannot help being amused at how the errant priest appears to have regained favour in his former mistress' estimation. "I guess to be consoled at the end of his life would have great appeal for the dear Father." His voice cannot conceal the sarcasm that he is feeling. It appears not to register with his hearer.

"Yes, it does. It does for me as well. That is what makes me so happy."

The spread of heresy through the community has continued. There are now ostals that have espoused the new way whilst there are others that remain orthodox. By now it is an open secret that Father Jean Vidal is a believer, despite to all outward appearances presenting as an orthodox parish priest. Arnaud, by now a convinced believer himself, is aware of how dangerous this infiltration of the village could be. He has heard stories of other communities where heretic goodmen have been arrested, imprisoned and in some cases burnt. Houses of believers have been requisitioned, even destroyed. Mostly these instances have occurred where the ecclesiastic authorities are strong. Arnaud hopes that in Vilanòva, far enough from the seat of the Church's power in the episcopal palace at Rodez, with a renegade priest and a weakened Priory, any possible heretical activity might be overlooked.

In any case he has other matters to worry about. He has tried to avoid having further conversations with Aimèry Targuier's father, Etienne, about the marriage pact. How is he to tell the pig herder that Grazide will not comply? And then, in a stroke of good fortune, the matter is resolved. It is Etienne who comes to him.

"Arnaud. I'm afraid our arrangement for your daughter and Aimèry will have to be dropped."

"Dropped? Why?" Arnaud tries hard to conceal his relief at this news.

"The boy has gone and got himself mixed up with those heretics and their leader, Galtier Foulcaut. He says that he is going to join them, he's going to be sort of baptised. Then he will become a 'goodman', or so he says." Etienne spits into the dust.

Arnaud knows he has to be careful in handling this. Etienne is clearly not a supporter of heretics. Arnaud must keep his own position concealed. "Become a goodman? What does that mean?"

"Oh, I don't know. It's so much heretical nonsense to me but one thing I do know. He will reject any kind of marriage. He is determined to be celibate, for heaven's sake. He'll have nothing to do with Grazide."

That'll be a relief to her, thinks Arnaud, relieved to hear the news as well.

"So, I'm afraid the marriage is off. That is unless Grazide wants to take on my other boy, Gervais. They used to be friends when they were kids."

Arnaud knows the other man is not serious. No one is going to let their daughter marry the cripple and his father must know that. "I don't think that would work, Etienne." He hopes enough is said to forestall that suggestion. Leaving Etienne Targuier he goes to the forge to find Grazide, anxious to tell her the news.

"Aimèry has taken up with this foolishness, has he? That does not surprise me."

"It's not all foolishness, daughter. There's a good bit of sense in it for us ordinary folk."

Grazide frowns. "Well, don't try and include me in it." Arnaud can take this rebuff. At least the stand-off over her marriage with Aimèry can be forgotten. A truce of sorts settles over the Lamothe ostal, heresy as a topic of conversation is avoided.

A week later he receives a visit from Father Jean Vital, an uncommon occurrence. "Arnaud Lamothe. I need to talk to you. You, as once senior prudhomme in this village, need to know what I have heard."

He is not used to the priest speaking like this. "What have you heard, Father?"

The cleric hesitates. "I think you and I share a common view about the…" he stops, apparently searching for a word, "unorthodoxy that pertains in this village."

Arnaud can see how the other man is struggling so he intervenes. "Let's call a spade a spade, Father. We're talking about the new way that some of us, and I think you too, support."

A look of relief crosses the priest's face. "Exactly. I can talk freely to you, I hope." Arnaud nods and continues to listen. "I have heard that the Bishop is determined to take action against what he considers to be heresy. His men are being ordered to root it out. I fear that Vilanòva is going to be one of his targets."

"That is not good news. Is your source reliable?"

"As much as I can tell, yes. I think this carries dangers for this community. I think we have to act. We, or perhaps you, need to talk to the goodman, Galtier Foulcaut. As long as he remains in the village we are in severe danger."

In the past Arnaud has not had much time for this priest, regarding him as a hypocrite, and venal as well. This concern for the wellbeing of the community is therefore surprising but what he proposes seems the right thing to do. "I will speak to him. I think he is going to need to move on." The priest nods his head in agreement.

Later that day Arnaud confronts Galtier Foulcaut with this ultimatum. He is surprised at how calmly the tall man receives it. "Such is often our destiny. We have no wish to endanger the good people of this village. Rest assured, Arnaud Lamothe, we will take the proper course."

Within a day they are gone. Galtier Foulcaut and the refugees that had arrived with him. The only exception is his nephew, Pierre, who is apprenticed in the forge. Arnaud agrees that the boy should move in with them in the Lamothe ostal.

Sybille has gone as well, as unobtrusively as she had arrived the previous year. Arnaud discovers later from Etienne Targuier that Aimèry, his elder son, has joined the heretic band and has gone with them.

"Good riddance," says Etienne to Arnaud. "That milksop of a boy has been a trial for me. A good thing that he has buggered off with those heretics." Etienne does not appreciate, thinks Arnaud, what fate could await an apprehended heretic. Perhaps that is fortunate.

In this way a notorious heretic leaves the village yet the heresy he preached remains in many of the ostals of the village including the house of the priest. The people of Vilanòva have the good sense to keep quiet about their unorthodox ideas though. When the Bishop's men do arrive in the village they fail to unearth anything other than benign, rural piety. They leave the people alone.

CHAPTER 13

Over the next few months a degree of peace settles on the village of Vilanòva. The departure of the refugee band has allowed the fires of heresy to dampen down. With no goodman in their midst to proselytise, most people give little thought to matters spiritual, taken up with the monthly pattern of agricultural work that their life demands of them.

Arnaud has returned to his work in the forge. The role of prudhomme had become an irritant to him; he was glad to leave it to Guillaume who had become more adept as his experience grew. The share-cropping agreement with the shepherd, Philippe, is proving to be profitable to both partners. Arnaud is enjoying a prosperity such as he had not experienced in the past.

Grazide is glad that the matter of her marriage has been dropped. Her father says no more about it. It seems to her that he is equally happy to leave the thorny subject alone. It is never a matter of conversation between them these days. Arnaud has changed his mind and allows her to continue to work in the forge, seemingly untroubled by the Bishop's disapprobation. Now that her father has taken up the hammer once again she is able to devote more time to her more artistic work, leaving the day to day mundane tasks to him and the apprentice, Pierre. What is pleasing to her is that some of her work has come to the notice of people beyond the village. Whilst most folk have neither the money nor the inclination to acquire decorative objects that is not true of the ecclesiastical authorities. She has received commissions for crucifixes, candle stands and other trappings that adorn some churches. Those on the pilgrims' routes, and thus the more prosperous of their kind, are amongst her best customers. Her father, whilst appreciating the extra income that his daughter's skill is bringing in, is dismissive of such artistry.

"Nails, scythes and door brackets. That's what a blacksmith's work is. That's what will always bring the money in."

Grazide no longer allows her father's prejudices to upset her in the way that they might have done in the past. She has grown in confidence; she is not going to let his attitude affect her.

It is a relief for her to get away from the overheated atmosphere of the forge from time to time. To that end she regularly undertakes the trips into the forest to collect supplies from the charcoal burners. It is a whole day away that she can spend on her own. The charcoal burners have become used to her visits. Whilst never over-effusive in their welcome their usual taciturnity has lessened to her. Grazide discovers that she likes them. Perhaps it is their dogged independence that appeals to her; determined to remain outside society, not to be embroiled in all its petty intrigues and nonsensical goings on. Grazide admires that.

Despite the recent lack of turmoil in the community, Grazide cannot share in it. She is not at peace; there is a restlessness in her soul that continues to disturb her. Perhaps it is this unease that drives her, one day in late summer, to retrace the journey that she made some years previously. She is on the road to the castle of Morlhon though she knows it is now a ruin, the village nearby deserted. She crosses the river Aveyron by ferry and makes her way up the wooded slopes towards her destination. There is a darkness under the trees, little signs of bird life in the branches, a sense of foreboding hangs in the air. She meets no one on the path. Finally the castle comes into sight. It is a sorry spectacle, its tower and walls collapsed, nine years of rampant growth is throttling the structure with bindweed, elders, nettles and entangling weeds. As she walks amongst the ruins she comes across the occasional evidence of what had happened those years ago; a rusted sword, its blade shattered, helmets that had been crushed by heavy blows, all conjure up an image in her mind that she has never lost. This is where her brothers died, fighting a pointless cause, no glory, no heroism, just a futile spasm of violence.

She can remember where she and her father buried the two boys. The iron cross that Arnaud had made is still there. The undergrowth has grown thick on the slope in front of the former castle walls. In its silence the scene could impart a kind of peace but none of that reaches into her mind. The sense of loss is overpowering. She sits on the ground next to the grave. Through her consciousness flit images from the past; play with her brothers when she was small, her father's occasional kindness to her, all these are lost to her now. Nowadays she is accustomed to that sense of being on her own, in a way she welcomes it; having her own autonomy. That is why she can never countenance being married, not if it involves surrendering such independence, which it surely would.

She has seen through the conspiracy of masculine domination, seen it for the distortion that it is. It is a story constructed from an initial misrepresentation, the rib of Adam, that has been fashioned over the centuries by male power into a denigration of women. It is a distortion that she utterly rejects.

She remembers those words of Sybille, '*No one can make you do what you don't want to do. No one has the right to do that.*' Just hearing those words from another human being had a profound impact. Having it confirmed by another has allowed her to incorporate it into her very self. '*No one has the right to do that.*' It is a gift to her from that enigmatic woman, a gift that will always be hers.

She remembers that night of passion, how unexpected it was and how exhilarating. Nothing that she had ever believed was possible. It had never been repeated. Sybille had continued to share her bed but nothing had ever passed between them again, neither in action nor in speech. Nevertheless it remained an invisible bond between the two women, unarticulated but nonetheless real. It was thus devastating when Sybille was suddenly gone, disappearing with the heretic Foulcaut and his followers. Grazide remains bewildered by that; more than bewildered, yet again bereft. It is a pattern that continues to repeat itself in her life. A pattern that has led her to decide that withdrawal into herself is the safest course to take. She knows that is true. It is with these truths reordered in her mind that she makes the journey home, back to the ostal, back to the place where she knows she has no place.

After Christmas she begins to notice a change in her father. He seems to tire more easily. Some days he has to leave the forge early, work left undone. She steps in at those times. There is a growing gauntness about his appearance, it is clear that he is losing weight. At times she is sure he is in pain but he never complains. She seeks out the help of one of the monks, Brother Raimond. He has skills with medicinal herbs and potions. He tries a number of remedies but none seem to make any difference, the decline continues. She is aware that her father is seriously ill. She seems powerless to help him.

Until that day when he asks to be taken to the goodmen.

END OF PART ONE

PART TWO

BASTIDE

CHAPTER 14
1223

Anger, like a rope tightening around her chest, threatens to overwhelm her. It restricts her breathing, becoming an unrelenting ache that she cannot shake off. Trapped within her, she cannot let it out. She said nothing to those two austere men that had consoled her father in such a strange ceremony; it would not have been appropriate, that she recognises. She doubts that her father had been aware of what was happening, the words being said, the actions performed but a change has occurred. The vomiting has lessened. In a way he seems to be more peaceful, yet still unresponsive.

Outside the house of the goodmen she is approached by an old woman. The two men that had carried Arnaud on his litter from the quay are still waiting in the shadows. "I can show you a hostel, my dear. It is on the other side of the village. You can take him there. Follow me." She leads the way, Grazide and the two men bearing the litter follow. There is no one about. The old lady stops outside the hostel. "Wait here. I will speak to the keeper." She hobbles inside.

It is quiet. Dusk has descended, birdsong is quieted as the night approaches; the only sound she hears is the rasp of her father's breathing.

The old lady reappears, there is a man with her. "This is Hugues de Port. He owns this hostel. He says you can stay the night here with your father."

Grazide looks at the man. His expression betrays nothing. She gets the feeling that the visitation of a person near to death is not unusual for him, something that he is used to.

"Bring him in, men," says Hugues. "The room at the back." It is a sparse room, just large enough to accommodate a mattress on the floor. It smells musty and damp. The reeds on the floor are old.

They lay Arnaud on the mattress and cover him with a rough blanket. A small stool is produced. "You can sit here. I will bring you food later."

Now she is alone with her dying father. She sits on the stool by the head of his makeshift bed. She does not move. Bit by bit the tightness of her anger begins to dissipate, a calmness returns. She looks at his face, his eyes closed, a sickly pallor. She wants to speak to him but cannot find the words. What to say when he cannot hear? In the end the words come, quietly, gently.

"I love you, Papa."

She wonders how she can say that, remembering the rows, the unkindness, the domination that she experienced from him. Yet also the awkward tenderness, the acceptance. Her mind is confused but she has to speak. "However much you might have hurt me, I have always loved you, my Papa." She squeezes his hand. Does she detect a squeeze back? The movement is infinitesimal, she could be mistaken. A serving girl appears with a bowl of gruel. Grazide sends it away, she has no desire to eat.

In the small hours of the morning her father dies. Nothing happens suddenly. His breathing becomes weaker, long pauses when he does not breathe at all and then a gasp as if he has remembered that he needs to breathe. In the end he is still.

At first light she is found, sitting at the head of her father's body, inert on the ground. They seem to know what to do; she acquiesces in silence.

Arnaud is buried in the graveyard alongside the small wooden church. A priest has been summoned to pray over the body as it is lowered into the earth. Grazide is left alone when the task is done. In her mind she pictures the iron cross at the site of her two brothers' resting place. Now she is alone. Completely, irrevocably, eternally alone. The feeling does not trouble her; somewhere within it there is tranquillity, a possibility that this is how things might be. Almost a freedom.

She returns to the hostel to pay her dues. Hugues de Port accepts her money. "Where are you going now?"

"Returning home, I suppose."

"I have another hostel in Montalban. It's on your way. Just outside the town in Sapiac."

She thanks him for the information though doubts that it is going to be of any use to her. She had noticed the walls of the town of Montalban, up on a hill above the river, when they had made the journey upstream to Corbarieu. She had not given it much attention as they passed it by.

She makes her way to the quay to wait for a boat that will take her homeward. There are no vessels to be seen. There is no one by the riverside except a young boy who is skimming stones across the water.

"Will there be a boat today?"

"Boat's just gone, miss. There won't be another today." He slings a flat stone across the water. "One, two, three, four. Four bounces; that's a record!"

Grazide turns away then calls back to the boy.

"Which is the road to Montalban, boy?"

"Over there, miss," he points to the north east. "You can't miss it." I'll have to walk, she thinks. She cannot wait until the next day's boat. She needs to get away.

It is a dry and dusty track that leads out of the village. The land here is flat; a few fields, occasional vineyards, very few people about. Soon the road leads into the woods; the trees are tall and there is deep shade. She knows the risks of travelling alone in such terrain. Bands of mercenaries, underemployed because of a temporary truce in the wars, are a danger to travellers. She has no fear though. She is almost indifferent to her fate.

She has been walking for an hour or so when she is aware of footsteps behind her. She looks back. There is a man following her. He must have emerged from the woods. She notices a thick leather jerkin; he is wearing a sword. She turns away and continues to walk but she cannot disguise the fear that is rising within her.

"Hey, lady. Not so fast. Where are you heading?" She continues to walk, more briskly now.

135

"Wait." Now he is running. She turns to face him, awaiting her fate. She is surprised when he stops about two paces from her. He is smiling. Now she notices his dark features, hair as black as hers hanging in ringlets to his shoulders. Across the right side of his face he has a livid scar that divides his rough beard. He is not tall, probably no taller than her but he is solidly built, his arms and legs are muscular, the skin taut over his bulky flesh.

"You should not be travelling this road on your own, lady. There are dangers in these parts." His voice is accented but not rough, there is almost a tenderness in his deep tone.

"I have no choice, sir. I have no companions to travel with."

He laughs. "Then let us put that right. Where are you headed? I can walk with you." He takes a step towards her and holds out his hand. "Giufré. Giufré da Costa. That's my name."

She does not move. Should she trust him? It only takes a moment's thought to realise that she has no choice. "I'm travelling home but it is a long way. I'm told that I can stop in Montalban tonight."

He smiles again. An amused smile, she cannot detect any trace of menace. Perhaps she can trust him. "Just where I'm going. May I walk with you? I think you would be a bit safer with me and my trusty companion," he pats the sword sheathed on his side.

She draws herself up to her full height, seeking to show she is no defenceless woman. "I will walk with you, Giufré da Costa, even though I do not know whether I can trust you."

This provokes more laughter from the man. "I wouldn't dare to compromise you, lady. You seem like a woman who would take no nonsense."

Quite right, thinks Grazide. She smiles back at him. "My name is Grazide Lamothe. I come from Vilanòva which is a few days' journey from here to the north east."

"Vilanòva. I know that name. Isn't that near Morlhon? Where the castle was destroyed by that bastard de Montfort?" He spits in the dust.

"Yes. My two brothers died in the fight. They are buried there."

"I'm sorry, Grazide. But de Montfort got his comeuppance at Toulouse. Killed by a catapult shot by a woman. I was there at that siege. You should have seen the celebrations. That woman has earned her place in history."

They walk on. Grazide is silent but her head overflows with thought. This man must be a mercenary, probably a Catalan judging by his accent and his name. Obvious that he is not a crusader though she knows that mercenaries can change their allegiances if they have sight of a better deal. Giufré respects her silence, he seems content to wait for her to speak.

The path opens out into a small glade in the woods. In the centre of the glade is a pool of water, sunlight glinting off the calm surface. The water is clear.

"Can we stop here? I need to rest and have a drink." She kneels down on the soft turf at the edge of the pool, cups her hands and drinks. Giufré follows suit and then lies back on the sward and closes his eyes. She stares at him lying there. Can she trust him?

"Giufré."

He does not open his eyes but grunts in reply.

"Where are you from? What are you doing in these woods?"

He still keeps his eyes closed. "Ah, you're wondering. Who is this devilish man that emerges from the forest and attaches himself to me?"

"I suppose so. Do I need to fear you?"

He raises himself on one elbow and looks her in the face. "Madam, you have no need to fear. I was in the woods having a sleep. I've been on the road for a long time. I come from over the mountains but that was ten years ago. I fought for King Peter of Aragon at Muret; what a shambles that was. Since then I've been all over the place, anywhere I can get money to fight. Plenty of lords willing to pay me to protect their precious castles."

"You're on your way to Montalban? Is there going to be more fighting there?"

"No. Probably not. It is a well-defended town. Good solid walls. In any case, what with this truce that has been agreed, opportunities for men like me are few and far between."

"So why Montalban?"

"Men have told me there could be employment there. The truce won't hold for long. Those Frenchmen are bound to return to sort out the young Count Raimond, just like they did with his father, God rest his excommunicated soul." He laughs and the sound echoes around the glade. "Now you know about me. What about you, my tall lady? How come you're so far from home and risking your life travelling through these woods with no companion?"

Reluctantly at first Grazide tells him of the journey with her dying father. She describes the ceremony that took place in Corbarieu. "The night after that he died. He is buried back there in Corbarieu."

"You brought him all this way to see the heretics, did you? Are you a believer?"

She bristles at this. "No. I am not. My father was taken in by their nonsense. He insisted that I take him to the goodmen. I had to do it for him."

Giufré whistles. "Phew. That's dangerous stuff, Grazide. I've seen people torched for less."

"He was my father. I had to do it for him."

"Like you I've little time for these Albigensians but I'll fight for them if the money's right." Grazide remembers that that was what the heresy was called. She knows enough about its followers and their beliefs to know that it is a challenge to the Church. Strange beliefs, quite different from those she had learnt from Bernard, the gentle itinerant that she met when she was growing up. She remembers he called himself a Poor Man of Lyon, people called them Waldensians. They were certainly not Albigensians.

They rest by the pool for around half an hour until Giufré looks up at the sun. "We'd best be moving on if we're going to reach the town by nightfall. Let's go." She follows him back to the path and they walk on. Conversation is desultory; she feels the late afternoon heat on her back. In her mind Vilanòva is receding. What is there to return for? With her father gone there seems little that might draw her to return home. Here is this itinerant soldier, happy to go wherever the money is good. Into her mind comes the impulsive gesture she made all those years ago, her request to go with Brother Bernard, to become a wanderer herself. She realises how unsure she is. That is uncharacteristic for her, normally a woman who knows her own mind.

The sun is low in the western sky as the path emerges from the woods and they see the town walls of Montalban ahead of them. "I was told the hostel is in Sapiac" says Grazide. "It's just this side of the town." As they get closer there are more people about. A man directs them to Hugues du Port's hostel, no more than a hundred paces from the river. The hostel seems full but the landlord says he can find them both a bed for the night. There is food for them. Grazide is glad of this, her hunger has returned after the day's journey. She shares a bed with a taciturn, one-eyed woman who snores loudly. Despite the trumpetings of her bedfellow she sleeps well. Giufré has been given a pallet on the floor in the men's room.

The following morning sees them making their way into the town. Giufré has a plan. "I've got a contact. A man called Bertrand de Castillon. A mate of mine told me that this de Castillon is the power in the town so I think I'll go and seek him out."

Grazide has not voiced her uncertainty about her plans. It is plain that Giufré is expecting her to travel on. "I spoke to the boatman," he says, "you can get a boat down river to the confluence with the Aveyron. From there you'll find other boatmen who will take you back up the river on your way back to Vilanòva. You should be safe on the boats, they're honest folk, these boatmen, they'll see you right."

Grazide is in a quandary yet is certain enough in her mind to know that she does not want to make the journey back to Vilanòva. There is nothing for her there now. She has no doubt that Pierre, the apprentice, will keep the forge running for what little work there is for blacksmithing. Philippe Noguès has proved to be a reliable share-cropping partner and his flock is burgeoning. She has no need to return for the time being.

"I'm not going back, Giufré. I don't know what I am going to do but I do know that I have no desire to return."

The Catalan stops and stares hard at her. In his eyes she can see that, by some instinct, he understands her. "Death changes things, does it not, my lady?" is all that he says.

She swallows hard, feeling her eyes fill with tears, fighting them off. She looks away, her right hand flutters by her side as if to take flight. She feels his hand on her shoulder, his grip firm but not commanding. She turns back to face him. "I never thought that it would be like this."

"No one does."

"I prayed for him to die. He was in such agony. The journey with him was awful but he made me promise that I would take him," she breaks off, her tears can be contained no longer. Why was she talking of this to this stranger, a man who must have seen so many deaths, violent deaths? And, of a sudden, that thought brings into her mind an image of Guillaume and Pierre, her brothers. The ache in her chest returns but now it is not anger, it is grief. Gut wrenching, chest tightening grief. Father, brothers and then, underpinning it all, the mother she cannot remember; just a memory of warmth, the warmth of once being loved.

"I can see that now is not the time to return," he says. "Come, let's both see what this town of Montalban might have for us." He leads the way through the southern gate into the town.

CHAPTER 15
1226

Grazide smiles to herself. She is seated by the window of a small room, staring into the street below. She remembers the impression the new town of Montalban made on her, that day three years previously when she and the mercenary walked through its well-fortified southern gate. Unused to any urban landscape as she was, the unity and formality of the streets, the buildings and the central square took her breath away. She could see at once that a new way of living was available here, different from the little village of Vilanòva with its ramshackle buildings, gathered around the monastery in a disorderly pattern like a gaggle of geese seeking protection from the fox. Here there was order that expressed an independence, a self-confidence that inspired the whole community. The houses were varied in design but all occupied identical sized plots. Most were built of wood, many with a second storey above the ground. Many had roofs of terracotta barrel tiles, some of the thatch that she was used to in Vilanòva. Some houses, mostly those that faced on to the central square, were brick and timber-built and expressed a munificence that reflected the general sense of order and autonomy. The streets, many of which were paved, formed a regular pattern meeting each other at right angles. Nowhere was there a dominating building; castle, monastery or church. A new church, built in pink brick, was near completion but was set away from the central square. Later she was to discover that there was a pre-existing abbey, dedicated to Saint-Théodard, that had been guarded by a castle and was surrounded by the small village of Montauriol. Count Raimond VII's great-grandfather, Alphonse-Jourdain, had created this new town to counteract the power of the Abbot of Saint-Théodard. The abbey had dominated the village and the important road that linked Toulouse in the south with Cahors in the north. Those that chose to move to the new town from the village of Montauriol or from the surrounding countryside were granted considerable freedoms, rights which still lasted to the present day. The Count's new town had displaced the domination of the Abbot.

She looks away from the window to a small cot in the corner of the room. Asleep there with his arms flung out above his head lies her small son, Pierre-Guillaume. His dark hair, as curly as his father's, contrasts with the pale skin of his face. She can hear the gentle sound of his breathing; it stills her mind.

It had been a shock to her when the unmistakable swelling of her belly and the nausea of the mornings told her that she was pregnant. Giufré had disappeared the previous month with neither a word nor any indication of where he was going. As far as she could tell he had no idea that he had fathered a child, perhaps not for the first time. She wondered whether she would see him again. Up until now there had been no word.

Their affair had been brief but torrid. On arrival in the town he had sought out the man, Bertrand de Castillon. Bertrand was undoubtedly an important inhabitant, a rich consul, who lived with his family in two houses adjacent to each other on the central square. Giufré had offered his services to the town and had been engaged to help overhaul the defences of the community. Despite the truce that pertained at that time the realists amongst the inhabitants, and Bertrand de Castillon was certainly one of them, expected that hostilities would be resumed sooner or later. The town needed to look to its defences.

That foresightedness was fortunate for now word has come of a fresh crusade from the north under the new King of France, Louis VIII. News has told of a siege of Avignon, away to the east. It would not be long before the invading horde, reportedly the largest ever mustered, would force its way into the westerly domains of the young Count Raimond VII of Toulouse.

The wife of Bertrand, Na Péronne, had taken Grazide in and had found her a place in the ostal of Magali de Gramazie. Magali was head of the ostal ever since the death of her husband in the previous year. With her lived two daughters, a son in his early teenage years, a cook and two servant girls. They were not a rich family but made a decent living from seamstress work. Magali had clearly been impressed

142

by this tall, capable stranger, declaring that she was just the sort of person she needed to help run the ostal and the business. Theirs was a simple house, wooden and fronting on to one of the streets that ran down from the square. Grazide slept in an upstairs room that she shared with the cook, Beatrice. Her duties did not include the seamstress work; that was down to the mother, her two daughters and the servants. Grazide ran the house, a task that she was well capable of. In addition she soon took over the running of the business, negotiating contracts, buying materials at the weekly market and keeping the books. It was little different from what she had been used to with her father's blacksmithing business, her experience in such matters soon became invaluable. It suited her well.

She had seen little of Giufré in the first few months of her time in Montalban. Occasionally they would meet, often in the marketplace on Thursdays. He might nod to her in passing, sometimes with a gruff word. She could see he was preoccupied with his work. She missed the man that she had met on the road, the day she had buried her father. Missed his humour, his understanding, his gentleness. Such disregard was not unusual. In her experience men had the capacity to switch on and off. Her father had been like that, as had her brothers. It seemed to her to be just another feature of masculine domination, a means of control. It was almost as if they saw women as dangerous; too much contact, too much involvement might undermine a man. In her growing years Grazide had learnt to play them at their own game. She too developed a detachment, a take it or leave it affectation. She was not going to show any trace of dependence. The sexual assault by Father Jean had reinforced her determination in that. If Giufré thought that she was curtailed by his indifference he was mistaken. She had the measure of him.

So it was surprising when, as time went on, she had allowed a relationship to develop between them. She came to welcome his affection, which he could display as if it were his true nature. She enjoyed his humour. It seemed a short step from that easy liaison to becoming, albeit briefly, lovers. But for Grazide there was none of the exhilaration that she had experienced in that night with the enigmatic woman, Sybille. With Giufré it had been impulsive, almost dangerous.

And then he was gone. Without a word, no indication as to why. Nothing changes, she had thought, nothing changes with men. She was not going to miss him so she mustered up her power to detach herself from any such feeling. It was her way. Then a few weeks later she discovered to her dismay that he had left a calling card. Seven months afterwards her little son was born. Fortunately Magali de Gramazie had supported her through the pregnancy and the birth. The older woman had the sense to see that Grazide was a more than valuable part of the ostal. A small child could be easily accommodated. The identity of the father was never discussed.

Hearing the little boy stir in his sleep she crosses the room to stroke his brow. She never knew that she could experience such an intense love for another human soul. Pierre-Guillaume has created a part of her that is quite new. To her he is her perfect creation, surpassing anything that she might have been able to mould out of metal.

Her little son opens his eyes and gazes at his mother. He raises both arms and she bends down to lift him from the cot. She carries him back to the chair by the window, sitting him on her knee. "There you are, my little boy. Have you had a good sleep?" The boy rubs his eyes and yawns, then nestles his head into her embrace. She rocks him gently as she hums a quiet tune.

In the three years that she has been in the town of Montalban she has come to see how different a community it is from her home village of Vilanòva. The rights and privileges granted in the town's foundation charter have fostered a sense of independence, a self-confidence of the community. The town is governed by twelve consuls, all appointed from different families that live in the town. Some of these families have lived in the town since its inception some seventy years previously; some are more recent incomers like the Castillons. They include rich merchants who bring a prosperity to the town which has been hardly curtailed even throughout the worst manifestations of the Northern French crusade. Simon de Montfort had never attempted to besiege Montalban, perhaps deterred by the stout walls, perhaps calculating that there were easier pickings to be had elsewhere. As a consequence the buildings and streets of the town are undamaged, suffering none of the destruction or despoliation of other castles and towns in the southern lands.

But a new crusade is worrying. In the three years that Grazide has lived in the town she has become aware that there are many supporters of heresy amongst the inhabitants. Not only supporters but a number of goodmen and a few women who have undertaken the consolamentum and have become ascetic goodwomen. She remembers how Morlhon became a target for the crusaders of Simon de Montfort once word got out that there were seven Waldensians sheltered in the Lord's castle. Here in Montalban there were many heretics, some of them Albigensian, these days labelled as Cathars, 'the pure ones'; Waldensians as well. The fabled walls of the town may not be the sure defence that the citizens might have imagined. Magali seems unconcerned. "It will pass us by, just as it has in the past, you have no need to worry, Grazide." Grazide is not convinced.

Carrying Pierre-Guillaume on her hip she makes her way down the wooden staircase and walks through to the main room. The two sisters, Arnaude and Bertrande, are sitting under the window that is open to the street outside. A gentle breeze relieves the heat of the afternoon. Sounds drift in, the calls of pedlars advertising their wares, the clip-clop of horses' hooves on the paved roadways, the chattering of sparrows tumbling in the dust. The girls are both sewing, singing to each other as they work.

"I have to go out," says Grazide. "Can you look after Pierre-Guillaume for me? He's just woken up."

Arnaude puts down her sewing and stands up. "Of course, Grazide." She holds out her arms. "Come here, my little pudding." Grazide hands him over to her. The little boy goes to Arnaude with no complaint, being rewarded with a kiss on his forehead.

145

"I won't be long. Just some bills to deliver." She leaves the house, a leather satchel slung over her shoulder. She welcomes the opportunity to get out. However much she loves her small son it is good to have a break from the constant maternal care that is such a part of her life nowadays. She walks with her head held high, still relishing the comforting formality of the streets, the uniform houses. There is a sense of freedom that seems almost to be carved into the paving under her feet.

If there had been gossip about her when her pregnancy had become obvious for all to see, and she was sure there was, she was determined to rise above it. She was not going to let any disapprobation oppress her. The shock when she had first realised that she was to have a baby was considerable. Giufré's disappearance had been disturbing enough, even though she had half expected it but pregnancy was different; a bitter-sweet gift from such a short encounter, part welcomed but part perceived as an invasion of her independence. It was nothing that she had sought out.

It had helped that Magali was so supportive. Grazide needed to have no concern about her outside reputation, being so accepted by those around her. Neither Magali nor any of her ostal were supporters of heretics and Grazide certainly had no contact with any goodmen at that time. That was fortunate. Later she would come to learn that they regarded pregnant women as carrying demons in their bellies. That was an affront that outraged her, it reinforced her determination to have nothing to do with them from that point.

Unlike in Vilanòva the influence of the Church on the community here was slight. Grazide did not regularly attend Mass but she did find a priest who was willing to baptise Pierre-Guillaume soon after he was born. She felt more comfortable having had that done.

She crosses the market square. Out of the shade of the houses the full heat of the sun beats down upon her uncovered head. She heads for the Castillon house that lies on the other side of the square. Na Péronne de Castillon greets her warmly. "Grazide, my dear. How good to see you. How is that adorable little Pierre-Guillaume?"

"He is well, thank you. Getting to be quite a handful these days."

"Oh, boys. They always are. My three were always giving me the run-around." Not really what I meant, thinks Grazide. No doubt the Castillon girls were all dutiful.

"I have your account from Na Gramazie. I hope the work was satisfactory."

Na Péronne throws up her hands in pleasure. "It was wonderful. Such beautiful work. I am very pleased with it. Please tell Na Gramazie so." She reaches out to take the proffered paper. "My husband's clerk will settle this as soon as he returns."

"Thank you, madam. Good day to you." She turns to leave but Na Péronne calls her back.

"Before you go. Has there been any word of that man, Giufré?"

Grazide had never acknowledged that the absent Catalan was the boy's father but from the way that Na Péronne is asking she is sure that the older woman has a shrewd idea that he is. "No. Nothing that I have heard."

"That must be difficult for you."

Grazide stares at her, her face set firm. "He is of no concern to me. He is a mercenary. They come and go as they please."

"Indeed that's true. My husband said he was a good man. Knew his stuff. I gather he smartened up our town defences. We could do with having him back."

Grazide's face flushes. The idea that Giufré might return has her conflicted. She would prefer not to think about it. "No doubt." She pauses, wondering whether to say more. "I must be going, madam. More of these to deliver." She indicates her satchel.

"Of course. Goodbye, Grazide. Give that little man a big kiss from me." Grazide smiles, turns and leaves.

By the time she returns to the house Magali has returned. Arnaude is feeding Pierre-Guillaume some broth. The cook, Beatrice, is preparing the evening meal. Grazide feels better now she is back in the ostal. The thought, engendered by Na Péronne's questions, that Giufré might return has unsettled her. Back in this ostal she feels secure. The return of Giufré could pose a threat for her and her place in this ménage in which she has found herself.

She is woken by an unusual sound. It is dark, the darkness of the dead of night, no starlight, no shafts of moonshine. She hears the sound again. It is a quiet moan coming from the cot where Pierre-Guillaume sleeps. Grazide slips out of the bed, careful not to disturb Beatrice. The cook sleeps deeply, she does not stir. Grazide feels her way across the room to where her son lies. She can make out the outline of his wooden cot. The little boy moans again. She reaches in to stroke his brow and is shocked to feel an unaccustomed heat. He has a fever. She feels his chest through the cotton shift and is alarmed at the intensity of his warmth. The little boy is ill.

Quietly she goes downstairs and returns with a bowl of water, a sponge and a towel. She soaks the sponge in the cool water then squeezes it out, shaking the drips from it. She leans over and mops his brow. He moves his head from side to side, reacting to the cold of the sponge and begins to cry. The sound has woken Beatrice for she whispers, "What is it, Grazide? Is he all right?"

"He has a fever. I'm sorry to wake you."

"Oh, the poor little lamb. Let me see." The cook rises from the bed and comes across to the mother and her son. She touches his forehead. "He's burning up, poor little thing. I'll fetch some broth." She disappears downstairs.

The commotion she makes has woken others in the ostal. Arnaude appears in the doorway. She has a lighted candle in her hand. She rubs her eyes.

"No need to worry, Arnaude. He has a fever, that's all." The young girl remains standing in the doorway.

Beatrice returns carrying a bowl of broth and a spoon. "Come on, now. Let's give him some of this. It will help."

Grazide lifts her son from the cot and holds him close to her, sitting him on her lap. Between the two of them they spoon a little of the broth into the small child but he is reluctant to take it.

"Come on," says Beatrice, "let's take his things off to cool him down." They pull his shift off over his head. Despite the heat radiating from his body he shivers. Grazide holds him close to her, conscious that he is breathing fast.

They stay there for some time. Arnaude returns to her room. Beatrice sits on the edge of their bed. A faint glimmer of dawn falls across the room, a cock crows. Somewhere across the town a dog is barking. Eventually the little boy falls asleep. He seems cooler now. Grazide carefully lies him back in the cot.

"I'll sit by him. Go back to bed, Beatrice. You need your sleep."

Over the next day the fever comes and goes. Pierre-Guillaume sleeps in snatches but is obviously distressed when awake. He holds his head from time to time. At other times he is delirious. Grazide sponges him down when the fever is high, wraps him tight when he shivers and shakes. They try to feed him but he will not take what is proffered.

Later in the day Beatrice reappears carrying herbs, marjoram, fennel and twigs of rosemary. She has been to their small garden plot on the edge of town. She pounds the herbs into a paste with a pestle and mortar, then makes them into a draught with water, fresh from the well. They manage to get him to swallow a few spoonfuls of the mixture.

"It will help to bring the fever down. My mother used to swear by it," says the cook. Grazide is doubtful but she does not voice her misgivings.

After two days the fever shows no signs of abating. The little boy is now coughing and his nose bleeds from time to time. He still holds his head, moaning inarticulately. The whole ostal is disturbed by his illness.

149

"Do you think we should get help?" says Magali on the third morning. "He does not seem to be getting any better."

"Perhaps we should," replies his mother. "Do you know anyone?"

"I'll ask around. I am sure there will be someone who can see the little boy."

She returns an hour or so later. "I spoke to my friend, Raimonde d'Avignon. They called a doctor to treat their son. Last year it was. He was one of those Poor Men of Lyon, Pierre de Vals. She said he brought about the boy's recovery."

"Is he still here, this Pierre de Vals?"

"Raimonde seems to think so. I'll make some more enquiries. Na Péronne is sure to know."

A Poor Man of Lyon. Immediately Grazide's mind is taken back to that gentle man, Bernard, that she met so many years ago in Vilanòva. Burnt with his companions when the castle of Morlhon was destroyed. The memory brings a chill with it.

"Please find out, Magali." The sense of impending harm has welled up within her.

Magali wastes no time in seeking out Na Péronne; both women return together. "Oh, Grazide. Magali has told me about your poor little boy. You must be so worried. I know that Pierre de Vals is lodging in the town. I have sent out my girls to find him."

The search is successful. That evening Na Péronne returns. With her is a man dressed in a simple brown tunic; he is barefoot. Dressed like Bernard, observes Grazide, but a different appearance. He is short, his bushy, dark eyebrows almost meet in the centre of his forehead. He has soft brown eyes and a sharp nose. What reminds her, though, of the Bernard that she knew is his air of tenderness. It is as if, when he enters the house, the disquiet, the agitation is subdued. His presence is calming. He smiles at Grazide. "It's your son who is ill, is it, madam?"

"Yes. He has had a fever for three days now. We cannot seem to get it down."

"I see. Has he any other symptoms?"

"He seems to be troubled with headaches. He is always holding his head and crying."

"Anything else? Does he vomit, any diarrhoea?"

"No. He has had nose bleeds in the last day."

Pierre de Vals frowns for a moment. "Well, take me to him if you would." Grazide leads the way upstairs, Pierre and Magali follow. He pauses when he reaches the entrance to the room, seeming to take in not just the sick little boy but the whole scene of the room of illness. Then he moves across to the cot. Pierre-Guillaume is asleep but his breathing is perturbed. From time to time he tosses his head from side to side. The doctor gently pulls aside the linen sheet that covers his body. Again he pauses, appearing to be doing nothing except observing. Grazide becomes impatient. "He is burning hot, sir. We have given him herbs in a draught but he is reluctant to drink."

Pierre raises his hand. "Peace, lady. Your son will be all right." He stoops down and observes the boy more closely. "Has he had this rash for long?"

Grazide is embarrassed. In her concern she has not noticed a rash. Pierre indicates a few rose-coloured patches on the little boy's chest.

"I'm sorry, sir. I hadn't noticed. I don't think they were there this morning. What is it?" He does not reply but is placing his hand on the boy's chest, then he gently feels his little belly; the boy groans.

Pierre de Vals stands up. He pulls the sheet back over the boy's body. Then he places his hand on the child's head and stays still for some minutes. Everyone is still. Finally he turns to Grazide. "Can we go downstairs?" He leads the way.

Downstairs he turns to Grazide. "I cannot be sure at this moment but I think this is enteric fever. It is serious."

A terror grips her heart. "Will he die? Is it that serious?"

"I cannot tell. It is a possibility. There are things that I can do. They may work but you must be prepared for the worst. I will pray earnestly for his recovery."

151

"But treatment. Can you give him treatment?" For a moment she feels the agitation overtake her.

He smiles at her. It is not a meaningless smile, no false reassurance. She is surprised to find that she is calming down. "Yes, as I said, there are things that I can do. Let us all pray that our Heavenly Father will bless us with his recovery."

There is no false piety that she can discern. His gentle demeanour radiates sincerity. She lowers her eyes. "Thank you, Brother Pierre. Thank you."

Over the following two weeks the Waldensian doctor wages war on Pierre-Guillaume's illness, specific herbal infusions, poultices, but always his calming presence. There are times when Grazide is sure that they are going to lose the little boy but each time he rallies. He is desperately weak, his body starved to a living skeleton but he clings on to life. Pierre de Vals is in the house every day, sometimes overnight when the illness is critical.

It is a morning, some three weeks after the illness has appeared that little Pierre-Guillaume opens his eyes, looks at Grazide and smiles, "Mama". She lifts him up. The fever is gone; despite his starved appearance she can feel his heart beating more strongly. She cannot hold back the tears of relief. He is going to live, of that she is certain.

Later that morning the doctor reappears. Seeing the change he too smiles. Only then does Grazide understand how much the boy's illness has cost him. He stands straighter now as if a heavy burden has been lifted from his shoulders.

"Thank you, Brother Pierre. From the depths of my heart, thank you."

"Let us give thanks to God for this. He is a merciful Father." Grazide closes her eyes, in her mind is an unformed prayer of thanks.

"God bless you both." He touches both their heads and leaves the room to the mother and her child.

In the weeks that follow Pierre-Guillaume recovers quickly. Perhaps it is the skill of Beatrice who prepares special foods for him, tempting his returning appetite with delicacies that soon restore the flesh to his bones. Though he tires easily his eyes are bright again, his childish wilfulness reasserts itself. With all that has happened Grazide recognises how deep is the love that she holds for this little person. Never mind that his father is absent, the seed that he implanted has grown into this little human being who carries the totality of her affection. Certainly she loved her brothers, the pain of their loss is still a sharp wound within her. Further she now recognises the love that she bore her father despite his oppression and cruelty to her on occasions. She regards the latter as inevitable in a patriarchal ostal, the contrast with her present state in the ostal of Magali and her family reinforces that perception. She is pleased that her own son can grow up in such an environment.

Now that he is fully recovered she likes to take walks with him down to the riverside whenever she can. This day the sun is bright in a clear blue sky though its warmth is declining in these early days of autumn. The river Tarn flows green in front of them as they sit on the bank. The intense heat of summer has turned the grass brown and brittle but already there are patches of green growth reappearing, watered by the damp morning dews of early October. They watch the boatmen manoeuvring their thin, long craft, sometimes loaded with barrels or large packages of cloth. These days the trade has built up again, profiting from the lull in hostilities that the temporary truce has afforded. Cargoes are shipped down river as far as Bordeaux and thence by ocean-going craft to foreign lands.

She spots a small white bird on the opposite shore. It stands on spindly legs watching the water. "Look, Pierre. Can you see the egret?" She points and the little boy shields his eyes from the angled sun's rays as he scans the further river edge.

"Yes. Yes. I can see it. Birdie!" The delight in his voice sings in her heart as her love for this little man overflows. Now she can recognise that memory, the recollection that she has had for as long as she can remember, the feeling of being loved. It surely must come from the mother she never knew, a presence lost to her conscious mind but still existing in her heart.

"Eaglet. I see the eaglet." He jumps up and down excitedly.

She laughs. "Egret, Pierre. It's egret."

"Egret," he pronounces it carefully, his face becoming solemn for a moment. He runs down the bank to pick up stones from the river edge, delighting in hurling them into the water and shouting, "Splash!"

"Be careful, Pierre. Don't go too close to the water." She keeps a watchful eye on him. Staring at the current she thinks back to that long journey that she undertook three years past with her dying father. What was the point of it? He must have suffered yet he was determined that she should take him to the goodmen at Corbarieu. Did that bizarre ceremony really make any difference? He died so soon afterwards, was it all worthwhile? Did it guarantee his soul a place in the heavenly realm?

Like all her contemporaries Grazide knew that salvation of her soul mattered. These goodmen with their deathbed consolamenta seemed to make it too easy. Even so the indulgences that were available at a price or the remissions off purgatory earned by the hated crusaders were just as corrupt, at least that is how she saw it. In her eyes living an upright, honest life must surely provide the best assurance of a life of eternal happiness, the prize promised to the righteous.

She knows that there are goodmen, and goodwomen too, in Montalban these days. She hears talk of them as she goes about her business on behalf of Magali. There are some families that are all believers, others where only some follow the strange calling that has been deemed heresy. There are quite a number of Waldensians too, the doctor Pierre de Vals is one. Despite this polyglot of beliefs most people are on the face of it orthodox. They attend Mass, albeit infrequently, in the impressive pink brick church of Saint-Jacques that was in the process of being completed, a testament to the relative prosperity of the town despite the troubled times; outwardly Montalban society appears untainted by heresy.

Since her son's illness she herself has returned to attending Mass. There was a strong need in her to give thanks for his recovery.

Beatrice encouraged her and went with her and the boy one Sunday morning. As far as Grazide can discern the Gramazie ostal shelters no heretical beliefs.

Yet despite this she retains an affection for the Waldensians. How could she not after all that Pierre de Vals did for her little boy? His gentle authority reminded her so much of Brother Bertrand. She remembers with some embarrassment her impulsive urge to join him on his travels all those years ago in Vilanòva. He was a gentle man, too. What he and his fellow Poor Men preached did not appear to her to be unreasonable, particularly in the light of the venality of her own parish priest. She shudders at the memory of that loathsome man and what he did to her. She had thought that time would assuage the hurt of that violation but it has not; it is still a wound in her soul.

Some months have passed since little Pierre-Guillaume's recovery from the fever. Now he shows no residual signs of the illness that threatened his life. Grazide delights in seeing him grow. He is beginning to develop a character of his own, often mischievous. The two servant girls in the ostal are inclined to encourage his wilful temperament. "Boys will be boys", they say to Grazide. She, for her part, is inclined not to accept that. Would they say "Girls will be girls" to excuse a similar egotism?

"It is not how I want to bring him up," she retorts sharply. "Boy or girl he needs to learn respect for others." She suspects that the relative tolerance accorded to grown men stems from just such a tolerance early in their lives. In her determination she finds an ally in Magali whose own son, Matheu, now in his early teens, lacks any degree of masculine swagger. There appears to be no distinction between him and his sisters. Grazide is glad that her own son is growing up in such an atmosphere.

Equally she herself feels very much at home in the ostal. She enjoys being the enabler that keeps life running smoothly, both in the domestic as well as the business sphere. It is an easy atmosphere that she is glad to be part of. Her duties take her out of the house, delivering completed goods, distributing invoices and collecting payments for work done. In this she has an easy access into many of the ostals of the town; she has become well known and never detects any hint of censure that she is mother to a natural child.

It is a warm day in early spring. Grazide is out on her own delivering a package of completed work to Na Péronne, wife of Bertrand de Castillon. She is one of the foremost customers of Magali de Gramazie, appreciative of the fine work that comes from her workshop. Over the last few years Na Péronne has become a good friend to Grazide.

She enters the market square at its south-west corner. Immediately she notices a small crowd on the opposite side of the square. There are sounds of laughter, occasional cheers and the banging of metal pot lids. The crowd is moving around the perimeter of the square, outside the covered market. They turn at the corner and are now coming towards her. She is shocked to see that at their head are two figures, totally naked. They are being led by one of the town constables who carries a long pike. As they get nearer she can see that one figure, a man, has a fine rope tied to his genitals. The second figure, a woman, is holding the end of this rope and is being made to walk ahead of the man. Some of the crowd are jeering, others chant bawdy rhymes.

She shrinks back against a doorway as the procession approaches. As they pass she catches the man's gaze, a pitiful look, a look of shame. Grazide cannot look away, she wants to speak, to say something but no words come. In a moment they have passed on and soon disappear down one of the streets that exit the square. For a while she cannot move. She has never seen such a spectacle in her life. What on earth was it all about? What has deserved such humiliation?

She hurries across the square to the Castillon house. Entering she is met by Na Péronne herself. "Did you see the procession?"

"I did. What was it all about? I've never seen anything like it."

Na Péronne takes her arm. "It is rough justice, Grazide. That couple were discovered in adultery. She is the young wife of Guillaume

156

Amiel, a fellow consul of my husband. The man is her lover, one Hugues Mazaler. He comes from Castelsarrasin. They were brought before the bailie and convicted. That procession was their punishment."

"But that is awful. It is so humiliating."

Na Péronne smiles, a rueful smile. "Yes, it probably is. But once it's done, it's done. The penance is laid down in the statutes of the town. In many other places they would have been strung up by the local lord. You could say that they have got off lightly, living in Montalban."

Grazide has no reply to that. The degradation that she has just witnessed disturbs her. If her intimate liaison with Giufré, father to her little boy, had been known about how would they have both been dealt with? It was not adulterous but who knows what attitude the judicial authorities would take towards it.

Na Péronne is looking at the package that Grazide is bearing. She smiles. "Enough of that. Is that my order you are carrying?"

"Yes. I'm sorry. Yes, it is. Here you are."

Na Péronne takes the package. "Do stop and have some refreshment, my dear. You look quite shaken." She calls for a servant who brings a small jug of wine and two elegant beakers. "Here, sit down and drink this," she pauses for a moment. "I'm glad to see you, Grazide, for there is a matter that I want to discuss with you."

Grazide tries to clear her mind of the scene that she has just stumbled across. She gives her attention to the older woman.

"You come from Vilanòva, do you not?"

"Yes, Na. It was my home village."

"And was your father Arnaud Lamothe, the blacksmith?"

"Yes, that's right. How do you know this?"

Na Péronne claps her hands in a gesture of delight. "I knew it. It is you."

"What do you mean, Na?" Grazide is mystified.

"We had a travelling merchant staying here last week. An old colleague of my husband's. He had passed through Concas, north east of Vilanòva, a few weeks previously. In the church of Sainte-Foy he had seen some beautiful metalwork, an elaborate candlestick holder. It occupied pride of place in the church. He was most impressed by it. He was told that it was the work of a woman, a woman blacksmith. They said she came from Vilanòva." Grazide blushes. She can see where this is leading. "Anyway," continues Na Péronne, "he passed through Vilanòva some days later and made enquiries about this woman. The blacksmith's forge was very run down, nobody seemed to be working there anymore. The people told him that the blacksmith himself had died three years previously but that his daughter had been working in the forge well before that and that she was the artisan who had created the candlestick in the church at Concas." Na Péronne folds her arms and looks straight at Grazide. "It was you, wasn't it?"

Grazide says nothing, her mind disjointed by this disclosure of her previous life. She had never spoken of it to anyone since the day that she arrived in Montalban.

"I am right, am I not?" continues Na Péronne. "I often wondered how you came by those strong arms."

Grazide cannot meet her gaze. She cannot understand why she should feel ashamed at being unmasked. Finally she speaks. "Yes. You are right. It was me. I used to work in my father's forge."

"There you are then," Na Péronne laughs. "I think that is wonderful. How did you come to be blacksmithing? Unusual for a woman, is it not?"

"Both my brothers died. They were killed at Morlhon. My father needed the help, there was no one else available so he taught me the trade."

"But that's magnificent. A woman blacksmith no less. You are a dark horse, Grazide Lamothe."

Grazide is regaining her composure. "But why are you so interested in this, Na Péronne. It's all in the past now."

The other woman's voice becomes quieter, more conspiratorial. "Well, there is a reason. You see my husband Bertrand would dearly love to have some smart decorative gates made for the new church. He has contributed a considerable amount to the building of the church and would like to see the whole project crowned with a commission from him. He approached the town blacksmith but he really is just a jobbing artisan, competent enough to make door hinges and the like but he himself would admit that making decorative gates is beyond his capability. When I heard about you I suggested to Bertrand that we should tackle you about it. Would you be able to do it, could you make a pair of gates for us?"

Grazide's mind is in further turmoil. Over the past three years she had resigned herself to the thought that her blacksmithing days were over. Secretly, however, she misses the work. She is proud of some of the artefacts that she had created. Now here was a glimmer of possibility. "This is a bit of a shock, Na. I will need to think about it."

"Certainly, my dear. Do think about it but perhaps you should not take too long. I fear my husband is an impatient man." She laughs again.

"But what about the town blacksmith? How will he take to a woman using his forge?"

"Oh, don't worry about that. Bertrand will see him right."

Grazide realises that Bertrand de Castillon has his ways of being an influential power in the community, mostly using his considerable wealth.

"Promise me you will think about it, Grazide. Bertrand is set on having his gates. This would be a wonderful solution."

Grazide's mind is racing as she walks back across town to the Gramazie house. This could be such an unexpected turn in her life. The prospect of returning to the work that she once loved excites her. Yet part of her wonders whether she could regain the skills that once were hers. Perhaps. The seduction of moulding and forming metal in the heat of the fire grows within her with every step that she takes. By the time she reaches home her mind is made up.

"Of course you must do it." Grazide has broken the news of her possible new commission to Magali de Gramazie. "I think it is a wonderful idea. You, a blacksmith. I would never have guessed it. Mind you," she pauses, takes a step back as if to appraise Grazide in a new light, "you have a fine strong build, and those arms," she pinches Grazide's biceps with a squeeze that seems friendly, "I should have known that that strength came from somewhere." She laughs and that is enough to bring a smile to Grazide's face.

"I will not neglect my duties here, Magali. You have been so kind to me."

"Tish. You have got everything running so smoothly, there will be plenty of time for you to return to the forge. The girls can take on some of the errands and deliveries, there is no need for you to do it all."

"Dear Magali. You are so good to me. Thank you." She takes a step towards her friend and kisses her on the cheek. "I promise I will not let you down."

"Of course you will not. It will be great fun to have a famous woman blacksmith in the ostal. I shall boast of it unmercifully."

Grazide frowns for a moment. "Hold on. I haven't been commissioned yet. Na Péronne has to speak to her husband first. He may reject the idea."

"Of course, of course. But I know he will agree," another peal of laughter bubbles from her throat. "Grazide, the blacksmith, what a marvellous thought."

It is with some trepidation that Grazide returns to the Castillon house the following day. She is to meet Bertrand de Castillon himself. She knows him to be a powerful man, able to make or break any enterprise. By now she has her heart set on the putative commission. She would be devastated if she were to be rejected.

Na Péronne greets her and escorts her up a wooden staircase to an upstairs room that is Bertrand's office. He is seated at a solid oak desk, reading some papers. Na Péronne pushes Grazide in front of her and calls "this is Grazide Lamothe that I told you of, husband."

Grazide remains stock still. He looks up from his papers, seeming to take time to scrutinise the tall, well-built woman in front of him. Grazide does not drop her gaze but looks him directly in the eyes. No one moves.

"Well now, you're the blacksmith, are you?"

"I was, sir. I haven't worked as such for some years now."

Bertrand grunts and frowns, then appears to remember his civility. "Sit down, won't you madam." He indicates a chair in front of the desk. "No need for you to stay, wife. Perhaps have some wine sent up." Na Péronne is no longer smiling as she turns and retreats downstairs.

He returns to shuffling the papers on the desk in front of him. Nothing is said. Grazide recognises a familiar scenario. It is not that the man in front of her is important, nor that he is rich, nor even that he is pre-eminent in society, he is deploying a power which she knows to be masculine, gender derived. It could unnerve her if she were to let it do so but recognising how he is asserting dominance is a big step towards dismantling its effect on her. She sits quite still, waiting.

He stops fiddling with his papers and looks at her. "My colleague, Rainier, saw some of your work in the church of Sainte-Foy at Concas, a candlestick was it?" Grazide nods in assent. "He was very impressed, particularly as it was done by a woman."

"Is that a surprise to you, sir?" Grazide is fighting hard to keep a level tone.

"No. Well, yes and no. I have to say I have never before encountered a woman who can do a blacksmith's work. Your father taught you, so I am told."

"Yes. I started when I was fourteen, when my brothers were killed."

"Oh yes. I remember. My wife told me of that. I am sorry to hear it." Grazide senses the atmosphere has become less chilly, she relaxes a little. "Well, candlesticks are one thing but gates are something else. Have you ever made a pair of gates, madam blacksmith?"

"No sir, I haven't but the techniques are the same. It's just there is much more to do."

Bertrand laughs. "I expect there is." Grazide senses that she has been approved.

Between them they negotiate the nature of the commission, possible designs, the timescale of the work and Grazide's fee. Bertrand promises to square things with the town blacksmith in the next few days. Grazide undertakes to prepare drawings for his approval.

The following week she returns carrying a bundle of drawings. In preparing the design she remembers the elaborate metal grill that encloses the chancel in the pilgrim church of Sainte-Foy in Concas. She had had plenty of opportunity to study the design when she was commissioned to create a decorative candlestick for that same church. Its Moorish influenced design would be a good model for these gates that Bertrand de Castillon is commissioning.

It is apparent to her that she has earned the respect of this man, the ambience is easier than at their previous meeting. As well as the drawings she carries another sheet which she places before him. "This is a draft contract between us. Perhaps you would like to read it and make any suggestions."

He gives her a look which seems to suggest that no woman has ever presented him with such a document before. She smiles in response. It takes him a few minutes to read the contract. Finally he looks up. "I have to say that is quite astonishing, not only a blacksmith but a literate businesswoman. You have quite surprised me, Grazide Lamothe."

She ignores the compliment. "Does the contract meet with your approval, sir?"

"Of course, of course. It's fine. I will get it copied up and we can sign it tomorrow."

"Thank you, sir. Then perhaps you could arrange for me to meet the town blacksmith. After that we will meet to approve the design and I will start work."

Bertrand laughs. "I think your father must have taught you more than blacksmithing, young lady. I've never met anyone like you before."

"Surely you have. You must meet many men of business. Some of them must know what they are doing."

"Yes, but they are men," something in her expression appears to stop him from continuing. "Well, there we are. Until next week then." He holds out his hand. Grazide takes it and they shake.

CHAPTER 16

It feels good to be back in a forge again. She had forgotten how much she enjoys the roar of the fire as she pumps the bellows to bring the raw metal to bright yellow heat. Pascaut, the town blacksmith, barely welcomed her to his smithy. His sullen demeanour combined with a perpetually furrowed brow and dark eyebrows makes for a forbidding character. Grazide supposes that Bertrand de Castillon has made it very worthwhile for him to allow a woman to use his workshop. With a conversation that seems limited to short utterances and grunts he shows her where all the equipment is kept. He has two apprentices working with him, the agreement has been that one of them, Stefe, a youth of around eighteen, should be assigned to assist Grazide. Pascaut himself has been commissioned to construct the basic frame and hinges of the gates' design, in accordance with Grazide's plan. The two skeletal frames are leaned up against a side wall of the smithy. Lengths of black metal strips have been ordered from the smelters by Bertrand and they lie waiting for Grazide to start work.

The design is intricate. Grazide brings to mind the ornate metal grill that surrounded the chancel in the church in Concas. Curls, crescents and circles, elsewhere fans of metal springing from a conjoined source, to be welded together in the heat of the fire. Grazide works methodically and steadily. Rarely does she spend more than three hours in a day working in the forge. It is a slow process but she likes to take time, working with the metal rather than against it, moulding it into the sinuous shapes of her drawings. Sometimes she modifies the design a little, her eye telling her that such a change would enhance the overall impact. Stefe is a capable assistant who appears glad to be learning techniques that are new to him, beyond the reach of his master, Pascaut.

The whole project takes around three months to complete. Some days Grazide is overcome with a fear that she might never be able to realise the final object. She has never created such work before, the scale of the undertaking unnerves her at times. Were it not for the support of Na Péronne, who takes a close interest in the progress of the commission, her nerve might have failed her. Bertrand de Castillon never visits the forge to view the progress but his wife is often there, encouraging and admiring. It helps Grazide through those times when her artistic endeavour threatens to dry up. "Don't despair, dear Grazide. It is coming on well. I am sure that it will be fine in the end."

Magali makes the occasional surreptitious visit to view Grazide's work. Bertrand had stipulated that the work should be kept secret so Grazide has to swear her friend to silence. On one occasion Magali brings Pierre-Guillaume to watch his mother work. He is entranced by the roaring of the fire as Stefe pumps the bellows but screams and puts his hands over his ears when Grazide starts wielding the hammer on the hot metal. The ringing clamour is more than he can take. Grazide is reminded of those times when her father took her to the forge with him when she was still very little. She can remember the excitement of helping pump the bellows, the hiss of the hot metal when doused in the barrel of cold water, the steam filling the air.

Reflecting on those memories she sees that this must have formed her ambition. Not once did he tell her that this was man's work. Despite his other overbearing ways she now thanks him for this. With a tug of sorrow she registers that she never thanked him in life. Now here she is, confident most of the time, competent and assured in her autonomy as both a skilled artisan and a woman.

Finally the work is completed. Grazide supervises the hanging of the gates and Bertrand de Castillon has laid on a celebration to show off the new acquisition. He had visited the forge for the first time on the previous day and had declared himself very satisfied with the work. Now he has gathered his five fellow-consuls and their families to view the new creation. Word has inevitably got around the town by now that the de Castillon family have donated a new adornment to the church of Saint-Jacques. People from all over the town, merchants, artisans, peasant farmers and labourers throng the square in front of the church. The gates themselves are hidden under a large grey sheet. Bertrand has made sure that there is plenty of wine available for all.

Throwing a good party has never done his reputation any harm in the past, he is not going to change his ways now.

Bertrand calls for quiet. "Fellow citizens of our beloved Montalban, it is my great pleasure to have added to the beauty of our new church by commissioning these magnificent gates that you see before you. It is my modest contribution to our lives and will, I most earnestly hope, continue to delight all for generations to come." With a theatrical flourish he pulls aside the sheet to reveal the new gates, dark burnished metal glinting in the midday sun. There are exclamations from the crowd. The secret of who made these magnificent gates has not been broached. Most people presume that they are the work of Pascaut, the town blacksmith, though many are surprised at how his skills appear to have miraculously blossomed.

Milking it for all he can, thinks Grazide, who is standing to the side in deep shadow. She smiles to herself and shares a glance with Na Péronne who pulls a face, as if to say, *here he goes again.*

"And now," continues Bertrand, "I would like to present to you the creator of this wonderful piece of artistry. Please step forward, Grazide Lamothe." He signals to Grazide to come out of the shadows.

A collective gasp rises from the assembled people. A sole male voice calls out, "It's a woman!" Grazide stands quite still, unsmiling.

There is a pause for what seems to her to be many seconds and then applause breaks out. To start with it comes from the women present, led by Na Péronne, but soon most of the people, women and men, are applauding enthusiastically. Now Grazide smiles. She raises her hand in a small gesture of thanks. The applause begins to die down and Bertrand is speaking again. "That is a surprise for you, is it not? A woman blacksmith." He laughs. "Women. They'll be wanting my job next, bless them."

The crowd guffaws. Grazide tries hard to fix the smile on her face at this patronising joke. She turns away.

"Speech, speech!" call people from the crowd. She hesitates and glances at Bertrand. Would he tolerate her speaking? He recognises her unspoken query. With a smile that is part mocking he indicates that she should speak. She turns to face the crowd again.

"Thank you for your appreciation of my work. Perhaps you are surprised that I, a woman, stand before you as creator of these gates. So I say to you now, why not? Who is it that has ordained that women should not, as much as men, undertake whatever they desire? So often do I hear 'this is man's work'. No, it is not. It is work and can be done by anyone with the necessary skill, man or woman."

There is a scatter of applause but most of her listeners remain silent. Grazide cannot speak any more. Bertrand comes forward. "Well said, Grazide Lamothe. So now everyone, drink and enjoy the sight of the new gates." The tension of the awkward moment is dispelled.

Magali comes forward from the assembled crowd and takes Grazide by the arm. "Come on, Grazide. Time we left." She steers Grazide down a side street and they are soon back at the ostal.

Grazide collapses into a chair. "I've had it, Magali. That's about all that I can take."

"I understand. It was a brave speech that you made just then. I think it will make many people think, women especially. It is not strange to my ears. It is different for us in this ostal. Since my husband died it has been quite natural to be without a man as head of our ostal. It works perfectly well for us."

"All I ask is that my skills are appreciated for what they are, not because I am a woman but because I am an artist. It should never matter whether I am a woman or a man."

"Exactly, but the world does not see it that way."

Grazide can say no more. She is tired, deeply, profoundly tired. She cannot sustain her outrage any longer.

If she had entertained the hope that making the gates for the new church would lead to other commissions she is to be soon disillusioned. No further approaches are made to her. It hurts her that the appreciation of her creation is short-lived, just the immediate excitement of a novelty but then nothing. It is disheartening.

Nonetheless she is happy to have more time to spend with her small son. He has grown fast in the three months that his mother had been so occupied at the forge. The differences in him might not be so noticeable to those in whose constant care he was entrusted. They are well-marked by her. He is now full of energy and inquisitiveness. It is good for her to experience this, to find ways to channel his exuberance into his developing character. At times she thinks to herself that this is also creative work, as much as creating beautiful metalwork. She thinks back to her own childhood family. Guillaume and Pierre were unlettered, they learnt some skill in the blacksmith's shop but in the end all that was required of them was to fight, ending in pointless tragedy. At least she, through her father's insistence, received something of an education. That it ended so abruptly and in such a humiliating way only fuels her determination that there are better ways for people to live together. It should be perfectly natural for her to express herself in whatever way she chooses. She wants the same for her son, Pierre-Guillaume.

It is obvious that Magali is glad to have her back in the ostal as in the days before she took on Bertrand de Castillon's commission. Despite the news of a return of hostilities, Grazide is aware that heretical ideas still flourish within the town. Some families and ostals are unaffected, her own and that of the de Castillon family included. In others there are all shades of opinion and belief. Strangely it does not seem that these confessional divergences lead to conflict in the community. Whatever some people purport to believe, in day-to-day life all seem to rub along together. Grazide is impressed with the thought that whatever it is that people believe, in the end it is what they do that matters. How they behave to each other, what contributes to the common good. It seems to her to be the long-standing way of life in the communities in which she has lived; an older tradition that is untroubled by belief systems, be they orthodox or heretical.

She still does not really understand why her father had been so insistent that he be taken, dying, to be consoled at Corbarieu those few years back. Grazide now regrets that she had not at the time tried to comprehend what it was that was driving him. She had simply done as bidden, taking him on his last journey despite its seeming pointlessness. The ceremony was strange. She had insisted that she stayed with him, she was not going to be put outside in the last hours of her father's life.

There had been that opportunity to understand, long before his last illness struck. Coming across the strange visitor, Galtier Foulcaut, a guest at her father's table, she could have stayed. Perhaps she would have learnt then but her anger did not allow it, she could not stay. Why was she so incensed at that time? There was something about that man, for all that he was regarded by many as a goodman, that she had reacted against. Now she would dearly like to understand.

It is some weeks later that an opportunity presents itself. Magali returns from the weekly market not only with provisions but also news.

"There is to be a grand debate. It's all the talk of the market. The two Carbonnel brothers, Jacques and Raimond have set it up, after Mass on Sunday, in the marketplace."

"What sort of debate?" There were often public meetings in the covered square, usually convened by the consuls. Boring affairs, mostly, concerning rubbish on the streets, rent collections or other mundane matters. Surely Magali is not getting excited about one of these?

"They say that it is a debate between the priest, a Franciscan brother, a Cathar and a Waldensian, Pierre de Vals, you remember him?"

Grazide did indeed. The squat little doctor who had tended to Pierre-Guillaume the previous year. "The doctor, of course I do. How could I forget him?"

"Yes, he's a lovely man. Na Péronne calls him an angel but not when her husband is around. I don't think Bertrand de Castillon would approve."

Grazide smiles. "And who else?"

"A Cathar goodwoman, Jeanne d'Avignon."

Grazide remembers meeting Jeanne d'Avignon once. An austere lady, thin and gaunt, doubtless due to her frequent fasts and avoidance of meat, eggs or cheese. She lives with another woman and her son, Bon, in a house just outside the town in Sapiac. What she had done with her husband, Grazide does not know. He must have left some time ago, marriage to a person who regarded carnal relations as a sin was probably not going to last. "Is she going to bring along that steward of hers?"

"What? Benoit? Benoit the Joker. I have no idea. That would liven up proceedings."

Indeed it would, thinks Grazide. He has not earned his nickname for nothing. His capacity for scandal and mischief is well known. She often wonders why his mistress puts up with him.

"Well, shall we go then?" says Magali.

"What, you and me? I didn't know you were interested in religious preferences?"

"I don't think I know what you mean by that but come on, it should be a laugh." She digs Grazide in the ribs as if to emphasise her point.

"A laugh is the last thing it is likely to be would be my guess but, yes, I'll come with you."

Both women attend Mass together in the church of Saint-Jacques the following Sunday. Grazide notices that the Carbonnel brothers are in the congregation. Presumably hedging their bets she supposes. There is no sign of Jeanne d'Avignon nor of her jocular steward, Benoit. Mass being over the two women, arm-in-arm, make their way to the central square. Quite a number of townspeople are heading the same way, bent on finding some entertainment to fill what otherwise could be a tedious holy day.

A small platform has been erected in the covered square. Around it are gathered rows of benches. To one side is an impressive carved chair, complete with a sumptuous red cushion. Grazide squeezes her companion's arm and indicates the seat. "Who's that for? Someone important?" Her question is soon answered. Bertrand de

Castillon, consul of the town, strides forward from his house. He looks around at the assembled throng and sits down on the chair. There is not a trace of a smile on his face.

Magali giggles. "I guess he's here to see fair play. There'll be no nonsense whilst he is sitting there."

Jacques Carbonnel has stepped up on to the rostrum. "People of Montalban," the crowd quietens, straining to hear what he is about to announce. "It has always been a tradition in our town ever since its foundation by the great Alphonse Jourdain, count of Toulouse some seventy years ago, that we can speak freely and without hindrance or fear of repression."

A small cheer goes up from one corner of the crowd, by its tone a cheer of sarcasm, thinks Grazide. Jacques continues, undeterred. "You will know that within our community there are many who hold different views on what it is to be a good Christian. We have been afflicted for some years by the oppressive forces from the North, seeking to impose just one way, what they call the orthodox way. But there are others who think differently so we have decided, my brother and I," here he indicates Raimond who is seated on one of the front benches, "to hold a public debate. We have invited prominent members of our community who hold views differing from the orthodox way to come and tell us of their faiths. Equally we will give ear to what our priest has to say and also brother Guilabertz, a member of the newly founded Franciscan order," he pauses to indicate a bearded figure seated on the benches who wears a grey habit with a hood. "Any one of you may question our speakers once they have delivered their address but please do not all speak at once. Let us conduct this debate in a civilised manner."

A buzz of conversation spreads through the crowd. Grazide and Magali have found spaces on a bench at the back. Jacques Carbonnel has come down from the rostrum and is escorting a hooded figure forward. It is the goodwoman, Jeanne d'Avignon, a gaunt and bent figure leaning heavily on a long thin staff in her right hand

172

Jacques helps her on to the platform and raises his hand for silence. The crowd acquiesces.

She speaks rapidly in a thin voice, often repeating herself. Grazide has to strain to catch what she is saying. The old lady starts hesitantly but bit-by-bit expounds her belief. The visible world and all in it are the creation of an evil god. Spiritual beings are trapped inside the bodies of men, women and animals. They seek to return to their spiritual home with the good God in heaven. That only happens if the person that they inhabit is consoled by the laying on of hands by a goodman. It is a blessing passed down the generations from the apostles themselves. Goodmen and goodwomen must fast regularly, abstain from meat or any other product that comes from the coupling of animals, must pray and preach so that all will one day return to their spiritual home. Only then will the world be saved. As she proceeds to elaborate on this Grazide recognises what she has heard, in part, in the past. Now she is hearing a full exposition.

"We must abjure carnal relations," the old lady continues, "women who are pregnant carry devils in their bodies, creations of the evil god." There are murmurs from the assembled crowd, mostly from women. Grazide is shocked and appalled. Is this the belief that her father espoused?

By now Jeanne has got into her stride. Her voice becomes stronger. "Baptism, the Eucharist, marriage, are all worthless. They cannot save you. Only being consoled will have effect, even if it is on your death bed."

A voice pipes up from the audience. It is the joker, Benoit. "There you are, folks. Sin away all your life but don't forget to get done before you die." There is laughter, quickly subdued by a black look on the face of Bertrand de Castillon. Grazide is surprised that this old lady puts up with her wayward steward; he hardly helps her cause. Jeanne d'Avignon has finished her speech. Jacques Carbonnel stands up. "Are there questions for the good lady? Raise your hands."

A few hands go up. An old peasant stands up. "I've heard that God made the first man out of clay and invited Lucifer to put a spirit in him. Lucifer said that would make the man too strong, he should make him out of silt instead, so God did. That's what I heard." He sits down, still mumbling under his breath. Jeanne d'Avignon says nothing.

Another person asks "what should we do with our wives, then? Kick them out?" This produces some coarse laughter and comments from the men in the crowd.

"No. Live with them but abstain from carnal contact for it is an evil sin."

"Abstain? Chance would be a fine thing," calls out a voice from the crowd. Grazide suspects it is Benoit again. He gets his laugh.

Next Jacques invites the priest from Saint-Jacques to speak. Father Arnault speaks eloquently, mostly relying on appeals to what "the Holy Father bids us do." Attend Mass and accept the holy sacraments, make confession and you will be saved. It is orthodox stuff with which Grazide is perfectly familiar. Back in Vilanòva Father Jean Vital preached the same, at the same time maintaining a scandalous life. This priest seems to be a different kettle of fish, she doubts whether he is afflicted with a similar hypocrisy.

Pierre de Vals is being escorted to the rostrum now. Grazide recognises the short doctor who cared for her son. His brown eyes, under the curtain of his dark bushy eyebrows, range across the assembled crowd. "I am a Poor Man of Lyon. Some of you know me as a doctor. Many of us followers of Valdes are practitioners of medicine. We are simple men who only seek to do the work of Jesus Christ. The Church of the Roman Pope tells you that their way is the only road to salvation. Yet they oppress us with tithes that enrich their prelates, they tell us that by giving them money and goods we can buy our way out of purgatory, that we can only be saved by the body of Christ blessed by a sacramental priest. There is no salvation in any of that. It is not the way of Our Lord. He led a simple life, preaching and healing, that is what we are called to do."

A quiet has descended on the crowd as he speaks. Grazide recognises the gentle demeanour that she first encountered with

Brother Bernard, all those years ago. How can these men be considered heretics?

Pierre de Vals is followed by the final speaker, the friar Brother Guilabertz. He comes from a newly founded house of Franciscan brothers. In his simple grey tunic he seems much like Pierre de Vals, the Waldensian. His speech is uncomplicated. "We are called to a way of poverty, of respect to all living things, to preach the Gospel. The way of us Franciscans is blessed by the Holy Father in Rome." Grazide finds this puzzling. Why do they have the approval of the orthodox Roman Church yet the Waldensians, whom they mostly resemble, are deemed heretics? It seems an arbitrary judgement. Perhaps it is more to do with the exercise of power and control by the established Church than anything else.

People are beginning to drift away now. Jacques thanks them all for coming. "Perhaps you can now make up your own minds, good people of Montalban. It is up to you."

As she turns to leave she notices a figure still seated at the back of the crowd. He is richly dressed, a dark robe wrapped around him, his head covered. Looking more closely she perceives the fine-boned features of a member of the nobility. She has not seen him before. He had been silent in the debate. As she passes him he stands up. "A moment if you please, madam."

She stops, surprised to be addressed by this stranger.

"Are you, as I believe you are, Grazide Lamothe?"

How does he know her? "Yes, sir. I am Grazide."

"My compliments then, madam. You are the artist who created those wonderful gates that adorn the new church. I must say they are magnificent."

Grazide is unsure how to receive this compliment from a perfect stranger. She says nothing.

"I am sorry. It is rude of me. I am Pons Grimoard. Not a resident of this fine town. I and my family come from Castelsarrasin, not far west from here. I heard tell of this debate and could not resist attending. What, may I ask, did you make of it?"

175

Grazide can find her voice now. "Somewhat confusing, if I am honest, sir. So many different views."

"But what appealed to you, or perhaps, you would prefer not to tell a perfect stranger?"

"To be honest," she sits down on the bench in front of her, Magali has gone ahead, "nothing very much. The Poor Man of Lyon seemed very sincere but I am not sure how much I could espouse his views. But overall all these religious people tend to address themselves to men. I feel somewhat left out by that."

"Being a woman, you mean."

"Yes. It has seemed to me that religion and religious debate is mostly addressed to men, even though some of the most devout followers are women."

"But is that not what is ordained in Holy Scripture? Are we not taught that?"

Grazide is intrigued. Why is this stranger with his rich clothes concerning himself with her? Never mind, she cannot resist responding. "For some years I have believed that there has been a misreading of Scripture. It stems from the story of creation in the second chapter of Genesis, woman created from an extracted rib of man. There is another account, though, of creation. It is in the first chapter of Genesis, man and woman created equally from the dust of the earth. Why has the Church, mostly men, emphasised the former over the latter?"

"Goodness me, a scholar as well as a blacksmith. You astound me, young lady."

"Do not patronise me, sir. It demeans you."

"I am sorry. I apologise, it was not intended."

"Never mind. I am used to it. It is the way of the world it seems."

He looks subdued. "I would like to debate this with you further, my lady. Perhaps we will have the opportunity one day. But now I must take my leave." He stands, bows, wraps his cloak around him and makes his way across the square. Grazide remains seated for a while, watching his retreating back.

CHAPTER 17

The twenty-fifth day of July is always welcomed by the inhabitants of Montalban. The Feast of Saint-Jacques, a day given over to a magnificent fair culminating in a grand meal for everyone in the covered market square. Tables are laid out, laden with food and drink; roasted pig, all kinds of vegetables, nuts, raisins and barrels of wine. The air is filled with chatter, excited laughter, bawdy songs. Even goodmen and goodwomen are to be seen, though they avoid the meat, contenting themselves with fish from the river Tarn. It is a day for forgetting business, forgetting labour in the fields, forgetting any divisions between rich and poor, high-born or peasant. A day devoted to pleasure, not profit.

Grazide enjoys the Feast of Saint-Jacques as much as the rest of Magali Gramazie's ostal. Little Pierre-Guillaume delights in the colours, the music, the company of other small children to play with between the tables. It is a tradition that the meal, which lasts for several hours, is interspersed with entertainments. Some people sing songs, some tell stories. On this occasion they are promised a show by a group of travelling players who arrived in the town on the preceding day.

The first to get up is Benoit the Joker. This is a regular feature at the feasts and he is greeted with cheers and thumping on the tables.

"Friends," he calls, "let me prevail upon you to tell you the tale of the Peasant's Fart." Much jeering at this point, many present have heard this story before. Benoit holds up his hand. "No, no. It is a sad and beguiling story, one to wring sorrow from the very depths of your heart."

He pulls a mock serious face and begins. "There once was a peasant who felt unwell, so badly that he feared he was on his way to Hell. There's no place in Paradise for peasants who have no love of clergymen. Believe me, he knew he was doomed. A devil was despatched to collect his soul. A simple fiend, he thought that the poor man's soul would exit from his arse. He held out a leather bag to collect the spirit. But the peasant, seeking a remedy for his ill had just downed

179

so much beef cooked in garlic that his guts and belly were as taut as the strings on a guitar. If only, he thought, I could fart my troubles would be over. He twists and writhes, strains and forces until at last a huge fart explodes, filling up the leather bag the little imp has been holding to his backside. Off goes the devil with the bag to the gates of Hell and tosses it down. Immediately the fart is vented and all the devils holler and scream, declaring curses on peasants' souls. It is decreed that henceforth no one should collect a peasant's soul – they stink! So peasants' souls can never go to Hell, that you'll be glad to hear. Where do they go? To sing amongst the frogs, you've heard the noise. A merry solution, you'll agree."

He sits down to cheers and catcalls. Grazide has not heard this tale before. She joins in the laughter. Pierre-Guillaume is under the table, playing with some sticks and stones. She hopes he has not been listening.

More food is brought out, beakers are refilled with wine as the cool of the evening comes on. Candles are lit along the tables, no one wants to leave. There is a sound of music coming from one corner of the square, the rattle of tambours and the piping of a lilting tune. Into the square come three travelling players, two men and a woman. They make their way to a rostrum in the centre of the square, surrounded on all sides by the tables of the feasting throng. As they mount the stage Grazide is surprised to recognise the woman. It is the same actor who played the part of Eve all those years ago, back in Vilanòva. Today her auburn hair is cut shorter but there is no mistaking, it is the same woman.

"Good people," calls out the woman as the music stops, "we are here to enact a salutary tale. It is known as 'The Four Wishes of Saint-Martin'. I take the part of an honest wife. Milos here plays my simple husband. And Gombert," here she indicates the third player, tall and dark-bearded, "will set the scene."

Gombert steps forward. "There was once a simple peasant. He was a lazy man, not fond of doing a day's work like the rest of you. One day he is leaning on his hoe when Saint-Martin appears to him."

Milos starts to mime the part of the peasant. Gombert speaks as Saint-Martin. "Put down your hoe, peasant, and listen carefully. I am here to grant you four wishes. You can wish for whatever you want but use them wisely. Once they are gone you can never have them back. Go home and tell your wife. I am sure she will be glad to hear your news."

"Thank you, Saint-Martin. I will do as you say." He hurries across the stage to the woman.

"Gods tooth! What are you doing here, you lazy man? It is only noon. Are you incapable of doing a day's work?"

"Hush, wife. I have great news. Saint-Martin appeared to me and has granted me four wishes. We can be rich. I need never work again. Just so long as I choose wisely."

"Well, that is a surprise," she strokes her chin. "Four wishes. Perhaps you could give one of them to me. You'll still have three for yourself."

"I don't know. Will you make a good wish? Can I trust you?"

"Of course you can, come on, my dear, let me have just one."

"All right then. Have your wish."

The woman turns away from him, scratching her head as if in deep thought. "I wish that you were given a hundred pricks."

The man jumps back in horror and starts feeling himself all over. The narrator takes up the story. "Immediately pricks burst out all over the man's body. Small ones, fat ones, long ones and one enormous one springing from his forehead standing up, big and strong."

The woman laughs. "Well, that is wonderful. Blessings on you, Saint-Martin. Instead of his one little prick that hangs like a fox stole, I've got a wealth of cocks at my disposal. What could be better?"

"Foolish woman. It's not funny. How can I go out with all these appendages? That was a bad wish you made." He pauses, "and yet, there are three wishes left." He raises his voice to address the whole crowd. "I wish that you had as many cunts on you as I have pricks on me. May your cunts pop out at once!"

The woman looks shocked. She starts to feel herself all over. The narrator speaks. "All at once the cunts arise, four on her forehead in a row, cunts above and cunts below, cunts behind and cunts in front."

The woman starts to wail. The audience collapses with laughter. The peasant shouts, "Now is my joy complete. One cunt wouldn't do for all the pricks you gave me. Don't be sad. With all those cunts you'll be famed throughout the land." He dances a little jig for joy.

"Husband, this is madness. That's two wishes thrown away. Quick, use the third to get rid of all these cunts and pricks."

"The stupid man agrees," says the narrator, "and wishes thereupon that all their cunts and pricks are gone." The woman screams.

"What ails you, wife?"

"You idiot! My cunt has disappeared."

He claps a hand over his groin. "Oh, what a shock! The wish has robbed me of my cock!"

"Oh, woe is me. We are undone but stop. There is one wish left. Quick, husband, beseech Saint-Martin to return us to our former state, no poorer will we be at any rate."

"He wished the wish that still remained," continues the narrator, "and thus they neither lost nor gained. He got his prick back at the cost of the four wishes he had lost."

To cheers and applause the three players take a bow. Then the woman steps forward and raises her arm for quiet. "Good people think about our tale. Who was the wise one, man or wife?" She picks up her flute and starts to play, the tambour joins the tune and they dance out of the square to cheers from the crowd. Grazide is aware that most of the applause comes from the women in the throng. The men look strangely silent.

Grazide turns to Magali. "I must go and see that woman. I've seen her before. Keep an eye on Pierre for me, would you?" Magali nods.

The feast continues as Grazide weaves her way through the tables, following the way the players had just gone. In a street just off one corner of the square she spots them standing by a stall that is serving out beakers of wine. Gombert, the narrator, is counting out some coins. He gives a handful to each of his two fellow players. Grazide approaches the woman. She looks up as the tall figure approaches.

"Thank you for that play. It made me laugh. Weren't you in the company that came to Vilanòva some years back? *The Play of Adam*, you were Eve, weren't you?"

The woman scratches her head.

"Vilanòva. That's east of here, isn't it? Yes, now I remember. We used to take that play to many towns and villages but I do remember Vilanòva. They paid us well there. Did you live there then?"

Grazide nods. "Yes. I grew up there. My father was the blacksmith. I'm Grazide, Grazide Lamothe." She holds out her hand.

"Aurimonde de Sella." The other woman takes her hand. Grazide notices a smile that only partly hides an enquiring gaze. It is in the actor's eyes that she detects a sharp intelligence. Her two companions put down their beakers. They have been taking no notice of the two women. Gombert speaks, "Come on, Aurimonde. We have to find lodgings. That's unless you want to spend another night on the cold stones of the church porch."

Milos shudders. "Lord, preserve us. That was too bloody cold for me."

Grazide is seized by an impulsive thought. "We can give you a bed for the night. I'm sure my friend, Magali, would not mind." In her head she hopes that is true. "Wait here. I'll go and speak with her."

Magali ponders a little. "I suppose we could. The girls could bed down with the servants. That would free up their bed for the two men."

"Aurimonde can share my bed," says Grazide. "I don't mind." For a moment she feels a brief excitement. So unformed, she does not understand its source.

The actors are happy with the suggestion. People are beginning to make their way home as the feast draws to a close. Grazide collects Pierre-Guillaume who has curled up on the lap of Magali's daughter Arnaude and is fast asleep. His mother carries him as Magali leads the way to their house.

Later, the ostal having reorganised the sleeping arrangements, she lies on her side and in the candlelight watches Aurimonde undress and climb in beside her. For a while they are silent but sleep does not come.

"That play. Have you done that often?"

"The Four Wishes of Saint-Martin? Yes, quite often. It is one of our most popular. Always goes down well."

"And that question that you asked at the end. Do you always include that?"

"Usually. Gombert and Milos don't like me asking it much. Sometimes it stirs up trouble."

"Trouble?"

"Yes, on occasions. One time the audience started fighting, nothing serious, just a bit of pushing and shoving. We were told never to return to that town. The boys were not happy, I can tell you." She chuckles at the memory.

"It made me think. It's not just a crude fabliau, is it? It's got a deeper meaning."

"Do you think that? Not many people do. They just think it's all about pricks and cunts."

"It seems to me to be saying something about pleasure and knowledge. The man's head, where his wisdom lies, is supplanted with a large penis, source of pleasure. His wife has undermined the idea that the man retains wisdom and rational thinking whilst the woman is only devoted to sensual pleasure. It turns that idea upside down."

"That's a very perceptive thought of yours Grazide. Maybe that's why I ask that question at the end. It baffles most men but the women in the audience seem to get it."

"Do you remember that bit in *The Play of Adam*? Eve being offered the fruit from the Tree of Knowledge. She asks the devil 'how does it taste?' That stuck with me. Knowledge and wisdom are not just attained by rational thought, the so-called male preserve, but also by sensual feeling, by taste. Always thought of as female and second-rate."

"You know, that had never occurred to me when we did that play. I see what you mean. I was always a bit mystified at that line."

Grazide feels pleased that she is being understood. The two of them continue to talk, quietening their voices so as not to disturb the ostal, until sleep overtakes them. The next day the actors are gone.

A few weeks after the Feast of Saint-Jacques Grazide is seated at the long table in the kitchen, collecting together invoices that she has to deliver the following day. The summer heat has abated a bit. It is a time of year that has always been her favourite. Always easier to work in the forge in autumn than in the high heat of summer, she remembers. Pierre-Guillaume is amusing himself in the corner of the room, playing with one of the kittens that the ostal cat had recently presented them with. Beatrice, the cook, is working in the corner, her back turned. She is making bread, kneading away and humming to herself. The fire has been stoked up under the heavy iron oven, ready to receive the shaped loaves. Grazide had collected the flour from one of the two boat mills on the Tarn earlier that day. She took Pierre-Guillaume with her. He always loved taking the short ferry crossing to collect the flour from the miller, was always entranced by the constant turning of the mill wheel whilst the boat strained against its moorings.

Her thoughts are back in Vilanòva. It is now four years since she left, escorting her dying father on his last journey. The decision not to return was impulsive, she can see that now. At the time she never really understood why she failed to return. Now, thinking back, she begins to understand her impetuous choice. Living in Montalban with its freedoms and open atmosphere has emphasised to her how oppressive her life was in the village of her childhood. No doubt that much of that was due to the assault that she suffered from the priest,

Jean Vital. Even now she still feels incensed at that attack though the strength of her anger has diminished over the years.

In her introspection she wonders whether that incident accounted for her brief liaison with Giufré, the father of Pierre-Guillaume. Where the priest had been violent, Giufré was gentle. They had become lovers almost before she had realised what was happening. It was unexpected, she did not seek it out.

When he disappeared she was not surprised. It seemed inevitable. A relationship to which neither party felt strongly committed. It was never going to last. Discovering that she had become pregnant had been a shock yet giving birth to Pierre-Guillaume was in the nature of a gift to her, a treasured gift, a deep grace.

Then when she nearly lost her son to the enteric fever the true value of that gift became apparent. Since then the idea of losing him is an unbearable prospect. Yes, there was the torment of the violent death of her brothers. There was even the anguish at the death of her father, the father with whom she had had such a turbulent relationship. But the loss that fuels the fragility of her feelings for her little boy seems implanted deep within her. An ache that is always there, the loss of one she never remembers but whose love she experiences as ever present, a paradox that has created the person that she is.

There is a knock at the door. Beatrice looks up, dusts down her flour-covered forearms on her pinafore and goes to see who it is. Grazide reapplies her mind to her invoices.

"Hello, Grazide." She turns to see who it is that addresses her. To her surprise she sees Aurimonde, the actor, standing there. For a moment Grazide feels a short tug in her chest, brief but thrilling.

"Aurimonde. How good to see you." She looks into the other woman's eyes. Can she believe that the excitement she feels is mirrored there? Aurimonde is smiling. She takes a step towards the taller woman and envelops her in an embrace. It is more than formal. Grazide would have it last for ever but she lets go for the sake of propriety. Beatrice and Pierre-Guillaume are both watching the two women.

"Come and sit down." She pulls out a stool from under the table. "It is good to see you again. Have you brought another play?"

In the corner Beatrice mutters under her breath "I hope not." Grazide does not hear the reproach.

"No. No more plays. I am afraid that we have split up. Gombert and Milos had had enough of my subversive ways, or so they said. I don't think they could tolerate a sparky woman any longer." She laughs. "I don't mind. I think I have had enough of pricks and cunts."

Beatrice gasps and quickly puts her hands over Pierre-Guillaume's ears. Her face is all disapproval.

"So, what now?" says Grazide. "What brings you back to Montalban? Have you plans?"

"I guess I'm looking for work. I know I've been an actor for the past few years but I can turn my hand to most things. Montalban always seemed like a thriving town when we visited it. Some of the places we pitch up at are really run down. Ruined by the wars. It is very sad to see."

Can Grazide entertain the thought that there is more to it than that? Is there another attraction that has brought this lively woman back?

"Have you somewhere to stay?"

"Well, no. I was going to ask if you know of anywhere. I'm not fussy."

Grazide cannot hide the excitement in her voice. "Stay here. There's room. I'm certain Magali will not mind." For a moment, though, she is not sure. She has presumed on Magali's hospitality once before.

"That would be good," says Aurimonde and she squeezes Grazide's arm as if to restrain her from taking too many liberties. "But I think I must speak to Magali myself first."

Grazide, noticing that Beatrice is frowning says, "Of course. Of course you must. I'm sure she'll be happy about it."

As it turns out there is no impediment from Magali. She is happy to incorporate Aurimonde in their ostal.

"So long as you don't mind sharing a bed with Grazide."

"That will be no problem. Naturally I will pay you rent."

"Oh that. We'll see about it once you get settled." Magali also promises to ask around to see if there is work that the newcomer can take on.

As indeed there is. Na Péronne, who seems to know most of what is going on in the town, tells her that Floris, the wine merchant, needs an assistant. Floris himself has doubts when he hears that a female ex-actor is interested in the position. However a few minutes interview with Aurimonde the next day convinces him that she would fit the bill. She is contracted.

"I think he thought that a young man would be a better bet. I told him that I had sampled wine from many different parts of this land. Travelling players get to go to most places." She laughs, a tinkling bubble of merriment, " I'm something of an expert when it comes to the drink." Grazide can see how her natural bounciness must have won the man over. She herself is entranced.

It is no surprise to Magali de Gramazie that the two young women that are now part of her ostal, Grazide Lamothe and Aurimonde de Sella, grow together over the next few months. With her astute eye she notices a change in Grazide, a lightening of affect perhaps, even a dreaminess. She knows her to be a serious young woman, determined at times, quite self-dependant. Now she sees something new.

She can see that the two complement each other, almost as if they were two parts of a join that interlock to make a perfect whole. In appearance they are contrasted. Grazide is the taller, Aurimonde just reaches the other's shoulder. Aurimonde has a head of short, auburn curls against the long dark sheen of Grazide's tresses. Her lively sky-blue eyes and her elfin features contrast with the seriousness of Grazide's green eyes and strong features of the taller woman's face. Magali knows Grazide to be naturally serious. It amuses her to see Aurimonde's lively ebullience infiltrate that reserve, an effect like yeast on dough, lifting and lightening. No, she thinks, there is no doubt that they are a natural fit.

However, it comes as a surprise to Grazide that she is falling in love with her new companion. Novel and unexpected, different from anything that she has experienced before. Certainly not in her brief affair with Giufré, there had been nothing like this. She is discovering what it is to live for another; something she experiences in her love for her little boy, Pierre-Guillaume. But this is different. It feels like an immolation, a sinking of herself into the other. Voluntary yet out of her control in a paradox that she cannot understand yet which might promise to fulfil her deepest needs.

So in a way it is inevitable that the two become lovers. Aurimonde is the instigator but her approach is cautious. It is her surprise that she finds that her tentativeness is met with a passion that she had not anticipated. There is a hunger in her lover which both thrills and, at times, shocks her. Their exploration of each other takes them both into an entirely new world, a world of resplendence and delight.

It is no surprise then that the dynamic of the Gramazie ostal is affected by the relationship that has developed between the two of them. Beatrice, the cook, disapproves. Barbed comments from time to time mostly fall on deaf ears. Magali is quite used to her servant's grumblings so this new impetus to the latter's grouchiness has little impact.

More serious, however, is the effect on Pierre-Guillaume. Young though he is it is apparent that he is disturbed by the sharing of his mother's affection with another. At times his behaviour becomes more impetuous. He is more likely to give rein to tantrums that can be explosive on occasions. Grazide is aware of this change and it disturbs her. Magali is quick to reassure his mother that such behaviour is natural in a child of his age. She does not explicitly link it to his mother's newfound romantic status. Perhaps there is no connection, thinks Grazide.

CHAPTER 18
1229

Bertrand de Castillon looks around his fellow consuls. All are seated on wooden benches arranged around the outside of the consuls' chamber, a square wooden room above the marketplace in the square. The ceiling is sloped, the occasional glint of sunlight is seen through small gaps in the barrel-tiled roof, the shafts of light cut through the gloom of the unlit room illuminating motes of dust floating in the still air. It is not a room in which to store documents and manuscripts; in a good storm the roof is as leaky as a giant colander. For that reason the room is bare except for the coat of arms of the Count of Toulouse on the south wall and the standard of the town on the opposite side.

A motley lot, thinks Bertrand. Many of them have only been consuls for less than three years. The usual practice is for all consuls to be reappointed every year. Some only last the one term, clearly not up to the task. Bertrand has been a consul for the last fifteen years. Rarely does anyone, not even the Count's seneschal, dare oppose him. He has a fixed place in the seating of the chamber, right under the Toulousain banner. First among equals, as is right and proper thinks Bertrand. Few would countermand him.

In the centre of the room is an elegant and solid chair, brought in for the occasion. A chair of a sumptuousness that befits its occupant, Pons Grimoard, newly appointed seneschal to Count Raimond VII of Toulouse. A small man but one who carries an implicit air of authority. Once but a minor noble from Castelsarrasin, his appointment as chief representative of the count has been unexpected. Bertrand studies his face. It is not entirely the face of inherited nobility. Much like me, thinks Bertrand, both of us self-made men.

A surprise, then, when Pons was appointed to his high office and not only because of the modesty of his origins. Bertrand knows that the seneschal is a heretic believer though this is knowledge shared with very few. With the way that the crusade has ended, to espouse a heretic cause is dangerous or, at least in Bertrand's eyes, foolish.

The recently signed Treaty of Paris which has ended the war is the current topic of discussion between the consuls and the seneschal. Since the summer before last minor lords across the region had offered no resistance to the overwhelming forces that the crusade had mustered. There had been a few pockets of opposition, but many had capitulated without a fight. The town of Labécède had been besieged by the crusaders, led by then by one Humbert de Beaujeu, Constable of France. When the town collapsed its men were put to the sword and many heretics had been burnt including a close friend of Pons the seneschal, Durand Barrère, a heretic goodman. Word had come that that same force was now moving on Toulouse itself, the town that had resisted all sieges and attacks since the death of Simon de Montfort some ten years previously.

"Toulouse will certainly stand against the crusaders, surely it will," said one of the consuls.

"I wish I shared your optimism," said Bertrand, mustering the innate authority that he had developed over the years. "Avignon collapsed two years ago; I doubt that even Toulouse has the defensive capability needed to resist the forces pitched against us. Time is running out for our Count, I fear. If Toulouse falls I fear that Montalban will follow, however good our fortifications might be."

There had been marked anxiety amongst the consuls. "We have to face facts," said Bertrand. "There is every possibility that the Count will have to submit to the Royal forces. Terms will have to be negotiated. If that happens I think those that have supported the heretics' cause will have to think hard about escape, there is bound to be retribution."

The end game was swift in coming. The crusaders under Humbert de Beaujeu, Constable of France, moved on Toulouse within a month of the consular debate in Montalban. Rather than directly attacking the city Humbert engaged in a strategy to destroy the lands around, thus depriving the people of Toulouse of their vital necessities. On Saint-Jean-Baptiste day in late June they set up camp on the hill of Pech-Aimèry, overlooking Toulouse from the east. Their technique was the same each day, first a line of crossbowmen was despatched, followed by a line of mounted knights. Systematically they moved across the terrain, killing anyone they found and mowing down the ripening corn. Others used pickaxes and mattocks to pull down towers and the walls of fortified places that they encountered. Vines were destroyed and burned. The ravaging continued for a full three months. By the end of the campaign the land, once rich and fertile, was a desert. By autumn a truce was agreed at Baziège, a town not far from Toulouse. By April of 1229 a Peace Treaty has been signed.

The terms agreed are humiliating for the Count of Toulouse. They are published in all the major towns of his jurisdiction within days of their signature. The consuls of Montalban have read them with mounting dismay, appalled at the implications for their town. Not the least of these is the agreement that the defensive walls of both Toulouse, Montalban and other towns should be dismantled. This is a stricture of great distress to Bertrand de Castillon who had previously spent so much time and energy, not to say money, on bolstering the town's defences just a few years previously.

In addition Raimond VII, who has agreed that his only child, Joan, should marry the King's brother, Alphonse of Poitiers, has undertaken to root out all heretics that can be found in his lands.

"That is going to put the cat among the pigeons in our town," says Bertrand to his fellow consuls. They have been receiving the news of the Peace Treaty with a mixture of apprehension and outright fear. The seneschal listens in silence. Bertrand looks around the assembled dignitaries with a mild contempt, recognising more than a few that have entertained heretical affiliations. Their retribution is bound to be swift, he imagines, glad that he has not been inveigled into what he has always regarded as naïve enthusiasms.

"What beats me," he later confides to his wife, Péronne, "is that Pons Grimoard, the count's seneschal who is going to have to institute this heretic chasing, is himself a secret supporter. I cannot see how he is going to manage that. He was very quiet at that meeting. I'll warrant that he will not remain seneschal for much longer."

Na Péronne looks troubled at the news. Many of her friends are known to be heretic believers. Even she herself retains a strong affection for the doctor, Pierre de Vals, an acknowledged Waldensian. "There will be dark days coming, husband. Let us pray that we will survive them." Bertrand's only reply is a non-committal grunt.

The destruction of the town walls demanded by the Peace Treaty is a blow to the morale of the people of Montalban. By now it is apparent that Raimond VII has agreed to extirpating remaining heretics in his domains. The grim reality of their impending fate leads many of the citizens of the town that have espoused Cathar or Waldensian sympathies to make an escape with the greatest speed. Many go north to the hinterlands of the Quercy and the Rouergue, hoping to find refuge in the smaller towns and villages. There might be a chance to evade capture and retribution. Amongst the refugees fleeing the town are Pierre de Vals, the Waldensian doctor. Also members of the Carbonnel family; Jacques de Carbonnel, however, who had set up the debate between the different persuasions, elects to stay, perhaps hoping that his even-minded stance might protect him from persecution.

Depleted though the town is by the egress of a number of notables who fear for their safety under the new regime that follows the Treaty of Paris, life still has to continue. A town like Montalban thrives on trade, merchandising and manufacturing, all functions that do best when there is peace in the land, even if power has swung towards the distant King of France and those political groups, primarily the Church, that have aligned themselves with the regnal supremacy. Bertrand de Castillon understands that. The upheaval has been disturbing. He is distressed by the stipulation that his precious walls are to be taken down but reluctantly agrees. The exodus of heretic supporters has also deprived the town of a few of its consuls. Bertrand is not sad to see them go; he had never rated what he regarded as their unworldliness as an asset to the efficient government of the town.

The Gramazie ostal and its business does not suffer unduly in the upheavals. Local demand for the work of the seamstresses seems not to have declined. In the past Magali de Gramazie has built up a significant export business, helped in no small part by the enterprise of Grazide. Orders from further afield were shipped by river to towns as far away as Bordeaux. That side of the business has suffered a decline in the past two years. Magali is hopeful that it will pick up again now that there is a relative peace in the land.

It is market day in early winter. Grazide has wrapped Pierre-Guillaume in a warm cloak that one of the seamstresses had made for him. She and Aurimonde wander around the stalls on the lookout for bargains. Beatrice has given them a list of requirements for the larder so their bags are soon filling up. Pierre-Guillaume holds his mother's hand, in his other hand he clutches a small rag doll, an inseparable companion these days. They stop to listen to a pair of minstrels who entertain the passing crowds. Pierre-Guillaume slips from his mother's grip in order to perform a little dance in the space in front of the performers. Passers-by stop to watch the little boy, their faces lit up with amusement.

At a stall of vegetables Grazide is searching for a good cabbage, her head down, carefully inspecting the displayed wares. Some are well-eaten by caterpillars, their leaves like green lace. At the back she spies one that seems more intact. She is about to reach out for it when from behind her she hears a man's voice.

"Grazide." The tone is low, almost guttural. She feels a shock of recognition even before she has turned to see who has addressed her. She knows this voice even though it is some years since she had last heard it.

She turns. Facing her is a man. She recognises the broad frame of his body, the head with unruly black curls, the livid scar on the right side of his face. He is smiling but that smile does nothing to lessen the rising panic that she is experiencing.

"Giufré. What are you doing here?" She tries hard to control her voice but the quiver in its tone is unmistakable.

He laughs, displaying an arrogance that she remembers of old. "What kind of a welcome for a long-lost friend is that?" He takes a step towards her. For a moment she is terrified that he is going to take hold of her. She steps back.

"Don't touch me." At last she has regained her self-control.

He pauses. "All right. All right. No need to be so wary."

By this time Aurimonde, who has been keeping an eye on Pierre-Guillaume, has noticed that her friend has been accosted by someone she must have assumed is a stranger. She comes across and takes Grazide's arm. She stares directly at Giufré but speaks to Grazide. "Is this man bothering you?"

Giufré turns towards Aurimonde, for a moment he displays a flash of anger. "Bothering her? Of course not. I am an old friend. I'm sure she will tell you."

Aurimonde looks at her partner, a quizzical look. Grazide is silent. By now Giufré has turned his attention to the little boy. "So, who is this little chap?" He stoops down to Pierre-Guillaume's level. "What's your name, my boy?"

Pierre-Guillaume looks frightened. He turns away and buries his head in the folds of his mother's dress. Giufré stands up again. "So, he is yours, is he? How old is he? Around five I should think." He points at the little boy's thick, dark curls. "And where did he get that head of hair? From his father, no doubt."

Grazide has regained her composure. "Aurimonde, this is Giufré da Costa. He is Pierre-Guillaume's father though perhaps he does not know it. He abandoned me before Pierre was born." It is obvious to her that Giufré has already worked out that Pierre-Guillaume is his son. He shows no surprise at Grazide's words.

Aurimonde intervenes. "So, you come back to claim your rights, do you? Do you imagine you have any entitlement here?"

Grazide interrupts her. She can see that her partner is shaken by this revelation. Grazide has never told her who it was that fathered Pierre-Guillaume. It has been a subject which both have consistently avoided. Magali, Grazide knows, has been discreet.

196

"It is all right, Aurimonde. Let's not continue this here." She turns to Giufré, her face expresses a cool determination. "Perhaps you would like to accompany us home. Then you can explain the reasons for your presence here."

They make their way back to the house. Grazide notices that the man is limping badly. Once in the house she turns to Giufré. "Have you been injured? You are limping badly."

"Good of you to be concerned. Yes, I did pick up a wound. During the fighting around Toulouse. A pike stab in the thigh. It laid me up for some time once the surgeons had stitched me up."

"So has the count kept you on?" She turns to Aurimonde. "He is a mercenary, you understand."

Giufré laughs. "I wasn't fighting for the bloody count. I was in the crusaders' army. They paid better."

If Grazide is shocked by this she does not show it. After all, he is a mercenary. His loyalty extends only as far as the person with the largest purse. "Then perhaps you would tell me why you are here. What do you want?"

"Just a chance to get to know my son. After all, I have a right to see that he is raised like a man."

Aurimonde explodes. "A right! You think you have a bloody right! Did he abandon you, Grazide? Did he just bugger off once he had fathered your child?"

Giufré is angry now. "Listen lady. What concern is it of yours? This is between me and his mother so stay out of it."

"Don't you threaten me, mercenary. You don't frighten me."

Grazide intervenes. She is glad that she left Pierre-Guillaume with Beatrice. She would not want him to see this. She puts her arm around Aurimonde. They both face Giufré. For a moment nothing is said. Giufré stares at the couple and a look of understanding comes over his face.

"Ah, now I'm beginning to get it. You two. You are a pair of sodomites. Fucking hell. That settles it. I am not going to let my boy be brought up by people like you."

"I think you have no say in the matter," says Grazide. "You lost that power when you disappeared."

"I'm still his father, or perhaps I'm not. Maybe you had it away with some other dark-haired stranger."

Aurimonde rushes towards him and beats him on the chest with both fists flailing. "Don't you dare make such filthy insinuations. Just piss off."

For a moment he is taken aback. Grazide pulls Aurimonde back, the smaller woman is now in tears. Giufré has not moved. "I do not know what you expected to gain by coming back here, by seeking me out. You have no place here. I think it would be for the best if you went." Grazide's jaw is set firm.

Giufré turns, takes three limping steps, then turns back. "I thought that you loved me, that's all. I thought that you'd want to see me again."

"I never loved you, Giufré. And I don't believe you know what love is. There is nothing here for you. You should go."

Giufré hesitates. Grazide holds her breath. What is he going to do? To her relief he turns and limps out of the house.

"I'm sorry I never told you the whole story, Aurimonde." It is later that night. The house is quiet.

"Well, I suppose I didn't ask you," says Aurimonde, "perhaps I was waiting for you to tell me. Did you not trust me?"

Grazide pauses, tears could flow but she holds them back. She swallows hard. "I was so ashamed. Even though Magali was so accepting, I could not speak of it. Still cannot."

"Not even to me? If that man had never turned up would you have told me?"

"Perhaps, I don't know. But I do trust you, Aurimonde. You are everything to me. Please do not let this come between us."

"Knowing who it is that is Pierre-Guillaume's father, that's not the point. It's not telling me that hurts."

Grazide takes her into her arms. For a while they lie still in the embrace. Now the tears come, two rivulets coursing down her face. She tastes the salt in them. Aurimonde is kissing her, holding her tight. There are no more words. In the end they both fall asleep.

The following morning comes disturbing news from Magali. "This has just arrived," she says, holding up a sealed document. It carries the town crest which means that it must come from the bailie, the administrator of justice in the town. Magali opens it and reads, the colour drains from her cheeks as she does so. She turns to Grazide, "I cannot believe this. It's my brother-in-law, Esteve. He has petitioned the court about my inheritance. He is claiming that my husband's estate should have passed to him, not me."

"Surely not," says Grazide. "How can he claim that? And after so long?"

"I don't know. I haven't seen him since Adalbert died. He lives over the Pyrenean Mountains, away to the south of here. Adalbert said he was always a difficult person, there was not much of a bond between them."

"So is he here in Montalban? Presumably he must be if he has lodged this petition."

Aurimonde joins them and Grazide quickly explains what is happening. "There is to be a hearing on the first day of next month. That does not give you much time, Magali."

Magali has sat down at the table, her head in her hands. "What can I do? This is awful."

Grazide lays a hand on her shoulder. "We can help you. You can fight this. He's trying it on, it'll be thrown out by the bailie. You wait and see. It's a nonsense."

Her optimism proves to be unfounded. On the first day of the month the hearing is held in the upper room of the covered market. The bailie is seated at a table placed under the arms of the Count of Toulouse. All the consuls, Bertrand de Castillon among them, are seated around the sides of the room. There are gaps. Some consuls are amongst those people that have recently fled the city.

Magali is accompanied by Grazide. There is no sign of her brother-in-law, Esteve Gramazie. A small man in a dark cloak sits in the far corner of the room. Once the bailie has opened proceedings the man stands up.

"May it please the court, I am here to represent the plaintiff, Esteve Gramazie, in this matter." It is obvious that this notary is known to the bailie, the latter simply nods in acknowledgement.

The argument is presented. Grazide cannot see how it has any substance. Then Magali is asked to stand.

"Did your husband write a will, madam?" says the bailie.

"No, sir. Not that I know of."

"And all his property and effects have come to you?"

"That is so. But it is my business that is carried on. I have a seamstress shop."

"Were you conducting this business whilst your husband was alive?"

"Yes, sir."

"In your name or in the name of your husband?"

"In his name."

The bailie is silent for a while, his head is down, studying his papers. Finally he speaks. "The plaintiff and defendant should withdraw whilst this matter is discussed in council."

Grazide and Magali make their way down the stairs to the market hall below. Esteve's notary does the same. They do not have to wait long before they are summoned.

The bailie does not look up once they are reassembled. His eyes are on his papers. "After deliberation the decision of this council is that Esteve Gramazie does have a right to the property and effects of his late brother, Adalbert Gramazie, as the only surviving adult male relative. The necessary transfer of ownership should take place in three months from now."

Grazide is stunned. Magali cries out and staggers, she could have fallen but Grazide catches hold to steady her. They are escorted out of the room.

Magali is in tears as they make their way slowly back to the house. "How can it be? It's terrible. What are we to do? The house, the business, my girls, all of you, we are ruined."

Back home the mood is sombre once the news of the court decision is out. "I cannot believe it," says Aurimonde. "How can they decide that? It's iniquitous."

"It is. Quite preposterous," says Grazide, "but we have to do something about it. There is something going on here, something nasty."

"How do you mean, nasty?"

"I think there are some people who have it in for Magali. They cannot accept an independent woman as head of an ostal, a woman running a successful business. I think they want to denigrate her."

"Who are these people?"

"I don't know. It must be some of the consuls."

"Bertrand de Castillon?"

"I'm not sure. He is a powerful man but I fail to see why he would have it in for Magali. Perhaps he was overruled by the others. You never know what shady politicking goes on."

"Is there anything we can do?" says Magali. She has regained some of her composure. "Can we appeal?"

Grazide can see that it is falling to her to take the reins. "I think so. Under the town charter there is a right to appeal to the higher lord. That would be the Count of Toulouse, probably to his seneschal, Pons Grimoard."

Magali speaks. "I don't think I could face that. How could I argue my case?"

"You could be represented. You are allowed to have someone to speak for you. A notary perhaps."

Aurimonde turns to her. "Grazide. You could do that. It surely doesn't have to be a notary." She claps her hands in enthusiasm. "You know all the ins and outs of the business. She would be good, wouldn't she, Magali?"

Grazide looks doubtful. "I'm not sure whether the seneschal would allow a woman to act. It's usually a notary, a man."

"But it does happen. I've heard of it in other places. You would be a woman acting for another independent woman. You could carry it off, Grazide."

So it is decided. Magali, with Grazide's help, lodges an appeal to the seneschal. He is to hear the appeal when he next visits the town.

The appeal hearing is quite different from the previous hearing in front of the bailie. Grazide has done her homework and has found many precedents for inheritance being directed to the wife of the dead husband. She calls witnesses who testify to the honesty and probity of Magali Gramazie. Her opposing notary does not call any witnesses so the seneschal calls on him to make his final address. He is brief for there is not much of a case for him to make.

At the end, however, he introduces a more sinister vein to his argument. "I would draw the seneschal's attention to the widely-known reputation of the Gramazie ostal. There are respected persons in this community who regard it as infamous. Many regard it as inappropriate that an ostal of women, headed by a woman, should be allowed to act independently without a man in ultimate control. I am able to reassure you, Seneschal, that my client is willing to exert that control. He will allow Magali Gramazie to continue to live in the house and to continue to conduct her business from there just so long as he retains control as the true heir of his brother's property and assets. In this way the common good of the community will be seen to be served." He sits down. There is a pause, the seneschal is quite still.

"Grazide Lamothe. Would you care to sum up your case for Magali Gramazie?"

Grazide stands. Her throat feels dry, there is a pounding in her chest. For a moment the words will not come. Finally she finds her voice. "Thank you, my lord Seneschal. I will be brief. You have heard from the witnesses that Magali Gramazie has a good reputation in this town. She is highly regarded as a woman of honesty and integrity. Her business is recognised as first class and she has many clients, both here

202

in Montalban and far and wide, who have testified to the excellent work that is done from her shop. You will know that it is a well-recognised custom that a woman can act on her own behalf. This may not be true in other lands but in this domain, in the County of Toulouse, a woman can assume the position of *femme sole*. Independent, taking her own decisions, making contracts and carrying out business. In addition there are precedents for the inheritance from a husband to a wife and that is surely what is right and proper. What the plaintiff is arguing for is an injustice, a travesty which goes against the freedoms that have long been held by women in our southern society. I would ask you to find in favour of the defendant and overturn the judgement of the previous court. Thank you."

She sits down and mops her brow with a silk handkerchief. She is sweating now. Magali squeezes her hands and whispers in her ear, "Well done. Thank you my dear Grazide. That was tremendous."

The seneschal is speaking. He summarises the arguments that have been presented to him. Finally he stands. "In this case I find that the appeal of Magali Gramazie is successful. My decision is final."

Magali lets out a gasp. Grazide is exhausted. They both stand as the seneschal leaves. As he passes Grazide he turns to her, a wry smile on his face. "Congratulations, madam. Is there no end to your talents?" He leaves the chamber.

There is relief and joy in the Gramazie ostal when they hear the news. That evening they all dine well; Beatrice has excelled herself in the kitchen. Aurimonde regales them with a vivid account of Grazide's performance. Even little Pierre-Guillaume joins in the merriment, happy to be included in the celebrations.

Grazide is about to put her son to bed when there is a knock on the door. Arnaude goes to answer it and ushers in a hooded figure, a woman. As she comes into the candlelight Grazide sees that it is Na Péronne, the consul's wife.

"Welcome Na," says Magali. "Can we offer you a beaker of wine?"

Na Péronne smiles. "No thank you. I must not stop but I have to speak to you, Grazide." Her face has become more serious.

"Me? What is it, Na?"

"Can I speak freely here?"

"Of course you can. These are all my friends."

"Very well. I heard of what happened at the seneschal's court today. You are to be congratulated. My husband told me what went on. It is he that has asked me to speak to you."

Grazide wonders why the consul is using his wife as an emissary. What is going on?

"Grazide. I have to warn you. There are people in this town that have taken objection to what you did today. Powerful people, some of them consuls."

Grazide feels defiant. "And is your husband one of these then?"

"No, he is not. He is doing what he can to restrain these people but it is difficult. He wanted me to tell you to be careful. It might be wise after today to be a little more retiring, a bit more discreet."

Aurimonde, who has been listening closely, explodes. "Discreet! What is all this about?"

Na Péronne's tone is sharp. "I think you know, young lady. There are those in this town who are not happy with what they think they see in this ostal." She turns to Magali. "I don't want to upset you, Magali, but I really think all of you must be careful. There are going to be changes in this town. Both my husband and I would not want to see you suffer in those changes. Now I must take my leave of you. I am sorry to interrupt your party."

Magali escorts her to the door and watches as she makes her way back to the square, her hooded figure dark in the gloom of the night.

When Grazide has put her son to bed she returns downstairs. Magali is sitting at the table, a single candle in front of her. The rest of the ostal has retired.

"Magali. I have to ask you," says Grazide as she sits down opposite the other woman, "is this a problem for you?"

"A problem?"

"Me and Aurimonde. Are we going to bring trouble on your ostal? I would hate to do that. If you want us to go just say so. Please be honest."

"Grazide. You coming here has been the best thing that has ever happened to me. You are part of the family, you and Pierre-Guillaume."

"Yes, but now it's me, Pierre and Aurimonde."

Magali smiles, reaches across the table and squeezes Grazide's hand. "And so it is and I am glad about it. You deserve some happiness, my darling."

"Thank you, Magali. I owe so much to you."

"Well, after today I think you've paid that off. I would have been ruined were it not for you. Goodnight, dearest Grazide." She kisses her and leaves the room whilst Grazide remains seated, deep in thought. The candle gutters and goes out.

CHAPTER 19
1231

It is two years since the signing of the Treaty of Paris which has ushered in an uneasy peace in the lands of the Count of Toulouse. The terms of that treaty are now widely known by most people. The County of Toulouse is much reduced and is no longer the powerful force that it once was. Montalban remains within the count's domain nonetheless but it is a substantially weakened town. Deprived not only of its walls but also many of its prominent citizens who have fled the threatened action against heretics that Count Raimond VII has agreed to undertake. With the disappearance of Pierre de Vals and other of his Waldensian brethren there is no one to maintain the work of the hospital. Gone also are most of the Cathar supporters. The Franciscan house has remained but it is not as well supported as in the past.

The papal legate, Cardinal Romanus, has directed all bishops and prelates to institute proceedings against heretics. In Montalban this has fallen to the Abbot of Saint-Théodard. He has demonstrated relish in undertaking this task but, like many other bishops and abbots, he seems to lack the organisation and efficiency needed to be effective. Until now no presumed heretics have been prosecuted.

Despite her success in defending the court case against Magali Gramazie, Grazide is well aware of the forces that threaten the ostal. Na Péronne's warning was apposite and all of them had taken notice of it, trying to keep as low a profile as possible in the town. Nevertheless there are instances of hostility from some people, a reluctance or tardiness in paying their bills, challenging the charges. It is noticeable that the Church, through its local prelates, is implicated in this enmity. On one occasion Grazide and Aurimonde had been refused entry to the Mass; for no particular reason the regular contract for work for the Abbey had been withdrawn.

Even Pierre-Guillaume suffers. Now growing into an active young boy he has many friends in the town with whom he can play; games of hide and seek in and out of the streets, making rudimentary model boats out of driftwood down by the riverbank, sometimes swimming in sheltered pools away from the current of the river. Then, for no apparent reason, he is excluded from the groups of youngsters. Grazide can see how much he is hurt by this. In her turn she aches with sorrow at the cruelty. She is sure that it derives from the antipathy that some in the town feel towards the Gramazie ostal.

It comes as a surprise then when one bright summer morning she receives a summons to the house of Bertrand de Castillon. A surprise because, even though he has not demonstrated any hostility to their ostal, the consul has made little contact with them over the last two years. She is ushered into the consul's study, a room full of papers, scrolls and books. Bertrand is seated at his desk. In the corner, sitting on a simple chair, is another man. Both stand when Grazide enters. "Please take a seat, madam," says Bertrand, indicating a stool on the other side of his desk. She turns to see who the other man is. "I think you know the seneschal," Bertrand smiles and indicates his visitor, Pons Grimoard.

Grazide blushes. "Of course. Good day to you, sir." She finds herself curtseying to the cloaked figure.

"Good day to you, Grazide Lamothe. It is a pleasure to see you again."

"Come on now," says Bertrand, "let's all sit down." He turns to Grazide. "The seneschal asked me to arrange this meeting so I think it's best if we ask him to explain why." He motions with an outstretched hand to Pons Grimoard. "Seneschal?"

"Thank you, consul." He turns to address Grazide. "I will try and explain the background to why I have asked to see you, madam. You will know much of what has been happening in the lands of the Count of Toulouse over the last two years."

Grazide nods but says nothing.

"The terms of the Peace Treaty," he continues, "are onerous, one could almost say humiliating. My lord, Count Raimond VII is seeking to comply with them yet retain his control for the benefit of all his people. You have seen how the walls of fortified towns have had to be dismantled, your Montalban for one."

Grazide looks across at Bertrand de Castillon. There is a grimace on his face.

"Toulouse as well. It has been very dispiriting, very dispiriting indeed."

"I can believe that, sir."

"Yes, well. The future is uncertain as well. The Count has no male heir, just a daughter, Jeanne."

Just a daughter, thinks Grazide, noticing the adverb.

"He has had to agree that his daughter should marry Alphonse, Count of Poitiers, who is, as you probably know, brother to the Capetian King of France, Louis IX. There is every likelihood that the County of Toulouse will disappear for ever, swallowed up into the Kingdom of France. But that is the future. There are other dictates that the Count has had to accept, not the least of which is rooting out any heretics left in the land. I am told that there are many of them."

Grazide cannot fail to notice the look on Bertrand's face. There is a stiffening of his features and a frown at the seneschal's words.

"The Count is determined to fulfil that obligation," says Pons. Grazide is surprised at this. The Count's toleration of heretics over the last ten years seems obvious to her. Is he now changing his attitude? "I have been directed to implement this on his behalf," says Pons. "There are other difficult obligations which have to be met. It is all going to be very difficult." He pauses, as if to collect himself. This is all very well, thinks Grazide, but why is he telling me all this? What concern is it to me?

Bertrand intervenes. "But it's not all bad, is it, Pons?"

"No, that is true. But I am coming to that. There is another matter which has been entrusted to me. It holds up some positive hope for the future of our afflicted lands." He leans towards Grazide, addressing her directly. "You may have heard of the new town of Còrdas, madam?"

Grazide has. Magali has had contracts with some people in the town, over to the east of Montalban. Built at the behest of the Count around nine years previously to replace a village destroyed in the wars. She nods.

"Còrdas was established with considerable rights granted to the people who settled there. It sits on a hill and has stout walls which have not had to be dismantled like these here at Montalban. I think the idea of such a new town was modelled on what happened here in Montalban when Alphonse-Jourdain was Count, back in the last century. Despite everything that has been going on the town has remained successful in these difficult times."

Where is this leading? thinks Grazide. She is soon to find out.

"The Count has been granted permission by King Louis to found other such towns. They are to be called bastides and will help to repopulate many of the areas devastated by the terrible wars that we have endured for the last twenty years or so. There is one stipulation, however. They are not allowed to have defensive walls. The King could not tolerate that."

Bertrand shows signs of becoming restless at this long preamble. Grazide knows him to be a man who prefers to get straight to the point. "With respect, Pons, I think you need to explain to this good lady why you are telling her all this."

"Yes. Yes, of course. Forgive me, Consul." He turns back to Grazide. "I have been searching out sites for possible new developments. Now I believe that you were born and raised in the town of Vilanòva, over to the north-east of here."

"Yes. That is right. I left there nine years ago."

"And I know that you are a skilled blacksmith. Those church gates that Bertrand here commissioned. Excellent work, quite remarkable."

"Thank you, sir."

"Well, Vilanòva was ceded to the Bishop of Rodez by the late Simon de Montfort after the collapse of the house of Morlhon. I expect you were aware of that."

Without a doubt, thinks Grazide, needing no reminder of what remains a painful memory for her.

"On behalf of the Count I have managed to regain the rights over Vilanòva from the Bishop. The Count has decreed that it should be the site of a new bastide of which he will be the founder."

This news is a surprise to Grazide. "But surely there is an existing village there. It was my home. A sauvatèrra protected by the Priory."

"Yes, of course. I have been there to see for myself. The new town, the bastide, will be built alongside the existing village. There will be a new charter which will apply to the whole of it, old village and new bastide. But I must explain why I have asked to see you. There will be much building to be done. The new people who move in will build their own homes and be able to pass them on to their descendants. They will only have to pay a rent for the use of the plot. When I visited the village I inspected the blacksmith's forge. It is very dilapidated. I was told that the young man who worked there had disappeared some years ago."

Pierre, thinks Grazide. Pierre Foulcaut. Son of the heretic goodman. What fate has befallen him?

"So, you see, Grazide, there is need of a new forge and a new blacksmith. I remembered my conversation with you and so I spoke to the consul here. He agrees with me that you would be just the person we need. I would like you to consider returning to Vilanòva to re-establish the forge and help to create a grand, new bastide. What do you say?"

Grazide is silent but her mind is racing at this unexpected offer. A jumble of thoughts, the first of which is what will Aurimonde think? Will she be willing to make the move? And what about Pierre-Guillaume? The Gramazie ostal is his home. How will Magali take it? Will she think that Grazide is leaving her in the lurch if she accepts the offer?

She looks at the two men. Part of her wishes she had never made those gates for Bertrand, then this dilemma that she finds herself in would have never arisen. "I don't know what to say, my Lord. This is a shock. I think I need time to think about it."

The seneschal's face betrays a trace of irritation. "Of course, yes. But don't take too long. The Count is anxious to move forward as quickly as possible. I have to leave after today so perhaps you could let me have your answer by the morning."

Precious little time to think about it, thinks Grazide, but a part of her, that impulsive side to her nature wants to accept. She tries her best to curb it.

"On what terms do you make this offer? Where am I to live? What about the forge?"

"We will build you a house once the plots are laid out. We can incorporate a forge as part of it."

"And the work? Will I be an employee of the Count or do I work for myself?"

"Either is acceptable. It can be negotiated in due course." Working for myself would be my choice, thinks Grazide. Already she is imagining what that negotiation might be.

"Very well. I will have my answer by the morning."

"Thank you, madam. Do give it your best consideration."

She curtseys once more to the seneschal. Bertrand escorts her out. At the doorway he says, "It is a good offer, Grazide. Think hard about it. Things are not going to get any easier around here."

An ominous warning, thinks Grazide. Probably best to take heed of what the consul says. He, above all people, is likely to know what the future holds for Montalban.

It is difficult to break it to Aurimonde. "Can you consider leaving here? Can we make a go of this?"

"And if I were to say no, what would you do? Would you turn the offer down?"

"Perhaps. I don't know. Are you saying no?"

Aurimonde snaps back. "I don't think you care what I think. You'll go your own way, won't you?" Grazide is silenced by this rebuff, she cannot find the words to say. Aurimonde stands up and leaves her sitting alone.

It is no easier to impart the news to Magali. The older woman's face falls. "I can't pretend that it won't be a blow to me. You do so much here. How would I cope?" then her tone softens. "But that is selfish of me. It is a great opportunity for you. How could I stand in your way? I suppose there will be others that I can find to take your place. But you, Pierre-Guillaume and Aurimonde, you are all part of the family. I shall miss you; the girls will miss you. Oh dear. I know that I am not making it easy for you."

Grazide puts her arms around her. "I understand. Of course I understand. We would miss you. These past few years have been the happiest of my life."

She does not know how to break it to Pierre-Guillaume. Her son is now seven years old. It comes as a surprise when he appears excited at the prospect of a move. "Great, Mama. We will have our own house. Will I have my own room?" His response is a relief to her.

Later that night she retires to her room. Aurimonde is already in bed, her back turned to her. "Are you asleep, darling?" This elicits no response. "Aurimonde, please talk to me."

Aurimonde turns over and stares at her. Grazide sits down on the edge of the bed. "The last thing that I want is for this to spoil things for us. You know how much I love you. I cannot bear to see you upset like this. I only want what is best for us both."

"So what is best for you has to be what is best for me. I just follow you on. Is that right?"

"No." There is pleading in her voice. "It must be for both of us. I do not want to lose you; I could not bear the thought of that."

Aurimonde sits up. "Look, Grazide. This is a great chance for you. I can see that. There is not much of a future for you in this town, I can read the signs. A chance to get away, I can see how that is good for you. But what about me? Where am I in this? Just to follow on? That is not an equal partnership, we are better than that. You say that you love me and I believe that. I love you, too, passionately, desperately but it seems at times that that entraps me. I have always been able, in the past, to make my own way, choose my own path.

213

Now I have chosen you but I cannot forget all that I have been, give it up, just for the sake of love. Of course I would but it could take its toll. I think my subservience would damage our love, maybe irrevocably."

There is a pause, the silence in the house is palpable. Then Grazide speaks, choosing her words carefully as if her future depends on what she says now. "I think I understand you. I am sorry. I can see how I have allowed myself to take your feelings for granted. What we have is too important for us to allow it to slip away, I could not bear for that to happen."

"Nor I. Come to bed, my love. Let us say no more now." Grazide acquiesces.

In the morning it all seems clearer. Aurimonde and Grazide agree that she should accept. They break the news to Magali who has the wisdom to agree that it is the best course for them to take.

"Thank you, dear Magali," says Grazide. "I don't think we shall ever have such a good friend as you."

"My blessings on you, all three of you. You will be missed, that is certain but I am glad for you. It will be a great new enterprise."

Aurimonde accompanies Grazide when she returns to the Castillon house. The seneschal is making ready to take his leave. "I am glad that you have accepted my offer, Grazide."

"We have accepted," says Grazide. "It has been a joint decision between the two of us, Aurimonde and me."

Pons allows himself a brief smile as he looks at the couple. "Yes, well, I'm sure that's good. My people will be in touch about the details. Much to be done, good day to you both." He mounts his palfrey and is soon gone.

CHAPTER 20

Géraud de Rabastens is a tired man. Making a long journey like this is getting too much for me, he thinks. No longer do I have a young man's energy. Now fifty years old he is the third son of Guy de Rabastens, a minor noble from a castle on the river Tarn, two days upstream from Montalban. All that is gone now. His father and elder brother were both killed at Muret, fighting for Count Raymond VI. Gilles, his second brother had been burnt as a heretic some sixteen years past. The castle and the surrounding village had been razed at around the same time.

He had been advised by the Count's seneschal, Pons Grimoard, to make the journey by river. "Somewhat safer by boat. Quercy is infested with brigands these days. I'll provide you with a couple of men as escorts."

He had been as good as his word. Now they are making their way up the river Aveyron. His two escorts, rough-looking men, help out on the oars from time to time. They make good progress, passing through impressive gorges, negotiating rapids. It is a long journey, even so. What possessed the Count to choose this far-flung village as the site of a new bastide, way out to the east of his reduced lands?

The seneschal had explained it to him. "Vilanòva. It's a village in the lands of the Lord of Morlhon, sadly lost in the wars. De Montfort passed the rights on to Pierre Henri, the Bishop of Rodez. The Count has been able to reacquire them in a deal made last year. That is where he wants a new bastide. It is a very run-down place, Géraud. Just a gaggle of houses around the church."

His commission is to survey the place and, if it is found suitable, draw up plans. He had done the same for the bastide of Còrdas some ten years previously. That had been a new urban construction on virgin land, a rocky hill. This would be a different kettle of fish, an existing village, a solid-looking church and a Priory. That could be tricky, he thinks. Dealing with the Church is never easy.

He has given good service to the Count and his father, Raymond VI, ever since he had moved to Toulouse in 1211. Much of his work has been to develop the impressive defences of the town but there had been, as well, plenty of work in upgrading and planning the infrastructure. And the young Count had been pleased with what Géraud had done at Còrdas. Both were equally distressed when the terms of the Peace Treaty dictated that the walls of Toulouse, Montalban and many other towns should be removed.

"There is a wall around this village," Pons had told him. "Not much more than a garden wall, really. There is to be no stronger defensive wall, though. It is not to be allowed. Vilanòva is a sauvatèrra, you know, a Peace of God place. Not that that has been much good to them. The place is plagued by brigands, I am told."

They have reached La Peyrade. "This is where you get off," says the boatman. "Vilanòva is half a day's journey to the north. Good luck to you and watch your backs through those woods." His words are not comforting to Géraud, glad of his two hulking companions. They make their way along a rough track that leads up from the river, following the boatman's directions. Different terrain here, thinks Géraud. Rocky, calcareous ground and scrubby vegetation. The trees here are not tall but are densely packed enough to make him glad of a clear path. Finding their way through the thick of the forest would be a nightmare. Already his surveyor's brain is sizing up the land. Seeking out good enough wood to build houses might be difficult in these parts. The trees, mostly scrub oak, are unlikely to provide trunks of timber that are long enough for construction.

They have been walking for about two hours when they come across a small hamlet, just a few scattered dwellings. On a mound above they come across a building, evidently a church. It is a tall barn of a place built in rough stone. Géraud's expert eye recognises it as an ancient building. He has seen others like it but they are few and far between. Probably built over five hundred years ago. Intrigued by this find he persuades his companions to have a break. They lie down on a grassy bank whilst he wanders around the building.

On the south side there is an arched doorway. He pushes open the door and enters the gloom. The only light comes from two or three apertures high up on the walls. He is aware of wall paintings on most of the surfaces but it is too dim to make them out. Here and there beams of penetrating light illuminate vivid splashes of colour but not enough for him to see the detail. The air inside is chill, despite the heat outside. An uncomfortable feeling overcomes him, he does not want to stay here any longer.

Collecting his two companions they make their way onward. On the edge of the hamlet they come across an old man. He is digging a hole but to what purpose it is difficult to see.

"Good day, fellow." The old man looks up, grunts and continues digging. "A fine church you have here."

"Oh aye," says the man. He stops digging, leaning on his long spade.

"What's the name of this place, sir?"

The old man coughs a rattling cough and spits on the ground. "Toulongergues, sir." He returns to his digging.

Géraud can see that he is not going to get much more out of the old man. He bids him farewell and the three travellers continue on their way.

Towards the end of the day they cross a rise and ahead they can see the tower of a substantial church, situated on an area of higher ground. It is surrounded on two sides by low, wooden buildings. "This must be the sauvatèrra of Vilanòva," calls Géraud to his companions. As they approach the village they can see smoke rising from some of the houses. Alongside the church are a few stone buildings, presumably the Priory, he thinks.

Pons Grimoard had told him that the Prior would be expecting him. They present themselves at the gate of the community and a monk escorts them to the Prior's chamber. Géraud notices that it is a small establishment, there are gardens to the east of the church but not much in the way of cultivation is noticeable. The cool reception that he receives from Prior Raimond does not surprise him. The Prior is an imposing figure, a tall man, his tonsured head and dark hair serve to emphasise his stern features. Perhaps such sternness is needed to

217

combat lax discipline in his community; Pons Grimoard had told him of troubles in the past. A senile old man, Prior Roger, who had allowed standards to slip is how he put it.

"Our guest room is at your service. Your two men can be put up in the village. We have made the necessary arrangements. Can you tell me how long your stay here might be?"

How much has Pons told the prelate of his assignment? He imagines that the prospect of a whole new town being built on the Priory's doorstep would not be all that popular. Perhaps for the moment it would be best to keep his cards close to his chest. "Difficult to say, Prior. Now that the Count has regained his rights over this village he wants the place to be surveyed. Just to keep the records up to date, you understand." From the expression on the Prior's face he can see that this explanation has not been convincing. Nevertheless Prior Raimond says nothing.

His chamber, as he had expected, is austere. A wooden bed and straw mattress. A small table and a single wooden stool. Géraud has been used to austerity in the past but faced with this basic lodging and the uncongenial welcome he has received he hopes that his task can be completed quickly.

He sets to work the following day, his only task being to survey the existing village and assess the available land to see if it is suitable for the construction of new dwellings. The church is the most imposing structure. There is a small marketplace at its western end. If there are to be possibly seventy new house plots added to the thirty or so existing dwellings, many of which are small and squalid, a larger central marketplace is going to be needed. He suspects that, in any case, the Count would not want the church as the centre of his new bastide. The design should reflect where the power resides. Géraud is experienced enough to understand such nuances.

Over the next two days he paces out the existing streets. Bit by bit he draws up a map of the existing village. He walks the perimeter of the village, examining the encircling wall. It is a poor structure, rough dry stone, collapsed in places and barely more than two cubits in height. The land falls away a little from the outside of the wall, some of it is cultivated but much of the remainder is scrub. The surrounding woods are not far away.

The church and Priory are placed on the south side of the area circumscribed by the wall, almost exactly halfway along. The village lies to the west of the church and occupies around one third of the whole area. To the east of the church are gardens and allotments, many are uncultivated and overgrown with brambles.

The measurements he makes are no more than approximations, once his map is complete there will be time for a later more exact survey, he thinks. He is able to outline an area for a possible new development on the land that is occupied by the gardens. It is good building land, well-drained and firm. He stares at the map and the boundary lines of the possible urban expansion. They make a pentagon, pointing east. In the centre of the pentagon he draws another whose sides are parallel to the larger figure but about one third of the size. This, he thinks, could be the central marketplace. Not a square but a five-sided area.

Then into his mind's eye comes an image. A shell. He has seen one carved on the walls of the church and on one of the houses of the village. Familiar to him, such carvings mark the pilgrimage way to Santiago de Compostela, the Chemin Saint-Jacques. Vilanòva is a resting place on one of the Chemin routes, the Via Podiensis. He has noticed the frescoes of pilgrims on the walls of the church. With his pen he inscribes on the smaller pentagon the site of the centre of his new bastide, Plaça des Concas. The five-sided shell of Saint-Jacques.

So intent has he been on imagining a new town on this area of overgrown gardens and scrubland that he does not notice a figure walking towards him from the direction of the church. A woman dressed in simple peasant's garb. She is bare-headed and her brown hair is cut short. "Good morning, sir," she says.

Géraud turns at the sound of the voice. Does he detect a beguiling note in its tone? At first glance she appears to be a young woman, an upright figure not bent by years of toil in the fields. As she gets closer he can see the lines on her face. Not as young as he thought, lines of experience no doubt. He returns the greeting but says no more. The woman persists. "You'll be a stranger here. Are you a pilgrim?"

"No, madam. Not a pilgrim."

"Well, you're not a monk, I can see that."

"My name is Géraud de Rabastens. I am here on the Count's business."

Her eyes widen for a moment. "The Count. That explains your fine clothes." She looks him up and down. Is she mocking me, he wonders?

"And you, madam. You are?" his voice trails off.

"Fabrisse Noguès. My husband is the sheep farmer round here."

"Well, I am pleased to meet you, Fabrisse Noguès, but now, if you would excuse me," he waves his arm weakly to indicate the land around him. She interrupts him.

"So what business does the Count have with Vilanòva? Are you planning a garden?"

"No. Just making some measurements, that's all." He dearly wishes this woman would go away.

"Measurements?" She raises her eyebrows. "What measurements?"

"Oh, this and that. Just for the records." He can see from her expression that she is not going to be satisfied with this explanation. Confound this meddling woman. He struggles to contain his irritation. The sooner that he can get away from this god-forsaken village the better. "Good day to you, madam." He turns away and walks towards the Priory.

Her meeting with this well-dressed stranger leaves Fabrisse frustrated. Her husband, Philippe, is away with his flocks on their summer grazing. She would have dearly loved to have been able to tell him about this unusual man that she found wandering around the village. Philippe would know what to do. He is one of the few people in Vilanòva who has prospered in the last decade. Since the death of Arnaud Lamothe he has been joint prudhomme with Guillaume Guiraud. It has been their lot to preside over the general decline in the village during that time. Perhaps the only saving grace has been the regular flow of pilgrims stopping off at Vilanòva on their journey to and from Santiago de Compostela. They are a steady source of income that has served to keep the economy of the village afloat, but only just.

Philippe has prospered, in no small part as a result of the investment made in his sheep business by Arnaud Lamothe before the latter's death. The daughter, Grazide, had taken her dying father south to be consoled by the goodmen and had never returned.

Soon afterwards Philippe's wife, Bethane, who had been Arnaud's mistress, had also died. A fever that had carried her off within days. The Lamothe ostal had been taken back by the Priory; subsequently rented out to Aimèry Targuier. Aimèry had returned to the village having left the band of heretics. It was said that when it came to the crunch he baulked at the idea of undergoing the consolamentum, becoming a heretic goodman, perhaps it was too much asceticism for him. Soon after his return he had married Margarethe, one of Grazide Lamothe's old companions.

It had been a surprise to Fabrisse when Philippe Noguès had proposed marriage to her. After being abandoned by Father Jean she had resigned herself to a life of widowhood. Taking up with the followers of the goodmen had given some purpose to her life but Galtier Foulcaut, the goodman and his companions had long since disappeared. She had not followed them. There had been rumours that they had been apprehended by the Bishop and Galtier himself had been burnt as an unrepentant heretic. She shudders at the thought of it.

Marriage to Philippe has worked out well. She was glad to discover that she had not lost her capacity to enjoy a good fuck. Her shepherd husband turned out to be a good enough lover, able to provide her with the satisfaction that she had missed in widowhood. Even her affair with the despicable priest had been disappointing, he had been smitten with the despicable *ejaculatio praecox* which left her in a permanent state of frustration. It was one of the brighter days of her life when he was carted off on the order of the Bishop and flung into jail.

No, she would have loved to tell Philippe about this man. Something is in the wind, she thinks to herself. Perhaps something that could be an advantage to them both.

Géraud has returned to Toulouse. There he gathers together all the notes and diagrams that he made on his visit to Vilanòva. Using his rough measurements, mostly made by the weary task of pacing out the village, he draws up a possible plan for the bastide. All in all it will create around one hundred dwellings, enough for a population of more than five hundred souls.

On the outside of the existing wall he marks out space for gardens. Outside the walls he draws field-plots, each one measuring three hundred by two hundred paces. There will have to be a considerable amount of forest clearing for the land for agriculture encroaches on the surrounding woodland. This will provide prospective settlers with ample timber for construction of their houses. Amongst the predominant scrub oak there are some good stands of taller oak and chestnut, trees large enough to provide the structural timbers.

He imagines that the charter for the bastide will follow that of his previous creation, Còrdas. The settlers will pay an entry fee and will be allocated a plot. On these plots they will build their own houses. After a rent-free interval (it was five years in Còrdas) they will pay an annual rent for the plot. Not a bad deal, thinks Géraud. It was certainly popular in Còrdas.

In his clear hand he writes a title for his plan across the top of the paper, '*A new Bastide for Vilanòva*'. Pleased with his work he sends for a jug of wine. Time to relax at last.

The following morning he presents himself to the offices of Pons Grimoard, the Count's seneschal. To his dismay he learns from the seneschal's steward that Pons is away. "He is at Montalban, sir. As he is likely to be there for a couple of weeks he left word that you should join him there. I can make the arrangements."

Géraud curses inwardly. Another tiresome journey is not welcome even though it is but two days by horse. He tries to force out a smile. "That would be kind. Thank you."

The steward arranges for a palfrey, a mule and an armed companion. "The seneschal asked that you attend him at the house of Bertrand de Castillon. It is on the main square of Montalban. I will send him word that you will be arriving at the end of this week."

Géraud spends the rest of the day getting his papers and the masterplan together. They are packed together into a box that will be strapped on to the mule that will accompany them to Montalban.

The journey is uneventful. No signs of brigands or any other impediments. This is a much-frequented highway, thinks Géraud, likely to be safe in daylight hours. Towards the evening of the second day the town comes into view. He notes the collapsed walls, dismantled like those of Toulouse. They find their way into the town and head for the central square. He sees a pair of imposing metal gates in front of the church. An elaborate design, almost Moorish which is surprising. Once in the central square he spots an opulent house. This must be the Castillon ostal.

He is right. He is escorted inside and taken up wooden stairs to a large room on the first floor. Impressive carpets and wall hangings, clearly this is a man of rich tastes. From the corner of the room comes an imposing figure; he wears a damask cloak with fine gold stitching along the seams. He is holding out his hand, Géraud takes it. "Welcome. May I introduce myself? Bertrand de Castillon. I am very glad to offer you hospitality."

"Thank you. I am told that I have to meet the seneschal, Pons Grimoard, here. Is that right?"

"Absolutely. Pons is staying here with us. He is out at present. But come, you must be weary after your journey." He flicks his fingers and a servant comes forward. "Please show our guest to his room."

He addresses Géraud once more. "You will join us for dinner? We shall eat in a couple of hours. I will have one of my people call you. Now please go and get some rest."

His room is a marked improvement on his cell in the Priory at Vilanòva. Small, nevertheless, but the bed is comfortable; there is a small desk and a table in the corner on which rests a small jug of wine and some bread. The servants have brought up his box and other effects. He pours himself a small beaker of wine and stretches out his limbs on the bed. Within minutes he is asleep.

He is woken by a gentle knock on the door. It is dark, he must have slept for some time. A servant enters carrying a candle which he sets down on the table in the corner. Its weak light is just enough to dispel the gloom. "My master requests the pleasure of your company at dinner, sir. Would you like to follow me, please?"

Back in the main room a table has been set out for a meal. Crowded around a log fire are members of the family. Two figures detach themselves from the group, Bertrand and the seneschal, Pons Grimoard.

"Ah, Géraud," says Bertrand. "I trust you are well rested. Here is the seneschal."

Pons Grimoard comes forward. Géraud is taken aback. It is only a few months since he last saw the seneschal but his appearance is much altered. He seems like a man who carries a heavy burden, more stooped, slower in his movements. His face is set in a fixed expression, worry lines that had not been evident before are plain to see. The seneschal holds out his hand. Géraud notices a marked tremor. Something is clearly wrong.

"Good to see you once more, Géraud. I trust that your journey was not too wearisome."

Does he mean the last two days' journey or the expedition to Vilanòva? "No. Not too wearisome."

"I imagine you have much to tell me but that can wait until tomorrow."

"Come, gentlemen," says Bertrand. "Let us eat."

The whole company settle down and the meal is served. Géraud discovers that he is unusually hungry but notices that Pons eats very little, just a few vegetables and bread. The seneschal's duties cannot be easy, he imagines. It looks as if they are taking their toll.

Towards the end of the evening Pons takes him on one side, away from the others. "Can we meet in the morning, Géraud? I am anxious to know what you made of Vilanòva. I hope you have good news for me. The Count is particularly keen that this project should succeed."

"I think you will like it, Seneschal, but let it wait until the morning. There is much to discuss."

"Agreed. Also there is someone that I want you to meet. A remarkable person who is possibly going to be crucial to the whole business."

Géraud is intrigued but by now too tired to pursue the matter. He takes his leave of the company and returns to his room. He is soon asleep.

The following morning finds Géraud, Pons and Bertrand de Castillon standing around the table in the main room. Géraud's sketches and plans are laid out for inspection.

"Here is the layout of the existing village. You can see that it is dominated by the church of the Holy Sepulchre. An impressive building. It is an important resting point on the Chemin Saint-Jacques which passes through the village. There are a fair number of pilgrims that take that route."

"That'll bring the money in," says Bertrand. "Regular income, just what is needed."

"Indeed so," says Géraud. "I have to say that the village is pretty run down otherwise so that income must be important."

"As long as it goes to the community and not to the Church," says Pons. "It is something we have to keep a careful eye on."

Géraud returns to the map. "As you can see the whole village and the gardens to the east of the church are surrounded by a stone wall. It is a feeble affair, collapsed in some places and certainly no kind of defence."

"That is good. The Count has agreed that defensive walls are not to be built."

"You know this village is a sauvatèrra. The limits of the sauvatèrra protection, such as it is, are marked by four stone crosses on the outside of the town. I have marked them on the map." He points to the small cross marks that are spread equidistantly around the village.

"What about water?" says Bertrand. "Is there a stream through the village?"

"No, no stream. The village is raised on a small elevation above the surrounding land. There is one well, situated here. In the square in front of the church."

"There'll have to be more wells dug then," says Pons. "One well is never going to be enough."

Géraud is anxious to move things on. "I have had a careful look at the ground to the east of the church, still enclosed by the boundary wall. It is a larger area than the existing village and is given over to garden plots, both for the village and the Priory. Mostly neglected and overgrown. The ground, however, is good. Limestone bedrock, perfectly suitable for taking buildings."

"So what are your suggestions then, surveyor?" says Pons. "Is it a feasible project?"

Géraud does not answer immediately. "You can see that I have outlined the area to the east of the village and the church. It forms a pentagon, pointing towards the east. Here is my suggested plan."

He pulls out the large sheet that he has titled '*A new Bastide for Vilanòva*'. The two other men bend forward to inspect it more closely. "I have placed the central market square here," he points to the Plaça des Concas, "except that it is not a square. It is also a pentagon which mirrors the larger pentagon of the whole area. A main street passes from west to east through the central plaça. Here are secondary streets at right angles to the main and here are alleyways that divide the whole

226

area into rectangular islands. Each island can hold two uniform plots, each of which can take one dwelling. All in all there could be another seventy dwellings in the new bastide to add to the thirty in the existing village. One hundred dwellings, maybe six hundred people, a substantial town." He stands back from the table hoping that he has not let his enthusiasm sound too triumphalist.

"One hundred dwellings. That is quite something," says Pons, still staring at the plan.

"That'll generate a tidy income for the Count," says Bertrand. Ever the businessman, thinks Géraud.

Géraud returns to the plan. "The central plaça is large enough to accommodate a market hall, perhaps with offices above. It moves the centre of the whole town away from the church and the Priory."

"That may not go down well with the Prior," says Pons.

"Too bad," says Bertrand. "Times are changing, your Prior will have to go along with it."

"I fear he will," says Géraud. "I think he knows that something is in the wind. I tried to remain discreet about the purpose of my visit to the village but he could not hide his anxiety."

"Géraud," says Pons, "I think the Count will be well pleased with this plan. May I take this now? I am due to have an audience with him back in Toulouse at the end of next week. I would imagine you will be returning tomorrow. This is good work; well done, surveyor."

"Thank you, Seneschal."

"And now there is someone that I want you to meet." He addresses Bertrand. "Has our visitor arrived yet?"

Bertrand calls over a servant who disappears downstairs. A few moments later he reappears and ushers in the visitor.

Géraud has been speculating as to who this other person might be. He is surprised to see that it is a tall woman. Strong face, dark hair and penetrating green eyes. She is dressed simply but carries herself with an air of quiet dignity. Bertrand is smiling. Pons steps forward to greet the newcomer. He turns to Géraud.

"Géraud de Rabastens. May I introduce Grazide Lamothe?"

CHAPTER 21
Lent 1232

Grazide had been relieved when she received the summons to the de Castillon house. Since her last meeting with Pons Grimoard she had not heard a word. Perhaps the seneschal had changed his mind. She recognises that he is going out on a limb, choosing a woman to be the blacksmith to the new development. There is no doubt in her mind that others may well be pressing him to engage a man. More appropriate. Less scandalous.

"Do you think I can trust Pons?" she says to Aurimonde. "We've heard nothing from him."

"Seems to me like a man of his word. Don't fret, my love. I'm sure he'll be in touch soon."

"I hope so. I want to get on with this, now it has been decided."

Aurimonde puts an arm around her lover. "Do I get the feeling that you have doubts about this venture? It would not be surprising."

Grazide turns to look her in the face. "Perhaps. I know I can do it but I haven't been in the forge since making those gates."

"I think you will be fine. Your skill will not have disappeared."

"There'll be a huge amount to do. I worry that I shall not be able to cope."

"Don't worry, my love. You fret too much. You can always take on a couple of apprentices."

A thought comes to Grazide. "What about you? How do you see this fitting in with your life?"

"Not blacksmithing," says Aurimonde, laughing. "I'm not cut out for that but I can turn my hand to most things. I don't think for one moment that there'll be nothing for me to do."

As requested Grazide attends the de Castillon house on the appointed day. A servant escorts her upstairs to the main room. Three men are standing around a long table. On its surface she sees papers, drawings and documents. Pons Grimoard detaches himself from the group and comes forward to her. Straightaway she notices a change

229

about him. He seems to have aged rapidly since their last meeting. With difficulty she restrains herself from staring too hard. She looks away and her gaze meets that of Bertrand de Castillon. He gives her a brief smile and inclines his head, a small gesture of welcome. Pons is speaking to the third man. "Géraud de Rabastens. May I introduce Grazide Lamothe?"

A short man, grey haired. She estimates that he must be around fifty. He wears a dark cloak, looking a bit threadbare. He is unsmiling but she notices kind eyes. She offers her hand and Géraud takes it; he has a soft grip. "I am pleased to meet you, madam." She can see from his face that he is mystified as to why this woman has been summoned to meet him.

Pons is speaking. "Géraud here is our surveyor." He waves a hand over the papers on the table. "This is all his work. He's just back from Vilanòva."

She feels a momentary jolt in her chest. He has been to Vilanòva. She wonders what is happening there, in the village of her childhood.

"Yes, indeed," says Géraud, still looking at her with a quizzical gaze.

"I had better explain," says Pons. "Grazide was born and raised in Vilanòva, were you not, madam?"

"Yes, sir. I left around ten years ago and have lived here ever since."

"I fear you will find the place changed," says Géraud. "It seemed very run down to me." That does not surprise Grazide but she says nothing. "I have asked Grazide to help us in this project," says Pons. "We shall have need of a blacksmith if we are to see seventy new homes being built. You may be surprised to hear that this lady is a very talented and capable smith. Her late father was the blacksmith in Vilanòva and he trained her. She is a quite remarkable craftswoman."

"I expect you noticed the splendid church gates," says Bertrand, "designed and created by this lady here. Quite superb."

Géraud looks doubtful. "There is sure to be a great deal for a blacksmith to do. Heavy work for a woman."

"You need have no worry," says Bertrand, laughing. "This lady is quite up to the task."

Grazide is feeling uncomfortable. This male appraisal is unsettling, almost patronising. For a moment she wishes she had Aurimonde with her.

"Come and see these plans," says Pons, taking her arm. "I think you will be impressed."

Grazide takes in what is laid out on the table. Pons is enthusiastically pointing out the projected design. The surveyor, who has drawn up these plans, is silent.

She is impressed. This new bastide will transform the village that she once knew. Immediately she sees the shift in focus that Géraud's projected plan entails. An expression of where power is going to be in the future. Away from the Church. She smiles with approval.

It appears that Géraud has noticed that smile for he leans over the plan. "You see, madam. The bastide will be a pentagonal design. The central plaça will also be a pentagon. It is the shape of a scallop shell, the emblem of Saint-Jacques, appropriate for a town which is an important stopping off point on the Via Podensis." He steps back, a proud smile on his face.

There are many questions. They discuss the project for over an hour. By now Grazide is excited, her doubts about her ability to take on her part in the project are banished. She is pleased to notice that the surveyor equally seems to have lost his doubts about her and her capability.

Pons speaks. "It has been agreed that we will build a house, and a new forge for Grazide. This will have to be one of the first projects once you have surveyed and mapped out the actual plots, Géraud." He addresses Grazide. "How much space will you need for the forge?"

Grazide looks at the plan, trying to imagine how it will look when constructed. "I think probably one plot for the house and another for the forge. Can they be adjoining plots so that they can be all one construction? Perhaps best to be on the edge of the town, because of the smoke and noise."

"Absolutely," says Géraud. "That seems sensible." He points to a spot on the plan. "Perhaps here. That would be on the edge but would have good street access."

Pons now outlines a timetable. First an initial announcement of what is planned, followed by publicity in the surrounding area. "We want to get as many people as possible to commit to the plan. There will be a founding ceremony, a Pau, on the first day of September and the Count will attend. After that the plots will be marked out by you, surveyor. I would hope that building will start later this year." He turns to Grazide. "We will find you and your family accommodation in the existing village which you can use whilst your house and the forge are being built. That will be our first priority." Grazide is pleased that he uses the word 'family'. At least the seneschal has recognised that their ostal will be the three of them, Grazide, Aurimonde and Pierre-Guillaume. Will they receive a similar broad-mindedness when she returns to her home village? she wonders.

Within a week the formal announcement is made. A member of the seneschal's staff journeys to the village and at the appointed hour stands up to address the inhabitants assembled outside the church. They listen intently.

"Good people of Vilanòva and of all the lands of the Count of Toulouse around. Be it known that his honour Raymond VII, the Count of Toulouse, is to institute a new town, a bastide, here in Vilanòva. The land will be surveyed and plots will be laid out. Any person, free or peasant, will be entitled to rent a house plot, a garden plot and, if so desired, a field plot. Each person will be free to build their own house on their plot. That house, and all their property, will be their own by right and they will be free to pass it on by inheritance,

232

by sale or by gift. Everyone who chooses to live in the bastide will have many freedoms granted in a charter that the Lord Count will draw up. On the first day of September this year there will be a founding ceremony, a Pau. That will be your opportunity to swear an oath of allegiance to the Count and apply for plots in the new bastide by payment of a fee of accession. You will then have one year in which to complete the building of your house and for the first five years of occupation your rental payment will be waived. All those of you who already live in the village are free to apply for a new plot if you so wish. If you remain in your existing house, by payment of an annual rent and by swearing an oath of allegiance, you will be entitled to all the freedoms and benefits of the bastide granted by the charter that will be drawn up."

These terms have been written out on a parchment which is then nailed to the door of the church of the Holy Sepulchre. There are not many in the village who are able to read it but those that are lettered read it out for the illiterate. Heralds are despatched to surrounding hamlets and manses to further advertise the new bastide.

In Vilanòva itself the announcement is received with a mixture of surprise and confusion. The two prudhommes, Guillaume Guiraud and Philippe Noguès, had been informed the day before the public proclamation, as had Brother Raimond, the Prior. The prudhommes find themselves overwhelmed with questions from the people of the village, most of which they cannot answer.

"I'm sorry," says Guillaume to a gaggle of men who have surrounded him as the public meeting breaks up. "I know no more than you. I agree this proclamation is very sketchy; there has to be more detail but I think that it is a great step forward for our village."

This is not received with universal enthusiasm. "How many new houses are going to be built?" says Aimèry Targuier. "We could be swamped with newcomers."

"At this stage we do not know," says Philippe. "They are sending a surveyor from Toulouse who will draw up plans. Then we'll know."

"Will we be able to see these plans?" This is Aimèry's wife, Margarethe.

"Perhaps. I am not certain."

"I'm certain we'll have no say in it," grumbles another. "The bloody Count will do what he likes. He won't take any notice of us."

The Prior has the advantage of a private audience with the seneschal's emissary. He is able to raise his own concerns. "I am worried about the status of the Priory. Will we still receive the taxes from the market as has been the practice since our Priory was founded? Then there is the question of the rents from the existing houses. Will we lose those?"

"I am unable to tell you, Prior. It may be that you will have to be supported in other ways. I can tell you that there will be a new, larger marketplace which will be under the Count's jurisdiction."

"And what about tithes? And the income from pilgrims?"

The man's voice has become testy. "I think you will find enough to survive. It is not the Count's intention to ruin the Priory let alone to upset the Church." From observing the other's face the emissary can see that Prior Raimond is unconvinced but the prelate says no more.

It is inevitable that rumours and scare-stories flourish over the next few weeks. These are fomented by the reappearance at the beginning of May of Géraud de Rabastens, the Count's surveyor. He arrives on horseback with a number of armed men and a baggage train of mules carrying surveying instruments, chains, poles, hammers and all that is needed to mark out the ground plan of the new bastide. Géraud starts his work by taking more accurate measurements of the area to the east of the church where the new bastide will be erected. With these measurements he draws up a revised plan and carefully delineates the lines of the streets and alleyways which then determine the placement of the house plots.

That completed he starts to mark out the plot on the ground, starting with the new marketplace. Poles are hammered in, distances are measured with chains and measuring rods. The whole process takes

234

some weeks to complete and is watched with considerable interest by the people of the village. Once completed Géraud summons the two prudhommes, Guillaume and Philippe. "My survey is done. There will be enough plots for seventy-two new dwellings as well as a provision for a new blacksmith's forge. You may be interested to hear that Grazide Lamothe is to return as the Count's blacksmith."

"Grazide Lamothe?" says Philippe. "She hasn't been heard of for nine years now. Why on earth has a woman been chosen?"

"Where has she been?" says Guillaume.

"As far as I have been told she has been in Montalban since she left here" says the surveyor, "Her father died. Perhaps there was no reason for her to return."

"Well, she was a handy smith when she worked in her father's forge, I'll grant you. Has she been working in Montalban?" says Philippe.

"Not all the time but I did see some impressive work that she did two years ago."

"With seventy-two houses to go up there'll be a huge amount of work for her to do here. Are you sure she's up to it?" says Guillaume.

"The seneschal is confident. We are building a substantial forge. She will be able to take on apprentices to help with the work."

Géraud is anxious to end the meeting. It is getting late and in the morning he sets off to return to Toulouse. "Gentlemen, there will be a chance to answer your further questions. The seneschal's man will be visiting about once a month to update you on progress, right up to September when the Pau will be held. Good night to you both."

Word comes to Grazide towards the end of May. A house in Vilanòva has been made available for them. The seneschal wants work to start on building the new forge and their adjoining house as soon as the Pau has been declared. They are urged to leave Montalban as soon as possible. Pons Grimoard is supplying transport and an escort party. Pierre-Guillaume is especially excited that he is going to be provided with his own pony for the journey, he appears to regard it all as a great adventure.

There is limited time to pack up. In addition Grazide has to purchase a set of tools for the future work in the forge, uncertain as to what remains in her father's old forge in Vilanòva. Such hardware is hard to come by in Montalban, the town blacksmith shows no enthusiasm for letting any of his implements go. She has to send to Toulouse for most of what she needs, hammers, pincers, pliers and the like.

The day of departure comes. A clear, bright morning in midsummer. Grazide has been dreading the moment of taking her leave of Magali and her daughters.

The older woman takes her in her arms. "Go well, dear Grazide. I am sure you all will prosper. We shall always remember you. You will ever be in my prayers, you, Pierre-Guillaume and Aurimonde." She kisses her fondly then turns to Pierre. "Come here, my little man." She hugs him and the boy's face reddens with embarrassment. "Look after your Mama. She is a very special person."

Finally she and Aurimonde embrace, tears flowing from the latter's eyes. "I know that all will be well for the two of you," says Magali quietly. "Do not let anything, or anybody, come between you, whatever happens." Aurimonde nods her head, wiping the tears away from her cheeks but unable to speak.

Grazide is glad to be setting off at last. She has never been able to banish the thought that Giufré might return any day. Now he will not be able to find us, she thinks to herself. It is a weight off her mind.

The journey is long but uneventful. Sometimes they are able to stop at taverns, more often they have to set up camp for the night. The seneschal has provided a good escort, five armed men and enough equipment and supplies to sustain them.

She is sickened to see the state of the land that they pass through. From time to time they come across villages that have been destroyed, houses burnt to the ground, fields and vineyards overgrown and untended. The road takes them over a high limestone plateau.

They spot shepherds' caselles but they are never occupied. Little sign of sheep, the land has indeed been ravaged by the wars.

They are setting up camp in the small hamlet of Toulongergues. Their escort leader tells her that there is only one day's journey left before they arrive in Vilanòva. Grazide knows this. She remembers the journey she made to the destroyed castle of Morlhon, the discovery of her two dead brothers. It all seems so long ago, a lifetime almost.

She remembers that there is an old church on higher ground above the hamlet. The men are preparing an evening meal. She turns to Aurimonde and Pierre. "Come and see the church. It is an ancient building. I used to come here when I was a girl." She wonders whether they are going to find it undamaged. It is quite possible that the crusaders might have found it a good target. Equally it would have made a good shelter for the local people in times of attack.

There is no sign of damage to the church. It still stands, a tall imposing hulk of a building, like a gigantic stone barn. They enter through the door on the south side, leaving the door wide open to allow the evening light to pour in.

Grazide remembers seeing wall paintings when she had visited as a girl. In those days she did not understand what they depicted, her predominant memory is of simple, primitive images painted in bright colours, reds, ochres, blues.

"Look at these paintings," says Aurimonde. Grazide can hear the awe in her voice. Pierre-Guillaume says nothing, he stands in front of a bas-relief sculpture that shows a middle-aged man, bearded, wearing a loincloth and accompanied by a child.

"Who is this, Mama? Why is he carrying a knife?"

She remembers. "It is the story of Abraham and Isaac. From the Bible."

"Is that the story of how God tells him to sacrifice his son?" Pierre shudders. "I hate that story."

237

Grazide seeks to distract him. "Look at these pictures, Pierre. Can you see that one? An eagle has caught a hare, he is holding it in his talons." What is the significance of that, she wonders.

She turns away. Aurimonde is standing, staring at an image, high up on the north wall. It is a naked woman; her arms are raised. Even though the depiction is primitive the sense of rejection is obvious. She stands beside a leafy tree, the Tree of Knowledge of Good and Evil. "The poor woman," says Aurimonde, almost whispering. "I know how she feels."

Grazide puts her arm around her lover and squeezes her. She wonders what is going through Aurimonde's mind. A momentary chill courses through her. "Come on, let's get back to the camp." The feeling of disturbance is becoming oppressive. She kisses Aurimonde on the forehead, anything to break the spell.

That night Grazide's sleep is disturbed by dreams. Half-remembered but disturbing. She is back in Vilanòva but it is not the familiar place that she once knew. The streets are straightened out, the houses are lined up in rows. Her father is there, wielding a heavy hammer in the forge. She is standing in the street watching him. Next to her stand her two brothers, Guillaume and Pierre. They stand upright but are disfigured by awful wounds on their arms and bodies.

She turns and looks down the street. She is staring at the figure of Aurimonde, naked, her arms lifted upwards. Grazide tries to run towards her but it is as if she is wading through thick mud, she can hardly move. Then the figure changes, no longer is it Aurimonde, it has dissolved into the figure of a woman in a long dress, wearing a cloak. She knows who this is, it is the image of the pilgrim woman that adorns the wall of the church of the Holy Sepulchre in Vilanòva. She is smiling at Grazide. A feeling of warmth floods the dream. Now Grazide can move freely. She runs towards the woman but as soon as she approaches her the image disappears. She is left staring down the long, straight street. Grazide cries out in desolation.

It must have been a real cry for she is awake now. Aurimonde is looking down at her. "What is it, my love?" she says. Grazide cannot speak, tears seeking to dissipate the agitation that she feels. Aurimonde holds her in a tight embrace until the crying ceases.

They arrive in Vilanòva the following afternoon. There are few people about to notice this small party of horse riders and pack animals. They dismount in the square in front of the church. Aurimonde stares around her at the squat, wooden houses, the mud-covered streets. "It's not much of a place, is it?"

Grazide cannot answer. It is not the place that she left, some nine years ago. The village seems to speak of neglect, of being uncared for. It was never like this before, she thinks.

A robed figure appears from around the side of the church. Grazide stares at him, then recognition dawns. "Brother Raimond, is it you?" He is older, of course he is she thinks, will he remember me?

"Grazide Lamothe. Welcome" says the Prior. "So many years, your poor father. We wondered what had befallen you."

"Much. And you, are you now the Prior?" The monk nods in assent.

She takes Pierre-Guillaume by the hand. "This is my son, Pierre-Guillaume. Say hello to the Prior, Pierre."

"Your son. What a charming boy, and with his uncles' names." Grazide can see that he is framing the next question. She interrupts to forestall him.

"And this is Aurimonde de Sella, my companion." She indicates Aurimonde, standing next to her.

Prior Raimond turns towards the shorter woman. There is a trace of confusion on his face. "Good day, Aurimonde de Sella. Welcome to Vilanòva."

"Thank you, Prior."

For a moment there is silence. Grazide breaks it. "Seneschal Grimoard informed you of our arrival, I believe. He told us that you would arrange accommodation for us."

The Prior appears to gather himself together. "Yes, yes of course. We have a vacant small house for you. Not your previous place, I'm afraid. That is now leased to Aimèry Targuier and his wife, Margarethe."

"Aimèry and Margarethe," Grazide laughs. "Well, there's a surprise." A couple of dreamy customers, she thinks, probably a good match.

The Prior summons his steward and instructs him to show the party to their temporary dwelling. It is not large, just two rooms, a thatched roof that looks as if it needs repairs, floors covered with reeds. Pierre-Guillaume looks worried. "Is this where we are going to live, Mama? Not much of a place, is it?"

"It's only for the time being, darling. We are having a new house built for us. It will be much nicer than this." Pierre continues to look disgruntled.

Later that evening, Pierre is asleep in the adjoining room, their luggage has been unloaded and is stacked in the corner.

"You're very quiet, Aurimonde, my love."

"Hmm."

"Are you upset?"

"Upset? No. It's not," she pauses, "it's not quite how I imagined. I didn't like that Prior. He was looking at me very strangely."

"Oh, don't worry. He was always a good man. He tried his best with father when he was ill."

"I don't think he approved. Of us, I mean."

"He probably thinks you're just a friend. I don't think it worried him." From her expression Grazide can see that Aurimonde is not convinced.

The following day the three of them make their way to the forge. Grazide is dismayed at the state of it. There are large gaps in the wood-tiled roof. The anvil is intact but there are scattered broken implements lying around the floor. She pulls on the arm of the bellows to discover a leak in the leather which renders them useless. "There's a lot to be done here just to patch it up," she says. "The sooner they build a new forge, the better. This is pretty grim."

Outside they encounter a woman. She grasps Grazide by both arms. It is Fabrisse.

"Grazide! How wonderful to see you. My goodness, what a beautiful woman you have become. And who are these?" She is looking past Grazide at Aurimonde and Pierre-Guillaume.

"Fabrisse. This is my son, Pierre-Guillaume, and this is my companion, Aurimonde."

"A son! How delightful." She bends down to address Pierre. "What a strong little chap you are." Pierre turns away in embarrassment at this effusive woman.

Fabrisse stands up again and holds out her hand to Aurimonde. Grazide can see that she has correctly apprehended what 'companion' meant. "So good to meet you, Aurimonde." She looks closely at her. "A good pair you make, I have no doubt." She is unsmiling.

"Thank you," says Aurimonde. Then she deliberately moves across to Grazide and puts her arm around her lover's waist. "That we are. A good pair."

There is a pause. Fabrisse claps her hands together, as if to break the momentary tension. "You won't have heard, will you? I'm now Fabrisse Noguès. I've married Philippe."

"You and Philippe!" Grazide's voice cannot conceal her amazement. "But what of Bethane?"

"Sadly she died. Soon after you left us. She had returned to Philippe."

Grazide tries to imagine all this going on. "So are you and Philippe getting on? Are you happy?"

"Blissfully! He's doing very well these days, quite prosperous. Did you know, he's now a prudhomme along with Bethane's uncle, Guillaume?"

Grazide is more interested in hearing that Philippe Noguès has now become a prosperous shepherd, wondering how much her father's share-cropping investment might have contributed to that revival of his fortunes. Maybe a subject to return to later.

Fabrisse prattles on, talking to Aurimonde. "Being married to a shepherd is not a bad thing. He's away a good bit of the year so he doesn't get under your feet. Then when he returns, wow!" Grazide hopes that Pierre-Guillaume is unaware of the woman's allusion.

"I'll tell Philippe you've arrived. He will be home this evening. And you are coming back to be our blacksmith. How about that? There are going to be big changes in sleepy old Vilanòva, to be sure." She is staring at Aurimonde, a fixed gaze of appraisal.

Grazide is glad enough when she takes her leave. "Come on," she says. "We must go and see what the surveyor has done." The three of them make their way out of the village towards the site of the new bastide.

The ground has been cleared of its previous overgrowth. Everywhere are stakes set in the earth and lines of rope that delineate the streets and the building plots. Grazide has a copy of Géraud's plan with her. On it is marked the site of their new home and forge. Using the map they work out where it is on the ground. On the south side of the development, two rectangular plots side by side. Their short ends face on to an alleyway, a street runs alongside the longer side of one rectangle. Grazide can picture how it will be. Substantial room for a forge, it should be able to accommodate three anvils and a furnace large enough to serve them. Her spirits begin to lift. She turns to Aurimonde. "This will be ours. Our house. Our ostal." She puts her arms around Aurimonde and Pierre-Guillaume as if to urge them into sharing her excitement.

On their way back to their lodging she stops at the church. "Come inside and see," she says to them both. As they step into the narthex she spots a figure in the corner. He is dressed in rags, his body contorted. He holds out a begging bowl. She reaches into her bag to find a coin and gives it to Pierre-Guillaume. "Give this to the poor man, darling."

As the boy approaches the beggar looks up. Grazide is shocked to see that it is Gervais Targuier, her childhood friend, brother of Aimèry. She is about to speak when she realises that he does not recognise her. Pierre-Guillaume drops the coin into his bowl, it makes a quiet ring that echoes around the narthex. Grazide says nothing. They pass on into the church.

Later that week the seneschal's man makes one of his regular visits to Vilanòva. Grazide outlines the repairs needed to make the old forge serviceable. She will need it as soon as the Pau is declared and incomers arrive to build their houses. He makes all the arrangements for the necessary work to be done.

In addition he brings with him a document for Grazide. It is the suggested terms of her appointment as the Count's blacksmith to the new bastide. Pons Grimoard has agreed that she should be an independent agent. Her new house and the forge alongside, along with all goods and equipment, will be her entitlement. She will be liable to pay a rent for the land that she occupies but this will only be levied after the first five years of her occupation. Inhabitants who have work done by her in the forge will pay her direct, a scale of charges will be drawn up. In the meantime the Count will pay her a generous retainer.

Grazide and Aurimonde agree that these are good terms but Grazide wants one change to be made. She writes back to the seneschal asking that both she and Aurimonde should share the title as equal partners. There is a delay in receiving a reply but when it comes it contains Pons Grimoard's agreement. Grazide is relieved.

"It is important to us, Aurimonde. I am determined that it is established that we are a couple. We are an ostal and we are partners. I want that to be known."

Aurimonde looks worried. "Will they accept it? You remember the trouble it caused in Montalban. Will it not be the same here?"

"It may be but I am determined. I want what you and I have, what we are, to be recognised."

"So do I, my darling, but I am worried how it will work out."

"It will work out fine. I think you will find that this place is different from Montalban. They may not have the sophistication of the town but there is an old sense, a sense of fairness, of acceptance, here. At least, there used to be. I hope it remains."

That evening they have a visit from Philippe Noguès. He is accompanied by his fellow prudhomme, Guillaume Guiraud. The latter is warm in his greeting to the daughter of his erstwhile friend, Arnaud. "He was a fine man, your father. I hope his soul is at rest. Did you find the goodmen?"

"Yes, I did. He died very soon afterwards."

"And you didn't return."

"No. It seemed there was nothing to return for. Life has changed for me."

"So I see. A fine boy you have now." The unasked question hangs in the air.

Philippe appears more subdued. Grazide is sure that she can guess why this is. "Congratulations on your marriage, Philippe. Fabrisse seems very happy. She tells me you are doing well."

Philippe frowns. "Tolerably well, thank you." He does not elaborate.

"That is good to hear. It seems the rest of the village does not share your good fortune."

"I know," says Guillaume. "We have suffered over these past few years. People have died, others have left. We do our best."

"So what do you think of the new plans? The Count's new bastide. Exciting, is it not?"

"I hope so," says Guillaume. "There are some folk who do not welcome it. Philippe and I think it is a good plan but we have trouble convincing some people."

"Is there interest from around and about? Seventy new dwellings is going to take some filling."

"I think so. From what I've heard there will be a good number bidding for plots in the new development."

"How about you? Will you be one of them?"

"Probably not. I'm happy enough with my old place. I think I'll stay put."

"How about you, Philippe?" says Aurimonde. "Are you going to? Fabrisse seemed quite enthusiastic."

Philippe speaks slowly. "Perhaps. Fabrisse wants to, I know. She thinks our place is a bit run down. She's probably right."

"It would be a good deal for you, surely," says Grazide. "You could afford to build a very smart house."

Philippe frowns. "Perhaps so. I don't know. I'm away a lot."

Grazide laughs. "Come on, Philippe. A new wife, you must put her in a smart new house."

This appears to be too much for the shepherd. "All right, Grazide. I know we have something to discuss. Can we get it over with?"

Grazide's tone becomes gentler. "Relax, Philippe. I imagine you are talking about my father's share-cropping deal with you, is that right?"

Philippe nods but says nothing.

"As far as I'm concerned that contract was with my father. Since he has died I wish to make no claim on it. It was between you and him."

A look of relief spreads over Philippe's face. "You mean that? That is very generous of you, thank you, Grazide."

"I have no need of his share, Philippe. Let's leave it at that." She reaches forward, arm outstretched and they shake hands.

The tension released the four of them chat on about the forthcoming Pau. Philippe and Guillaume have been told that the Count himself will be present. "And also the Bishop of Rodez, though I think he'll have gritted teeth. I'm told he is not at all happy at the deal that has been made which restores the rights of this place to the Count," says Philippe. "It's going to be fun to watch." Grazide can see that the bishop is not a popular man in the village. She is not surprised at that.

After they have gone Aurimonde turns to her, "That was very generous, what you gave him. By rights your father's share should go to you."

"I know, love, but it won't go amiss to spread a little bounty about. We don't need that share, not with the deal that the Count has granted us."

Aurimonde laughs. "You're a crafty woman, Grazide Lamothe. Come here and kiss me, you wily politician!"

Even so Grazide wonders whether she has done the right thing. She lies awake whilst Aurimonde sleeps beside her, feeling her lover's body pressed tight against her. Will the gesture that she made to Philippe have the desired effect? Can she buy a reputation like that? Are they destined to be the subject of infamy, the way that Magali was, back in Montalban, she worries.

CHAPTER 22
September 1232

It is the first day of September, the day of the Pau. Autumn comes early to these southern lands. The trees are turning, browns through to vivid reds. In the few vineyards that remain the vendanges will soon begin. There is still a warmth in the air.

It had been confirmed that the Count himself, Raymond VII, would be present at the ceremony. Some are amazed that such an illustrious person would ever deign to visit their small village. Fabrisse is ebullient. "The Count, coming to Vilanòva. How wonderful!"

Grazide can guess how her mind is working. Fabrisse, wife of one of the two prudhommes, surely she will be presented to the noble Lord. "I'll have to smarten Philippe up a bit," she says to Grazide. "Philippe is busy putting his ewes to the tup at the moment. He can't turn up in his filthy working gear."

Grazide imagines that such a project will not meet with much enthusiasm from Philippe. Perhaps at least she will be able to get him to wash before receiving the comital handshake.

The Count had arrived on the previous day. A large party, fifteen mounted knights accompanied their Lord along with fifty foot-soldiers and a considerable baggage train. Camp was established on flat land to the east of the projected bastide. Aurimonde and Pierre-Guillaume had found a good vantage point to observe the arrival of the procession.

Aurimonde had been surprised at the Count's appearance. Still a young man, unbearded and with that cast of face that speaks of noble birth he had appeared, even so, to be a burdened ruler. He did not smile, even when cheered by the small crowd that had gathered to meet him. When he dismounted she could see how slight he was. War and politics had taken their toll on Raymond VII, Count of Toulouse. She was surprised that he had made this journey to an obscure little village. Perhaps he attached great importance to the project.

Pierre-Guillaume had been visibly excited by the jamboree. Returning home with Aurimonde he had rushed inside to his mother.

"Mama! I saw the Count. There were hundreds of soldiers, lots and lots of horses. It was fantastic!"

Grazide's mind went back to all those years ago. Her brothers, equally enthralled at the prospect of military service, of fighting, of glory. Surely her own son was not going to be seduced in the same way? "That's good, Pierre, but the Count has done with fighting. There is now peace, that's why he has come here. To help us all live in peace."

As she spoke these words she wondered whether they were true. What is it with young men? How easily are they stirred up into violence, how simple for their leaders and rulers to recruit them into meaningless conflict. She did not want her own son to grow up into this farrago of masculine vaingloriousness but how to prevent it? That old lie 'boys will be boys' came into her mind. She had always been determined that in bringing up her own son that calumny would be exposed.

Today people have been arriving in great numbers from before dawn. The villagers are emerging and crowds gather on the site, east of the church, where the outline of the new bastide has been so carefully marked out. In the area where the central plaça is to be a long table has been erected. Three clerks, each with a large sheaf of papers in front of them, are seated at the table. The seneschal's man moves between them, giving last minute instructions. Armed soldiers line the sides of the area. There is no sign of the seneschal, Pons Grimoard, nor of his master, the Count. A quiet hum rises from the crowd.

From the camp to the east a fanfare of trumpets sounds. The morning sun illuminates a procession that is wending its way to the central plaça. It is headed by two enormous soldiers carrying pikes. Behind them come two men, one carrying a long, thick stake, the other bearing a wooden shield-like shape and a heavy mallet.

Then come the worthies. The Bishop of Rodez, preceded by a cross-bearer, is followed by Prior Raimond and the new parish priest, Hugues Dubois. After them come the two prudhommes, Philippe and Guillaume, both looking very uncomfortable to be in such exalted company. Grazide notices, with a wry smile, that Philippe has indeed

248

been smartened up by Fabrisse, he looks quite presentable. They are followed by the Count's seneschal. Grazide cannot fail to see how his health has deteriorated. He hangs on the arm of a servant and walks with small, stumbling steps, his facial expression fixed and staring. In his right hand he carries a stick, she can see the tremble as he uses it to steady himself.

There is a small gap in the procession before a dozen knights, on foot, precede the mounted figure of the Count, astride a magnificent destrier, a huge warhorse draped with cloths of purple and gold. Finally come two flag-bearers. One carries the colours of the Count, a yellow cross on an orange background. The other displays a flag bearing the Lion of Morlhon, emblem of the displaced lord of the area.

The whole company arrive at the site of the plaça and the Count dismounts. For a moment silence falls on the whole crowd, a cock crows in the distance. The Count steps forward to address the crowd. Grazide is surprised to hear his voice. She had expected a strong, firm masculine tone. Instead he speaks in a light, high voice, a trace of a stammer is evident.

He does not speak for long, just enough to announce a new bastide of which he will be the sovereign lord. There will be new freedoms, a new prosperity and opportunities for all his subjects. He steps back and the men with the stake and shield come forward. A hole has been dug in the bedrock and a platform has been erected beside it. The stake is hammered into the ground. It stands firm, six cubits high. The shield which bears the Count's coat of arms is fixed to the top. The Pau has been erected.

A herald steps forward bearing a rolled parchment. He unrolls it and reads out in a strong, loud voice the terms of establishment of the bastide. Every man who wishes to settle in the town must swear allegiance to the Count, pay the accession fee of ten Toulousain livres and will then be allocated a building plot. The house that they construct must be of sound design and its construction must be completed within one year. In due course the Count will grant a charter to the new town and a governing body of a bailie and four consuls will be appointed. All those wishing to accept the Count's invitation to settle in the new bastide of Vilanòva should now present themselves. The herald steps back.

No one moves at first. There is a murmuring amongst the assembled crowd. Finally a man strides forward and is directed to the clerks at the bench. This breaks the logjam and others follow. Soon there is a long queue, waiting to be processed at the clerks' bench. The Count and his retinue return to their camp. The Pau is over.

Later in the day a giant feast has been prepared. Benches are laid out in the square in front of the church. There is food and wine in abundance, plenty enough to enhance the excitement that the day's events have engendered. Many clutch their contracts of accession, showing them to their friends, comparing their allocation. There is little rivalry, all the plots are the same size and shape, an equality which has a significance that many have yet to grasp.

"It will be a great town!" This is Philippe whose tongue has been somewhat loosened by the drink. "Just imagine the wonderful houses, the wide streets and the magnificent plaça. What a place to live."

The feasting continues until the evening draws in. The crowds disperse, many have a long journey back to their hamlets and manses. Grazide and Aurimonde are left outside the church. Pierre-Guillaume has returned to one of his friends' houses, they will collect him later.

Grazide takes Aurimonde's hand. "Come with me." She leads her into the church. It is deserted and nearly dark. A single candle burns on the altar in the eastern apse, just enough light to find their way. Grazide guides her to the northern apse. It is just possible to make out the frescoes on the walls. She stops in front of the image of the pilgrim woman.

For a while she remains motionless, her eyes fixed on the image. Aurimonde stands next to her. The light from the candle flickers in the growing dark, creating shadows that dance on the walls of the apse.

"Why have you brought me here, my love?"

Grazide does not reply immediately. It is as if she has lapsed into some kind of trance. Eventually she speaks. "I have always believed that this painting is my mother. I don't know why. I have no memory of her but I do know it is her."

Aurimonde looks harder at the image. There is no doubting the gentleness of the portrait. She slips her hand into Grazide's and squeezes.

"I have always been able to feel her love, all my life. For many years I had no idea where the feeling came from yet I knew it was there. Now I know its source. It is a bitter-sweet feeling. I have it yet I have never known the person from whom it came."

Aurimonde turns her gaze from the picture to look at her lover's face. There are no tears, no smile. It is a face set in certainty, almost a face at peace.

"Is this what you wanted me to see? Is this why you have brought me in here?"

"There is more. I want to tell you, Aurimonde my darling, that I now know what that love is for. All these years I have held it within me. Yes, there is my love for Pierre-Guillaume. That is a burning, welding love that binds me to him. It is beyond my control. But this other love has need of an outlet. Now I know. It is that love that I give to you. Freely, abundantly, without condition. In that love I am yours, I am yours forever."

Aurimonde is silent. Tears now roll down her cheeks. She does nothing to wipe them away.

"Aurimonde," says Grazide. There is a gentleness in her voice, a firm gentleness. "Can you be mine as I am yours, forever?"

Aurimonde swallows hard, her voice choked. "Darling Grazide, I am yours. Never in my life have I known such love as I bear for you. I can."

"There is something that I dearly want to do. We cannot be married in the way that man and wife are married, but we can make vows to each other. We have no need of priests or witnesses, we can do it alone, together. Are you willing?"

Aurimonde hesitates. She turns to look at the picture, then says, "With all my heart. I am willing."

So there, under the unseeing gaze of her mother Grazide and Aurimonde exchange vows, vows to love each other, care for each other, share for as long as both will live. Their contract is sealed with a kiss, a long, all engulfing, unifying kiss.

Neither of them knows where this simple act is destined to take them.

END OF PART TWO

PART THREE

INQUISITION

CHAPTER 23
1232

As some had predicted, the establishment of a new bastide at Vilanòva turns out to be remarkably popular. Within a month of the ceremony of the Pau more than half of the plots have been reserved and the accession payments have been made. Most have come from folk who live elsewhere, from hamlets and manses spread far and wide. The attraction of the promised freedoms and rights that will be granted to the settlers is too good to resist.

The seneschal has arranged for the old forge to be patched up; soon it is in working order. Grazide feels strange as she walks into the renovated building. There are so many memories but the most overpowering of them is that of her father, patiently teaching her the rudiments of the smithing trade. For the first time in recent years she misses him.

She anticipates that there will be an immediate demand for ironwork once people start building so prepares a stock of hinges, iron bars for doors, tools of all kinds and nails of all sizes. The Count's men have arranged a consignment of 'blooms', pig iron bars each weighing around thirty pounds. These are transported in batches of six, some coming from as far away as Castile, raw material for Grazide to work on.

Well aware that she is going to need help with all the work that has to be done, she recruits two young men as apprentices, two brothers, Josèp and Lois. Their father, Andrieu Fauré, is one of the first to sign up for a plot in the new bastide. The Fauré ostal plan to move from the hamlet of Toulongergues, the two brothers glad to find employment. Grazide is a good teacher so they learn fast. Soon the old forge is ringing with the tones of hammers on metal.

Meanwhile work is starting on the construction of the new forge and the adjoining house for Grazide and Aurimonde. The seneschal is well aware that this must have priority and be completed as quickly as possible. A workforce of ten carpenters and builders is recruited. They soon set to work. Blocks of stone are hewn out of a nearby quarry and laid out to form a firm foundation for the walls.

Woodworkers search the surrounding forests for stands of tall trees. They can provide trunks of a length that can be cut into beams. First they climb the trees to thin out the crown and cut off the side branches, this to prevent the trunk from splitting when it falls. The wood gathered is used for kindling or is collected by the charcoal burners. Then the woodworkers set to work to fell the trunk with their heavy axes. The sounds echo throughout the forest.

Carpenters use axes to square up the trunks, marking out the lines of cut with string soaked in ochre. Piece by piece they cut away the surplus wood. Finally, using hand axes they finish off the work to end up with a strong, well-formed beam. These beams are then transported to the building sites. The framework of each wall is laid out on the flat ground, the joints are fashioned and fastened with stout pegs of wood, 'tree nails'. Where the greatest strength is needed iron straps are hammered in with metal nails. Gradually the superstructure emerges.

The wooden constructions are hauled into the vertical, their feet sunk into square holes cut into the foundation blocks. Once all the woodwork is in place the spaces between the stanchions and the transoms are filled with cob, a mixture of compressed clay and straw. Window frames with pointed arches are made in wood, enough to provide good light in all the rooms. The ridge of each house runs along its greater length. This allows rainwater to flow down into the androne, the narrow gap between each of the house plots.

Aurimonde watches the construction of their house with particular interest. "I remember my father building our house back in my home village. I was fourteen at the time. Most people used reed thatch for their roofs but my papa was not going to settle for that. He used clay tiles. He taught me how to tile. I loved that. I became pretty good at it in the end."

Grazide is impressed. "You, a roofer! Well I never. We must have a word with the foreman. Maybe they could use some help."

258

"Do you think so. I'd love to give it a go."

The foreman has initial reservations. "I'm not sure if a lass can do this work," he says, but Aurimonde's persuasiveness overcomes his reluctance. He agrees to give her a trial.

Aurimonde presents herself the following day. She has found herself a man's short tunic, just falling above her knee, woollen hose to her mid-thigh and stout boots. "I can't scramble around on the roof in my long tunic," she says to Grazide. The tunic is sleeveless, exposing her arms, soon to become tanned in the bright sun. She appears oblivious to the comments that her masculine dress attracts from the other builders, half a lifetime spent as a travelling player has habituated her to ribald heckling.

The foreman is impressed. She shins up ladders and scrambles along the roof timbers like a monkey. She is even able to carry a hod of heavy tiles, nearly as many as the male workers can manage. Soon she is busy, nailing the flat clay tiles into neat rows, overlapping each row to make a watertight covering. Barrel tiles are used along the ridges. It is a neat job and Aurimonde completes both roofs within a month. Despite this facility for the work she is aware that some of the other roofers do not welcome her presence among them. On occasions she finds her tools going missing, once she is trapped on a roof when her ladder is taken away. These are petty aggravations though. Once she has had a word with the foreman they die down.

Harvest-time is over; most of the new settlers who have sworn an oath of fealty to the Count and paid the accession fee have started work on constructing their houses. Unlike the house that Grazide and Aurimonde are to occupy, theirs are single storey, built in wood. Many settlers who are moving into the bastide demolish their existing dwellings to re-use the materials in their new building, transporting beams of wood and cob material into the new town. Where they can afford it they copy the example of the blacksmith's house and roof their houses with tiles. The seneschal's steward has arranged for a kiln to be constructed on the outskirts of the town. Although much of the surrounding terrain is calcareous rock there are patches of marly ground that serve as a source of clay for the tile makers.

It is hardly surprising that Aurimonde finds her skill as a roofer in great demand. She likes nothing better. "It is good for me, contributing to the income of our ostal." Grazide is happy to agree. The extra revenue will enable them to furnish their house more lavishly.

Grazide herself is busy in the forge. Nonetheless both she and Aurimonde find time to prepare the garden plot that they have rented, just outside the perimeter of the bastide. Their allotment, known as a cazal, measures twenty by twenty-five paces. The ground lacks fertility, being very stony. They dig over the entire plot and work in large quantities of manure. Guillaume Guiraud, who owns a pair of oxen, is a good source of supply of the latter. Pierre-Guillaume with his small barrow-load of well-rotted manure becomes a familiar sight in the streets of the new development. Grazide is still able to find time to teach him to read and write, passing on the skills that her father had encouraged her to acquire.

But not everything goes on as swimmingly as the construction of Grazide and Aurimonde's house. Some of the incomers do not appear to have the skills adequate enough to construct good dwellings. There are a few examples of sub-standard huts and lean-to's appearing on some of the plots. The seneschal's men are alert to this, in some cases demanding that people dismantle their ramshackle constructions and start again, encouraged to seek help from others that have more skill. As time goes on good building practices are disseminated, there is a greater uniformity in the houses that are springing up.

All this does nothing to help weld the join between the existing inhabitants of Vilanòva and the incomers. Aimèry Targuier is particularly vociferous, surprising in such a mild man. "It's going to ruin our community, all these newcomers. Pushing us out, taking away our livelihoods, it's a bloody disgrace."

His dreamy wife, Margarethe does not contradict him. Her life is taken up with their three young children, twin girls and an infant boy. "I leave all those matters to the menfolk," she says to Fabrisse Noguès one day. "They are better equipped to deal with these things."

But these are the growing pains of a new community. As time goes on they lessen in their intensity. Within a year of the Pau the first houses are completed. Philippe and Fabrisse are ready to occupy their grand, two-storey house that fronts on to the plaça. It announces how prosperous the shepherd has become these days. Even so Fabrisse cannot get her new husband to dress in anything other than a peasant's garb. She herself is now the proud possessor of a fine wardrobe of dresses and cloaks. Befitting, she thinks, a woman married to a prosperous sheep farmer.

Most of the building plots are now allocated and never has there been such a hive of activity as is now seen in Vilanòva. It is not just the house building, the main streets are paved, new wells are dug which is not an easy task in such rocky terrain. The town wall is repaired but not to a point that could be regarded as defensive, that is not allowed.

Naturally most of the inhabitants will work the land. Each is able to rent a sizeable plot of land known as an arpent. There is much assartage of the surrounding woodland needed to provide enough land for around fifty arpents. In addition some of the plots are terraced to provide for the planting of vineyards. The dry, stony terroir is known to be excellent for the growing of vines. Aurimonde is one of the new settlers who opt to rent land for the cultivation of grapes. Her previous experience in the wine trade in Montalban stands her in good stead.

The weekly market is now established in the Plaça des Concas, the centre of the new bastide. Some of the house plots on the plaça are occupied by shopkeepers; butchers, grocers, drapers amongst them. Their frontages on to the plaça form a shopfront from which they can carry on their trade. In addition there are two or three fine houses, rivalling the Noguès domicile in size, which are occupied by merchants who have moved into the new bastide. Vilanòva is situated on the Via Podensis, one branch of the pilgrimage route, the Chemin Saint-Jacques. This makes it not only a stop for pilgrims but also for

261

traders passing from the east to both Toulouse and the river systems that flow to ports on the west coast. The speed of transition from a sleepy, clerical-dominated peasant village to a thriving and burgeoning town, augmented by the new merchant class, is startling. Its success in rejuvenating the whole area is a matter of pride to most of the inhabitants.

However this new prosperity and civic optimism is not matched by the fortunes of the Priory. Brother Raimond's early anxieties that the new bastide might deprive the monastic house of its revenue prove to be well-founded. Not only is the revenue from the existing market run by the church appropriated by the new comital market in the Plaça des Concas but there is a growing resistance to the payment of tithes to the Church. The new secular authority of the Count leads the bastide dwellers to resent the old ecclesiastical levy and many refuse to submit to it. The authority of the Bishop of Rodez has been diminished, as has his ability to exert his control over the people of the new town. Even the new priest of the parish, the Northerner Hugues Dubois, is unable to influence his parishioners. He refers to this fiscal rebellion in some of his homilies but it is clear that his heart is not in it. How can he succeed where the Bishop and the Prior have so manifestly failed?

The end result is that the Priory is becoming run down. The monks are, by now, mostly quite aged; when death intervenes they are less than likely to be succeeded by younger recruits. It all amounts to a crisis in ecclesiastical confidence.

Grazide, for her part, has resumed a regular pattern of attendance at Mass. She likes Father Hugues Dubois, a most welcome successor to the disgraced prelate, Jean Vital who now languishes in an episcopal prison in Rodez. She remains as sensitive to the prevailing clerical misogyny as ever but finds little of it in the new priest. He has an air of toleration about him, unusual in men of his calling. More particularly he never appears to be critical of her domestic ménage, a welcome observation that is nonetheless surprising.

It is now two years since the declaration of the Pau. Over that time most of the building plots have been allocated. The population has grown enormously. No longer a paltry village it has become the prosperous town that its founder, the Count of Toulouse, must have hoped for. Paved streets and well-constructed houses testify to that aggrandisement. There is an air of confidence about Vilanòva which must be pleasing to him, a man who must have been demoralised by the strictures of the Treaty of Paris.

As has been promised a town charter is drawn up. It allows for the appointment of a bailie and four consuls, each to serve for one year. The former is the local representative of the Count. It is to these five appointees that the governance of the town is delegated. It comes as an unpleasant shock to the original inhabitants that none of their number is appointed as consul. In particular Guillaume Guiraud and Philippe Noguès, prudhommes in the old village, are overlooked.

What comes as a greater surprise to the community as a whole is that one of the four consuls appointed is Grazide Lamothe, a woman. There are grumblings amongst some of the people when this appointment is announced. Most of these cavils are petty misogyny. Some who do not know Grazide wonder how could it be expected that a weak and mindless woman could take on such an important role?

A more sinister opposition makes itself known the day after the announcement. A deputation of four men, all incomers to the new town, presents itself to the bailie. Its spokesman is a gruff merchant, one Donat d'Arnal and himself an appointed consul. Donat is new to the town. One of the new breed of hard-headed businessmen that have emerged since the wars; men who have found a way to exploit the economic growth of recovering communities like Vilanòva.

"Bailie," he says, "we wish to protest at the appointment of a woman, Grazide Lamothe, as consul."

The bailie, a tough character quite used to disputations, looks unimpressed. "Oh yes? And on what grounds do you protest at the Count's appointment?"

"It is most unusual for a woman to be appointed to such a post. It seems to us to be inappropriate and dangerous."

"It may be unusual, Consul Donat, but this is a novel project. Unusual decisions may be made. The woman, Grazide Lamothe, has exceptional capabilities; she was also born and raised here so she represents a link with the existing community."

"There are other considerations."

"And what may they be?" For a moment the merchant does not reply. He turns to his companions as if to look for permission to continue. He receives brief nods of encouragement.

"The woman in question lives in an ostal which is, shall we say, somewhat irregular."

The bailie's voice becomes firmer. "The Count and his seneschal are perfectly aware of the lady's domestic arrangements. She lives with her companion and her young son. There are many women in such situations; so many men have been killed in the wars. There is nothing irregular about it."

"With the greatest respect, Bailie, there is more to it than that. Their ostal could become, indeed has become, the subject of scandal. We would not want this great project of the Count's, this bastide, to be threatened in any way."

"What are you implying, Consul? What scandal?"

The consul smiles, a weak thinning of the lips. "It is said that the two of them, Grazide Lamothe and Aurimonde de Sella, are more than companions. They live together as man and wife. Surely such immorality should exclude her from taking office."

At this point one of his fellow consuls, Lucatz Barasc who has been becoming visibly agitated blurts out, "They're a pair of sodomites, it is well known."

Donat glares at the companion, perhaps he is aware that this outburst is not going to help. He turns back to the bailie, "Please excuse Consul Barasc, Bailie. As you can see, feelings run high in the town."

"Oh yes?" says the bailie. His face has taken on a thunderous look. "Is this town to be governed by popular prejudice? I do not think that the Count or his seneschal would be pleased to hear that. That will be the end of the matter. The Count's decision is not going to be overturned. Grazide Lamothe will remain a consul."

It is not an auspicious start for Grazide. She never gets to hear of this deputation to the bailie but she has no difficulty in recognising the antipathy that comes from her fellow consuls, particularly Donat d'Arnal. "He's a difficult man to deal with," she says to Aurimonde after the first consular meeting, "but then I should be pretty used to that kind of thing by now. He will just have to get on with it."

She is not aware of the full nature of Donat's antipathy, supposing it to be the kind of casual misogyny that permeates society. By now she has learnt to never allow such common prejudice to trouble her. She knows that her appointment has the approval of Pons Grimoard, the seneschal, even though he is hardly ever seen in Vilanòva nowadays.

Then an episode occurs that is to shake her equanimity. Aurimonde, returning to the house one afternoon, finds Pierre-Guillaume sitting alone in the kitchen. Grazide is still working in the forge. He does not look up when Aurimonde enters.

"Hello, Pierre. Are you here? I'd have thought you'd be out with your friends." He does not move. She notices that he is red-eyed, he has been crying. "What's the matter, love? What are these tears for?" She sits down beside him and puts an arm around him. She feels him stiffen. "Come on, Pierre. You can tell me." He says nothing but lets out another sob. She squeezes him and he relaxes a little. He lets his head rest on Aurimonde's shoulder. As she turns to look at him she notices a swelling below his left eye. It seems to be visibly increasing in size. "Have you been in a fight, Pierre? What's been going on?" He says nothing but nods his head.

"Who've you been fighting with? This is not like you; you don't get into fights."

"Other boys," his voice is indistinct.

"Oh, Pierre! What was it all about? What started it?"

Pierre-Guillaume pulls himself away from her. No longer crying, his face has darkened. "It's you and Mama. It's your fault." For a moment Aurimonde is taken aback by the venom of his tone. This is not like Pierre.

"They called me a bastard. They said I was a son of sodomites. Then they started punching me." He breaks down in tears again. Aurimonde goes to hold him once more but he shrugs her off. Her mind is racing. Who are these boys? A chill runs through her mind. Is this what is being said about her and Grazide? Have these ruffians picked up on it?

"I am so sorry, Pierre. This should never happen to you."

He shouts, "Well, it has happened. It's not fair. It's not my fault you two…" he breaks off, appearing unable to complete what he is saying.

"Us two?" says Aurimonde. "Come on, you can say it."

"I don't know. I don't want to talk about it. Leave me alone."

She pauses. Perhaps she should not persist. "At least let me bathe that eye. It's a nasty swelling." The boy allows her to administer to him. After bathing his face she finds some goose fat to apply to the swelling. No more words are said.

Grazide is distressed when she returns later to find her son in this state. "What's been going on?"

Aurimonde puts her finger to her lips. "I'll talk later." His mother can see how upset Pierre-Guillaume is. After they have eaten she puts him to bed. The boy is clearly exhausted.

Alone together Aurimonde relates what the boy has told her. Grazide is incensed. "I don't mind if people talk about us. That we are used to. But for Pierre to be dragged into it. That is too much."

"It is hateful but what can we do? Can we have these boys punished for it?"

Grazide looks doubtful. "That is very difficult. I imagine that all we can do is teach Pierre-Guillaume how to deal with these bullies. He must stay out of their way."

"They used that awful word. Sodomites. Do you think Pierre understands what that means?"

"I doubt it, but I am sure he knows it is not complimentary."

"Is that what we are, you and me? Sodomites?"

Grazide cannot answer. Her mind is racing, thoughts are tumbling over each other. She tries hard not to panic. In her heart she knows that there is nothing evil about her relationship with Aurimonde. How could there be? The love she feels for her partner transcends any such idea but it is wounding to hear that it is debased by people in her own community, her neighbours, the people she works with, even her fellow consuls. A loving relationship between two women is nothing new. Why should it cause such affront here in Vilanòva?

Perhaps some people fantasize about her sex life. Perhaps that causes the revulsion, the prejudice that they experience, she and Aurimonde. Using that word 'sodomite', that seems to suggest why they attract opprobrium from some in the town. The physical love between the two of them is something beautiful, something good. How can that hurt others? They both know that they are enriched by it. Grazide knows that for her and Aurimonde it is both natural and fulfilling.

Perhaps it is because they are women? Grazide has little experience of male same-sex relationships but is worldly-wise enough to know that they are quite common. She hears talk about such liaisons occurring in monasteries. By the way it is spoken of it appears to be acceptable. Perfectly obvious that monks should behave in that way.

But not for women. The more she thinks about it the angrier she gets. Are women like her and Aurimonde hounded down because they dare to be women, dare to expect that the society in which they live should deal with them as fairly as they deal with men?

Surely it has not always been like this? In the past, here in the south, she has always believed that life has been gentler. For women as much as for men. An old, accepting tradition which she sees as being swept away. She is aware of the agencies that have brought about this change; the wars of the last two decades with the subsequent imposition of Northern lordship and culture, and the Church, obsessed with Adam's rib, whose whole structure is predicated on that story of male dominion. It need not be so. Perhaps it was not always so. Perhaps there once was a gentler age, an age of acceptance where women could claim a more equal place in society.

That night she and Aurimonde make love passionately. It is as if it fulfils a deep need for both of them, a refuge from the threats to their love. Afterwards Grazide lies awake, exhausted but content. Aurimonde lies beside her, naked and asleep, her head resting on her partner's shoulder, their legs intertwined. For this moment at least Grazide feels at peace.

A week later the consuls are summoned to a meeting with the seneschal and the bailie. By now the covered market in the plaça has been completed, together with offices for the administrators of the town. This is the day when the town's charter is to be presented to the consuls and inhabitants.

Grazide attends along with her three fellow-consuls. She is greeted by the seneschal, Pons Grimoard. She is shocked to notice his physical condition; he has further deteriorated since their last encounter some two years earlier when he attended the Pau. He is much reduced. He shuffles in, supported by a manservant. His face is fixed in a rigid stare, his voice is mumbling and feeble. He holds out a hand to Grazide, the tremor is now coarse and extreme.

The bailie does all the talking. "Consuls, I have here the charter that our lord, the Count of Toulouse, has granted to his new bastide town of Vilanòva, delivered to you in person by his seneschal and representative, Pons Grimoard." With his right hand he indicates the bowed figure of the seneschal. "You will see that the charter contains thirty-seven clauses and here," he points to the bottom of the document to a seal of yellow wax, "it is signed and sealed by the Count himself, I leave it with you for you to peruse and then advertise to the people of Vilanòva."

The short ceremony over, the bailie and the seneschal withdraw. For a moment all four consuls remain motionless, staring at the document that lies on the table before them. Eventually Donat d'Arnal stands and points to the charter. "Well then, fellow consuls, let's see what is in this. Perhaps I should read it out for you all."

There is a murmur of assent and he starts to read the charter out loud. It begins with a renunciation of most of the old feudal taxes and goes on to establish the right of the inhabitants to freely dispose of their goods and property by sale, gift or transfer to others. Other freedoms, sure to be welcomed by the people of the bastide, are clearly stated. Arrangements for the governance of the town and the administration of justice are set out in detail, including the various fines for misdemeanours and offences. The liability to rents and taxes is delineated. The right to hold a weekly market and two annual fairs is established.

Much of this sounds familiar to Grazide. It echoes many of the statutes that had pertained in Montalban. She notices that a similar punishment for adultery, the naked procession through the streets, is included in the new document. For a moment her mind wanders. What will be the response to same-sex liaisons? Will they attract a similar humiliation? She tries to put the thought from her mind.

Consul Donat has come to the end of his reading of the document. "Well Consuls, what do you make of that?" There is little to be discussed for it is obvious that the terms of the charter are bound to be beneficial to the people of the town. In any case, as one consul points out, they are not up for debate. The charter is a decree from their sovereign lord, the Count himself, and is not open for negotiation. Even so Grazide can see that most people are going to be happy with it.

Arrangements are made for the charter to be displayed in a prominent place in the covered market. For a few days it is closely perused by those who can read, dictated to those who lack the facility. Very soon all the existing inhabitants are familiar with the terms of the charter. Word spreads throughout the surrounding area. Soon others

269

are encouraged to apply for the remaining vacant plots in the town. Vilanòva has become a thriving, lively community. There is an optimism in the air that replaces the years of degradation brought about by the recent wars.

Work in the forge continues at a pace. The two former apprentices, Josèp and Lois, are now skilled and accomplished smiths. They are able to take on the bulk of the work needed to support the building of new dwellings. Grazide's work as consul keeps her away from the forge for a good deal of the time but she is still able to supervise and monitor the work of her employees.

She herself has time for more artistic metalwork. She has no shortage of commissions. This work is a great solace for her, particularly when her consular duties are burdensome. She has it in mind not to accept reappointment at the end of the year but others, amongst them the priest, Hugues Dubois, persuade her to continue. She is heartened that there are a few in the town who have come to appreciate the value of having a woman consul.

It is during a private meeting with the bailie, sorting through the minor disputes that arise from time to time, that she learns some surprising news. "We have a new seneschal, Grazide."

"Really. What has become of Pons Grimoard? I know he is not in good health. Who is to replace him?"

"The Lord Sicard d'Alaman. A man of considerable talents, well respected. He should be an asset to the Count."

"I shall miss Pons Grimoard. He was always a good friend to me."

The bailie clears his throat. "I'm afraid the news is not good. You have no doubt heard that the Holy Father in Rome has commissioned inquisitors. They are to carry out the terms of the Peace Treaty that demand the rooting out of remaining heretics. One such, I regret to say, is Pons Grimoard. It appears he has been a secret supporter of the Cathar heresy all this time. He was supposed to have been active in ridding the land of heretics on the Count's behalf. It turns out that all along he has been one himself which is why so little has been done up until now. The new inquisitors very quickly discovered his treachery."

Grazide is stunned, hearing this news. Eventually she finds her voice. "What is to become of him? He is not a well man."

"True. I believe the inquisitors took that into account. He has been handed over to the civil powers. By rights he should burn at the stake but they have been lenient. He is in gaol in Toulouse."

He will surely not last long there, thinks Grazide. The poor old man will not survive such privations. "God rest his soul," she says. "He was a good man, for all his errant beliefs."

The fate of Pons Grimoard hangs heavily on her heart over the following days. Aurimonde is quick to see that her lover is troubled. "What is it, my dearest? Something is troubling you."

Grazide is glad to share her disquiet and Aurimonde is a good listener, her sympathy and understanding are valuable.

"I suspect that there is more to this than your sorrow at the fate of poor old Pons."

"What do you mean, more?"

"This talk of inquisition. This is something new. I heard of it last week from one of the travelling merchants. The inquisitors are mostly Dominican friars. I am told they are spreading throughout the land, establishing bases from which to conduct their inquests."

"Do you think they will come here?"

"Perhaps. It would not be surprising. You told me there was an enclave of heretics when you lived here before. Not that I've heard anyone speak in support of the them but I gather these friars are good at rooting out any vestiges of heresy."

Grazide says nothing but her mind goes back to that last journey with her dying father. She knew she was taking him to the heretics, the goodmen, even though she shared not one bit of the belief that had ensnared him. For a moment a shiver of fear comes over her.

Aurimonde looks her in the eyes. "I know what you are thinking, my love. What you did for your father. No one is going to condemn you for that."

"Perhaps not. Perhaps you're right," but the fear has been implanted. Grazide is worried.

The new seneschal, Sicard d'Alaman, has cause to visit Vilanòva quite soon afterwards. He meets with the bailie and the four consuls in the home of Consul Donat. A tall man, an imposing even haughty presence; he is a marked contrast to his predecessor.

"I am glad to see how successful this comital bastide has become. Consuls, you are to be congratulated. The Count himself is very pleased that his foundation has taken such strong roots."

There is surely going to be something else, thinks Grazide. He has not come all this way simply to congratulate us.

Sure enough she is right. "You may have heard," says the seneschal, "that the Count has undertaken to rid the land of those heresies that have brought such devastation on us all. Skilled inquisitors have been commissioned and they will be journeying throughout the land and conducting their courts of enquiry in various cities and towns. One such town is Vilanòva here. As things stand at the moment you will not be visited for a year or two. They have larger fish to fry. The exact timetable has yet to be drawn up but it will be a good idea to prepare your people for the visitation. There will be an opportunity for any who have been involved with contumacious heretics to come forward and confess during a period of grace. They will be dealt with leniently. As well as that any who know of others' involvement have a duty to give testimony to that effect. Their witness will be secure and private. Those accused will not know who has given evidence against them. It is vital that all vestiges of heresy are rooted out."

Grazide is horrified. There is no justice in this. Her fear is magnified when she contemplates the implications of this process. Even so she can see from his expression that Sicard d'Alaman does not expect any dissent. She keeps silent.

The thought of the arrival of inquisitors, even though it is not imminent, weighs heavily upon her in the following days. Its deadening effect cannot be ignored. She tries to keep on with her day-to-day work but it is hard. Being creative when there is a constant nagging worry deep within her is difficult. Her artistic work suffers, she finds it easier to restrict herself to mundane smithing tasks; repairing and sharpening tools, making door hinges, bolts and nails.

At times like this she finds refuge in visiting the church. Sometimes she stands for hours in front of the fresco of the woman pilgrim. She can experience a degree of peace as she contemplates the image, convinced that it is modelled on her mother. Most times she is alone in her contemplation, undisturbed but on this occasion she becomes aware of a figure standing behind her. She turns to be met by the smiling countenance of Father Hugues Dubois, the parish priest. He takes a step towards her. She is frozen into immobility.

"Grazide. What brings you here?"

"Nothing, Father. I just like to come here on my own."

He smiles again. "It is peaceful, is it not?" Grazide cannot reply. She is discomfited by the intrusion but at the same time perhaps she can detect a trace of empathy in his tone.

"And you, Grazide. Are you at peace?" For a moment she is shocked by the directness of his question. She wishes that this man would leave her alone. She cannot find the words to say.

The priest turns to look at the figure that she has been gazing at. "She is a lovely lady. I've always thought that. A devout pilgrim no doubt. I wonder if she made it to Santiago. Perhaps she did. Perhaps it changed her life."

Is he talking about her mother? Does he know something? "She died." says Grazide " She never made a pilgrimage to Santiago." There is a silence between them. She is beginning to feel deeply uncomfortable, talking to this man.

"Perhaps there is something that you want to tell me, Grazide, to unburden yourself." In a moment her demeanour changes. Is this someone that she can confide in, can open herself to? The gentleness of his speech is beguiling. Is it safe for her to speak?

273

"There is something that troubles me, Father, but it is hard to talk about it to anyone." He says nothing but in his half-smile she recognises that he is encouraging her to speak, she can see that he is willing to listen. "I fear the inquisition coming. I have never been a heretic but I did take my father, when he was dying, to be blessed by the heretics. He was desperate that it should happen. How could I refuse him?"

"That must have been a dilemma for you. Yet perhaps you acted out of love for him. You were being a good daughter."

"I don't know about that. We had our differences." She looks down at her hands, clenched together. "He was a difficult man, especially after my brothers were killed."

"But you carried out his wishes in the end. That was the loving thing to do."

Grazide feels tears welling up in her eyes. "Maybe," she pauses, "but I fear that there are people who know what I did. If it gets to the ears of the inquisitors they are bound to think that I was a supporter of heretics, which I was not." She begins to sob, her long dark hair draped over her down-turned face is wet with tears.

The priest puts a hand on her shoulder. "Who knows what will happen but I know you to be a good Christian soul, untainted by heresy. That is bound to count for something. I will speak out for you if I have to."

"Thank you, Father, but will they listen to you?"

He spreads his hands in a gesture of not knowing. "Perhaps they will. We can only pray that justice will prevail."

Grazide is silent for a moment. There is more that she wants to say. Is it safe to do so? She takes the risk. "There is something else. Something else that worries me."

"Yes, daughter?"

"It is Aurimonde and me. I know that there are many in this town that do not approve."

"Do not approve?"

274

"That we live together. Like man and wife. Sometimes they call us awful things."

"Perhaps that is so."

"What do you think of us, Father? Are we not sinners in the eyes of the Church?"

Father Hugues sighs. "There are some that would say so. To be honest with you I have been under pressure from the Bishop to do something about the two of you. I have resisted that pressure."

Grazide's eyes widen. "You have defied the Bishop?"

He laughs. "That is not so unusual. Perhaps it's because I am not from these parts. I was trained in Paris. Things were different there. Loving relationships between two men, sometimes two women as well, were quite common. Tolerated, even if they were not encouraged. Certainly nothing to be condemned."

Grazide takes courage at these words, enough to say, "So what do you think? What do you think of me and Aurimonde?"

"It is clear to me. You are a loving couple. You care for your boy and bring him up in love. Why should I condemn you?"

A wave of relief washes over Grazide. She could never have expected such toleration, even love, to come from a servant of the Church. Yet here he is, a lone figure prepared to stand out against the oppression and misogyny of the powerful body of which he is just a small part. She falls to her knees in front of him. "Thank you. Oh, thank you, Father." She is sobbing again.

He places a hand on her head. "God bless you, Grazide Lamothe, you and your family." He holds out his hand to her and helps her to her feet. With the back of her sleeve she wipes the tears from her face.

"And you do not condemn us? Can I believe that?"

"No. I do not condemn you, neither does your Heavenly Father. He loves you as you are, one of his children."

Grazide finds it hard to believe this but she knows one thing; the heaviness has gone, for this moment at least she feels liberated.

Later, when she is recounting this encounter with the priest to Aurimonde, it is hard for her to remember all that was said. Aurimonde smiles. "I can see what a difference it has made. You are quite changed. The old Grazide that I know and love. Come here." She holds out her arms to engulf her lover in a long embrace. Their lips meet, a passion stirring between them.

CHAPTER 24
1236

These days the bastide town of Vilanòva enjoys a period of peace and prosperity. Thanks to the easy governance of the officials, happy to administer the terms of the town charter, the people prosper. In the markets and fairs trade flourishes and the profit thus engendered swells the coffers of Vilanòva. The consuls are able to initiate works to enhance the town. All the main streets are now paved, a watermill on the edge of a lake below the town has been constructed. This relieves the women of the town from the endless, tedious grinding of corn by hand. Few of the inhabitants, basking in these new benefits, see any clouds ahead. In a type of collective amnesia they have forgotten the ardours of the past, imagining that the good times will surely go on for ever.

Mischance, when it comes, hits hard and to no one more than to Philippe Noguès, the prosperous shepherd and his wife, Fabrisse. The latter has revelled in her new life in their smart house on the Plaça des Concas. Material wealth has come late in life to Fabrisse and she is determined to make the most of it.

For many years now Philippe has been used to summer grazing his flock on the limestone causse that lies well to the north of Vilanòva, beyond the valley of the Lot. There his animals flourish on the wiry grasslands that can never be cultivated and are too barren for cattle or pigs. It is sheep country and Philippe's large flocks prosper.

Those familiar with the land are well acquainted with the many rifts in the rocky terrain, some of which lead to subterranean caves. These are often good places for shelter from the summer storms but few venture far into their dark passageways. But there is one place that wise shepherds do well to avoid. The Gouffre de Padirac, a huge chasm, a hole in the ground seventy-five metres across and one hundred metres deep. Many tales are told of how it came into being, superstitious minds speak of it as the entrance to hell, giving it as wide a berth as possible.

It is late summer. Philippe is preparing for the long task of returning his flocks to the home pasture around Vilanòva, their winter location. On this particular morning the sun is clear in the sky, the declining warmth a welcome relief from the baking heat of high summer. In the search for good pasture not previously close-cropped by his flocks, he has allowed his sheep to spread close to Padirac. Other shepherds are cautious enough to avoid this area. Perhaps Philippe has grown careless in his success, doubting that anything can go wrong.

Then something extraordinary happens. About an hour before noon the sky begins to darken. Philippe looks up to see if a storm is gathering. There is not a cloud in the sky. Bit by bit the light is fading. Squinting his eyes he looks up at the sun, a dark shadow lies across its orb. All the time the shadow is enlarging as the light fades. Within minutes there is nothing left except a black circle with a thin ring of light around it. The sky is now dark enough for stars to appear. The songs of skylarks, a constant feature on the causse, are quietened.

A shiver of fear assails him. This is nothing that he has ever experienced in his life before. Images of the end of the world flash into his mind, like those seen on the portals of many churches. Is this the Last Judgement?

He becomes aware that the sheep are disturbed. Their bleating becomes louder, more agitated. In the gloom he sees that they are beginning to move, milling about in an ever-increasing circle. Then his dogs begin to howl and the eerie sound seems to disturb the sheep even more. Suddenly the circling stops and the whole flock is pouring off towards the north. In a flash he is on his feet, calling his dogs but they pay no heed. The gouffre, they are heading towards the gouffre. In a panic he chases after them but they are already a long way ahead of him, now rolling down a hill, a direction which takes them straight towards the awful chasm.

Reaching the top of the slope he realises he can do nothing. The whole flock is cascading down towards the gouffre, he is powerless to stop them. He is gripped with horror as he sees them disappear in a suicidal torrent, those behind forcing those in front over the lip of the vast hole in the ground.

Within minutes there is silence. The dogs have quietened down and are whimpering around his feet. Slowly the light reappears. Philippe is rooted to the spot, unable to move, unable to believe what has just happened. Finally he makes his way down to the gouffre, dreading what he might see. He edges to the lip of the chasm and stares down. The midday sun lights up the base of the huge pit and far below he can make out the corpses of his whole flock, piled on top of each other, motionless and silent.

It takes him two days to make the journey back home, his dogs at his heels. It is a dejected figure that makes its way to the grand house in the Plaça des Concas. Fabrisse looks up as he enters.

"Philippe? You are back. So soon? I was not expecting you for another month at least. Is something up?"

Philippe can hardly speak. "Get me some wine," his voice is cracked and weak.

Fabrisse reaches for the jug on the table and pours out a beaker of the rough, red wine.

"There is something. I can see it in your face."

"The sheep," he breaks off, unable to complete the sentence.

"What do you mean, the sheep?"

"The sheep, damn you woman," he shouts. "They've gone."

"Gone?"

"Yes, gone. I've lost them, lost them all. Every single one." He sits down heavily, his head in his hands.

"But how? How did you lose them? Can they not be found again?"

"They've gone, I told you. All dead."

This news appears to stop the flow of questions from Fabrisse. She moves forward and puts an arm around her husband. She speaks more gently. "Tell me about it, Philippe. Tell me what has happened."

He takes a deep gulp of wine from the beaker and wipes his mouth. "The sun disappeared, God knows why. That spooked the flock. They stampeded; I couldn't stop them. They just drove themselves over the edge, into the gouffre."

"The gouffre. You were at Padirac?" Philippe nods.

"You took the flock near to the Gouffre of Padirac? You idiot. Whatever for? You know how dangerous that is."

"Of course I bloody know that," his voice is raised. "It was the only place that I could find enough good grazing. How was I to know the sun would go dark in the middle of the day. I couldn't believe it."

"I know. It happened here; it went as dark as night. No one knows what it means."

"It means we are ruined, Fabrisse. The whole flock, gone. Everything I had was invested in them."

"But surely we have savings. You have done so well in these past few years. We must have money saved up."

Philippe's tone is sarcastic. "Perhaps you may have noticed, wife. All this." He waves his arm around to indicate the house and its contents. "We have spent it all. You haven't exactly been frugal either. All those posh gowns and your stupid fripperies. It's used up all our money. There is nothing left. We are ruined."

Fabrisse appears to be struck dumb. She is silent in the face of her husband's distress. She turns away and leaves him alone, sitting and staring into the empty beaker in his hand.

The disastrous news of Philippe Noguès' flock soon spreads through the town. Many folk have been frightened by the eclipse of the sun. No one has ever experienced such a phenomenon before. Hearing of the tragedy that has befallen the Noguès' flock leads many to speculate on the significance of the darkness at noon. Some see it as an omen, a sign of divine disapprobation. Rumours of other misfortunes abound. Others see it as a judgement though opinions differ as to why such judgement is deserved. Some put it down to the easy affluence that has been a feature of the new community, pointing to the ruin of Philippe and Fabrisse Noguès as a harbinger of what is to come. Yet others, perhaps mindful of the prospect of a visit from the inquisition lay the blame at the doors of those who had supported and encouraged the heretics, perhaps still do. Fabrisse herself is mindful that she was one such supporter though nowadays she has returned to a more orthodox belief; more befitting, she imagines, to her new social position, a position that she now sees as having been cruelly taken from her by her husband's stupidity. Out of this turmoil she has discerned a cause for the expression of divine displeasure.

"It is those two women," she says to Margarethe Targuier as they draw water from the well.

"What? Grazide and Aurimonde you mean?"

"Exactly. We have allowed them to live amongst us in a disgusting cohabitation. It is unnatural, two women living like husband and wife, sharing the same bed and indulging in perverted, disgusting practices."

Margarethe looks shocked at this outburst. "I thought she was your friend, Grazide I mean."

"Perhaps she was but now I see her for what she is. Nothing more than a sodomite. This is a judgement on them both. We should never have allowed it."

It is fortunate that this interpretation of the solar phenomenon does not spread. The demise of the Noguès' ostal overtakes any attempt by Fabrisse to disseminate her inflammatory opinions. She and Philippe are forced to sell their house to a merchant, come lately to Vilanòva. They are reduced to renting a small, run-down cottage in the original part of the town. Philippe, no longer the prosperous shepherd, becomes a manual labourer, an employment that provides just enough for them to eke out an existence. Fabrisse is not seen out and about much, becoming something of a recluse.

Certainly no word of her prejudice reaches the ears of Grazide and Aurimonde yet both are aware of an increased coolness towards them in recent days. Not being something they are unused to they pay it scant regard. As time goes on and ordinary life seems to continue untrammelled by divine displeasure the rumours and predictions of doom quieten down.

Such has been the prosperity of the town the consuls have been able to build a new house of hospitality for the increasing number of pilgrims that pass through Vilanòva on their way to and from Santiago. It is a fine stone building erected in one corner of the Plaça des Concas. A ground rent is payable to the Count but otherwise the considerable proceeds enrich the coffers of the bastide.

Everyone has noticed the increase in the numbers of pilgrims that pass through the town. There is even talk of extending the church to accommodate them. "If we could get hold of a decent relic to place in the church that would be even better," says Donat d'Arnal to his fellow consuls. "That would bring them flocking in."

Grazide wonders how Father Hugues would feel about this. She doubts that such commercial considerations would be prominent in the priest's mind.

It is a dull morning in late autumn. Grazide is returning from the administrative offices when she spies a tall figure slowly making its way from the direction of the church towards the pilgrims' hostel. A woman, hooded and wearing a rough cloak. Grazide notices that she has a large yellow cross stitched on to the front of her dress. She leans on a long walking stick and is barefoot. Scars and bruising are visible on her feet. There is something that is familiar about this figure. As she approaches Grazide she wearily pulls back the hood from her head. Grazide is shocked to see that her scalp is shaven, just a rough stubble remains. The woman's expression is desolate, her gaunt face spells out hunger and privation.

And then, with a greater shock, Grazide recognises her. It is Sybille, the quiet woman who had lodged with her and her father those many years ago. Sybille, who had been one of the company of heretics led by the charismatic weaver, Galtier Foulcaut, the goodman. She has aged.

"Sybille. Is it you?"

The woman stops, staring at Grazide. Her desolate expression changes. "Grazide," she murmurs. "Grazide Lamothe." She does not move.

Grazide takes a step towards her, the look of concern on her face is matched by her words. "But why? Why are you like this? What are you doing? What has happened to you?"

Sybille's head drops, she sways. Grazide jumps forward to support her. "Poor woman. You are exhausted."

"I will be all right," murmurs Sybille. "Just take me to the hostel."

"That I will not. You are coming with me." She nods her head towards the stone building in the corner of the marketplace. "You need rest and better food than the bread and gruel that you will get in that place. Here, hold on to my arm."

Grazide leads her down the side street to her house. As they enter Aurimonde and Pierre-Guillaume look up. "Who is this?" says Aurimonde. Sybille sways on her feet. "Here, let me help you." The two women help Sybille to a chair. Pierre simply stares at the visitor.

"This is an old friend Sybille. Perhaps you remember her, Pierre. She lived with us for a while when you were much younger." From Pierre's puzzled expression she can see that he does not remember.

"Aurimonde. Have we food we can give her? The poor lady is starving."

Within moments food is found and they all sit and eat. The sustenance is enough to restore Sybille to a degree. She begins to talk, to explain her presence in Vilanòva. "I am making the pilgrimage to Santiago. It is not my choice. I was convicted by the inquisitors in Toulouse. Someone denounced me as a Cathar heretic, many of us were denounced including Galtier, our leader. Do you remember him, Grazide?"

Indeed I do, thinks Grazide. The man who brought trouble to Vilanòva, who instilled his heretical ideas into her father's head. She simply nods.

"The punishments were severe. Galtier and two others were burnt at the stake. I escaped with a lighter sentence. I have to make a pilgrimage, wearing this yellow cross, first to the church of Sainte-Foy at Concas and then all the way to Santiago. Barefoot, I am allowed no footwear. That's where I am on my way to now. I have to complete it by next Easter. Then I shall be absolved as long as I never again consort with heretics or offer any support to them."

Grazide is shocked by this. Certainly she had heard rumours of the range of punishments dealt out by inquisitors but seeing the sight of Sybille, almost broken by the penance exacted upon her, brings home the severity with which the inquisition is going about its task. It strikes a fearful chord in her heart.

A bed is made up for Sybille and she is soon asleep. Aurimonde and Grazide remain sitting in front of the kitchen fire.

"The poor woman," says Aurimonde. "I had no idea that the inquisitors were being so harsh. I certainly had little time for the heretics but this seems too cruel."

Grazide does not respond. She is lost in thought. The fire dies down and they retire to bed.

Shortly before dawn Grazide hears movement in the kitchen downstairs. Pulling a gown around her she descends the wooden staircase. Sybille is up and dressed, her cloak around her shoulders.

"Sybille, surely you are not leaving. Stay with us another day. Get some rest." Grazide notices again how gaunt and drawn the pilgrim is. A night's sleep has not changed her much.

"No. I have to go. If I am to complete my journey in time I cannot afford to stop. I will go and hear Mass and be on my way."

"At least have something to eat before you go. I will come with you to Mass if you like. Then we can come back here for some breakfast."

"If you wish." Her voice is tired. "You must do what you think right."

Grazide is thinking back to that night with this woman, so many years ago. Sybille had awoken a passion within her, exhilarating and unexpected. Now she appreciates how much she owes her first lover. To see her now, degraded and humiliated by her sentence, arouses Grazide's anger. It does not take much to stir that feeling. A sense of cruelty and oppression is never far from the surface of her mind.

Father Hugues is just starting to say Mass when they enter the church. A gaggle of pilgrims is gathered in the centre of the church, some resting on their long walking sticks, some standing erect. Her mind relaxes into the rhythm of the Latin incantation, responding automatically at the familiar junctures in the liturgy. It is all so habitual, these days it brings a modicum of peace to her mind. Father Hugues has a way of saying Mass which enhances the recitation of the words, not overemphasised and neither like the gabble that she had used to hear from his disgraced predecessor, Jean Vital. She warms to the new pastor.

Aurimonde and Pierre-Guillaume are up when they return to the house. A pot is bubbling over the fire. She sits Sybille down whilst Aurimonde brings food for them all. Finishing hers Grazide searches out victuals for their visitor's journey. "Enough to keep you going until you reach the next refuge." She knows that what is generally provided at such places is limited and meagre so she packs the bag with dried meats, biscuits and apples.

The meal over, Sybille takes her leave. There are few words but Grazide is surprised at the force of the older woman's embrace, almost sensing in her a reluctance to let go. Would she stay if I asked her? wonders Grazide. Could I dissuade her from continuing her penitential journey? Perhaps we could hide her? A further moment's thought tells her that that would be fruitless. The long arm of the inquisition, aided by informants and intelligences would seek her out, such is the tight net that has been cast over the land. She releases her hold on Sybille, her voice not much more than a whisper. "God go with you, dearest Sybille. We may never meet again but I want you to know how good you were to me. I thank you for that."

Sybille has gone. Aurimonde turns to Grazide. In her lover's face Grazide believes she can see understanding. She has never told Aurimonde about the night with Sybille. Now she knows that she has no need to. "I'm going out," says Pierre, rising from the bench beside the table. "Things to do." He is almost at the door when Aurimonde calls.

"Can you bring back some leeks? I'm making soup."

"Maybe." His voice is irritable. "If I have time." He bangs the door shut as he leaves.

Aurimonde glances at Grazide then smiles. "He's growing up."

"That's no reason for him to be rude."

"Oh, don't worry, darling. It's his age."

Grazide is not so sure. There seems to be more to it than adolescent tantrums. She has sensed a distancing in him, perhaps ever since the bullying episode. She finds the change uncomfortable. He has not been so assiduous in his gardening duties, their small patch is beginning to look unruly, part overgrown with weeds. She wonders what he is getting up to all day.

She is soon to find out. A few days later she is in the forge, talking with Josèp and Lois, the two Fauré brothers who are now responsible for most of the regular smithing work. There are routine matters to be sorted out, delivery of pig-iron, charcoal collection and the like. It is Josèp who surprises her.

"Saw your boy in the woods the other day."

"In the woods?"

"Yes. I was bringing back a cartload of fuel from the charcoal burners. Saw him in a clearing, talking to some man I didn't recognise."

"What man? What did he look like?"

"Burly looking bloke. Curly black hair. Thought he might be one of those brigands."

For a moment Grazide feels a chill of recognition strike through her. "Was he scarred? On his face, did he have a scar?"

"Yes, that's right. An ugly brute he looked. He was talking to your boy. Quite intently. I don't think either of them noticed me."

Surely not. Grazide's mind is racing. Surely it cannot be Giufré. The boy's father. Has he returned? In a panic she runs back to the house from the forge. Aurimonde is tending the fire but jumps up when she hears the door slam.

"What on earth? What's the matter, Grazide?" Grazide is too overcome to speak. Eventually she finds her voice.

"Giufré. Giufré is back. Josèp saw him in the woods. He was talking to Pierre-Guillaume. Why has he returned?" She collapses in tears.

Aurimonde hurries across to her and puts an arm around her shoulders. "Are you sure? Are you sure it was him?"

"Josèp described him. I know it was Giufré. What's he doing here? What does he want with Pierre?"

"I'm not sure I know. Perhaps he just wanted to see him."

"How long has this been going on? Do you think they have been meeting up regularly? Perhaps that is why Pierre is being so difficult. Oh, Aurimonde, I can't bear the thought. What can we do?"

"We can do something. We have to talk to that young man, and soon. I have a bad feeling about this. I think his father is up to no good."

Aurimonde's suspicions are justified. The two women tackle Pierre-Guillaume when he returns later that day. "Where have you been all day?" says Grazide. "You haven't been working in the garden."

Pierre's face is set in a stubborn look. He does not meet Grazide's gaze. "Around and about," is all he says.

"Where? What have you been up to?" says Aurimonde.

"None of your bloody business," he shouts. "You're not my Mama. Why should I tell you?"

Grazide is aware of a deeper resentment beyond his words. "Pierre. Do not speak like that to Aurimonde. She is like another mother to you. Show her some respect."

"I don't need another mother. In fact I don't need either of you. You don't care about me, about how I feel. All you care about is each other. It's disgusting."

This is too much for Grazide. Taking a step towards him she slaps him around the face, hard. He staggers backwards, his hand held to his cheek. Immediately Aurimonde rushes forward to restrain Grazide. "Stop, Grazide, stop. It doesn't help."

"I hate you," Pierre squeezes out the words as if to add extra venom to them. "I hate you both."

Grazide tries hard to calm herself. "I'm sorry, Pierre. I should not have struck you. I'm sorry." Pierre just grunts and turns away. "I need to ask you. Have you been seeing that man Giufré? Tell me the truth."

Pierre's face reddens. "And what if I have? He says he's my father, he cares about me. A lot more than you do. Why shouldn't I see him?"

"Oh, Pierre, you can't. He is a dangerous man. Please don't see him."

"You can't stop me."

"I beg you, don't. He will only lead you into trouble."

"He won't. He cares about me. He told me so. A boy like me needs a father, not two bloody mothers."

Aurimonde comes forward, her palms raised in front of her. "Enough. Both of you. That is enough." This stops the two of them. They both stare at Aurimonde. "There is nothing to be gained by carrying on like this. Let's leave it for the moment. Both of you, just calm down. We can talk about it later."

"There's nothing to talk about," Pierre is muttering under his breath. "Just forget it."

The two women stand motionless as he leaves the room. For a moment nothing is said. Eventually Aurimonde breaks the silence. "Don't fret, my love. It will pass. I don't think for a moment that Giufré will show his face here. Whatever he has promised to Pierre the poor boy will soon see that he is not to be trusted."

"I am not so sure. I just don't understand Pierre. He has never been like this before."

"He'll come around, just you wait and see. Giufré will disappear as he always does and the whole episode will be forgotten."

But three days later events serve to prove her wrong. Pierre has disappeared. He does not return at night. Grazide is frantic in her search for him. No one seems to have seen him.

Then on the morning of the fourth day, shocking news is revealed. The offices of the town on the first floor of the covered marketplace have been broken into. The bailie discovers the break-in when he arrives to open up at first light. More disturbingly he discovers the oak chest that contains all the town's documents and the substantial amount of money collected in revenues and taxes has been forced open. All the money has gone.

There is an immediate hue and cry. Word spreads fast, a crowd gathers in the Plaça des Concas, agitating and speculating. Is it one of the townspeople that has carried out this felony? Has anybody seen anything?

Later in the morning a lone figure is seen emerging from the woods, making his way towards the milling crowd. One of the charcoal-burners, the stockier of the two. As he approaches the crowd he calls out. "Hey there. Where is the bailie? I need to see him."

The crowd parts to allow him through. The bailie is standing at the base of the staircase that rises up to the offices above. "Well, fellow. What do you want of me?" The suspicion in his voice is obvious to those around him.

"Information, Bailie. I have information for you."

The bailie looks flustered. "Well, come on then, man. Out with it. What information?"

"A civil tongue would help, sir. And a cup of something to drink. I've come a long way."

The bailie quickly orders someone to bring the man a beaker of wine. He swallows it down in one gulp. "Brigands, Bailie. A whole band of them. I saw them early this morning, coming away from the town. They seemed in a big hurry. Led by a dark-haired man, scar on his face. He had a boy with him."

Grazide, who has just arrived in time to hear what the charcoal-burner has to say, turns ashen-white and staggers as if to fall. Willing arms around her steady her.

"Pascaut," she calls to the charcoal-burner. "A boy? What was he like?"

"A young lad. About fourteen, I guess. Well-dressed, not like the rest of the band of those ruffians."

"And was he going with them? Which way were they going?"

"Looked like he was. They were heading south. They'll be long gone by now."

The bailie intervenes. "It must be them. They must have been the criminals that have robbed our town. Call out the militia, we have to get after them."

The militia that he summons are nothing more than volunteers from some of the younger and more able-bodied men of the town. Formed simply to protect the bastide they are not likely to be much help in pursuing a band of brigands who are most probably heavily armed and many leagues ahead of them. Nevertheless the bailie orders them to follow the road to the south.

They return later that evening. There has been no sign of a company of brigands. They have searched as far as Toulongergues but there has been no word of them. "Most probably hiding out in the forest," says their leader. "Not a hope in hell of finding them there." There is a trace of relief in his voice. They would not have relished a fight with brigands. Such men were generally feared, many being ex-mercenaries who had fought in the wars, a tough lot and quite ruthless.

But for Grazide this news is horrifying. "It must be Pierre," she says to Aurimonde. "It must be him. He has gone off with his father. Oh, Aurimonde, I cannot bear it. My Pierre, my little boy."

Aurimonde does not speak. She holds Grazide tight, feeling the tears that flow down her lover's cheeks. They are back in the house by now. Word has now spread that it is Pierre-Guillaume Lamothe who has disappeared with the brigands. The sense of shock is almost universal yet there is one person who does not share the general consternation. "Only what you can expect," says Fabrisse Noguès to her husband. "A boy like that, living with those two women. Of course he'd want to get away. Anyone would. Having to live with those two perverts."

"Shut your mouth, woman," says Philippe. "What do you know? Grazide has always been a good person. She was kind and generous to me, don't you forget it. I won't have you bad-mouthing her." This riposte has the effect, for a short while at least, of silencing his wife but it is not long before she is spreading her vituperation abroad.

For Grazide the next few days are desolate. She feels unable to move, remaining inside the house, crying from time to time, refusing to eat despite Aurimonde's cajoling. "How could he do it? It's that bastard, his father. He has corrupted Pierre. Oh, I wish I had never met Giufré. I wish Pierre had never been born."

Aurimonde can find no reply to this. Grazide seems set on punishing herself. "It's my fault. I should never have struck him. I should have given him more attention. My son, my little boy." She is wracked with tears, sobbing as if to empty herself of her grief.

If there had been hope that Pierre-Guillaume might return it fades as the days turn into weeks and, inexorably, the weeks into months. There is no sign of his return, no word of him. These days Grazide seems like an empty husk, able to do little more that eke out a basic existence. She cannot work in the forge, any creativity that she might have had has disappeared.

She is unable to face her duties as consul. Donat d'Arnal grumbles about this when talking to the bailie. "Just what you would expect from a woman, Bailie. I said she should never have been appointed. Can't be relied upon. Giving in to their blasted emotions all the time." The bailie does his best to ignore the consul's rant but Donat continues. "The three of us are flooded with work these days. It's a bloody disgrace. She will have to go. Perhaps the seneschal will appoint a man next time, like we said before."

The bailie says nothing. Perhaps he has learnt that this is the best way to deal with Donat's tirades. There is no doubt that in the past two months the other three consuls have struggled without the considerable input that Grazide has provided in the past.

Then there is a change. Spring is coming and with the warmer days Grazide's desolation seems to melt a little. At times she can smile, she is more able to devote some energy to her work in the forge. Initially she busies herself with the humdrum, routine work; there is no inspiration for more than that but it is enough to fill a space in her mind that had been previously occupied with her grief. She is reminded of the death of her brothers, those many years back. Were it not for the constant solace of her relationship with Aurimonde she might have regarded the loss of those that she has loved the only defining feature of her life. At least she has Aurimonde. As she gradually emerges from grief the depth of her love for her companion is revealed. It is a strong, burning love, a constant flame, a continuing passion. No one is going to take that from her now.

CHAPTER 25

It is a clear night. The light from a crescent moon dimly illuminates the plaça. In the shadows cast by the surrounding houses a solitary figure is seen moving quickly in the direction of the church. It is Aurimonde. She wears a dark cloak, a hood covering her head. There is no one else to be seen.

She makes her way towards the west door of the church. Pushing it open she steps into the gloom of the narthex. She has not noticed that she is being followed. Two figures, equally cloaked and hooded. She does not hear them follow her into the church.

In a moment she is seized from behind. She lets out a cry but it is immediately muffled by a rough hand across her mouth. She struggles to release herself. In her past as a travelling player she has been used to unwanted attention, usually from men inflamed by too much drink. She has always been quite adept at dealing with that. This is different. The second man grasps her arms and forces them behind her back. She kicks backwards, aiming for his shins. She cannot make contact. The first man pulls off her cloak and tears at her tunic. She now realises that a third man has joined them. A small man, unhooded. His face is contorted in a sneer of aggression mixed with lust. His high voice echoes around the narthex. "Hold the whore down. Let's give her a dose of what she needs."

In a flash she recognises him. It is Lucatz Barasc, one of Grazide's fellow consuls, one of the deputation that tried to oppose her partner's appointment. Aurimonde cannot believe it. She finds her voice. "You bastards! Let me go."

It is no use. The first two men force her to the ground, holding her legs apart as Lucatz Barasc advances, his exposed member in a state of high excitement.

All three of them rape her in turn, holding her down and beating her whilst violating her. In the end she cannot resist, she allows them to use her as if she were a lifeless corpse.

Finally they stop. She lies curled up on the floor, bleeding from a cut over her eye, whimpering in distress.

"That should teach you, sodomite. Maybe you'll get a taste for real fucking now," says Lucatz. "Come on men, let's get out of here."

Left alone, lying on the cold stone, Aurimonde cannot move. She lapses in and out of consciousness. After an interval of time that she cannot judge she is aware of a person standing beside her. She is covered with a cloak and her head is lifted from the hard ground. A gentle voice, enough to calm her fear that this might be a further assailant, says "You poor lady. What has happened here?" A strong arm helps her to sit up, she drinks from a proffered beaker of water.

Grazide feels concerned when her partner does not return. She had said she would only be a few minutes, now she has been gone for an hour. There is a quiet knock on the door. Opening it she gasps. It is Father Hugues. He is supporting Aurimonde beside him. "Let's get her inside. She needs attention." Grazide sees the blood running down Aurimonde's contused face, her clothes dishevelled, the blank look in her eyes.

"Aurimonde. Whatever has happened, Father? Where has she been?"

"I found her in the church, lying on the floor of the narthex. Help me get her in."

Together they help Aurimonde into the house and lay her on a bed. Grazide fetches a bowl of water and lint and stems the bleeding from her forehead. Aurimonde says nothing, as if unaware of what is happening to her.

Father Hugues speaks quietly. "She has been assaulted. I saw nobody, I just came across her when I entered the church. I fear she has been violated."

"What? Who can have done this? In the church? It's unbelievable. The bastards!"

"I have no idea who it could have been. I saw nobody."

Just then there is a groan from the prone figure on the bed. Grazide kneels down beside her, she is trying to speak.

Her voice is weak. "Lucatz Barasc. It was Lucatz Barasc and two others with him." Her voice trails off.

294

Grazide can see the shock on the priest's face. "Lucatz Barasc?" he says. "Surely not. He is a consul."

A fellow consul of mine, thinks Grazide. Her mind is racing now. Not a man that she has ever warmed to. Is it he who has raped her Aurimonde? She is overtaken with a fierce anger. She turns to Father Hugues. "This is an outrage. It is shocking. An attack like this from a consul."

Father Hugues nods in agreement. "Yes, it is Grazide, but first we must attend to poor Aurimonde." Together they bathe her wounds, wash the dirt from her arms and legs and settle her into bed. She is soon asleep.

"I will return in the morning, Grazide. We can talk then."

The following day he joins them after he has said Mass. By now Aurimonde has recovered enough to sit up in bed and take some sustenance. Bit by bit she tells the two of them what happened the previous night.

"Did you recognise the other two, my love?"

Aurimonde shakes her head. "No. They were hooded and it was very dark. It was only Lucatz Barasc that I recognised."

"And they all three raped you?"

Aurimonde nods. Grazide is overcome, not now with rage but with pity. She takes her in her arms. "Oh my poor love. My poor love."

Father Hugues stands watching the two of them. "We have to decide what is to be done," he says.

Grazide turns sharply to him. "What is to be done? We have to report this. We cannot let those rapists get away with this." For a moment Father Hugues says nothing, his face pursed. "Father. We cannot let them go unpunished. Surely you agree."

Father Hugues appears to be searching for his words carefully. "Yes, but it will be difficult. He is a man of some standing in the town."

"Bugger that!" Grazide cannot hold back a shout. "He is a filthy rapist, however important you think he is."

"I agree, Grazide. But there could be difficulties for Aurimonde, and also for you. It may not be easy."

"Difficulties? What difficulties? She has been raped. That's the only 'difficulty'."

"Peace, Grazide. I am only thinking of the two of you. A rape trial will not be easy, believe me."

"Why not? It is quite straightforward. Aurimonde recognised him."

Father Hugues coughs as if to conceal embarrassment. "The thing is Grazide, Aurimonde's relationship with you may come under scrutiny. It may be difficult and painful for the two of you."

"We can deal with that. We are used to putting up with what some folk think. We must report this."

Father Hugues gestures agreement. "If you wish. I will support you as best I can," but his face betrays his continuing concern.

It is a few days before Aurimonde is well enough to accompany Grazide to see the bailie. They are alone with him in his office in the market hall.

"Bailie. We have a serious crime to report," says Grazide. "As you can see Aurimonde has been injured so, if I may, I will speak for her." The bailie nods his assent. "She wishes to bring an accusation of physical assault and rape."

"Against whom?"

"Against Lucatz Barasc and two others, unknown."

The bailie cannot disguise the shock on his face. "Lucatz Barasc? Are you sure?" He has turned to address Aurimonde.

Her tone is quiet but firm. "Yes, Bailie. I saw him with my own eyes."

"When was this? Where?"

"Three nights ago. In the narthex of the church."

"Did anyone witness this alleged attack?"

Grazide intervenes. She does not like his use of the word 'alleged'. "No one witnessed the attack as far as we know. Father Hugues discovered her soon afterwards. He helped her back to our house."

The bailie's hand covers his mouth for a moment as if appearing to ponder the matter. Then he says "this is a serious accusation. I will have to make some enquiries and consult the seneschal. In the meantime I would urge you to say nothing of this to anyone. Not until I decide what is to be done."

"With respect," says Grazide, her lips pursed, "there is no question of what is to be done. This man must be brought to trial."

"Thank you, madam consul, but I will be the decider of that. Good day to you both. You will be hearing from me."

Back home Grazide cannot restrain herself. "I know the bailie to be trustworthy and straightforward but I am worried. I get the feeling that he may come under pressure to cover this up."

Aurimonde does not respond. It seems as if the visit to the bailie has depleted her of what little energy she has. "I need to rest, Grazide. No more talk, please."

"Of course. I am sorry, my love. You must rest." Leaving Aurimonde sleeping upstairs she returns to the kitchen. In her indignation she has hidden away from the truth of what the attack must have done to her partner. Now she fears for her lover, she fears for them both.

The seneschal, Sicard d'Alaman, studies the papers in front of him. He is seated behind a long table set out in the larger of the two rooms that comprise the administrative offices of the town. On his left sits the bailie, on his right sits the consul, Donat d'Arnal. On his right is seated the recently appointed fourth consul, Aimèry Targuier.

Facing the table in the centre of the room are three chairs. On one side sits Lucatz Barasc, the accused, and on the other side sit Aurimonde and Grazide. Aurimonde is hunched up, her head lowered. Grazide stares directly at the seneschal.

"This hearing is convened." The seneschal has looked up from his papers. He addresses Aurimonde. "Are you Aurimonde de Sella, a resident of this town?" Aurimonde, without looking up, mumbles her assent. "And what is the complaint you bring before the Count's justice?" His tone is abrupt, commanding. For a moment Aurimonde says nothing.

Grazide intervenes. "With your permission, my Lord, may I speak for my friend? As you can see she has been greatly distressed by what she has undergone. It is hard for her to make the accusation."

The seneschal frowns. "Well, at some point she will have to give evidence but for the moment you may speak for her. Please proceed."

Grazide stands. "Thank you, Seneschal. My friend, Aurimonde de Sella, wishes to accuse Lucatz Barasc of physical assault and rape. An attack which occurred in the narthex of our church two weeks ago, at night. She submits that she was raped by Lucatz Barasc and by two other men whom she was unable to identify." She sits down.

"Thank you, Grazide Lamothe." He directs his gaze to Lucatz. "What do you have to say to this accusation? Is it true?"

Lucatz stands. "I am entirely innocent of these charges, Seneschal. I was nowhere near the church on the night in question."

"Can you tell me where you were at the time of the alleged offence?"

"Certainly. I was at home with my wife and family."

"Is your wife willing to confirm this?"

Lucatz Barasc shoots a glance at Donat d'Arnal who nods his head almost imperceptibly. "Yes. I believe she is."

Donat leans across to the seneschal and whispers something in his ear. The seneschal pauses for a moment, as if in thought. "For the moment we will accept your wife's testimony."

Grazide is fuming. She knows Lucatz Barasc's wife is sister to Donat d'Arnal. What she also knows is how dominated she is by her brother. To Grazide's mind the possibility of coercion is very strong.

"Excuse me, Seneschal, but perhaps we can hear this lady's testimony here."

Sicard's face darkens. "I have no need of that, madam. The testimony will stand." Grazide sits down again, for the moment subdued by the latent anger in the seneschal's voice. "I must now hear from the plaintiff, her account of what happened that evening. Madam, please stand." Slowly Aurimonde rises to her feet. She lifts her head to look at the seneschal. "I realise this is difficult for you," his tone has lightened, "but please tell me what happened to you."

Slowly, hesitantly Aurimonde gives her account of the attack. More than once she has to stop to regain control of her words. The seneschal is listening intently. After she has finished he speaks. "And you were found in this state, on the ground, by the parish priest, Father Hugues?" Aurimonde nods in assent. The seneschal turns to the bailie. "Can we hear from the priest? Is he here?"

"Yes, my Lord. He is waiting outside. I will bring him in."

Father Hugues is ushered in and stands before the seneschal. "Please tell me what you saw that night."

The priest looks across at Aurimonde. "It was dark. I entered the church and I found her lying on the floor."

"And what state was she in?"

"At first I thought she was dead. She was quite inert. When I lifted her head I could see she was still living. I covered her and gave her something to drink."

"Please tell me how she looked."

"She was bleeding from a wound above her eye. Her clothes," he pauses for a moment, "they were somewhat dishevelled. It was then I suspected that someone had violated her."

"Someone? Did you see anyone? Somebody coming away from the church?"

"I saw no one, my Lord. There appeared to be nobody about."

"Thank you, Father. You may leave us." Father Hugues turns to leave, for a moment his eyes meet Grazide's. She can read the concern in his eyes.

The seneschal is speaking again. "If there is no more testimony to be given you may leave for the moment." With a peremptory wave of his hand he indicates Aurimonde, Grazide and Lucatz Barasc. "I will consider this case and call you when I am ready to pronounce justice." The three of them retire. Lucatz Barasc does not look at the two women but goes down the wooden stairs to the marketplace. Grazide and Aurimonde remain in the anteroom. Grazide puts her arm around Aurimonde and whispers in her ear. "You were very brave, my darling."

"I don't know. It's just my word against his. This is hopeless, the seneschal will never convict him."

"Hush. We don't know that yet. Sicard d'Alaman is a fair man despite his austere manner."

It is not long before they are called back in. The bailie comes to collect them.

"I have consulted with my colleagues here about this distressing case. I have no reason to doubt that the plaintiff, Aurimonde de Sella, was attacked and raped by three men. She has clearly identified one of them as being Lucatz Barasc, and I have no reason to doubt her." Grazide's heart misses a beat. Is he going to convict Lucatz Barasc? She cannot believe it.

The seneschal is continuing, his face has hardened. "However, in the case of rape, the accused cannot be convicted if the victim is a person of low repute. It has been brought to my attention that Aurimonde de Sella and the consul, Grazide Lamothe, live in very irregular circumstances." Grazide, in her shock at these words, fails to notice the slightest smirk on the face of Donat d'Arnal. "These circumstances are such that they bring their reputation into question. I have good reason to believe that not only do they live as man and wife, a liaison which must offend God's holy law, but theirs is a union which involves unnatural practices. In these circumstances an accusation of rape from a person of such low repute cannot be upheld. My judgement therefore is that the accused has no case to answer. The hearing is ended."

Grazide cannot contain her anger. "Seneschal, my Lord. This cannot be."

"Silence!" The bailie is on his feet and forcibly guides them to the door. Aurimonde is in tears. In the anteroom they find Father Hugues.

"Grazide, Aurimonde. What on earth has happened?"

Grazide speaks, her lips are pursed. "Those men, they have no right. It is a travesty. Come on, Aurimonde. Let's get out of here." She turns to the priest. "I'm sorry, Father. I can't explain now. It is disgraceful."

Father Hugues is speechless as the two women disappear down the staircase and hurry away from the plaça. They forge a way through a small crowd that has gathered, presumably to hear of what has transpired at the seneschal's hearing. Word gets out about the verdict; the shock waves reverberate through the whole community. Rather than generating support for the two women, the finding of 'low reputation' gives licence to many to speak out, one of whom is Grazide's former friend, Fabrisse Noguès.

"Just as I have always said. It is disgusting, what these two women get up to. It is a disgrace to our town." Fuelled by the anger at the collapse of her own good fortune she is able to whip up a growing body of opinion that turns against Grazide and Aurimonde. Even people whom they had considered their friends find ways of avoiding the two women. What is noticeable is that the majority of these protesters are women themselves. The men of the town, in the main, do not align themselves with this tide of disapprobation.

Over the weeks that follow Grazide and Aurimonde are not often to be seen. They find it easier to confine themselves to the house as much as possible. It is there that they receive a visit from Father Hugues. In more than one of his homilies during Mass he has made veiled references to the furore that is raging in the community, so veiled that they are hardly noticed.

"I have tried to get some sense into people," he says to the two women, "but I doubt if they hear what I am saying. I am afraid, also, that I am getting more pressure from the Bishop. He seems to think that I must speak out against the two of you. I am resisting him at the moment."

Grazide lays a hand on his. "Thank you, Father. You are a good friend. Perhaps the only one we have."

"Maybe it will die down in time. Folk will get tired of gossiping about it. Something else will come along to occupy their minds."

"Maybe," says Grazide, though in herself she doubts it.

But the effect of all this on Aurimonde is what worries Grazide. Her partner has remained withdrawn and uncommunicative, even seeming to avoid any physical contact with Grazide. Sometimes she sits, inert, for hours. Grazide cannot lift her out of herself however hard she tries. At night Aurimonde often wakes in a terror, she is clearly afflicted with nightmares. She has removed herself to the bed that Pierre-Guillaume used to sleep in, in the attic room. "I don't want to disturb you," is how she explains it to Grazide. "You will sleep better if I leave you on your own." She has lost that zest for life that she once had. Grazide worries that she may never regain it.

For herself Grazide decides that she can no longer continue as consul. She hands in her resignation to the bailie. Donat d'Arnal is with them at the time. "I am so sorry that you feel bound to do this, Grazide," says Donat, "but I quite understand why." Weasel words, thinks Grazide. She can see through his false commiserations. She is in no doubt at all that it was he who swung the seneschal's mind around to acquitting his brother-in-law, Lucatz Barasc.

"Never mind, Donat. No longer will you have to accommodate a tiresome woman," she cannot disguise the disdain in her voice. "No doubt a compliant man will be found to fill my place." Donat smiles weakly but says nothing.

And so what to the outside might seem a minor scandal dies down. It is soon overtaken by events infinitely more seismic in their consequences.

CHAPTER 26

The fears and rumours engendered by the unexpected solar eclipse have diminished over time but now there comes news of the activities of inquisitors, Dominican friars appointed by the Pope. They have been active further south in the lands of the Count of Toulouse. Many in Vilanòva do not believe that they will ever extend their inquisitions as far north as their town.

It comes as a shock, then, when notices are posted on both the church door and the entrance to the administrative offices announcing that the inquisitor, the Dominican Brother Ferrer, will be visiting the town on the first Sunday of Lent to initiate his enquiries. The people of the town are instructed to gather in the church of the Holy Sepulchre immediately after Mass on that Sunday. After all Vilanòva is not to escape the reach of the inquisitors.

On the day appointed a large congregation attend Mass. The ceremony over they remain in the church as instructed. The west door opens and the bailie enters escorting an imposing figure who wears a white habit and a black cloak. It is Brother Ferrer, the inquisitor. Grazide, who has been amongst those attending Mass, observes him closely. She imagines she can detect a kindliness in his face though he is not smiling. He does not look about him; his gaze avoids contact with any of the people, rather being focussed on an invisible point in the middle distance. He is tall in stature, only diminished by a slight stoop. A man whose life is devoted to studying papers laid before him, thinks Grazide. Nonetheless she cannot ignore a chill that spreads through her body at the sight of this mendicant friar.

Father Hugues has joined the two men and the three of them ascend the two steps in front of the altar in the eastern apse. Father Hugues raises an arm to call the attention of the people.

"Good people. This is Brother Ferrer who has joined us today to explain how his mission of inquisition into the possible presence of heresy in our community will be carried out."

He stands aside and the inquisitor steps forward. His voice is firm, his gaze now ranges over the assembled congregation. He speaks in formal tones, as if this is a well-rehearsed address. "Good people," says the Dominican monk, " it is my duty and purpose to seek out heresy wherever it can be found and to bring any that have been tainted by its vile apostasy back into the arms of Mother Church. I urge each one of you to examine your conscience. If you have ever held heretical beliefs or have ever sheltered or aided those who are heretics you have a period of grace. It will last for twelve days from today, time to make full confession of your involvement. You will be dealt with leniently. However if you fail to come forward and are subsequently convicted of such heinous and deviant practices you are liable to excommunication and punishment.

In addition, if you know of any who have been mired in the swamp of heresy you are to make it known. Your evidence will be given in secret and your identity will not be revealed to those against whom you testify. Failure to give such evidence, if subsequently discovered, will be subject to penalties.

All testimony will be recorded and preserved. Once again I urge each one of you to make confession within the allotted period of grace. I can assure you that you will be treated leniently. My hearings will be conducted in the Priory attached to this church and will commence tomorrow. Present yourselves to my assistants and your evidence will be taken. May God bless our endeavour and the Holy Saints look kindly upon our enquiries."

The inquisitor steps down from the altar steps and, preceded by the bailie, moves through the people to leave the church by the south door, the exit that leads to the Priory. There is silence. Grazide sees the looks on people's faces. The impact and severity of this announcement has shocked many. She can see fear in the eyes of some, smug complacency in others. Uncomfortable in the presence of so many of the townspeople she leaves as quickly as she can.

Her mind is in turmoil. What is she to tell Aurimonde? Her partner is still withdrawn, still hurting. Grazide wonders if she will ever recover. Whatever she tries to do to help her seems to no avail, she seems entrapped in her passivity, out of reach. How can Grazide share what is dominating her mind now? Should she come forward? Should she tell the inquisitor of that journey with her dying father? Surely not, she has never espoused heretical beliefs. Certainly she knows of some who have, many of whom still live in the community. Those that were taken in by the heretic Galtier all those years ago. Of one thing she is certain. She is not going to be coerced into giving evidence against anybody. The inquisitor can threaten all he likes, she is not going down that road.

Over the next couple of weeks the town is in turmoil. Fear and anxiety course through the community like a lava flow of threatening destruction. There is talk of nothing else. Most days people can be seen outside the Priory gates, some looking uncertain as to whether to enter. The general unease is infectious, no one is spared.

On the Monday morning one of the first to present themselves to the Priory is Fabrisse Noguès. She is admitted and conducted to a small room. Seated at a table is the inquisitor, Brother Ferrer. He is reading documents laid in front of him. She is ushered in by one of the Bishop's guards who have been provided to protect the inquisitor. At the far end of the table is another white-robed figure who is acting as a scribe. Fabrisse is ordered to sit in a large chair in the centre of the room, opposite the inquisitor.

The scribe asks for her particulars and enters her details on the manuscript in front of him and administers an oath. Then Brother Ferrer speaks. Fabrisse is surprised at how gentle his voice is. "What is it that you have come to tell me, sister? Please speak clearly so that your words can be taken down."

There is a tremble in Fabrisse's voice. "I wish to confess my past sins. Some years ago this town was visited by heretics. I attended one or two of their meetings. On one occasion I joined in a meal with them. Since then I have realised that what they preached is a foul heresy. I am a good Christian. I attend Mass regularly and I believe in the holy sacraments."

"What did you hear them preach?"

"Oh, I don't remember well. Something about our souls not going to heaven after we die."

"Did you believe them?"

"No," her voice is adamant. "No. It was just that they seemed to be nice people. I know now that they were wretched heretics. I regret ever having anything to do with them."

"Very well, sister. Thank you for your confession. You will return later when summoned. I will decide what is to be done about your contact with heretics."

Fabrisse becomes agitated, her voice raised. "Please, sir. I was misled," then her voice changes. It takes on a steely tone. "There is something I can tell you. Not about me but about someone else."

There is a pause. The inquisitor is studying her closely. "You have evidence to give? Against whom?"

"Her name is Grazide Lamothe. She still lives in the town. She is the town blacksmith."

"That is a little unusual. Is that what you want to give in evidence?"

"No, no. More than that. Her father was blacksmith before her. He became very ill. She took him to Corbarieu when he was dying. I believe she took him to the heretics."

"Do you know her to be a heretic or a believer?"

"I don't know but she would not have done that if she hadn't been."

"Perhaps," Brother Ferrer's voice tails off.

"There is more. She is a notorious woman. She lives with another woman. They co-habit as man and wife. It is a scandal."

"Sister," his voice is more severe. "My task is to root out heresy. Common gossip is of no concern to me. Nevertheless I will bear what you say in mind. You may go. You will be informed when to return."

Fabrisse is escorted out from the Priory and makes her way back home. Philippe is not there. She slumps in a chair beside the kitchen fire, feeling exhausted.

Over the subsequent eleven days of grace there are many who appear before the inquisitor. Some are quite open about it; others try to keep their attendance quiet. On the last day of the twelve the twisted figure of the beggar, Gervais Targuier, is seen hanging around the Priory gates. No one takes much notice of him.

The period of grace is over. Well over one hundred of the residents of the town have come forward. Over the subsequent weeks their evidence is heard and carefully transcribed in Latin by the inquisitor's scribe. The substantial pile of documents is locked away and guarded by the Bishop's men. There are many in the community who fear what jeopardy for them lives within those inscribed manuscripts. The sense of fear in the community is palpable; it colours all conversations, all transactions. If Vilanòva was once a town basking in self-satisfaction that has all gone now.

One by one individuals are summoned to appear before Brother Ferrer. It is a few days before Fabrisse Noguès' call comes. Despite knowing that most of those that have preceded her have been discharged without punishment, she is almost paralysed with fear when notice of her attendance is served. Philippe, her husband, is little help to her. "You got yourself into this mess, you foolish woman, you can get yourself out of it on your own." He is a changed man since the catastrophe of losing his whole flock in the Gouffre de Padirac. Withdrawn, sullen and prone to violence, much of which is directed against his wife. Perhaps he does not want to confront his own involvement with the heretics. Certainly he has not presented himself to the inquisitor.

As it turns out Brother Ferrer is lenient with her. On payment of a small fine she is absolved. "But please take care, madam, not to ever have anything to do with any heretics in the future. For you to be found guilty of that will invite the severest of penalties."

"Thank you, sir. Of course I will not. I want nothing to do with such foul people. I am a good Christian."

The inquisitor, unsmiling, dismisses her.

Others are called who have had something to confess. A few are ordered to wear a yellow cross, stitched to their clothing, for a year. Some are ordered to support a pauper for the rest of their lives. It becomes apparent to the community that their inquisitor, Brother Ferrer, is a fair and just man.

"His remit is to root out heresy," says Donat d'Arnal in conversation with the bailie one day. "The light touch seems to be more effective in doing that than any heavy-handed retribution."

His optimism is shortly to be shown misjudged. The whole process of inquisition is taking a considerable length of time. Some people summoned to appear are detained for up to two days whilst they are interrogated by intensive cross-examination. One such is the lately appointed consul, Aimèry Targuier. Evidence had been given anonymously implicating him in his involvement with the heretics. He had not presented himself during the period of grace. His wife, Margarethe, is distressed when she hears of his fate. "I thought that he would escape more lightly," she says to Grazide. She is one of the very few people who have maintained their relationship with the blacksmith, her old friend. "I told the stupid man to come forward in the period of grace but would he listen to me? The idiot. Now he has to pay a huge fine. I don't know how we are going to be able to find that sort of money. If he doesn't they will confiscate our property." Grazide is sympathetic but this news does nothing to calm her own apprehension.

It is early morning. Grazide is woken by a loud knocking on the street door. She pulls a cloak around her and hurries downstairs. Opening the door she is confronted by three armed men. They wear the Bishop's coat-of-arms on their sleeves.

"Grazide Lamothe?" one of them demands.

"Yes. That is me. What do you want?"

He hands over a rolled parchment. "You are to attend Brother Ferrer in the Priory tomorrow morning. Failure to do so will lead to your arrest."

Grazide takes the document. It weighs heavy in her hand; her chest is gripped with fear.

"Do you understand?" The man's voice is commanding. Grazide tries to get a grip on her dread. In as firm a voice as she can muster she says, "I understand. I will attend." The men turn and leave. She remains standing in the doorway, clutching the parchment, watching their retreating backs.

"What is it, Grazide?" It is Aurimonde. She has come downstairs, still in her night shift.

"Oh, it's nothing." Grazide attempts a reassurance but at once sees that it is pointless.

"That didn't seem like nothing, all that beating on the door. What is that in your hand?"

Grazide does not reply. She unrolls the parchment and lays it on the table. She remains silent whilst Aurimonde reads the document. Finally her partner turns to her. Grazide can see the panic in her eyes.

"You are summoned? Surely not! You have done nothing."

"That is not what they seem to think."

"But what do they have against you? You were never a heretic."

"No, I wasn't. Someone has testified against me; it has to be."

"But who? Who would?"

Grazide smiles, a wan smile. "We have enough enemies in this town, my darling. It could be any one of them."

There are tears in Aurimonde's eyes. "I cannot lose you, Grazide. I cannot lose you."

"Peace, my love. I am sure it will come to nothing. Nothing is going to separate us, I promise. Come here." She holds out her arms and Aurimonde falls into her embrace. Grazide strokes her hair, gently, as if to calm her. "I will tell him the truth. It will be all right. He is a fair man," but within her the words carry no conviction. This is what she has been dreading.

The following morning the inquisitor is polite when she appears before him. Polite enough to calm some of Grazide's anxieties.

She is in no doubt that someone has told him of her journey with her dying father. She hopes she will be able to explain that. Perhaps she will just receive a fine, that would be bearable.

The scribe takes down her details. Brother Ferrer remains motionless, arms folded, his eyes fixed on the woman seated in the large chair in front of him. Once the initial formalities are completed he starts. He looks down at the papers in front of him. "Well now, Grazide Lamothe. You were born in this town; is that correct?"

"Yes, sir. It was a village then, a sauvatèrra. My father was a blacksmith."

"Yes, so I understand. And you had two brothers?"

"Yes. Guillaume and Pierre."

"What happened to them, are they still around?"

"No, sir," she feels a lump in her throat. For a moment her voice falters. "They both died defending the castle of Morlhon, over twenty years ago."

"Ah, yes. I have heard about that. The Lord Morlhon was resisting the forces of the King, is that not so?"

"The army of Simon de Montfort, sir. The castle was sacked."

"And I believe some eight heretics were burnt."

"I know nothing of that, sir."

The inquisitor pauses, examining her face closely. "I see." All this time the scribe is writing continuously. "I gather that your father taught you the blacksmith's trade after that."

"Yes, sir. He did. There was no one else to take over from him."

"Mmm. Most unusual. Did you manage the work? It hardly seems like a womanly occupation."

Grazide says nothing. The inquisitor continues. "Later on I believe, your father became ill and died?"

Grazide tries to hide the tremor in her voice. "Yes, he did, sir."

"And you left the village. Where did you go?"

"I moved to Montalban."

"Ah, Montalban. We know a great deal about that town. Heresy was widespread there, was it not?"

"I know nothing of that."

"Perhaps not. How long did you live there?"

"For around five years." For a moment she feels a glimmer of hope. He seems to have glossed over her father's dying journey. "I moved back here when the bastide was planned. To work as blacksmith. I was appointed by the Count's seneschal, Pons Grimoard."

"Yes," he frowns. "Pons Grimoard. No longer seneschal, is he?" Again he looks at his papers. "When you returned you were not alone, I understand."

"Yes. That is correct. I had my son, Pierre-Guillaume, with me."

"A son. But no father?"

"His father deserted me before Pierre was born."

"Most unfortunate. Were you married to this man?"

Grazide blushes, immediately annoyed at herself. "No, sir. We never married."

"And have you seen this man since?"

"Only once. Some years back. He returned but I told him to leave."

"That is surprising. Did you not want a father for your little boy?"

Grazide purses her lips. "He was not the sort of man who makes a good father. He was not a trustworthy man."

"So that was the last time that you saw him. Is that right?"

"Yes. That is right."

"And your boy? He must be quite a young man now. He still lives with you?"

Why is he asking me all this? thinks Grazide. What is he after? "No, sir. I am afraid he disappeared last year."

"Disappeared?" Brother Ferrer's eyebrows are raised. "Where has he gone?"

"I am afraid I do not know, sir. He disappeared around the time that a band of brigands were seen in these parts."

"Gone off with the brigands? That must have been a shock for you."

For a moment Grazide says nothing. She has brought up her fist to cover her mouth. "I believe his father was one of those brigands. I fear he has gone off with his father."

"That must be most upsetting for you." Again Grazide does not reply. "I can see that it is. I will not dwell on it." Grazide feels relief when she hears these words. He is continuing. "I understand that when you returned here to Vilanòva you were accompanied not only by your son but by one other person."

Here it comes, thinks Grazide. The gossip has obviously reached the inquisitor's ears. "Yes, I was."

"And who was that?"

"Her name is Aurimonde de Sella, sir."

"Ah yes. I believe I have been told about her. She was a travelling player, a joglaresse is that not right?"

"She was, sir. She is no longer."

"You met her in Montalban?"

"Yes."

"And that was when you started to live together?"

"She joined the ostal that I lived in. The ostal of Magali de Gramazie and her family."

"Again, no husband."

"Magali's husband had died. She was a widow. She had to carry on her business."

"I see. An ostal of women."

Grazide feels her anger arise within her. She fights to control it. "It was a respectable ostal, well regarded in the town."

"Yes. Well regarded in Montalban, I have no doubt. Was this Magali de Gramazie a follower of heretics?"

The abruptness of this question throws Grazide. She feels flustered. "No, sir. Not at all. She had nothing to do with any heretics."

"And you?"

"Certainly not."

"I see." Again he is shifting his papers, apparently looking for a particular document. Finally he finds it.

"I understand your son became very ill when he was quite little. He nearly died, is that so?"

"Yes. He did."

"And he was attended by a man named," here he looks down at the document, "Pierre de Vals, a doctor in the town."

Pierre de Vals. Grazide has nearly forgotten him. The doctor who dressed in a brown tunic, whose ministrations saved her boy's life. Now she remembers him. An unnamed dread rises within her.

"Were you aware that Pierre de Vals was a shameless heretic, follower of the abominable Valdes of Lyon?"

"No, I was not, sir. I took him to be just a doctor. He was very good to me."

"Perhaps so." He pauses. "Perhaps so. Perhaps you were attracted to who he was. After all he saved your child."

"He was simply a doctor, sir. He never spoke of his beliefs, at least not to me or anyone else in the ostal. That is the truth." Grazide is aware that her voice is becoming too shrill. She tries to calm herself.

"Very well. We will leave that for now. Perhaps I could return to Aurimonde de Sella, the trobairitz. She moved here with you when you returned. Is that right?"

"Yes. That is right."

"And what is the nature of your relationship with this Aurimonde de Sella? "

"We are companions, sir."

"Companions?"

"Yes, companions."

"So you set up home here without a husband but with a young son and," he pauses, perhaps to create a dramatic effect, "a companion." Grazide nods but does not speak. "I have heard that there is some disquiet in the town about your ostal. Would you care to comment on that?"

"No, sir. I have no knowledge of how people think. I do believe there are some who think it unnatural that a woman should be a blacksmith. They see it as man's work."

"Grazide Lamothe. You dissemble." His voice has taken on a sharper tone. "May I remind you that you are under oath to tell me the truth? I know, for instance, that your 'companion', Aurimonde de Sella, had occasion to accuse a prominent citizen of this town of assault and rape."

The anger in Grazide is rekindled. What else has this inquisitor been told? The extent of the malice against Aurimonde and her is beginning to be revealed and this mendicant friar has been soaking it all up. "That is true, sir."

"And as I understand it the man in question was acquitted. Why was that?"

"I am not sure if I know, sir. Aurimonde was certainly raped and she clearly identified her attacker."

"Come now, madam. I think you know more than that. Why was he acquitted?"

Grazide is silent.

"I think you know perfectly well. He was acquitted on account of the reputation attributed to his accuser. She was deemed to be a woman of low repute and thus unable to bring a charge of rape against any man. That low repute stemmed from her relationship with you. It was a matter of shame to the community that the two of you live together as man and wife."

Grazide cannot contain herself. "That is foul prejudice and tittle-tattle. I am surprised that I am being questioned about this. I thought that you were supposed to be seeking out heresy, not collecting small-town gossip." Her face is flushed with anger, her breathing rapid, her fists clenched.

314

Brother Ferrer's face looks like thunder. "Control yourself, madam. I will decide on what I investigate. It would serve you better if you were to control yourself."

"I apologise, Brother Ferrer. I withdraw my remarks."

He turns to the scribe who is frantically writing. "You can expunge that last exchange from the record, Brother." He turns again to Grazide. "We will take a break for the moment, madam. Your interrogation will continue in an hour. You are to remain here." He calls out, "Guards!" The Bishop's men appear and escort Grazide to one of the monks' empty cells. She is brought a beaker of water and a crust of bread.

During the hour's recess Grazide goes over and over what has passed between them. He seems to have skated over the matter of her father's death. She is dismayed at the attention he has given to her and Aurimonde. Is this going to influence him?

For a moment she wonders if escape might be possible. She could slip away from the Priory, collect Aurimonde and the two of them could flee the town. But where could they go? There is no one who would shelter them. By now she knows that the long arm of the inquisition stretches throughout the lands of the Count of Toulouse. Their records, as she has seen, are extensive. It is obvious that their contents are shared amongst the several inquisitors wherever they are active. It is a network of information that has any possible heretic inextricably trapped.

There is a subtle change in the inquisitor when she returns. Perhaps his approach is a little more emollient. He does not return to the subject of her and Aurimonde. Instead he begins to submit a series of what appear to be standardised questions. He is reading from a document in front of him. He looks up and smiles. "I hope you are a little rested, madam. May we continue?" Grazide nods a silent assent. "I have some questions to put to you about your beliefs. To start with, do you assert that all living things were not created by the Living God?"

What a strange question, thinks Grazide. "Of course not. God, our Father, is creator of all."

"Was Jesus born of the virgin Mary?"

"Yes, I believe that."

"Is it wrong to eat meat?"

"I eat meat."

The questions continue. Now it is obvious to Grazide that he is seeking to implicate her in Cathar beliefs, to get her to admit heresy. She continues to bat away his questions, hoping he might tire of asking them eventually.

But then her equanimity is disturbed. "What do you know of the consolamentum?"

She struggles to find an answer. Does she deny any involvement in such a ceremony? What does he know? Has someone told him of Corbarieu, where she took her dying father? "I am told that the heretics perform it as a ceremony that will save a person's soul."

"Do you believe that is true?"

"I know little about it, sir. I could not say."

"Well, what about administering the consolamentum to the dying? What do you know about that?"

Grazide has determined that she will be honest about this subject if questioned but how much should she reveal? "I understand that it is a custom amongst the heretics."

"A custom you approve?"

"I do not have a view, sir."

"Come now, Grazide Lamothe. Surely you do." Grazide says nothing. Brother Ferrer is shuffling papers again. The scribe pushes a document across the table to him. He peruses it for some minutes. There is complete silence in the room. "I understand that shortly after your father's death you left Vilanòva."

"Yes, sir. As I said, I moved to Montalban."

"And your father did not die in the village. You took him away when he was gravely ill. Why was that? Surely such an arduous journey when he was near to death must have caused him much suffering?"

"It was his wish, sir. I was doing his will."

"His wish? That is strange. Please be honest with me now, madam. Where were you taking him?"

She hesitates, a grim expression on her face. "To Corbarieu."

The inquisitor looks up sharply. "Corbarieu. Indeed. Did he have family there? Is that why he asked to be taken to Corbarieu?"

"No. His family have always lived in these parts."

"So why Corbarieu?" he pronounces the name with exaggerated care.

"It is where he asked me to take him."

"And you concurred? Taking a dying man on a long, hard journey. Did you not ask him why?"

"He insisted, sir. I was his only child. I was bound to do what he asked."

"Enough of this!" The inquisitor's words are spat out. "Once again you dissemble. Are you not aware that Corbarieu was a nest of heretics at that time? That dying persons were taken there to be consoled by the 'goodmen'?" The sarcasm in his voice on using this appellation is obvious to Grazide. "A consolamentum intended to save a dying man's soul. Is that not why you took your father there?"

"I only did what he asked me. I thought it was pointless. I begged him to change his mind but he was adamant." She notices that his face lightens a little.

"Perhaps," he says, "you simply followed his wishes."

"Yes, sir. He would not reconsider. He was very ill."

"A dutiful daughter, then." He smiles. For a moment it disarms Grazide.

"I tried to be. He was my father."

"Quite. Quite understandable." He pauses and is still. The scribe stops writing. In a quiet voice, almost imperceptible he says,

"Tell me what happened, Grazide Lamothe. Tell me about the consolamentum."

Grazide panics. What should she say? She had insisted on staying in the room. Observing her father being consoled. With a stab of fear she remembers kneeling before the goodman, his hand on her head in blessing. "I did not understand it, sir. There were lots of words. I wasn't really listening. They placed a book on his chest. It was quite quickly over. I stayed with him. I stayed with my father. I feared he might die and I wanted to be with him if he did." She is crying now, tears freely coursing down her cheeks.

"And did he die then?"

"No. The following night, in the lodgings that we were staying in."

"Do you believe his soul was saved, Madam?"

"I don't know. He was not always a good man. I pray for his soul to this day."

Perhaps the conviction with which she says the last sentence has an effect on the inquisitor for he says "That is all I think we need to know on that matter. Can you tell me truthfully, were you a believer in heresy?"

"No, sir. I was not, nor am I now." Can she believe it? It seems to her that he is going to accept that denial. Relief floods over her. She feels faint but then steadies herself. The scribe is writing. Brother Ferrer leans across and whispers something to him. The scribe searches out another document and passes it over to the inquisitor. Surely there can be no more, thinks Grazide. She has admitted her role in her father's contact with the goodmen. It seems that he has accepted her testimony. Perhaps he will levy a fine, that will be all.

"You were raised in this village, is that correct?"

"Yes, sir. I told you that I was."

"And your mother?"

She swallows hard. "I never knew my mother, sir. She died when I was very young."

"That is sad. Did your father marry again? Did you have a step-mother?"

"No, sir. He did not." She is not going to mention his liaison with Bethane Noguès, wife of Philippe the shepherd, who left her husband to move in with Arnaud, her father. Not unless he asks directly.

He does not. "Do you recall, when growing up, a visit to the village by a man named Bernard? He would have been recognisable. He always wore a brown habit."

This comes like a stab in the heart to Grazide. She had declined to mention the itinerant Bernard, not for a moment thinking that she had anything to hide. She can recall his gentle manner, somewhat of a contrast to the demeanour of the mendicant friar in front of her at this moment. Then, with a growing horror she remembers his words. '*I am a Poor Man, a follower of Valdes.*' A Waldensian. A sect pronounced as heretics. She begins to panic. "I'm not sure, sir. I vaguely remember something of the kind. It was a long time ago. I was very young."

He is staring hard at the document in front of him, obviously someone's testimony. He measures his words carefully, "Not too young to stop you wanting to join him. Do you deny that you sought to join his sect, to travel with him?"

It is as if the ground has opened up beneath her. She is staring into a deep chasm, a rift in the earth. She tries to speak but the words will not come.

"Do you deny it, Grazide Lamothe? You wanted to join the despicable Waldensians."

How does he know this? Even she had forgotten the incident until now. Her impulsive outburst all those years ago. '*Let me come with you, brother. I can be your companion.*' And suddenly, with that memory, returns another. The boy with the limp, her crippled boyhood friend, Gervais Targuier, the hidden observer hiding in the shadows.

Gervais, the beggar that stands at the church door.

CHAPTER 27

The sentence, when it comes, is harsh. The following day she is escorted back to the inquisitor. Entering the room she sees that he is joined by the parish priest, Hugues Dubois. She can immediately see the distress on the priest's face. He makes no sign of greeting, remaining silent, avoiding her gaze.

The inquisitor is speaking. "Grazide Lamothe. I find that you have been a vile consorter with a contumacious Waldensian heretic. In the power vested in me I hereby excommunicate you forthwith. You are to be denied the comforts of the Church. Your property is to be confiscated and you lose all your rights to dispose of your assets. You can only be reconciled with the Church after you have made a solitary pilgrimage to the shrine of Saint-Jacques in Santiago de Compostela. You must make that pilgrimage barefoot and it must be completed by the Feast of Pentecost next year. You will make the pilgrimage at your own expense. From now on you are to wear a yellow cross stitched to your tunic. You will carry a sealed document and present it to the monks at Santiago. It contains instructions that you are to be publicly scourged by them in front of the cathedral. Only then will your sins be remitted.

If, in the future, you are found to have any contact with heretics you will be burnt at the stake. This judgement is final."

They have won, thinks Grazide. Finally, irrevocably, despotic male domination has overwhelmed me. The Church, the inquisition, my own community, my son's father, even my childhood friend Gervais, they have all torn away everything in my life. I have nothing left. I am defeated, I can resist no more. Once I imagined that I was a person in my own right, now I can see that that was a fantasy. I was fooling myself. There is nothing that I can say now, nothing I can do that can change things. I am emptied.

She is escorted from the room. Father Hugues has said nothing. Even you, she thinks, you who said you would protect me. You have abandoned me. She is overcome with desolation.

Aurimonde takes it badly. "Where are we to go? What will you do?"

"There is nothing I can do, my love. I have to make this journey."

"I will come with you."

Grazide looks at her tenderly. "You cannot. I have to make the pilgrimage on my own. It is my sentence." Aurimonde, her lover, now a husk of her former self, thinks Grazide. Her spirit, her zest for life has been knocked out of her. Her fear for Aurimonde is overwhelming.

"What will become of me? I cannot live without you."

"You can, you must." says Grazide. "We will find a way." Already her mind is exploring possibilities.

Back in the Priory the scribe is collecting up his papers. Brother Ferrer turns to Father Hugues. "Thank you for your counsel, Father. I had a mind to exact a more severe penance on that woman. You changed my mind, perhaps that is for the best."

"I believe her to be a good woman, Brother, for all that she has been implicated in heresy."

"That is as may be but my task is to root out all vestiges of heresy. I cannot flinch from that. The true Church, our faith must surely prevail. But I am a merciful man. I can see that this woman, for all that she has been misguided, has qualities that are not seen in many. It is a pity that she took the path she chose."

"You believe she chose heresy?"

"Perhaps. But she has chosen to live life differently. There is only so much deviation that the Church, and society, can tolerate. Perhaps she pushed the boundaries too far."

There is nothing that Father Hugues can find to say. He has seen the desolation in Grazide's face. He feels that same desolation in his soul.

Events, once this punishment has been proclaimed, move on at a pace. Grazide and Aurimonde have to leave their house, the forge is confiscated and put up for sale. The two Fauré brothers are ready buyers, anxious to continue their hard-learned trade. The house is sold to an incoming merchant and his family, the proceeds of the sale going to the coffers of the town, a matter of some satisfaction to Donat d'Arnal.

The two women have gone. Grazide has found a refuge for Aurimonde in a convent in the nearby village of Puylaroque. The sisters take her in with a kindness that is reassuring to Grazide. Her lover will be well cared for in their community, she can see that.

Their parting, when it comes, is agonising for them both. There are few words that they can say. They cling to each other as if to retain for ever the love that has bound them together. Finally one of the nuns takes Aurimonde by the arm and gently leads her away. As Grazide stares at her departing back she knows in her heart that she will never see her lover again.

Little is heard of Grazide from then on. Sometimes reports come from pilgrims passing through Vilanòva. They tell of a tall, dark-haired woman seen on the road. A large yellow cross is stitched to her tunic. Barefoot and silent, she shuns any contact with fellow pilgrims. In time these reports become less frequent, eventually dying out altogether.

POSTLUDE

The June sun beats hard on the wooded landscape. Hills unfold in a panorama that leads away to the distant mountains, immersed in the heat haze of summer. The track winds toward the summit of a low hill. A solitary, gaunt figure is ascending, a woman. Reaching the crest the scene opens up in front of her. Away in the distance she can see the spires of a great cathedral, granite-dark in the sunlight. Larks rise from the scrubby grass of the hillside. They balance on the wind, their incessant song as persistent as a choir of surrounding angels.

The woman stands, alone, unmoving. Then from her satchel she pulls out a rolled parchment scroll. Holding it in her left hand she begins the downward journey, down towards the distant spires.

THE END

GLOSSARY

Albigensians	name given to southern heretics, later labelled as Cathars*(qv)*
androne	The narrow gap between houses in a bastide
arpent	a field plot on the outside of a bastide town
assartage	The clearing of forest to provide agricultural land
bailie	an officer of a town, appointed by the lord
bastide	a medieval new town established by the lord of the region
caselle	a stone-built shepherd's hut, in shape like a beehive
Catharism, Cathar	a dualist heresy prevalent in SW France in the 12th-14th centurie a follower of the same
causse	a limestone plateau
cazal	a garden plot in a bastide
chemins Saint-Jacques	the various pilgrim routes to Santiago de Compostela
Concas	(Occ.) modern day Conques
consolamentum	an initiation ceremony in Catharism
denier	a coin, one penny
destrier	A war horse
fabliau	a scurrilous tale
femme sole	the right of a woman to hold property and to represent herself in law
goodman/woman	the title given to one who has undergone the Cathar consolamentum
Gouffre de Padirac	a huge sinkhole in the causse of Quercy
joglaresses	female travelling minstrels
joglars	male travelling minstrels
marly ground	a soil consisting of clay and silica
narthex	the entrance area of a church
ostal	a household, referring both to the building and the people who li therein
Pau	a ceremony to initiate the building of a bastide town
Peace of God	movement initiated by the medieval church to protect ecclesiastic property and non-combatants from violence
'perfect'	another term for a Cathar goodman/woman *(qv)*
plaça	a square in the centre of a bastide
Plaça des Concas	the main square in Vilanòva

prudhomme	a trustworthy citizen, appointed by the lord of a village or town
Quercy	a county, part of the lands of the Count of Toulouse, incorporating Montalban
Rouergue	a county, part of the lands of the Count of Toulouse, incorporating Vilanòva and Rodez
sauvatèrra	a village or town where the 'Peace of God' *(qv)* pertains
seneschal	the principal minister of a lord
terroir	environmental factors that affect the growth of grapevines
trobairitz	a female troubadour
vendanges	the autumnal grape harvest
Via Podensis	one of the chemins Saint-Jacques *(qv)*, that passes through Vilanòva
Vilanòva	a village in the west of the Rouergue, modern-day Villeneuve d'Aveyron
Waldensians	itinerant preachers, followers of Pierre Valdes, known as 'Poor Men of Lyon', deemed heretics

ACKNOWLEDGEMENTS

Once again I am deeply indebted to John May for the editorial help that he has given me at all stages of this project. His discernment and judgement have been both invaluable and unerring. Unfortunately he was unable to complete the final stages of the task and I am grateful to Christopher Sturdy who edited and proofread the final draft with his usual keen eye and impeccable judgement. Thanks also to Liz Colman who generously agreed to type up the whole manuscript and to Carol Miller who read the final draft and whose advice was invaluable.

Thanks too to Annie Pickering Pick for the striking cover image. It has been good to have all of my books illuminated by the same talented hand. Thanks also to Sera Pickering Pick for the cover design.

For a historical novel of this kind there has been a great deal of research. Chris Dennis gave me invaluable help in pointing me in the direction of many sources, both primary and secondary. I am once again glad to be able to thank the staff at the Bodleian Library in Oxford for all their help in seeking out those sources of the extensive reading that was made in preparation for writing this story of a woman blacksmith living in a turbulent era. I particularly valued the published work of Professor Claire Taylor of the Department of History at the University of Nottingham, undoubtedly one of the current leading authorities on the subject of medieval heresy.

I have indicated in a reading list below some of the main sources of historical writing that have helped me to understand this era. Like all writers of historical fiction I am acutely aware of the debt that we owe to those whose painstaking work has illuminated the culture and people of this time and place. I am happy to acknowledge the guidance obtained from such writers as Hilary Mantel (in particular in her 2017 Reith Lectures) and especially from Sarah Dunant from whom I have learnt so much about the craft and creativity of writing.

I must emphasise however that whatever failings this frail vessel has are down to me and me alone.

Whilst the story of a woman blacksmith in 13th Century southwest France is fictional many of the events and some of the characters are in the historical record. I have tried to be as accurate as possible about the former but in two instances, the date of the total eclipse of the sun and the initiation of the Papal inquisition by Brother Ferrer, I have brought the events forward.

Being blessed with seven granddaughters I thought that it was high time that I should write a novel that has a woman as the main protagonist. For this reason I have dedicated this book to them.

Finally my deepest thanks to Jill. It is hard to live with someone who spends a good bit of his mental life eight centuries back. Her toleration, love and support have been inestimable throughout.

Andrew Chapman. December 2019

Further reading

If you seek to explore the times and themes of this book here are a few suggestions that might be helpful.

On **heresy**, both Cathar and Waldensian, there is a vast literature but these are some of the best sources

The Cathars Malcolm Barber. (Pearson 2013)　ISBN 978-1-4082-5258-1

Heresy, Crusade and Inquisition in Medieval Quercy Claire Taylor. (York Medieval Press 2011)　ISBN 978-1-903153-38-3

Medieval Heresy Malcolm Lambert. (3rd edition 2002 Blackwell)　ISBN 978-0631222767

The War on Heresy. Faith and Power in medieval Europe R.I.Moore (Profile Books 2014)　ISBN 978-1-84668-200-1

On the **bastides** of Southwest France there is much less. The best book without doubt (but it is in French) is

Histoire des bastides Jacques Dubourg (Éditions Sud Ouest 2002)　ISBN 978-2-87901-492-0

There is a growing literature of **medieval feminist** studies. Here are three sources that I found very helpful.

Medieval Misogyny and the Invention of Western Romantic Love R. Howard Bloch (University of Chicago 1992)　ISBN 978-0-22605-973-1

Bodytalk. When Women Speak in Old French Literature E. Jane Burns (University of Pennsylvania 1993)　ISBN 978-0-81221-405-5

The Oxford Handbook of Women and Gender in Medieval Europe ed.Judith M. Bennett & Ruth Mazo Karras (OUP 2013) ISBN 978-0-19-877938-4

Also available by Andrew Chapman

BEYOND

THE

SILENCE

It is 1890 and the painter Vincent Van Gogh, convalescent from severe mental illness, arrives in the small village of Auvers-sur-Oise, north of Paris. There he is befriended by the local doctor, Paul Gachet, whose attempts to help the painter become more and more fruitless as time goes on.

Over a century later another doctor, Richard Avery, comes across the portrait that Van Gogh painted of Doctor Gachet. Its effect on the modern doctor is overwhelming.

The two narratives, one in the nineteenth century and one straddling the turn of the millenium, tell similar stories about the nature of doctoring, its disintegrating effect and the possibilities of redemption.

PILRIG PUBLISHING

£7.99

ISBN:978-0-9564421-0-9

www.andrewchapmanikon.com

First published in Great Britain in March 2010

IKON

It is early in the 15th Century and a strange procession, wending its way up a mountainside on a small Greek island, is witnessed by a young goat herd, Ioánnis. He can see that something is being carried but has no idea what this covert ascension is all about.

As he grows up on the island he comes under the influence of an old priest who opens the young boy's eyes to perceptions that are quite new.

All this is disrupted by a cataclysmic event which pitches Ioánnis into a lifetime's odyssey throughout the Near East, a journey of the mind which brings him, in the end, to a revelation and a startling conclusion.

PILRIG PUBLISHING

£9.99

ISBN:978-0-9564421-1-6

www.andrewchapmanikon.com

First published in Great Britain in June 2012

THE
LEAVING

Nick Propert, a clergyman in a Midlands town, suffers a devastating shock when his wife disappears. Although their relationship has been strained there appears to be no explanation for her leaving and Nick is left to reconstruct his life in her absence. This leads him to a remote peninsula on the west coast of Scotland, a place where he can seek to understand what has happened to his life and whether a future on his own might be possible. The answers are surprising to him.

PILRIG PUBLISHING

£9.99

ISBN:978-0-9564421-2-3

www.andrewchapmanikon.com

First published in Great Britain in September 2015